Encomiums

"Sade's neglected masterpiece... can be considered not only a decisive turning point in the author's development, but also a significant milestone in the history of the philosophy of emotion."

— Marco Menin, University of Turin

"For those of us who have been waiting a lifetime for a translation, *Aline and Valcour* is the final piece of the puzzle that is Sade, and a key work in French literature."

— Steven Moore, author of *The Novel: An Alternative History*

"Sade may be diabolical, but he is also devilishly adroit."

— Beatrice C. Fink, University of Maryland

I0650590

"*Aline and Valcour* shows an epistolary novel that is very much in and of the Revolutionary moment, which only enhances its appeal. That Sade produced a book this good is an occasion for surprise and pleasure. *Aline and Valcour* has the capacity to not only deepen the popular conception of Sade but the popular-academic conception of him as influenced by Barthes and Foucault. I also greatly admire the translation, which is kept in period but is not at all a pastiche. It is both formal *&* direct."

— Prof. Nicholas Birns, New York University

"Jocelyne Geneviève Barque and John Galbraith Simmons have triumphantly met the manifold challenges of this fascinating, often prolix novel, rendering Sade's words into a sparkling English that never lapses into faux-'modern' anachronism or pedantic literalism."

— Christopher Winks, Professor of Comparative Literature, Queens College

Aline and Valcour will force readers on this side of the Atlantic to re-think everything they've ever learned, heard, or read about the Marquis de Sade. The translation of this formidable novel... is accurate, clear, loses nothing of the Sadean voice, and makes for compelling reading.

— Alyson Waters, PhD, managing editor of *Yale French Studies*

"This remarkable translation of this extraordinary novel, done into English with such talent and devotion, will be a landmark contribution to French studies in the English-speaking world."

— Donald Nicholson-Smith, translator, Chevalier des Arts et Lettres

afin que... les traces de ma tombe disparu
comme je me flatte que ma mémoire s'e

"so that... all traces of my grave may disappear from the surface of the earth, just as I like to think my memory will be effaced from the minds of men..."

*nt de dessus de la surface de la terre,
ra de l'esprit des hommes... D.A.F. SADE*

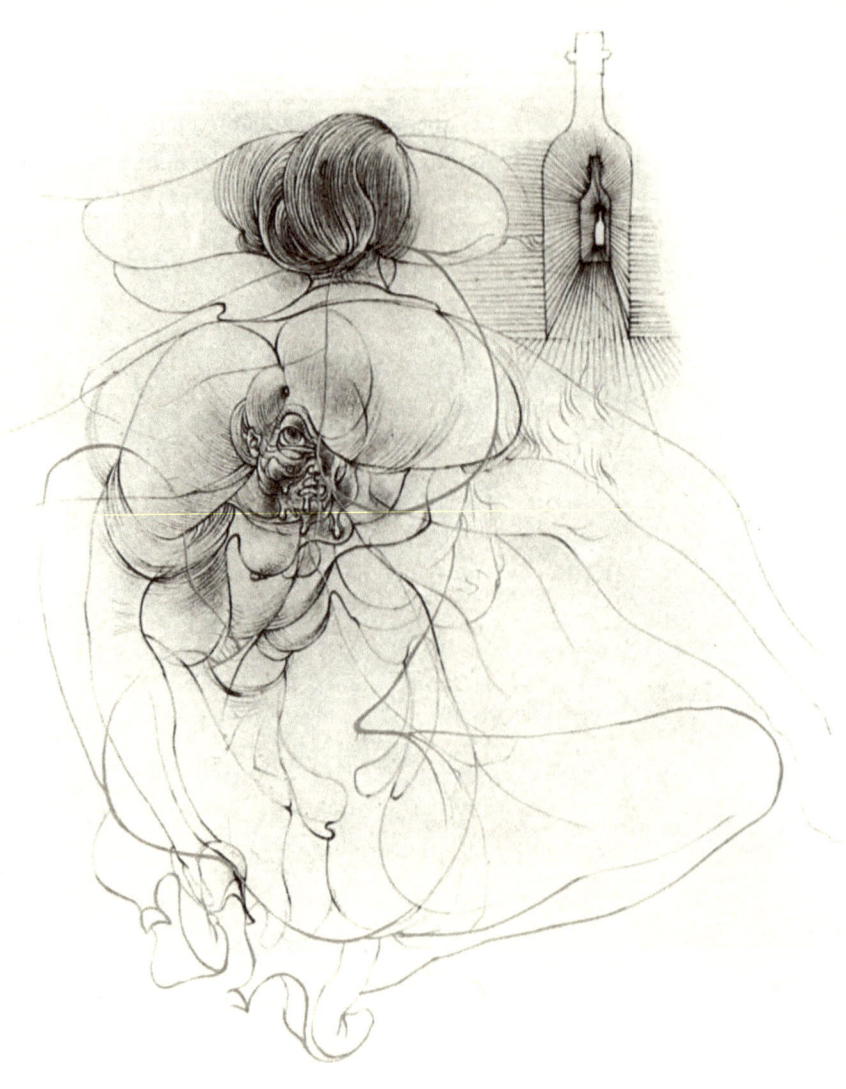

Hans Bellmer, *Aline et Valcour* (1968).

"so that … all traces of my grave may disappear from the surface
of the earth, just as I like to think my memory will be effaced
from the minds of men …"

nt de dessus de la surface de la terre,
ra de l'esprit des hommes… D.A.F. SADE

Hans Bellmer, *Aline et Valcour* (1968).

ALINE AND VALCOUR
or, the Philosophical Novel

by

Marquis de Sade

Vol. III

Translated by

Jocelyne Geneviève Barque

&

John Galbraith Simmons

Contra Mundum Press   New York · London · Melbourne

Aline and Valcour © 2019 John Galbraith Simmons & Jocelyne Geneviève Barque; Introduction © 2019 John Galbraith Simmons.

This translation is a recipient of a Grant from The National Endowment of the Arts.

NATIONAL ENDOWMENT for the ARTS
══════ arts.gov

Letters I–V appeared in slightly different form in *The Brooklyn Rail* (February 2009) and *Fiction Anthology 2* (2013); "The Crime of Passion, or Love's Delirium" appeared in *The Brooklyn Rail* (September 2013).

First Contra Mundum Press Edition 2019.

Library of Congress Cataloguing-in-Publication Data

Sade, 1740–1814

Aline and Valcour, Vol. III / Sade; Introduction by John Galbraith Simmons

—1st Contra Mundum Press Edition
488 pp., 6×9 in.

ISBN 9781940625331

   I. Sade.
  II. Title.
 III. Simmons, John Galbraith; Barque, Jocelyne Geneviève.
 IV. Translation.
  V. Simmons, John Galbraith.
 VI. Introduction.

2019946562

Table of Contents

Introduction

Aline and Valcour

Endnotes

Illustrations

Translators' Note

In accordance with recent editions in French, our translation is based on the third state or printing of the novel in 1795. The text in English is complete and integral. Footnotes are Sade's own, added at the time of publication. At the end of each volume we provide contextual endnotes that gloss historic and unfamiliar events, names, and places.

ALINE AND VALCOUR
or, the Philosophical Novel

Written in the Bastille a year before the Revolution in France
by Citizen S***

Nam veluti pueri trepidant atque omnia cæcis
in tenebris metuunt, sic nos in luce timemus
interdum, nilo quæ sunt metuenda magis quam
quæ pueri in tenebris pavitant finguntque futura.
hunc igitur terrorem animi tenebrasque necessest
non radii solis neque lucida tela diei
discutiant sed naturæ species ratioque.

Just as children in the night tremble & fear everything,
so we in the light sometimes fear
what is no more to be feared than the things
children shudder at in the dark
and imagine will come true. This terror,
this darkness of the mind's eye must be scattered,
not by the rays of the sun & glistening shafts of daylight,
but by a dispassionate view of the inner laws of Nature.

— Lucretius, *De rerum natura*, Book III

Important Note to the Reader

The author must inform the reader that, having sold and submitted his manuscript at the time he left the Bastille, there was consequently no question of his being able to revise it. How then can this work, written seven years ago, remain fully current with the order of the day? He asks his readers to think back and recall the very extraordinary circumstances of that time; and he invites them to form a judgment only after reading from beginning to end. For a book of this sort, it is not the appearance of one or another character, or of some isolated system of thought, upon which an opinion may be based. One who is just and impartial will only ever pronounce upon the whole.

Principal Characters

Monsieur de Blamont	"The President," a magistrate judge and libertine
Monsieur Dolbourg	a banker, best friend & Blamont's companion in crime
Madame de Blamont	"The President," Blamont's wife
Aline	daughter of Monsieur & Madame de Blamont
Valcour	Aline's young suitor
Monsieur Déterville	friend to Aline, Madame de Blamont, & Valcour
Eugénie	fiancée then wife to Déterville
Madame de Senneval	mother-in-law to Déterville
Sophie	spurned mistress to Dolbourg
Sainville	young man & world voyager
Léonore	Sainville's wife & lover
Clémentine	Léonore's companion
Ben Mâacoro	King of Butua (a dystopia)
Zamé	Chief of Tamoé (a utopia)
Brigandos	Leader of Bohemian Gypsies

Letter XXXVI

Déterville to Valcour

Vertfeuille, 17 November

Is it not truly odious, my dear Valcour, that an unfortunate
young man, guilty only of sentiments that give rise to virtue,
after having covered the earth and braved every peril, encoun-
tering only obstacles and torments and misfortunes — that he,
now returning to his native land and soon to be home, could
see it only to curse it? Such calamities, I dare say, make for
reflections I'd just as soon pass over in silence. The amity that
Sainville inspires would spread great bitterness.

'Twas he and Aline, my dear Valcour, who were the cause
of the great tumult. *Aline and Sainville.* I can imagine you
saying: "Whatever can you mean? What sort of strange turn
of events would involve these two?"

Read on and all will become clear.

Needless to depict for you the fright our women suffered
when they saw the house fill with police, spies, and soldiers
— not to mention all manner of disgusting rabble whose despotism strikes terror in humanity at the expense of reason and
justice, as if the government required assurances beyond virtue and, among men, a bond besides one's honor. I need not tell
you what became of our charming group when there emerged,
in the midst of this uproar, an ugly little man — short, fat, stupid looking, all atremble — a sword in one hand and a pistol in
the other. He bore the titles *King's Counselor & Commanding
Officer* of the courts of Paris. And here he had come and now
stated that, for purposes of national security, he must insure
that if an army officer who goes by the name *Sainville* (a name
usurped, as the order he bore proved) — if such *Sire de Sainville* were present at the Chateau of Vertfeuille, near Orléans,

it was the duty of himself, Nicodem Poussefort (as this Commanding Officer was named), to arrest said soldier in said chateau together with a young woman whom he had abducted and made to pass for his wife. He was to conduct them both to a place as indicated by the Court.*

I leave you to guess, after such a preamble, what each of us was thinking. I can only tell you what happened — and the singular role the President de Blamont plays in in all this.

Once the little man's speech was done, like a priest down from his pulpit he stood sweating, twitching, and poisonous. While our ladies revived and poor Sainville and his wife wailed and wept in one another's arms, Count de Beaulé, stepping forward with that air of nobility and superiority with which he had once commanded the French in the face of the enemy, ordered the fellow to stand down and discharge his men from the room. How could he have the gall to enter the chateau of an honest woman with so little formality? To this question, masterfully formulated with the titles and decorations that supported it, Nicodem Poussefort, Superior Officer of Paris Security, responded with some confusion that he believed he was authorized both by the order he carried and by instructions that he had received from the concerned parties. But the Count, after a second round of upbraids and insults, informed him that orders pertaining to parental *lettres de cachet* were not to be announced in barking orders like the highwayman and thief Louis Mandrin but, rather, signaled by the organ of the assigned officers in each district. The *chimeric* supremacy or *illusory* authority of the tribunal of the Paris Security Court

---

* Everything barbarous is preserved in barbarity's own idiom. It seems that we must use the language of our cruel ancestors each time we imitate their atrocious behavior. See the style of monitory letters, of letters of assignation, of *lettres de cachet*. Fortunately, it is impossible to kill or imprison a man using good French.

did not extend beyond the city limits. He again demanded the   o
order's provenance and by what solicitation it was obtained.
In response the officer handed him papers and the Count,
before opening them, told him:

"At ease, Monsieur, I shall take care of this."

Then, turning to Monsieur and Madame de Sainville: 5

"You are to be my prisoners," he told them. "Give me your
word of honor that you will not leave this house without me."

"You are mistaken, Monsieur," piped up the officer. "The
lady whose compliance you demand is not the person whom I
must arrest. The one whom my instructions indicate —" and   10
he pointed to Aline — "is this young woman. She must be
Madame de Sainville."

"The error is yours," said the Count. "Your instructions are
false. The young woman whom you designate is the daughter
of Madame de Blamont."   15

And indicating Léonore:

"She and she alone is Madame de Sainville."

"Monsieur le Count," replied the officer, "the thing is all
the more improbable because my instructions owe to the President, Monsieur de Blamont himself. Would he have ordered   20
me to arrest his own daughter? Let us bring them face to face."

The given description of Aline could not be bettered. No
feature of hers resembled Léonore and to mistake one for the
other was impossible.

"Ah — but now it's clear!" impetuously burst forth Ma-   25
dame de Blamont. Addressing the officer: "Please, Monsieur,
shed some light. What are your exact orders concerning this
young lady?"

"To leave her at the convent of the Benedictines on the
way to Lyon, Madame. To say that she is awaiting her family,   30
soon to come and make arrangements. Then to continue with
Monsieur de Sainville to the Île Sainte-Marguerite, where he
shall be imprisoned for ten years."

"And what person provided you with these various instructions?"

"My first order, Madame," replied the officer, "general and rather vague, came from the President. He told me to follow orders set out by Monsieur de Sainville's father, who did not wish to sign onto the task of having his own son arrested at the home of Madame de Blamont, where he knew he was to be found, unless it were done in conjunction with Monsieur le President. Consequent to this consideration, more than one day was required and I was brought next morning to a second meeting. There I found the two men and received from them the various particulars that enabled me to take action."

And that, my dear Valcour, was all we could learn, and since nothing further has been clarified, I imagine that even before finishing this letter you'll be given over to a million speculations. Let us formulate some together, even if it interrupts the interesting course of events I have yet to relate.

It appears clear, first of all, that Monsieur de Blamont had conferred with Sainville's father and asked — indeed, entreated the man — to allow him to make use of a *lettre de cachet* for his own daughter. He claimed she was far guiltier than Léonore; and as no one laid claim to the latter, he would take responsibility. The important thing was to separate Léonore from Sainville, which objective would be readily achieved since Madame de Blamont was likely to let her to stay at Vertfeuille. Later he planned to fetch her in order to install her in a convent, from which she could always be summoned if needed. Sainville's father clearly had little interest in Léonore and only desired to disjoin her from his son, so he accorded the President everything he wanted, provided the latter assured him that the arrest take place at Vertfeuille. All this, my friend, with the aim of detaining Aline and taking her to Lyon, once and for all becoming Dolbourg's wife; and the President would not be long in joining them.

These are my conjectures, my friend, and those of all of
us here. Let's now look to the crucial details of what actually
happened.

"You may withdraw, Monsieur," the Count said to the officer after these clarifications. "Return to tell those who sent
you that Count de Beaulé, Commandant in the province of
Orléanais and Lieutenant General of the army, takes your
prisoners in charge and gives you his word that he will bring
them to the minister three days hence."

"*Monsieur le Comte*," said the officer, prostrating before
him, "I shall obey without question; but you understand my
situation and know I risk losing my position if you've not the
kindness to give me a receipt."

The General ordered an escritoire and immediately provided what the officer wanted. After which, the Alguazil and
his troops decamped, not without filching here and pilfering
there, as is common among such rascals, absconding with
anything they could lay their hands on.*

Scarcely had they left than we made prodigious efforts to
make sense of the President's despicable and clumsy maneuvers. As I just included everything we said in my description
of what transpired, let me pass quickly to the essential upshot.
As calm returned, all reflections made, the Count opened the
order and after reading a few lines:

"What! Monsieur!" He turned with surprise to Sainville:
"You are in fact the Count of Karmeil? I know your father well."

---

* You can see what we call civilization in France and the price we pay for no longer
gathering food in the forest — a multitude of crimes tolerated, authorized, and rewarded. The government punishes two or three delinquents who would be astonished
to have committed as many horrors as these villains come to tear apart a family. Here
is what in our country we call good order, security, the police. Come virtue — see how
the French worship and serve you! *(Author's note.)*

  We must recall that the author here refers to the government of the old order.
(Editor's note.)

"The Count of Karmeil!" cried Madame de Blamont, thoroughly distraught and confused. "Are you sure? Are you not making a mistake? Great heavens! Léonore, no! I cannot resist the blows of fate! Unhappy child! Open your arms — to me — *to your own mother!*"

And so overwhelmed by all that just transpired, by such a touching scene, she fainted. She fell into the arms of Léonore herself.

"Great God," said Léonore. "Surely the goodness of this kind woman has misled her. What's she trying to say? Me, her daughter! Please Heaven were it only true!"

"But it is, Mademoiselle," I said. "Let's help Madame de Blamont. She's far from wrong. We've everything needed to convince you. Sainville, help me introduce your wife to the most adorable of mothers."

I leave you to imagine the universal uproar. The Count, completely unaware of the facts, had no idea what was going on. Madame de Senneval, who knew everything, assured Léonore there could be no mistake. Madame de Blamont, with prompt help from Aline, who had no idea which way to turn, regained consciousness, and cast herself a second time into Léonore's arms. The confusion cleared when, for my part, I produced both the letter from the Chevalier de Meilcourt and the depositions we took at Pré-Saint-Gervais. Together they made a powerful case. It was impossible that Claire de Blamont, called Léonore for purposes of this story, could long remain blind to the facts of her birth.

"So that explains why Madame de Kerneuil hated me so," she said, prostrating herself at the feet of her real mother. "That's why they detested me. Oh, Madame," she continued — but more by outward gesture than genuine emotion, a feature of her character that must be always kept in mind — "let me ask you on bended knee to provide those sentiments that the unfortunate hand of fate never permitted me to know. My soul was made to enjoy them but the most barbarous of women refused to allow it. Sainville, hasten to kneel like me before this tender mother. Beg her forgiveness for our errors and aspire to her blessing."

That interesting young man, more genuinely affected than his wife, wept prostate at the feet of Madame de Blamont. "Oh, Madame, will you deign forgive my crimes — my many crimes?"

"By the Good Lord above," said that delicate and sensitive mother, "you've committed no such thing. Your only error was to have loved. Like you, I would have loved her, too. Arise, Sainville. I want you to receive her from my hand."

I shan't picture for you the lovely woman and the charming couple. Aline kissed them in turn, her mother and her sister. No, my friend: Only Nature's palette could render this tableau; artistry could not.

We were meanwhile recounting, as succinctly as we could, the whole story to Count Beaulé.

"Singular adventures indeed," he said as he approached Madame de Blamont. "My old and dear friend," he continued, taking her hands in his, "they truly bring me to tears. But you are the mystery. Why didn't you tell me? Now he's become like a son, dear Sainville. And poor Aline — they've acted against her, too. What a horror! Come, come, let us all be calm, I shall take all three under my wing and if the least misfortune threatens again, I will put my life on the line before seeing harm come to any of them."

All turned to this gentle & honest soldier. We came around him and thanked him and caressed him. Madame de Blamont in an excess of joy wrapped her arms around his neck and said:

"My dear Count. If ever you loved me, you'll save these three fine creatures from unhappiness."

"I give my word," replied the Count, quite moved. "How could I not when I see before me a divine marriage, love and friendship, all in the name of what's right? Karmeil has been my friend for 30 years; we fought together in Germany and Corsica." However, he continued, "No doubt the question of 100,000 écus drives him to despair." He turned to Sainville and Léonore: "And you both passed for dead?"

"It's true, monsieur," replied Léonore's young lover, "and also one of the circumstances in our story that I believed best to pass over in silence. After she'd fled the cloister, Léonore wrote her parents that, unable to abide the horror of her situation and burning to be united with the object of her desire but now restrained by decency, she dared not go further. Faced with losing either her honor or the one she loved, she wrote that she'd decided to end her life. To insure her death not be doubted, she placed the letter inside a box with one of her dresses, and together we tossed it into the river. When recovered, her clothing would be recognized and the letter read; her body would be given up as lost, leaving no room for doubt in the province. For myself, I wrote my father that I was going to Russia out of despair, and he would never again hear from the son he had wished to make his victim. To confirm my definitive disappearance with a view to preventing further search, I asked a friend in that country to wait three months, then inform the Count of Karmeil of my death. I know he did so and that my father sooner recovered from that than from my plunder of one 100,000 écus."

"All this makes sense in light of Chevalier Meilcourt's letter," replied the Count with heartening frankness. "Courage, my friend. We'll overcome all this. I repeat: your father's only concern was losing the damned écus. A shame, for if we had even half the ingots lost to the Inquisition, I could certainly make him change his mind. I shan't renounce the gold;

I'll talk to the minister. We must write him. It's a vile injustice. 0
The King of Spain himself must rectify this — he must."

And he turned to Aline:

"As for you, my child, don't worry. Of all three, you've the least to worry about. The President's effort was nothing but a subterfuge bound to fail as soon as the mistake was recog- 5
nized. There is a *lettre de cachet* for you. The only one that exists implicates Madame de Sainville. You've nothing to fear. The instructions were an error that fails the test. Only Léonore is in danger, and I will take care of it."

Effusions of gratitude poured forth anew. As suppertime 10
approached we sat down to table, where hope soon reawak-ened in every heart the sentiments consumed by so many un-fortunate events. On everyone's face could be read renewed joy and tranquility.

The next day it was decided that everything concerning 15
Léonore would be carefully concealed from the President. The young woman would appear in public only as the daughter of the late Countess of Kerneuil, who had raised her, whose name she bore, and whose property she'd inherit. After recti-fying with Versailles the story of the *lettre de cachet*, which 20
the Count guessed would take just 24 hours, we would seek an intelligent and reliable man of affairs to go to Rennes and work to secure Léonore's assets.

"Let your conscience remain at peace," said the Count to Madame de Blamont, seeing that she disliked the arrange- 25
ment. "I understand your sensitivity in these matters, but here it's uncalled for. Between two inevitable evils, the wise man must always prefer the lesser. While Léonore ought to be declared your daughter, to do so would be impossible with a man like the President, who from the cradle conspired against 30
the poor creature's happiness and would only find some new way to torment her. She must be recognized as the person

she's always been believed to be, so she must also lay claim to what's hers."

"But what if among the heirs of Madame de Kerneuil," asked Madame de Blamont, "there might be some who will be ruined?"

"That would be unfortunate," said the Count, "but quite easy to repair through sacrifices that Léonore would assuredly make and, in any case, a far lesser evil than handing her over to the President. Can you imagine the multitude of indecent explanations that would necessarily be made public if we adopted that tactic? The President has no need of another daughter; he believes he has one already in Sophie, and abused her horribly. Let's incite nothing further in that perverted soul. May Léonore, already made unhappy by a mother not her own, not become more so with her true father. And besides, what fortune could you provide for this young woman? You know how much this concerns me. You mustn't think I'd allow you to endanger Aline's dowry, meant to provide the fortune of our dear Valcour, the best and most honest of men!"

"Oh, Monsieur!" cried Aline, "Let no such consideration stop you; Valcour doesn't want the money and I don't want it either unless I can share it with my sister."

"No," replied the Count. "Léonore would only accept her older sister's kind offer if she had no other fortune; but she has what she needs to live on without you; and she must claim the inheritance of Madame de Kerneuil and enjoy it. Believe me: better to leave things as they are."

"The heirs we dispossess still worry me," repeated the honest President.

"Good heavens and so what!" said the Count, "We'll assign them ingots from Madrid."

That last sally brought laughter and all agreed on these three points:

First, we must see to voiding the court order with no   o
harm to Aline; it was an act of gross deception that could not
stand the least scrutiny; yet, as concerns that damnable ruse,
for the sake of the President's honor it's wise to just keep silent.
We can be quite sure he'll conceal it, too, once he realizes it's
got no chance of success.   5

Second, approval by the Count of Karmeil of the marriage between Sainville and Léonore, with both religious and
civil formalities to ensure validity.

Third, we provide proof that Elizabeth de Kerneuil, believed dead, had only eloped with her husband, which makes   10
her immediately accepted as legitimate heir to the assets of
the Count and Countess de Kerneuil.

With these resolutions adopted and preliminary letters
written, and after shared reflections concerning the singularity of Léonore's provenance, concealed from her at birth by   15
her real father, only to come to light as she fell a second time
into a trap set by that villain, we made gestures — of attachment, of tenderness, and of gratitude — deliciously done on
both sides.

That left us with the pleasure of listening to the adven-   20
tures of the beautiful Léonore. These will come to you, in view
of all I've had to put down here concerning today's events,
in my next letter.

Letter XXXVII
President de Blamont to Dolbourg

Paris, 18 November

Well then, Dolbourg, in spite of your spurious systems and absurd reasoning, will you agree that Heaven frequently favors what you call crime and casts aside what you call virtue? Where in the devil have you seen it otherwise? In all honesty, you still have some childish prejudices that always make me blush. Much as I call you my pupil, no one can believe it as soon as you open your mouth. Recently I brought you into good company with academicians and faculty lights, placing you amidst our century's Socrates and Aspasias. What did I find but you were ready to mount the pulpit to prove the existence of God! They all laughed and looked to me. With you old as Methuselah, I unfortunately couldn't use your age as an excuse. I chose to disavow you. Educate yourself, I beg you. Declare war on all those stupid and offensive illusions that still clot up your mind! Leave me out of your foolishness.

All that aside, have you ever seen anything more pleasing than the arrival, *chez ma femme*, of that pretty adventuress? Or the touching and saintly hospitality my good dear spouse accorded her? Or how I was immediately apprised of it all? Or, so too, that fine gentleman and father from Brittany who begged I approve his boy's arrest at my wife's home, where rumor had it he could be found. Then, too, on this singular occasion you had our wholly natural capture of the charming Aline instead of the lady love of our angry father's son. Well, then, what say you? Dare you now claim there exists no divine hand by which we may ensnare those two tender creatures?

However, as we are now embattled, though I in no way doubt our eventual success, it's time to sketch the way forward.

According to my calculations, Aline will be in Lyon with the Benedictines on the 21ˢᵗ or 22ⁿᵈ of the month. I have written to the Abbess, whom I count as a friend, and the young lady will be held under close watch until we arrive. We will leave her there a week or two while we take hold of the other one. The old Count from Brittany seemed worried, to say the least, about the young lady of Kerneuil with whom his son had chosen to elope. He'll be happy if I take her out of the picture and, with no pension to pay, thoroughly delighted. The pretty damsel appears to be a genuine creature left for naught: she has neither father nor mother. She was believed to have died near where she was born — bad behavior and not to be helped. You understand what I'm talking about? Caught in our nets, wouldn't she be a pretty little eel? Would it be anything but unjust not to take advantage of the situation, when heaven abandons her to us without respite? And more: looks of an angel, just 18 years old. Not first fruit, I know, but so many ways to compensate for that; besides, for a certain kind of libertine, such things are a matter of indifference. Aren't we sure of new and piquant pleasures when we ourselves propose them?

In order to avoid the appearance of being in too great a hurry, we will only return to Vertfeuille in four or five days; and there, with all possible decency and requisite *politesse*, we'll take away this dear Léonore de Kerneuil — whom my wife, astonished by the confusion, shall assuredly have kept with her for the sake of propriety — and we'll transport her immediately to the little house in Montmartre, where our victim shall remain until it pleases the Sacrificial Priests to offer her in homage to Venus.

That will entail another scene at Vertfeuille, as I hope you understand. The Senneval woman will grouse and grieve; virtuous Déterville will frown and curl his bottom lip; and the President shall weep, demand her daughter be returned, call me her tyrant and so forth —all those pretty epithets that these women lavish upon us when our fantasies and tastes don't harmonize with the stupid monotony of their own.

And what are your plans in all this? Will you assuage and pretend? To what end? Does the hunter need a snare when his prey is already in the dog's jaws and a gesture will fetch it up? The marriage will happen and to my wife I shall insist: *You constantly imposed new obstacles. I had to overcome them. Your daughter is not dead and you shall see her again. But only with the name* Dolbourg.

She can cry and shout all she likes. We'll have won the day. That's the important thing.

These preliminaries taken care of and with the demoiselle of Kerneuil safe in our hands and, indeed, *ours* if you like, we shall set off for Lyon to see to your marriage, which shall be consummated, fresh from the flowered banks of the Rhone, at the impenetrable Chateau de Blamont. What do you think of this plan? Do you not find it well conceived? With these arrangements, the demoiselle Augustine, whose inclinations have begun to make me very happy, will become quite useless to us. But no matter. We'll put her to the side for the time being. It often happens in life that libertines like ourselves need a reliable woman, and an accomplished minx like her is never just a useless piece of furniture.

As for the young damsel from Brittany, my friend, you cannot imagine to what extent she occupies my mind. I don't know but that I feel something for her far more exciting than for anybody else. All this without knowing her or even having seen her, yet a secret voice seems to promise my heart the kind of voluptuous sensual delight it's never known. Nature's inspirations are indeed a pleasant fine thing; a philosopher who paid attention to them would find some quite extraordinary.

Is it not already quite singular that Nature titillates us within, inexpressibly, at the least promise of some dastardly deed? What becomes of men's laws when Nature so delights at just the thought of breaking them?

Always a bit of a lesson, to be sure. With another there would be something to crow about but with you it's not worth the trouble. You take less pleasure by half in misdeeds because you don't analyze. They're only truly delicious when you combine and savor them. Only then do you have voluptuous memories that provide pleasure a thousand years after being committed.

Don't suppose that all these projects have made me forget young Sophie. New desires never eradicate the old; like a bee in flowers, I roam indifferently amidst the sweetest, and I soil and profane everything that comes my way; I leave the rest for idle hours — always, in my case, rare. We shall search, lie in wait, and pounce, to be sure, upon that charming fugitive.

Once found, you can well imagine how we must use her to *set an example* and treat her with all due rigor. I insist on *examples*, I confess. More than a score of times in my life I've imposed the death sentence for some unfortunate soul with the sole aim of *setting an example*. Nothing, I find, is so advantageous to society — because corrections require we break on the wheel and hang people every day! To us alone the *example* does not apply — and do you know the reason? So that we're not hanged ourselves and no one even dare accuse us. So it is we enjoy a sense of impunity delightful for souls such as ours.*

---

* Certainly, if we condemned judges who erred when it was a question of life and death to the same torture as those they pronounce upon, we would no longer see such infamy. Less blood would run from our gallows. For something to amuse the people, one or two mophead judges consigned to the gibbet would save the lives of a thousand innocents.

o To me it seems essential, besides, to severely punish the
compassionate Madame de Blamont, who accords hospitality
to every young woman who comes down the pike and ends by
being talked about everywhere. An honest husband with his
own reputation to protect needs still must look after that of
s his wife.

Oh! Bid all good night — 'tis two in the morning and I'm
falling asleep.

Letter XXXVIII
Déterville to Valcour

Vertfeuille, 16 November

Part Two — Léonore

"If anything," *said the lovely young woman to Madame de
Blamont,* "might excuse the hazardous course Monsieur de　　10
Karmeil made me take (permit me, in recounting our adventures, to call him Sainville, as he's better known) — if anything,
I say, would make me worthy of your indulgence, I dare lay
claim to such consideration in light of the odious treatment I
regularly received from Madame de Kerneuil. Weak justifica-　　15
tion, to be sure; a daughter must endure everything from her
parents. That I know, but when nothing compensates for such
harshness, when the woman you take to be your mother re-
peatedly tells you she's not related to you in any way, that she'd
been duped, that her infant had been exchanged while under a　　20
wet nurse's care, and that the child returned to her was assuredly only the daughter of a peasant, and that such comments
rained down with threats and blows, you may understand that
my patience wore thin; and when, after all this, you're torn
away from the man you adore to be sacrificed to someone you　　25
hate, at 15 years old, at least with my disposition, you're liable
to behave foolishly."

　　"Your disposition?" asked Madame de Blamont.

　　"Yes, Madame," returned Léonore. "I am about to reveal
too many proofs of its vivacity not to forewarn you and ask　　30
that you forgive its many faults."

I shall not repeat, Madame, *our heroine continued,* what you already know of the beginning of my story. I can see how anxious you are to learn about the awful event that separated me from Sainville in Venice and so immediately pass onto the issue of that catastrophe.

Foolish caution, for which I've often since blamed myself, was the only cause of my awful separation from Sainville.

A noble named Fallieri was the man who so cruelly afflicted our union. He didn't conceal his plans from me; I learned of them in a signed letter delivered by one of our gondoliers. I simply told this emissary to inform his employer that he was wasting his time and energy. To avoid arguments and justifications, I tore up the note and said not a word to Sainville; then, without revealing my reasons, I made him discharge our people because now they were all suspect. He complied, but it was useless; the plot was too far advanced. Fallieri was rich and had too many people working for him; his prey would not escape. And what sort of man? What kind of monster intended to steal me from my love? I don't know how possibly to describe him without disgust and can't remember him without horror. All the twisted features Nature can unite she wove together to create the appearance of this terrifying man; and the only thing worse was that dedicated libertine's heart and mind. Don't imagine love played a role in the awful man's scheme; he proudly avowed he'd never known it. Guided by intemperance and aspiring only to satisfy it, anybody with a few charms was the same to him. The letter I'd received simply put me on notice. If it didn't get results, he had other means.

It was four days after my unpleasant response to Fallieri's impudent letter that Sainville made plans that would leave me alone in the fig tree garden on Malamocco Island. Disturbed by dark premonitions I could not comprehend, I tried to stop

him a dozen times; I considered telling him everything, then   o
tried arousing his jealousy without saying a thing about the
real cause. I vacillated, mumbled a few words, and could not
hold back a flood of tears. His virtuous trust heard nothing
and I couldn't find the courage to reveal my dark secret before
he left. No sooner was he gone the whole horror of my situa-   5
tion came all too clear with a sudden warning.

The garden's miserable owner, whom we believed honest,
had disclosed the most reliable information about our activi-
ties to Fallieri, and she alone convinced him that capturing me
in her yard, whether my husband was there or not, would be   10
the easiest thing in the world.

She approached me just after Sainville left to tell me, as
I'd requested she do, that others were coming to visit her garden. But dropping the respectful tone she'd always taken until
then, she rudely told me either to leave or come inside her   15
house if I didn't want to be seen.

What she said, her tone of voice, and the way she addressed me all made me tremble with anger — and fear.

"How is that, Madame?" I said to the arrogant creature,
"Don't you remember our agreement? Only a short while and   20
my husband will be back."

"Oh! Your husband! You little wh--e" she replied. "The
likes of him can be found anywhere. The one I'm going to get
for you is worth far more."

At those cruel words I broke into a cold sweat. Feeling   25
lost and helpless, I fell on my knees and clasped my hands.

"Dear lady!" I exclaimed "Are you abandoning me? You're
going to hand me over? I dare implore you as my protector —
don't sacrifice innocence —"

But it was too late. She vanished. Immediately six men   30
surrounded me and brought me almost fainting into a gondola

that rapidly departed the island, reaching the Brenta Canal,* and about four hours later docked at a remote palace where my abductor was waiting.

They brought me before him more dead than alive. Whatever the extent of his debauchery, some little sensitivity remained in his coarse soul — such that he clearly understood my condition would not permit him to fulfill his desires just then. For satisfaction, it was wiser to wait a few hours, the better to give rise to at least some sensation in the unfortunate object he planned to sacrifice for the sake of his own.

Here Léonore flushed deeply and began to stammer.

"Madame," she continued, embarrassed, *still addressing the President*: "You enjoined me to hide nothing from you, and I shall dare tell all. I guarded my virtue as best I could and hope at least you won't condemn me for the transgressions that shame the assailants of my modesty even without, on my part, the least weakening."

"Indeed! Who does not know of such things," exclaimed the old general. "We all know that a lost young woman cannot protect herself from a man's recklessness; in all this there is no suspicion that you committed even a venial sin. A woman is never guilty but by her own free will; everything taken from her by force is at the charge of her abductor and forever a stain upon his conscience. But there are scoundrels who care not a whit about one misdeed more or less; so long as they get what they want, they're unconcerned about how they obtain it."

"Alas! This libertine would be counted among them, Monsieur," continued Léonore. "He ordered me be put to bed. He had a woman do it in his presence, and permitted his eyes devour all.

---

* The channel links Padua and Venice; superb country estates of Venetian nobility line its banks.

"Were you undressed?" asked the Count.

Léonore reddened. "Monsieur!"

"She may spare us the details," said Madame de Senneval. "Truly, Count, you are too curious. You can see that this Venetian was an impudent man who permitted himself every liberty except the one that he believed he ought to put off for a time in the interest of his own pleasure. Is that not the case, lovely girl?"

"Yes, Madame," Léonore replied. "Your deft honesty tells all and spares me the shame; it is the height of thoughtful sensitivity."

"Something I would like to know —" said the Count.

"That you will not, however," Madame de Blamont interrupted. "You see how you make these young ladies blush. Continue, Léonore, continue. You've already described this person and we can imagine what he might do."

The turmoil I experienced, *resumed our beautiful adventuress,* the intense grief that consumed me, the endless tears, soon rendered my condition even more serious than Fallieri could have imagined; and when he came the next day to enjoy the success of his criminal doings, he found me in such agitation and so tormented by a raging fever that it became impossible for him to do with me as he wanted. My state raised more bile than interest; he went away grumbling and fulminating against French women who, prettier and more delicate than others, he said, always made for such scenes. He would have no more of them. He added: "I cannot stand these prudes who faint away for a thing that would make others come running." And he went off, leaving orders to be informed when my health improved.

It is said that when fate torments us at the height of misfortune, the gods are sure to help. To that I trusted and shall never repent of it.

Dolcini — such was the name of the surgeon who treated me — was about 30 years old, handsome, with a sweet and honest nature. As soon as I realized his soul was open to me, that he not only sympathized with my plight but felt moved by the evils intended to befall me once I recovered, I showed my gratitude with vivid expressions that both touched him deeply and inflamed his heart. Soon I could see that Dolcini had fallen in love. I let him talk about it and did everything possible to make him believe I was not indifferent. The fact was that escape from imminent danger, no matter the price, was clearly essential. If Providence spared me this time, I told myself, it would not abandon me the next. She'd help me escape from the weaker man just as she helped me with one more powerful, so I'd find the means to get away from the one as from the other.

"Kindly take a moment to consider my line of reasoning," *said Léonore to* the *assembled.* "False though it might appear, it served as my dependable guide: to never be afraid of putting myself in danger a second time to escape the fate of the first."

Indeed, when Dolcini saw I approved his passion, he sought to help me in every way. Eagerly he told me one day: "The essential thing is to take you out of this place."

"That's all I want."

"It's not as easy as you think or as I would like. We're surrounded by spies. Among them, the woman who attends you — we must not even think of dismissing her. As for myself, whether the thing succeeds or not I shall be left ruined and penniless. The safest choice, in consequence, if you really care anything for me, is to agree to accompany me to Sicily, my

native land. There — I give you my word — I'll marry you   o
as soon as we arrive. But how to proceed?"

"And if you really love me, need you ask? Can't your affection overcome every obstacle?"

"Ah! Believe me, only the insurmountable would stop me
for even a moment." Then, after a brief reflection: "I see only   5
one way out: we take advantage of your illness to escape."

"How do you imagine that could help?"

"Listen to me, and above all, have no fear. 'Tis frightful
to be sure but it's all we have."

"Explain yourself."   10

"My reports will change concerning your health and
symptoms. I'll say you'e in great danger, at death's door. Little
by little you will seem to worsen and finally pretend to die. I'll
be the only witness to your last breath. I'm quite sure your
abductor will allow no one else versed in the medical arts to   15
attend, nor even let a priest offer absolution. We only must
keep your caretaker in the dark; we can't shut her out but
we'll mislead her. The plan shall work. I alone will attend to
your burial in the parish near the chateau. The gravedigger is
a commoner and indebted to me. He will place you in a vault   20
to which I alone have access. The same night I'll come to take
you away and we'll promptly depart for Sicily. Tell me: do you
find this plan too frightening?"

"'Tis extreme. If the least bit goes awry or were anything
neglected —"   25

"Great heavens! With the love you inspire, how can you
doubt? Would I try anything like this only to abandon you?
I'm taking you away in the face of all possible peril."

"Certainly — but there must be attention to every detail.
Once I'm locked inside the vault, what if something happens   30
to you? Misfortune always threatens and can strike at any
time. If you alone know the secret, imagine the risk."

"The gravedigger shall be in my confidence. How could he not? If something were to happen to me, would he not save you?"

"All right! I put myself in your hands. My trust dispels all fear."

"But, my beautiful Léonore," continued Dolcini, kneeling beside me, "will you agree at least to repay such love and zeal?"

I gave him my hand and looked away for fear I might reveal my true feelings. Over and over he caressed my hand, then left straightaway to prepare.

He returned the same evening.

"I've just come from the city," he told me, "where I ordered a coffin. It will be cushioned with three inches of horsehair and feathers, and lined with white satin. In one corner two drawers will be made, one to contain salts and spirituous waters, the other dried jams, biscuits, and Spanish wine. You will easily be able to breathe and have everything you need at hand to sustain you for 24 hours; you will be as comfortable as if you were in a chaise lounge. The coffin, to be made by a worker employed by friends of mine, will be shipped to a relative in Padua, where I shall pick it up. I'll bring it here by night, in order to divert spies and evade discovery. Does your courage hold? Do you waiver?"

"No," I said. "Your careful attention so convinces me of your true feelings that I put myself entirely in your hands. Count on my gratitude."

Inflamed by these words, Dolcini thanked me a thousand times twice over and declared he would always be worthy of my feelings for him.

"I'm only a poor surgeon," he told me, "but an honest man — confused, humiliated, full of remorse for serving the gross and vulgar fantasies of such a master, who's in charge of my fate. I'm only too happy to find a way to quit him forever.

O Léonore, what a change of fortune! Yesterday I was the   o
slave and agent of vice; today, I become avenger and brace of
virtue!"

From that moment the daily reports to Fallieri changed
completely. My illness became dangerous and might turn for
the worse; it was impossible to guarantee my recovery; and   5
Dolcini, certain that the request would be denied, asked for
assistance from another physician.

"None of that," answered cruel Fallieri — truly, debauchery smothers all natural feelings.* "Bury her secretly when she
dies. You'll tell the priest that he'd better keep quiet, take his   10
money, and recite paternosters for the soul of the poor creature — whom I didn't have the pleasure of sending to hell."

"Look — what a soul," Dolcini told me, showing me the
awful note. "He would have obtained your last favors and
thought nothing of it. But in the end you've got permission to   15
die — not bad for such a monster."

Now it became a matter of deceiving the guardian, who
was sharp, clever, and dangerous; but I played my part with
skill, trembling, agonizing, simulating faints and swoons. I
completely succeeded in making her my dupe. A final crisis   20
seemed to do me in. Dolcini told her I was dead and therefore
he was going to execute his master's orders. He advised her to
keep quiet; the bier was brought. Together they laid me upon it.

"Go and rest," Dolcini said to the guardian. "You've done
your duty. They'll come for her tonight and we'll bury her. To   25
assure secrecy it will be only myself and one other man. Go."

---

* Libertinage does not stifle Nature's sentiments but it fosters selfishness. The libertine's desires, located in his soul, are almost always in contradiction with, and more
powerful than, social conventions, annihilating them in accord with principles infinitely more powerful; he does not throttle Nature but only makes her cede to egotism.
This general axiom, however, does not hold in this case, for in words and actions
Fallieri speaks with gratuitous bleakness.

The woman wanted nothing more than to take her leave; and once delivered of her presence, Dolcini helped me settle into the casket.

If it weren't for the suffering such a situation can inflict upon the mind, it would have been impossible to be more comfortable. The body, certainly, was shielded from harm. I lay nicely within, breathing marvelously well — in spite of which I was plunged into a lugubrious state that made my plight seem frightful.

The time for our departure arrived. Dolcini, who had yet to make final preparations, wanted to be absolutely sure I was willing, and then he required 16 hours to make ready. We set our watches to the same time. I was to be taken away at four o'clock Monday morning, to be delivered the same day at eight o'clock in the evening. One keeps track of the minutes in situations like these. The gravedigger was to make sure I was alive and I made him promise to release me exactly 16 hours later, whether Dolcini was back or not. He took one key to the casket; my lover, the other. I was taken away. The priest, as ordered, was waiting without ceremony at the door of the church. The prepared vault opened, I was placed inside. The door shut. There I was, alive in the abyss of the dead.

Inconspicuous openings in the vault allowed air to circulate through the holes of the coffin and let me breathe; but then I grew cold. Dolcini had made sure I was dressed warmly but not completely and I was gripped by irrepressible and violent shivering. Fear sprang forth and my imagination darkened. I felt on the verge of losing consciousness when, remembering the liqueurs, I opened one of the drawers as Dolcini had shown me. But I was astonished — my cold hand, instead of finding relief, wrapped around a dagger!

If I ever believed myself at death's door, it was now. *Betrayed & abandoned,* I told myself. *The weapon is yours to use,*

another favor from the barbarous monster. He doesn't want   o
you to die from despair. Don't hesitate. Anything else would be
more dreadful still.

But a little reflection brought me back from the brink. Such
deliberate care had been taken. Was it possible they could have
done all that for someone they planned to sacrifice? The coffin   5
so skillfully organized, small vents so carefully made — could
all that fit with a plan of prompting me to so miserably take my
own life? The fright from the awful discovery dissipated and
put an end to the breakdown from such dark thoughts. With
strength recovered, I undertook another inspection. Feeling   10
about the sides of coffin once more, I came across the drawer
of supplies Dolcini had told me about. I was so relieved and
told myself: *More proofs of attention, the more I'll be certain
nobody wants me to die.* But why the dagger, evidently forgotten? From a small flask of Spanish wine, I drank few drops and   15
felt calm enough to await the hour fixed by my abductor.

But the hour arrived and nothing happened.

"Great heavens!" I thought. "Doubt no longer — this is my
final resting place. I'm about to meet a dreadful end in death's
own temple, prey to reptant creatures within this awful vault   20
intending to eat me alive. Ah! Let me avoid such a terrible end.
Hasten the moment. I must die."

Grabbing the dagger, I tested its point and put it on my
heart. I shed a flood of bitter tears.

O Sainville! Disconsolate: *How young was she who was*   25
taken from you! So many years she could have made you
happy! Yet here she is, lost to you. Detestable trust, traitorous
state — but the misfortune is my own, I've only myself to blame.

Such awful thoughts engulfed me when suddenly I heard
the stone being lifted.   30

Nothing can describe the profusion that assailed me —
hope, worry, joy, fear, all those conflicting feelings overcame

me, though which was the most powerful I couldn't say. The coffin was drawn from the vault and Dolcini appeared.

"We must hurry," he said. "Your guardian suspects something and she's warned Fallieri. We're lost if we don't move quickly. Everything's ready; the felucca awaits at a hundred paces. The gravedigger and I will transport you in the coffin and you'll remain confined to it during the voyage. Covered with an oilcloth, it will pass for a trunk full of merchandise. Our plan cannot but succeed."

"No, cruel man! Explain the dagger. Why was it here? For what reason?"

"Good god! It scared you. A foolish mistake — why didn't I tell you? My first idea had been to disguise you as a man, so a weapon was called for. Foolish — forgive me! But we must leave, Léonore; there's no time. Every wasted moment could cost our lives. Your life is in my hands and I took an oath to save it. No useless delays. Don't make me break my heart's promise."

They carried me off again. The coffin was loaded onto the felucca and placed in a corner covered again with the oilcloth. We sailed immediately.

Three times daily, under the pretext of retrieving something from one of the crates, Dolcini opened the coffin to give me air, a little food, and provide a few tender words. His fear that we were being followed obliged him to make me suffer.

On the fourth day a violent storm rose along the coast of Malta. It was the same that battered Sainville. But the roiling sea pitched the felucca to one side and it sailed like that for more than 80 leagues, so utterly exhausting that I lost consciousness. That explains the moment Sainville described, when he saw a coffin brought into a room at the inn — and witnessed both Dolcini's sorrow when he opened it and first feared he'd found only a corpse, then his joy in perceiving I

408

was still alive. He was getting ready to bring me around when
Sainville left me behind — in order to search for me.

After Dolcini bled me, I quickly recovered. The same
wind that decided Sainville to leave also prompted us to set
sail. My suitor, meanwhile, now convinced there was nothing
more to fear, finally allowed me out of my funereal dwelling.

For us just as for Sainville, the favorable weather that made
us sail further than Catania, as we'd planned, turned out to
be deceptive. Soon an eastern wind pushed us furiously off
course and sent us into the African ocean. There a privateer
out of Tripoli perceived our distress and in a few fatal moments his vessel swept impetuously down upon us. Far too
weak to think of putting up even token resistance, we were
forced to choose between death and capture. Dolcini, inflamed by love, dared dispute the conquest. He lost his life
defending me — slaughtered.

His decapitated head tumbled beside me.

And on we sailed along the African coast.

The same wind that had prevented us from reaching
Sicily was favorable for landing in Africa and we soon headed
for port. The corsair to whom I now belonged hoped to sell
me for a good price. He caused me no grief and from that
good Turk, whether by sympathy or pity, I received far more
solace than I might've expected.

But then the French consul. When early next day we
landed in Tripoli, he happened to be in the harbor and as
we disembarked he immediately recognized me as from his
country. He inquired about my adventures, indicated a desire
to help me and, to better convince me, purchased me from the
pirate on the spot.

"Now you're free, beautiful Léonore." The consul offered me his hand and took me to his home. "May your destiny I offer be more pleasant that the one you've just left behind."

"Monsieur," I replied meekly, "no fate could be crueler than the one from which your generosity has saved me. Believe me, my gratitude shall be eternal."

"It remains only to prove it," said Duval. "With your beauty and the sort of debt you've acquired, it's not hard to imagine what species of tender might repay it."

Duval's fresh impudence made me realize that if I'd changed masters after being nearly taken into a Turk's harem, now I was in a Frenchman's home on a footing not much different. Into whomsoever's hands a woman of my age might fall, the risks were pretty much the same.

That thought — deeply painful for a delicate young woman who aspires only to keep herself pure for the sole object she adores — made me shed tears. Surprised, Duval asked me the reason why; I told him everything.

"You may rest easy, beautiful Léonore," he told me. "Though you've landed on the African coast, you've not fallen into the hands of a barbarian. I've all the sentiments your beauty inspired and will not harm you. To deserve them will be my sole charge and you shall see me work toward that alone."

"Alas! Monsieur," I answered, moved by appearances that would prove deceptive, "what you hope for over time concerning my hand and heart are not mine to give. But if you're generous to the end, kindly seek information on the fate of the husband from whom I was so brutally separated in Venice, and inform him that I'm with you. You may be sure he'll immediately remit the sum you just paid and you'll have made three people happy."

"Three?"

"Yes, three, Monsieur. I find your soul too refined not to place you amongst those made happy by doing a good deed."

Duval, angered by my little outpouring, replied that I o
seemed not to understand my own interests, that when I
wished to turn away a man like him, it wasn't wise to show
such pluck.

"Do not think," he continued, "that the feelings you arouse
in me allow for the disinterest you seem to want to inspire. I 5
shall not assert my rights, yet nor will I give them up by handing you over to a rival. I've just 24 hours left in this city, as I've
been posted to Alexandria, a consular appointment far more
pleasant and rewarding than this one. I hope you'll agree to
follow me there and leave you to reflect. But once arrived in 10
that Egyptian city, whatever decision you take, I'm warning
you that you must behave like the wife I intend to make of you."

"But Monsieur!" I replied, confused. "You just promised
not to abuse your rights!"

"Certainly," Duval continued imperiously. "It would be 15
abusive to treat you like a slave. But I'm asking you to become
my wife."

"Cruel ploy!"

"So it is. Think about it."

Imagine for yourself this last comment, pronounced 20
with the tone of a man who would brook no further rebuffs
— imagine, I say, how deeply it affected me. His frightful manner plunged me into sorrow. Alas! I told myself, perhaps the
bargain was a bad one after all. The corsair who captured me
might have been more compassionate. What was to become 25
of me! What awful fate awaited?

I concealed my distress while, based still on first principles, I determined to deliver myself blind to the danger that
awaited, hoping soon to come across another that I could use
to set me free. 30

So the next day, with Duval's assignment in Tripoli ending, we embarked for Egypt. My new lover feigned indiffer-

ence during the journey. Perhaps he thought his attitude would afflict my self-esteem, not realizing that my tranquility of heart gained more than vanity lost, and that in the sorry spot heaven placed me, I preferred humiliation to love. Still looking for ways to deflate my pride, he told me:

"We arrive tomorrow. I'm expected and shall enjoy a rather important function. I think I've waited long enough for your answer. No more indecision. Kindly tell me now what role you'll play in my household. That of an adventuress suits neither you nor me. Rejecting the idea of being my wife, leaves you in the position of a domestic servant."

"Servant!"

"The word has its proper effect. You must choose. Either you are my wife when we arrive in Alexandria — or my slave."

"Rude you are. Is that what you know of love? You told me you wished to become worthy of my feelings for you. Do you think you'll obtain them with such pronouncements? Put me back in the shackles you saved me from only to serve me up to your own shameful desires. Send me back to those pirates where I'll find softer hearts and be less unhappy."

In blinding despair, I was ready to fling myself off the boat, intending to drown myself in the waves.

"Stop!" Duval seized me when I was almost in mid-air. "What are you doing?"

"Giving myself up to death's embrace, less frightful than what you intend."

"O Léonore! Do you hate me so?"

"I don't hate you now, but I shall if you continue to do violence to a heart that cannot be yours."

"All right then. I set you free and won't keep you. But I ask one favor and implore at your feet: agree merely to play the role of my wife. I will claim my rights only when I triumph over your distance and detachment."

With still too little experience to realize where the Consul's demands would lead, I consented. He solemnly pledged
to ask for nothing further unless my repugnance vanished.
I allowed him hope in order to purchase tranquility while
avoiding the odious title in which his cruelty would otherwise
force me to submit.

Once arrived, Duval was made welcome at the home of
one Monsieur Duprat, a French merchant. As we agreed, I
was introduced as his wife. The next day we settled into the
official residence.

In Alexandria, as in all foreign cities, Europeans meet
as often as possible to enjoy better entertainments than the
country has to offer. Duval's circle came to include just-men-
tioned Duprat; the consuls of Spain, England, Holland, and
Portugal; and some well-known merchants. They were always
accompanied by their spouses, who became part of my social
circle and regarded me as wife of the Consul of France.

Meanwhile, Duval was falling more deeply in love, and
moving from words to deeds. There was nothing he wouldn't try.
His attentions went so far that he was mocked in public for the
amusing spectacle: in Egypt, a husband enamored of his wife.

A young Portuguese from the colonies of Zanzibar, a
nephew of his nation's Consul who was posted to Egypt for
commercial affairs, was the first to discern the comic intrigue,
which he pleasantly ridiculed.

"Don't be surprised," Duval sometimes said to him. "My
passion is extreme and I'm far from keeping it a secret. Don't
imagine that sensual pleasure can extinguish the flame love
sets ablaze, for the more a wife puts her charms on offer, the
more she excites. An attachment taken lightly when a wife
is unloved becomes deliciously sweet when she's worshipped,
harmonizing one's heart with heaven's vows, with the law and
with Nature. No, there's no woman on earth as worthy as the

one we possess. When she freely abandons herself to the passionate transports of her soul, it's with delight we lavish upon her all those names that can bolster and brace the one she already has. She becomes at once spouse, mistress, friend, confidant, sister and goddess. She represents everything that can contribute to life's most thrilling felicity; all passions arouse, erupt, and are united in her alone. We live only for her and desire only her. Ah! My friend, you don't know what it is to be a husband: no bonds are more flattering, no pleasure more valuable than that of marriage, nothing on earth so scrupulously sensual. Woe to him who's not known it, who prefers a sort of pleasure apart, for he'll have only skimmed life's surface without ever having found happiness."

Such was the way Duval expressed himself to Dom Gaspard, the young Portuguese I just mentioned — and who would soon take up a role in my adventures. In praising marriage, Duval was still in love with love. Would he have thought the same had he really known the pleasures he described? Who doesn't know how men are fickle and inconstant!

Whatever the case, young Duval was impetuous, amiable, constantly exacerbating his passion with sweet nothings and trawling the depths for things supposedly unknown to vulgar and uncultivated souls who, more like animals and not made for subtlety of detail, know only the *materiel* of pleasure. By such invidious schemes, in short, the most honest of women couldn't refuse the man in whose house she was obliged to dwell, where such things are never requested but always pinched and pilfered. Duval became ever more pressing, losing no occasion he believed might bring victory.

One day, exhausted by the oppressive heat in a new climate, I fell asleep in a small room infused with jasmine. Imagine my astonishment when I was awakened by Duval and found myself nearly naked in his arms.

"Great heavens!" I screamed and struggled to escape. "Is   o
that how you abuse —"

"O divinity of my heart!" Duval, inflamed with love and
desire, held me fast with one hand while the other he fr---ed
himself. "My idol, my mistress, don't refuse the pleasure offered by chance and circumstance; let me imbibe to insobriety   5
the charms you deny me. Let me enjoy them together, love
and voluptuousness. Don't hide them from my worship and
veneration. I will take solitary pleasure for I have no choice;
and I leave to you — so cruel — what I cannot obtain. But
don't conceal what good fortune offers. Such grace and fresh-   10
ness, such fine and delicious contours! Everything about you
is so beautiful, so delicate! O Léonore — are you the work of
a god? Are you yourself a goddess? But good heavens, don't
quash the all-consuming effects of blind love! You see them —
feel them — traitress — the sacrifice is offered — and it leaves   15
me only more unhappy!"

However I might resist, I couldn't escape his tribute and
homage. But I so struggled in the arms of this crazed lover
that he didn't come away with a sense of victory. If the incense
burned, it sputtered so far from the altar that goddess herself   20
could scarcely believe it.

"Traitor," I said furiously, fleeing, "since you're coward
enough to take advantage of me this way, coming upon me
as I slept, I break our fancied bonds. I'll tell the whole world
about you and leave your house forever."   25

Duval desperately rushed after me; I escaped and locked
myself in my apartment and refused to see him the whole day.

From now on I had to reflect seriously on the dangers
facing me. I told myself: "You are at the precipice. How even
imagine victory?"   30

How could I escape a man so combustible! He followed
me everywhere, never letting me out of his sight. Would I be

as lucky tomorrow as I was today? I quickly decided: flight was the only choice.

Planning my escape, I looked to Dom Gaspard, seeing him as the only one in our circle who might help. First, I simply inquired about his plans. He told me that he must shortly return to Monomotapa although he was not eager to do so, being obliged to go there only to report on his current mission. He then intended to sail to the Cap before returning to Portugal. This plan suited me well enough; the journey back to Europe was long but when one is not free the road taken doesn't matter if the destination can be reached. Determined to trust this young man, I thought the best way to reach him was through the organ by which Almighty God's voice unites every heart. Recall again my first principles and don't blame my indiscretion.

So it was I spoke with my eyes. Dom Gaspard, lively, spirited, young and full of wit, candor, and honesty, readily understood what they told him. His own reassured me that his feelings were reciprocal and sincere, and that the only question was how to make arrangements. Dom Gaspard wrote me in French, which he spoke fluently; I replied. We finally agreed on a meeting at which I fully confided in him.

"In no wise am I Duval's wife. An unfortunate adventure pitched me into his hands in Tripoli and he purchased me. He wants to abuse his rights with me and make me accept a union I don't like or want. Are you the man willing to free me from such enslavement?"

"Certainly," replied Gaspard. "I'll do whatever's required. You'll find me more patient than Duval, and I swear I'll bring you back to Europe before asking any reward."

"O Dom Gaspard! I trust and believe you. You return an unhappy woman to life. Count on my gratitude."

And from that moment we both worked to a single end.

The venture was not easy. Besides Duval's jealousy, we were afraid of his stature in the city and environs. To reach Monomotapa from Alexandria, Dom Gaspard would have to join one of the caravans departing from Cairo; and that meant first sailing up the Nile to the Egyptian capital. All this would take time and the Consul could have us arrested.

Thus we conceived a stratagem that was fairly bizarre. The young Portuguese had in his service a Negro about my age and size. We agreed to use a kind of makeup, the secret composition to which Gaspard was privy, that involved blackening my face and arms. Painted this way, I'd secretly escape in company of the Negro servant, disguised as the young man's brother. We would sail up the Nile first and wait for Gaspard to arrive in Cairo just in time for the caravan's departure. That would enable Gaspard to remain in Alexandria after I fled, and he'd be in a position to disrupt Duval's searches and to apprise me of the pleasant repercussions of my escape. We also decided that, in leaving, I would send Duval a letter telling him that, not being free to respond to his love and not wanting to do so, I'd decided to run away to Damietta, where a merchant of my acquaintance, whom I had contacted while in Egypt, offered me the means to return in Europe. Once there, I promised to send him the sum he had paid to purchase me. In this way, Duval would have considered another possible destination since he'd at first suspect that I was off to Cairo. Searching in two places, he would risk losing his quarry. And if in pursuit he came upon the caravan, could he recognize me in disguise?

A perilous adventure, I could feel it. Even assuming little risk in the escape itself, was this the right way to go about it? Could I be sure the young Portuguese deserved my trust? Might he not take advantage of my situation and his power over me? And if somehow we were separated, what would happen to me on the caravan, alone and forsaken! These great dangers, however, were potential; those I faced with Duval were all too real. Another siesta cradled amidst jasmine and I'd be a fallen woman. So I hesitated no longer. Resolved, I worked to execute the plan: I wrote my letter and fled swiftly under cover of darkness. The first night I hid in the home of the Portuguese, where he renewed his solemn oath to wait until we returned to Europe to demand reward for his help. As planned, I painted my face and arms, dressed, and placed myself in the care of the Negro servant.

We reached Cairo without the least difficulty and five days later, Gaspard arrived. He hauled me up onto the camel with his baggage, just as he would one of his servants, and we joined the caravan as it left.

On the journey Dom Gaspard apprised me of the turmoil that followed my escape. He said that Duval, furious, not doubting the contents of my letter, launched his search only in Damietta. The event amused the whole city and he was reproached in spite of his sorrow. People said he must have behaved badly with me; I seemed too sweet to be the one to blame. Women sympathized with me while the men made fun of him.

But let us put Alexandria behind us and allow me to give you a few details concerning the singular and little frequented road I traveled.

Although the assembly of travelers known as a caravan includes people of various countries and religions, the reigning sense of order was incomparable. Excellent policing kept us as safe as we might be on our roads in France. A regular army is not organized so well. The chief alone has the right to settle the few disagreements that arise, and his decisions are always fair.

We usually started off two hours before sunrise, and apart from an hour near midday, the journey continued until three

hours after sundown. The guides used kettledrums to send   o
signals: all must be ready on time; the least delay is unaccept-
able. No one is tempted to make a mistake that could cost a
life; and it's very difficult to rejoin the caravan once separated
from it. Although the route was unmarked, the guides were
so skillful that we were never lost. The order decided on the   5
day of departure was rigorously maintained during the whole
journey. Most curious of all was the patience of the animals;
they were even-tempered and never tired; they seemed to
adapt to all discomforts that might arise from chance or due
to weather, and they could go for days without food; however,   10
several perished. Skeletal remains scattered on the road, serving as signposts for the guides, gave proof both of courage and
the fact their strength eventually gives out.

Thus we started out and on the first day encountered a
frightful desert storm. A terrible wind began to build that sent   15
sand hurtling into the skies and falling like rain. It not only
blinded our guides but made them lose track of the route they
intended to follow, forcing them to call a halt until the next
day. I grew worried for, although I was well-disguised and far
from Duval, I still feared he would come after us and I would   20
be recognized. But Dom Gaspard, ever attentive, comforted
and reassured me.

After the first day's adventure, we safely moved forward
without incident until we reached Hélaoué, a charming city
that lives up to its name, which means *"place full of sweet-*   25
ness." It is the furthest city under the authority of the Grand
Seigneur, and we saw beautiful gardens deliciously cooled by
streams to refresh travelers after crossing the arid deserts,
often deprived of water. We filled our goatskin flasks and re-
plenished our supply of wines.   30

Fully past my fear about Duval pursuing us, my disguise
began to bother me and I proposed to Dom Gaspard to give it up;

but he was afraid the change might spread gossip amongst the travelers. Out of concern for my safety, he asked me to remain as I was until we reached the Portuguese colonies.

After leaving Hélaoué, we crossed other deserts no less arid than the previous ones.

"Léonore," Dom Gaspard said to me one day as we plodded on through the dreadful climate, "to what purpose do you think the Divine One made such grave mistakes in the composition and construction of our planet?"

"I've no idea."

"Clearly, the defect exists. Is it intentional or accidental? If intentional, God is malicious; if accidental, He is weak. In any event, He's wrong."

"That's irrefutable and I wouldn't know how to respond. But I content myself with the intimation of it and confess it's hard to evince passion for the greatness of a being whose faults are so very real."

"But could you, if you found yourself were amongst a band of rascals and rapscallions?"

"Surely not."

"All that exists is thus not perfect. Yet perfection alone is what's worthy of praise. If this quality cannot be found in God's works, He does not deserve it. What conclusion do you draw from this syllogism — the surest of all ways to reason? Tell me what you think of this one, I beg you."

These were the first philosophical darts Gaspard launched my way and they revealed how his mind, matured by study, was loath to accept fallacy. My respect for him redoubled. Perhaps I should take the opportunity to tell you more about these systems — but for the moment let me continue our journey.

After Hélaoué we reached Machou, a large town on the eastern bank of the Nile where we came upon two islands of palm trees, flowering senna, and bitter melon; a week later

we arrived at Dongola, on the Nubian border. For about a
league roundabout the country is superb but beyond it lies
only a fearsome expanse of desert. The Nile flows through this
charming plain but the soil is not inundated by its periodic
flooding; rather, its inhabitants irrigate it by an exhausting
kind of transport. Dom Gaspard bade me admire the beauty
of their horses, far superior to those so highly praised in Europe. These people, most of them disciples of Mohammed, are
prone to every sort of vice, and the most common is *blasphemy*. Nothing they say does not involve it and it's hard to
explain how artfully they employ it. Formerly Christian, its
laws much interfered with their customs and soon displeased
them; but their disorder makes their present cult difficult to
understand.

Their surprising inclinations toward blasphemy, indeed,
gave Dom Gaspard occasion to discuss some of his principles;
let me continue to tell you about them.

"How is it that men could think," said my brave, honest
traveling companion, "that the great Supreme Being whom
they worship, the Sublime One they consider their creator,
might be offended by the various invectives they use in addressing Him? Does not the Great Being they take to be author of everything and sole principle of all things created, rise
above such insults? Can we even presume they reach Him? As
for those imprecations that unhappy and suffering men hurl
his way, aren't they legitimate? Is not the first natural reaction
when one is harmed to complain? And whom to better blame
but the author of one's ills? In spreading so many men across
the earth, did not God know that He was exposing himself
to their reproaches? And for all that, did he put an end to
scourges? If He allowed men to fall, knowing they will avenge
by complaint, He must be indifferent to their invective. If He
deserved their complaints and defied them while deserving

them, how can He be angry? The strong man who offends the weak knows that the latter will react with insults. Can He fear such words knowing His conduct incited them? If God were sensitive to our reproaches and master over all, would He not have created the universe in a way that deserved our praise? In not doing so, not believing Himself so compelled, sure that He would be cursed, it becomes certain that such blasphemy was in no way His concern. There is consequently no risk in so addressing Him; He hears blasphemes without wrath or woe, thoroughly convinced He deserves them. Without taking offense at what ensues, He laughs at our ignorance and complete inability to discover or understand His views. It is a barbaric absurdity that in Europe an act of the weak against the strong should be punished so severely as it once was or is even now considered a crime against religion. Nothing done by the former, blunted in effect before reaching the latter, can be an outrage. What the powerful do to the weak is dangerous, not the reverse. And I don't want to hear tell, either, of the armed valet who offends his master by striking him with the master's own weapon; in that case not the master but the valet is powerful. The master's power is illusory while the valet's power is real. This is nothing like the case with God, the omnipotent; and no matter with what weapon we dare threaten Him, He will always triumph. Whatever we attempt is but a frail impulse of the weak against the strong; nothing can touch Him. He will not feel offended by insults that He deserves but cares about not a whit. In their eternal madness men forever want to cast God in their own image. They believe themselves offended by an insulting word and imagine that God, like them, is displeased.

"Let us stop, in short, insisting on a God made from the same stuff as us, a God irritated by invective, fond of praise, and obliging of our prayers. We forever want to see Him as a

human monarch who must listen to us and judge. In that way   0
we diminish His views and His most celebrated worshiper becomes finally nothing but an idolater. God is too mighty and
spiritual for all such human considerations. He leaves us to be
good or bad, to acknowledge or deny Him, to worship or hate
Him according to the kind of organization we received from   5
Him. He is unconcerned what we think about any of these
matters, indifferent to our homages, always far above us and
absolutely untouched by our blasphemies. He cares nothing
about what we do because all is necessity and we act only according to His laws. Let us not imagine He will reward us for   10
our prayers or punish us for cursing Him; He will no more
show more mercy in the first instance than inflict torment in
the second. It is laughable to see that men, puny frail beings
who cannot possibly change the course of the smallest star,
think that their insults or prayers can reach on high much less   15
please or irritate the one who crafted the works they are unable to disturb in the slightest? It is a strange blindness owing
to vanity that man prefers viewing himself as a criminal rather
than acknowledging his weakness. Imbecile that he is, he'd
prefer to pass his life trembling before the thought of impos-   20
sible offenses rather than stand strong, accepting the power-
lessness that so offends his pride.

"O Léonore, pray or blaspheme, worship or profane, it's
all the same in the eyes of the Being powerful enough to
have decided good and evil in everything that we see. A god   25
touched by our cults and offended by our faults — wouldn't
that just be human? And how, if He were endowed with all our
passions, could He possess the creative energy which is the
most sublime combination of virtues? If we blaspheme and
address the Divinity with some feeble insult, whether by anger   30
or from tiresome suffering or for any other reason, let's do so
without fear, certain He won't be resentful. He is too mighty to

seek revenge. Would He have deprived us of the faculty to see His faults, or would He have committed any if He feared reproaches dictated by reason? They may be addressed to Him with peace of mind."

"It seems to me," I said to Dom Gaspard, "that your systems regarding religion are simple and fitting."

Gaspard replied: "You're mistaken, Léonore. My systems concerning religion are neither. They are nonexistent. I've dispensed with the puerilities that weigh down the minds and memories of young people. I spent my time learning rather than thinking nonsense; and I've adopted principles on this matter as well as on other subjects concerning morals. From these constants I never deviate. I believe in some agency, God or Nature, for there is always a motor force upon us. That I admit but I do not serve Him through any cult. I'm sure He requires nothing of the sort and quite uncertain He deserves it. Why worship? I prefer to virtuously employ the time that others waste on prayers; and the agent, if just and fair, will be grateful to me for being useful to men instead of being a devotee, ever kneeling at the altar. When I see less malice on earth and encounter fewer rascals and more honest men, perhaps then I shall think that the author of the universe deserves gratitude; but as long as malice assails me from all directions, so long as I see only the dark side — evil, cruelty, betrayal, perfidy, and viciousness among men — I will stay within sensible limits and not overwhelm with invective the One who permits it. I still laugh at the folly of religion, I mock the diversity of cults and listen only to reason and my heart. To the Being who deserves only reproaches — I don't make them, for they are useless. I remain silent."

"But what of your morality?"

"Pure! Must we revere illusions to have the right to be honest? I love my fellow man; I relieve his suffering with good-

ness in my heart. I deplore my own mediocrity only because it
deprives me of the pleasure of making people happy. I respect
the property of others and would never steal another man's
wife or his assets. You may be certain that I would not have
taken you away from Duval if I believed you to be his wife.
To love I am sensitive, for it is the pleasure of honest people.
I hate vice while virtue inspires me and I will end my days
in tranquility with its maxims, in no wise wishing for the ridiculous joys of heaven or fearing the ludicrous flames of hell."

These sentiments pleased me. I found Gaspard estimable
and resolved to make him my friend and wanted to know more
about him. No matter that it might prove perilous, and despite
unfavorable circumstances, I felt the urge to see if this young
man, who'd cast off so many constraints and shown respect
only for those of an honest man, would remain faithful to the
moral principles he proclaimed. For I'd given Gaspard some
hope, having kept silent about my union with Sainville; and
my hand, we agreed, would reward his help once we reached
Europe. But shortly after our conversation, I took the opportunity during a halt in the journey to confess I'd deceived him,
that I could never repay my debt to him, that my hand belonged to another. He was now master of my fate and ought
to punish me for having abused his trust. He could abandon
me here in the desert. But if he decided to keep his word, such
decency being all the more generous for being unselfish, he'd
be assured of my undying affection.

"Perhaps I ought to have deceived you to the end," I added,
"but the way you explained yourself, the feelings you revealed,
your philosophy and aversion for the false entanglements that
restrain men — all that, Gaspard, makes me think so highly
of you that I should keep nothing from you. You're now my
master, I surrender."

o   Gaspard, moved, stared at me in wonder before quickly regaining his composure.

"O Léonore!" he exclaimed, wrapping me in his arms, "I owe you such gratitude! I sacrificed only for love; but I would have done it all for virtue."

5   He pressed upon me his purse; I forbade myself to take it.

"Let it remain with you at least," he continued. "In case I die before accomplishing what I promised. When I saw you as a mistress, I neglected to provide the care and attention that I supposed would come about with our marriage. But to

10 a friend, I owe much more."

Fallen at his feet, I let him to raise me up with my heart's first impulse, I confess, to shed a torrent of tears.

"Generous mortal!" I cried. "You absorbed all those religious illusions and in that way freed your mind from those

15 fables, so useless to mankind, the better to lend ascendancy to all that might bring happiness to your fellow man. Accept my love and gratitude, let me regard you as friend and brother, even as the deity whose virtues you deny and who only would deserve our praise were He as noble as you. O! Gaspard, I

20 would not have found sentiments like that in a pious soul."

At this juncture Léonore's character, or at least her way of thinking about religion, was fully revealed and Madame de

25 Blamont. However delighted by Gaspard's actions, she made known her anger with her daughter in seeing her praise the signal quality of a man hostile to religious principles. It was impossible for the great piety of this honest, sensitive woman not to manifest alarm at what had just been said.

30   Léonore calmly listened to her mother's reproaches.

"Oh, Madame!" she said, "I would've breached the sincerity you demanded of me had I concealed my principles; I must

stop here if they outrage you. For I will be obliged to reveal
still more shocking things, which you would condemn all the
more in that I might have avoided taking part in them. Neither Monsieur de Sainville nor Dom Gaspard, nor anybody else
with whom you'll see me allied, may be blamed for the lack of
conformity between my system and yours; my husband will tell
you that from age 13 he recognized in me strong aversion to
all religious ideas. At that age I'd already read almost everything written to counter your opinions. A friend of Countess
Kerneuil lent me books that I devoured; we discussed them
and she reasoned with me, reinforcing their principles. She
explained them carefully and over the course of two years nur-
tured my soul with a philosophy that enthused her. Later experience, my misfortunes, and the sights of the world brought
these systems to life. They became so familiar to me that today
I could scarcely adopt others. I see them as compatible with the
soundest virtues. Perhaps subsequent events in my story will
convince you. For nonetheless I've in no way done away with
the idea of God; that, Madame, is not to be imagined. But I believe in a God elevated far above all cults. I'm firmly persuaded
that He neither deserves nor wants them; and that, of all of
them, ours being the least reasonable, would offend him most
grievously, if He involved himself in the follies of mankind."

"You poor child," said Madame de Blamont, wrapping
Léonore in her arms. "You'd not have run all these risks without the early tragedies of youth. But you ought and must
believe that moral virtues are more vivid with the help of
religion, and that one who serves God well will better love
his fellow man."

Here tears filled the tender mother's beautiful eyes and
brimmed too in Aline's — who held her sister's hands in hers
and gazed upon her with gentle pity. Not that the dear young
woman imagined herself as better than the other but only,

rather, persuaded by the religious maxims upon which she believes all present and future happiness depends. Anyone who does not adopt them offers a picture of unhappiness that concerns a soul as delicate as hers.

The Count quickly saw that mediation was required to restore peace of mind.

"Madame," he told the President, "Léonore's errors are in no way your fault; they must not give you remorse. You must sympathize without trying to change her mind, for you won't succeed; nothing is more important to us than our ideas concerning religion. You know very well that even the approach of death itself changes nothing in that regard."

"Quite right!" Léonore responded energetically. "And to assure tranquility at that moment, we early try to liberate ourselves from anything which might make it horrible. I'm far from renouncing what I adopted for my own happiness just to put myself in accord with sentiments I owe my mother and my spouse. All that troubles me is the sorrow my mother feels — she for whom I stand ready to make every sacrifice that could be of use to her, yet with the sole condition that she not require me to accept beliefs I could only adopt myself with horror."

"Well, then — posed in that fashion —" said the Count, "I think the best thing we can do is to listen to Léonore's further adventures and request more than ever that she hide nothing. My dear and charming friends," he continued, addressing Madame de Blamont and Aline, "with your strength and virtue, you may hear all without risk; and with your wisdom and kind hearts you can feel compassion and forgiveness for the guilty — and continue to love her."

Urged by all to go on — immediately her mother and sister kissed her — Léonore continued her story, taking up her account *as follows*:

When our caravan arrived in the vicinity of Dongola, its leader   o
requested the King's permission to pass through his capital.
Granted immediately, yet in truth no great favor for no city
is more dreadful. Wretched and deserted houses line that
streets obstructed by mounds of sand swept by wind storms;
desolation everywhere. A poorly fortified castle, guarded by a   5
garrison of Arab pastoralists, occupied the center of the city.
Dom Gaspard and I, together with a few Dutch merchants,
were honored with an invitation to dine with the King at tables
separate from but as well-served as his own.

My position as Dom Gaspard's servant had lasted just   10
one day; as soon as we believed we were out of danger, my
friend introduced me as the nephew of an African king whom
he was returning to his uncle; and as he had taught me Portuguese, I spoke only that language.

Four days after leaving Dongola, we entered the kingdom   15
of Sennar. Fearful of being looted by the people living above
the town of Korti along the Nile, we were constrained to travel
at a distance from the river and to enter Bihonda, a desert
landscape less cultivated than Libya, but with at least a few
trees. On reaching the other side we met inhabitants camped   20
in tents who let us want for nothing. We finally reached Har-
gabi, where everything for the traveler was to be found. Such
delicious abundance, after crossing such arid land, inclined us
to stay for a time. Leaving, we passed through beautiful acacia
forests, their coolness enlivened by a multitude of green par-   25
rots, grouses, and other birds that contributed much delight
to our journey. We emerged to cross fertile plains and soon
came upon the city of Sennar.

By reason of a deadly adventure that was to befall us,
allow me a moment to draw your attention to this capital city   30
of about three thousand souls — as filthy as it was badly po-
liced, with the King's palace of sun-dried bricks — a cluster

of buildings remarkable only for disorder and bad taste. The apartments, decorated with tapestry, are furnished in the style of the Levant with surrounding gardens. It is all unpleasant in the scorching heat, unbearable from January to April. The people, who are of Mohammedan faith, are dishonest, malicious, superstitious, and depraved. No sooner had we arrived than we would have liked to leave.

We were presented to the King, a man about 50 years old, an unbridled libertine of unbelievable cruelty. He was only to be approached barefoot and his face, covered with a gauze veil, was never to be seen, as if the fool was afraid of dazzling his subjects. When he traveled from the capital to his country house two leagues away, he was preceded by 400 guards on horseback and surrounded by 200 valets singing his praises, with a dozen more bearing him in his palanquin followed by 700 naked women who carried on their heads baskets full of various foods to be served to His Majesty. 300 cavaliers brought up the rear and the procession was so long that the front of the column often reached the country house before the end of it had left the city. So long as the King contented himself with ostentatious display as long as his treasuries could provide, he needn't expose himself to reproaches of passersby. But his extreme cruelty truly warranted them. He revolts his subjects and fears them, like all despots; and recently has revealed his dark side to passing caravans. Although we were warned about this, thanks to accursed curiosity we fell into one of the traps he often sets for travelers, the better to garner victims for his villainy.

One of the keenest pleasures of this monstrous prince, which arouses him most vigorously, is to have every offender he can snare impaled before his eyes without distinction as to age or sex. Standing at an open palace window, 15 or 20 feet from the place of execution, surrounded by women, he enjoys

in fine comfort the cruel pleasure of watching victims suffer.   o
To increase their number, he overburdens travelers with taxes
and prohibitions, in violation of which punishment invariably
comes at the end of a pointed stake.

The prohibition that endangered Gaspard and I, putting
not only us but several others in mortal peril, as I shall explain,   5
was trumpeted whenever a caravan passed through Sennar. It
forbade anyone to go near a small pavilion located at half a
league from the city.

Locked away inside, so we were told, could be found
Mohammed's *organ.*   10

Despite the wretched King's decree, a multitude of flun-
keys incessantly chat up travelers, arousing their curiosity as
to this wonder, so strange that anyone with a little imagination
is bound to succumb. Some offer to take you to the place, assuring you the prohibition is not serious and there's no danger   15
even if caught. So we let ourselves be seduced and off we went.

You shall see what came of that.

For, so thoroughly convinced that the injunction against
a visit to view the famed organ of Mohammed was a mere
formality, and genuinely excited by the idea of admiring one   20
of the greatest wonders of the world, we were stricken with
the liveliest desire to go visit: Gaspard, three Arab women,
two Turks, four Dutch and Portuguese merchants, and me.
All traveling with the caravan, we allowed ourselves to be
tricked. At dawn two days after we arrived in Sennar, we let   25
a pair of lying rascals take us to Mohammed's pavilion. We
were within 20 paces when a group of soldiers armed with
muskets rushed out from nearby bushes where they'd lain
in wait. They pounced on us like hunters snaring game. All
eleven of us were taken back to the king, who burst out in   30
laughter at the sight of such a catch — and he promised to
take care that we would not long languish on earth. He looked

us over carefully one after the other, unmoved by the youth and beauty of the three Arab women who threw themselves at his feet, begging for mercy. He found them guilty like the rest of us, and assured them he would take great pleasure in seeing whether they could withstand torture and suffering with the same courage as the men.

My gender went undiscovered as I was still in the same disguise. The King thought I was a boy. Gaspard implored him to spare my life, reminding him of his alliances with an African king to whom he claimed I belonged — hoping to incite compassion by making me out as of royal blood. He had no success.

"Fend for yourself," said the barbarian. "Don't trouble yourself about the others."

In spite of all, we were served an excellent dinner in the palace itself and were left alone in a room until the hour of the spectacle that the king was mounting at our expense. I need not depict my condition, for you readily can imagine the horror of it. All my thoughts turned toward Sainville. *Unfortunate beloved!* I cried. *Never shall I see you again. It's all far worse than the dagger in the coffin in Venice. An early death — but by* impalement!

I wept copiously with only the hand of good sweet Gaspard to wipe away my tears, forgetting all danger to himself.

The same sense of despair reigned throughout our small group. The men ranted and raved; the women, always gentler even when suffering, merely wept and wailed. Only screams and imprecations were heard in this place of doom — doubtless a charming melody to the ears of our cruel executioner, who meanwhile dined with women in a nearby room.

In the end I heard the fatal hour sound. Trembling, I huddled close to Gaspard. The one who was to perish like me, I thought, still owed me comfort and support. The King took

his place of observation, his gaze fixed upon the blood-soaked
arena. The monster watched the executions — the two Turks,
then the four Europeans and three Arab women. Gaspard
and I were last. They came to take me first. I kissed my friend.

"I shall die happy," I said, "spared the pain of seeing you
perish before my eyes."

Then, gathering courage and strength, I threw myself in
the middle of the circle. The executioner seized me.

Léonore trembled from the recollection: "O, Madame! If I was
ever convinced death was nigh, I dare say it was on this most
horrible occasion."

To carry out the ceremony, *she continued,* almost like one
might inflict corporal punishment on a child, the particular
part of the body which Nature locates beneath the small of the
back was to be exposed so that nothing would obstruct view
of the place into which the pike was to be introduced. That
awkward juncture was promptly revealed to the eyes of the
monarch.

But imagine: no sooner was I naked than tumultuous
screams filled the whole assembly. The executioner himself
thrust me away in horror. Overwhelmed by what was to be my
fate, I failed to consider the surprise caused by my presenting,
beneath the expanse of black flesh of my back, so very white
a bottom. So complete was the shock that some took me to
be a god and others, the devil — and everybody fled. Only
the king, slightly less credulous, ordered me brought before
him; Gaspard, too. Interpreters came forward to ask me the
meaning of my mixed state, found nowhere in Nature. No use
dissembling, I had to confess. The king made me wash in front

of him, and put on women's clothes. After this metamorphosis, he unfortunately found me quite to his taste and declared
I must make ready to receive him that same night, with the
honor of serving his pleasures.

Tragic fate, I told myself — not much difference between
the torment to come and the torture from which I'd just escaped. *O SainIle... Sainville! Would you not love me more were
I impaled?*

In consideration of the pleasures that the King of Sennar anticipated, he spared Dom Gaspard but immediately
separated us. The young Portuguese was placed among the
slaves and I was consigned to a small bedroom adjacent to the
seraglio.

But then, good fortune. A terrible riot broke out that
the same evening, incited by our fellow travelers. They were
infuriated by what had been done to us and retaliated with
violence, causing such tumult in the city that the king himself
found it necessary to personally head up troops in an effort to
put down the disorder. He returned quite late and, too tired,
he retired to his apartment. He sent word that only the next
day would I enjoy the favors he so obligingly planned to bestow upon me.

The news calmed me. To the ill-fated, time is treasure.
However much is granted, the soul blossoms in proportion
to the welcome delay and there always seems enough to help
find some means of escape.

It was already past midnight. I stood at the balcony, exhausted, devising a thousand plans, each one more singular
than the next, all aimed at delivering me from evil. Comforted
by my lucky star, I felt sure that fate would always turn in my
favor — and, suddenly, I heard someone call my name.

"Who's there?" I asked. "Who could still care for the un-
luckiest woman alive?"

"Her best friend in the whole world," came the answer.   o
"The unfortunate Gaspard has come to save her."

"Gaspard! Can it be you?"

"O Léonore! Let yourself down. I can tell the distance
is short. Risk and don't be afraid. One of the tyrant's guards,
bought by my generosity, awaits us and shall escape with us.   5
Let's be off. The caravan has just left in the wake of the riot
and isn't more than two miles distant. We'll easily catch up.
You must hurry."

Neither balm on scorching wounds nor dew cooling
the sepal of flowers withered by burning winds would have   10
ported to my heart more welcome relief than those words. I
didn't waste a minute. Without looking down, I threw myself
into Gaspard's open arms. He and his guide carried me off and
after a forced march, less than 45 minutes later, we rejoined
our fellow travelers. They were surprised by my changed state   15
and appearance but we were received with inexpressible joy.
All men become friends in face of danger; the noble soldier
who saved us received further compensation and I covered
Gaspard with a thousand kisses. Words could not describe my
gratitude. In good order we located our belongings and the   20
Negro servant, too, and we continued our journey.

"Finally — I can breathe again," said the Count. "You let me in
for a terrible fright — a feeling with which I'm rather unfamiliar. And it owes only, I believe, to the interest you inspired and   25
aroused in my soul. Perhaps this is the first time a beautiful
woman evaded punishment the way you did. Many thousands
more have perished for showing what you revealed."

"Really, Count!" cried Madame de Blamont.

"Madame, allow me to laugh at this quite singular adven-   30
ture. I assure you that the white body in contrast with the black
visage must produce a most pleasing effect."

"Continue, dear daughter. The Count's foolishness is insufferable."

After leaving Sennar, *continued Léonore,* we reached Bakas, a small village on the Nile at a place where we found the river dried up. We then came to Giasim, considerably larger but similarly situated with respect to the river and nevertheless within a forest whose tree trunks ten men could not encircle; one of those huge creations, hollowed out by age, made for a room that could easily hold 50 people. Here we had to leave our camels behind, for the mountains we still had to cross were covered with poisonous herbs that would immediately kill them.

From Giasim, we passed through beautiful forests of evergreen tamarind bearing some variety of plums the taste of which was not unpleasant; these forests, so thick that the sun never penetrates, are often dangerously cold. But my strength and good constitution spared me all ills, and were it not for relentless anxiety, the journey, dangerous as it was, would have offered only pleasure. We reached Serka, a small city in the mountains, situated in a beautiful valley, cooled by a stream that forms a border between Ethiopia and the kingdom of Sennar. Everywhere in this region we found the richest and most beautiful fields of cotton and bamboo, ebony forests pleasantly enriched by the soil, a multitude of aromatic plants. Only the distant roar of lions distracted from the enjoyment of traveling through this beautiful country. We had to make large fires to keep the animals away — without such precautions their company would not be so pleasant. In the days that followed we crossed several perilous rivers and soon after traversed a plain shaded by pomegranate trees, the fruit of which we devoured.

The seigneurs of the lands along our journey guarded our
baggage. Throughout the time we were in Ethiopia their vas-
sals carried it from one territory to the next.

Although we did not go so far as to enter the capital, I
saw enough of the countryside to be able to say briefly that it
is too little visited; it has much to offer the philosopher and
naturalist alike. No province in Europe is more artistically
cultivated; cardamom and ginger plants lend beauty to the
plains and through the air percolate atoms most pleasantly
perfumed; vast rivers flow through the land, their banks lined
with lilies, jonquils, tulips, and violets. It can seem a Garden
of Eden. One need not be surprised that in this clime fervent
imaginations located that place of pleasure from which the
first man was expelled for partaking of an apple, a fruit nowhere to be found here. Forests, even more delightful than
the plains, are full of orange, lemon, and pomegranate trees,
and still more, ever flowering among them, are some with
blossoms that have a fragrance at once stronger and more
delicate than ours.

People of this region have been often confused with
those of neighboring Nubia, though they are much different
in appearance: tawny, tall and stately with pleasant faces; almost all have beautiful eyes and well-shaped noses, thin lips
and white teeth, in contrast to those who are powerfully black
with no defining features besides those of the Negroes with
whom you are familiar.

Ethiopians follow the Coptic religion, a sort of cult that
melds Catholicism and Greek Orthodoxy. They are highly
devout and great worshipers of saints, profoundly moved by
the possibility of miracles and, especially, by the idea of transubstantiation. But among them some are reasonable enough
to reject such dogma that uses faith, that most misleading of
guides, to suppress rebel reason.

"How admit such things!" said one of the Ethiopian philosophers to Gaspard, who was pleased, in my presence, to
hold a brief discussion in Latin. He continued:

"How can we believe in a dogma as improbable as transubstantiation? Is that not to willingly blind oneself instead
of preferring the real meaning of the words of Jesus Christ?
It is an inexplicable mystery the acceptance of which runs
contrary to all insights that reason provides. Can a righteous
being go that far in abusing men's credulity? Is it not equally
absurd and disgusting to imagine that God would ask us to eat
His own flesh? Isn't it ridiculous and horrific to dare believe
that a man, even a saint, could evoke God by a few words and
make him willfully descend into corruptible and destructible
elements? Or that this God comes down to enter the host
corporally or spiritually? Would not His substance inevitably
enlarge it? Why would the volume of the host not change after
incorporation? If God came down only in spirit, how could
this divine essence penetrate matter without making it live?
After corporal introduction, the host must be enlarged or,
in the instance of a spiritual junction, it must be enlivened.
Complete metamorphosis is absolutely impossible; no change
of any kind operates by ideas alone; and any such mutation
implies extinction of visible parts of the original body and a
swift conjuncture of the elements of the second body in the
decomposed parts of the first — a process that can only succeed through the force of atoms in the former operating upon
those of the latter. But all this must be witnessed or else it is
only illusory and may be denied by all reasonable minds. Only
thus can the Eucharist be viewed as incorporative; yet, as was
just made clear, such incorporation is impossible.

"You cannot argue, moreover, that for God nothing is impossible. Such reasoning is false, irrefutably connected to His
own first actions, after which it can no longer be the case that

the effects of His creations have different qualities than those   0
which He first embedded in them. It is impossible for Him,
for instance, to modify the nature of the elements or suppress
their properties. One who uses miracles to explain what he
cannot understand is a fool we must pity and never listen to.
A miracle, for him, is the work of an Almighty God who devi-   5
ates from the fundamental laws He Himself established. Can
we attribute such sentiments to a Supreme Being? If He needs
to ignore His own first actions to turn men into believers, we
must agree that what He did earlier was not powerful enough
to merit our faith. He thus must confess that at first He made a   10
mistake and must now do better. A first absurdity — but what
persuades you that God reasons this way?

"With respect to what you call miracles, who proves to
you that God ignores His own first actions? Whatever your ill
will with respect to God, whom you so mistreat, how can you   15
believe that He conducts Himself as you would have it? Are
you so familiar with all God's laws that you dare defend your
system? And for even the most astonishing phenomena, how
do you know that what surprises isn't actually one of God's
laws of which you have simply been ignorant until now? And   20
in that case, what gives you the right to call it a miracle? Unless somebody convinces me that the phenomenon in question could not possibly be in accord with the universal laws
of Nature, I would never believe it. A miracle is possible only
for an event that is contrary to the laws of Nature. But what   25
is that event? What could it be? Is it for us to decide? We
still have plumbed and understood not a quarter of Nature's
incomprehensible mysteries. Suppose, however, some kind
of event actually occurs and is visible, triggered by the magi-
cal words of a priest, without knowing whether it conforms   30
to a law of Nature. Even as a witness I would not suppose a
miracle. In recognizing it, I might draw no conclusion as to

cause; but what of it when I see nothing of the metamorphosis? When it works because you tell me it does, with nothing
else to convince me? And what if I see that what you claim is
contradicted by accidents that make it impossible to know if a
miracle had actually taken place? When I see holy flour identified with the body of God, withering, putrefying, allowing
itself to be devoured by worms, burning, dissolving, ingested,
turned into chyle and excrement, at last, profaning itself indu-
bitably — can I then reasonably believe that it contains a God,
that God Himself might submit to such degradation? And is
it not a thousand times preferable that I reject what you tell
me about all this rather than accept it with all the powerful
contradictions, repellent to reason and repugnant to my heart,
which degrade God Himself?

"So do you say that a mystery must confound reason
and make it buckle under its incomprehensibility? All empty
words. My reason owes to God, it is the only torch He provided to guide me and to know Him. It is absolutely impossible that He requires me to accept things clearly opposed to
it. If He wanted me to believe such things, would He not have
given me some reason to do so? That would be far simpler
than forcing me to admit things at the expense of God-given
good sense. Why do you think God did not choose the better
of the two options?

"You seem moreover to make a point of depicting a hate-
ful God whereas I seek to love Him. Do you believe yourself that this Incomprehensible Mystery is worthy of belief?
Don't fool yourself. Centuries before Jesus Christ, Confucius
included it in his dogma. The Chinese and Mexicans who descended from them believe, as you do, that mysterious words
incorporate the Holy Spirit into sanctified bread and wine.
These disgusting fables were taught in Egyptian schools that
accepted all manner of metamorphosis and reincarnation.

They were taught by Confucius, Pythagoras, and Jesus Christ
at different times, and each of them borrowed elements of the
doctrine for some of the ideas they used to form their own
systems. Your religion's doctrine regarding the Eucharist can
be more readily grasped than the ideas of all the great men
just mentioned.

"And that," continued our Ethiopian philosopher, "is a reflection not understood by your deists, although some here
give me credit for this insight. Listen to me and reconsider
your fantastical beliefs.

"Everything is purely symbolic in all the teachings of Jesus.
When he told his apostles shortly before his death: 'Eat, this is
my body; drink, this is my blood,' he meant to say: 'The food
offered is paid for by the money Judas earned from the sale of
my body. It is my body you eat, my blood you drink.' Listen
carefully to the other words of this prophet; try to penetrate
their meaning and you will recognize in them all the same
song and style and always the same symbolic character — a
peculiar aspect that sometimes makes him admirable. But to
take his discourse literally is not only to lose its sweet substance but also to risk, as in the case just mentioned, falling
into execrable worship and committing revolting impieties.
Let us renounce, therefore, such dangerous errors and abjure
forever the frightening system of transubstantiation. Don't
imagine we're atheists when we dare proclaim from the depth
of our heart, together with the Capharnaite: '*Quomodo potest
hic nobis dare carnem suam.*'"

Such was the reasoning of the Negro philosopher. Gaspard was enchanted.

"I would never have thought that such enlightenment
could penetrate the depths of Africa," he told me enthusias-
tically. "Much as we might try to propagate the error to the
ends of the earth, it will come up against limits and encounter
enemies wherever human reason is free to be heard."

I concurred with both Dom Gaspard and the black philosopher, for my thinking was profoundly the same as theirs.

The Holy Scripture is accepted in Ethiopia. The people
use the same sacraments as Catholics but they receive communion of two species and their devotions conform to the
Greek religion. Their confession is much simpler than ours,
perhaps more edifying; they concede they are sinners and
prostrate themselves at their priests' feet, imploring absolution and penance; but they do not enter into the details, which
are as humiliating for the one who commits them as dangerous to the one who listens — not to say useless as to what God
may require from sinners.

Their churches are clean and beautiful; the utmost respect is observed within. A few paintings are displayed within
but they admit no bas-relief representations, cannot stand
them, and quite rightly see them as irrefutable proof of the
most absurd paganism. Their choir chants, mingling nicely
with the sound of musical instruments, are in tune and pleasant even if they do not use scores. Like Jews and Turks, they
practice circumcision but they have no idea attached to it
besides imitation of their God whom they worship and who
submitted to it like themselves.

Once arrived in Ethiopia, Dom Gaspard wished to show
me the famous source of the Nile. A small group from the
caravan joined us to visit that natural wonder.

From a summit among the Mountains of the Moon roar
forth two huge sources of water, one from the east, the other
from the west. They form two streams that rush with amazing
impetuosity into cane- and rush-covered marshland. These
sources disappear only to be sighted again 12 leagues distant,
reuniting to create the River Nile whose channel is further
swelled by a multitude of other streams. Not far from here,
the river shows a great peculiarity, its majestic flow crossing a

great lake without becoming part of it.* The magnificent palace of an Ethiopian emperor stands amidst these waters but
we had no time to visit it. We did come across an extraordinary animal, almost the size of a cat with a man's face, beautiful white beard, and plaintive humanlike voice. It lives in trees
and can hardly be domesticated; it evinces the same love of
freedom as men; in captivity it wastes away and dies.

Most cities in Ethiopia are alike, with low buildings em-
bellished by roof terraces, separated by flower- and fruit-cov-
ered hedges with trees planted at regular intervals. I would've
liked to journey through all the provinces but that would have
meant following that part of our caravan whose route ended
inland and descended into Monomotapa, passing through the
Kingdom of Monoëmugi and crossing the awful deserts of
Cafres. Dom Gaspard did not want me exposed to the terrible
dangers along that route and so, as here the caravan divided,
we followed Portuguese and Dutch travelers on their way to
the banks of the Zambezi River, and from there to sail down
to Mombasa, on the coast of Zanzibar, where we would find
a Portuguese trading post. This promised a more comfortable
and less eventful journey. In Mombasa, Dom Gaspard introduced me to his fellow citizens as a young French woman
whose numerous misfortunes had brought her under his care,
and whom he planned to take back to Europe as soon as his
business in Monomotapa was complete.

Dom Gaspard's nobility was such that he only wished to
be my friend and always introduced me to Europeans in this
way — that generosity, I tell you, together with everything he'd
already done for me, brought tears to my eyes. Were all his

---

* Ptolemy believed the lake to be the source of the Nile; but one must add that (although Léonore's account seems in no way mistaken) it is nevertheless possible he
was in error, and no real details have come down to us.

countrymen as good and honest as he, I wouldn't have been subject to all the disasters — those already befallen me and ones I've yet to depict.

We stayed only a short time at the first Portuguese trading post; Dom Gaspard's obligations and his eagerness to take me back to Europe as soon as possible did not permit us to stay long in Mombasa. Although Portuguese settlements dotted the coast and it would have been simple to reach our destination by passing from one to another, he found it expedient to take a Dutch vessel sailing toward the Cap along the coast, and to disembark at the Bay of Guama where Portuguese small craft could always be found, in order to swiftly transport us to Fort Sena, the nation's most important trading post on the border of Monomotapa. There my friend concluded some business on behalf of the Consul of Alexandria, and we soon left for Fort Tete to wait an opportunity to return to Europe.

This outpost, headed by a chief officer about 45 years old, included four administrators and a garrison of some sixty Portuguese and mulattos, under the command of three officers. In the company of the chief, whose name was Dom Lopès de Riveiras, was his very pretty and witty Spanish mistress, Clémentine. Educated, well-read, with a talent for music, she was 23 or 24 years of age and spoke two or three foreign languages. Of prodigious vivacity, with a pleasant and cheerful nature, she was devoid of religious faith and without principles, yet her morals were not yet completely corrupt.

As you'll see, I was to remain for some time in the company of this new friend; so allow me to describe her in a little more detail. Clémentine was from Madrid. Although raised amongst courtesans, she never exercised that occupation. Inasmuch as her mother was notorious for her many lovers not to say charm and lack of scruples, it was unlikely that her young stripling would long remain morally pure. Although

she had known only two lovers — the Duke of Medinaceli,   o
who had purchased her from her mother and kept her secretly
in his palace from age 12 to 17, and Dom Lopès de Riveiras,
who took her to Africa at the request of the Duke, his protector — although, as I said, the beautiful Clémentine had known
only these two men, she possessed a libertine spirit that, for   5
a young woman of my age, made her dangerous company.
Add affability to wit, kindness to charm, and nothing could
have been simpler for her than to spread her depraved way of
thinking to those around her. The word *virtue* had no place in
the imagination of this singular young woman while *love* was   10
only an illusion. That sentiment, she alleged, existed only in
old novels, where it was for a woman to give but never to take.
Attaching value to friendship while supposing it possible only
between those of the same sex, she avowed that we can give
our heart to a friend, but only when tastes and character are   15
in perfect accord and no rivalry exists. For the rest, bonds and
duties meant nothing to her. Clémentine viewed good deeds
as trickery; sensitivity, a weakness from which we must protect ourselves; modesty, an error that always disadvantages
the charms of one who's pretty; sincerity, an idiocy that makes   20
a fool; humility, an absurdity; temperance, a deprivation for
the best years of one's life; and religion, laughable hypocrisy.

Such was the moral fiber of my dear companion. Physically, she was voluptuous. She was tall and formed like Venus
with skin stunningly white, yet hair and eyes beautifully   25
dark. In her mischievous gaze reigned languor that seemed
to arouse and kindle love in both sexes; it was amazingly ex-
pressive without her even quite knowing it, and even the simplest things she said were ever resonant of sentiment. When
she wanted to say something, she had a way of half-opening   30
her eyes, softening their intensity in a way that that made

whatever she wished to convey sweeter and more interesting. But when enlivened by sensuality and pleasure, their fiery glow was insistent. She had a small nose, narrow and delicate, thin ruby red lips, and a small mouth with perfect teeth. With a slender waistline, she was not at all plump yet her figure was shapely, her bosom round and developed, so too her arms, hips, and the turn of her ankle — all with a fresh and healthy appearance that arouses every man's desire.

Yet despite such charms — kindly forgive this little display of pride — whenever we appeared together, my own triumphs were more certain. True, I was seven years younger than she, but unlike her I had the look of candor and innocence that nothing could destroy. Try as we might to treat them as chimeric, the sentiments of our soul exert a singular influence upon our physical features. Our habit of making them convey the movement of the passions that act upon us makes it difficult not to retain by preference the tone set by our favorite among them; and in cases of equal beauty, modesty will always inspire for these traits the sort of interest and majesty not to be found in a prurient woman who disdains the innocent graces by which virtue softens the strident radiance of beauty.

Clémentine's duenna was an elderly woman; she was also served by a young maid and the servants of Dom Lopès.

Dom Gaspard introduced me to this new company, as he did everywhere; but here, unfortunately, he found himself only a subaltern, so our reception was in accord with the mediocrity of his rank; and, as our relations were doubted to be entirely virtuous, we were soon teased. Six weeks was enough to clarify things and I was happy to bring people around to a more honest appraisal. Respect replaced calumny; prejudices challenged, justice was done and through good conduct, Dom Gaspard and I earned respect.

Every day my young friend told me how sorry he felt that
affairs impeded his eagerness to keep his word, but he assured
me that by year's end he'd obtain permission to return to his
country.

Meanwhile, Clémentine provided much warmth and
friendship; and I cheerfully reciprocated. The first sign of her
trust was to confide that she in no way loved Dom Riveiras.
She desired, no less than I, to return to Europe but there was
little chance of that and she did not harbor the same hope.

"Yet I think Dom Lopès's ardor has cooled; as I never
loved him, it is easy to tell. We must be cold with men to understand them. It's far more important to *know* than to love
them. I'd like to be certain of Dom Lopès' indifference. What
might hurt another would fill me with joy; once I no longer
please him, he won't oppose my leaving; but from fear of being
abandoned I must carefully manage the way I snuff passion's
flame, something which makes the task still more difficult as I
must feign love while forcing him to hate me."

Such was the situation when an awful event plunged me
into the greatest grief I'd experienced since the fatal moment
that separated me from Sainville. For Dom Gaspard fell ill.
Seized with a raging fever, just four days later, he died in my
arms. He died full of concern for me, anxious about my future,
foreseeing misfortune in the wake of his own end, regretting it
only for the sorrow of no longer being able to help me.

And my plight was indeed dire! Here I was, deep in Africa, more than 2,000 leagues from my country, among virtual
strangers, without resources, not knowing what the future
would bring, comforted only by new friendship with a young
woman whom I knew to be a bit less than morally upright.
The last thing I needed was the further torment of bitter grief
for Dom Gaspard. The young man's honesty, purity of feeling
and constant attention deserved my esteem. My tears were

sincere. His dying words were advice and hurried prayers that Dom Lopès would take over and fulfill his pledge to me. The unfortunate young man breathed his last — swearing he loved no one but me.

"Sainville," interrupted the Count de Beaulé. "After a relationship such as this, nothing less than the sort of examinations you performed for Ben Mâacoro would seem to be required."

"My dear Count," replied Sainville pleasantly, "for anyone who knows her heart, there's no need of further proof of Léonore's modesty. Delicate and sensitive love is in no wise jealous of the rights that friendship bestows."

"Truly, Count," said Madame de Senneval, "spare us your thoughts because they are so indecent!"

"I knew it. *Indecent* — when *we* suspect *you*, mesdames. As if, unfortunately for you, we didn't have constant good reason."

"I vouch for Léonore," said Madame de Blamont. "With respect to Dom Gaspard I would wager she is guilty of not even a single bad thought."

"*Thoughts*," said the Count, "are things for which women never take the blame. I beg you, let us say nothing of thoughts. If theirs were known, not a single chaste woman would be left on earth."

"Then I must be the only one," resumed Sainville's wife. "Throughout my existence my mind has always followed my heart and I've never had a single thought for anybody but my husband."

"Let us then continue, beautiful Léonore," said the Count. "You are made for singularities; that is a question of blood — is it not, my dear President?"

Madame de Blamont lowered her gaze and blushed.

After the silence that followed, *our lovely adventuress took the*   o
opportunity to continue as *follows*:

At the time Dom Gaspard died, serious efforts were
under way at Fort Tete to unite the colony in Benguela by an
inland route that would establish a settlement to be located
in the Kingdom of Butua. The minister in Lisbon in charge   5
of the project, initiated by Count de Souza, urged it forward
and Dom Lopès had obtained about Ben Mâacoro, the king of
that central part of Africa, such useful information as needed
to succeed. He envisaged opening negotiations. Just a week
after my loss, as I considered how I might return to Europe,   10
Dom Lopès asked me into his office together with Clémentine.
Here, behind closed doors, he asked us to listen carefully and
spoke as follows:

"Clémentine," he addressed his mistress: "I know what
you want. Your sentiments for me are extinct. You long only   15
to return to Portugal. I am not to be toyed with." He added
intently: "Seductive and clever as you are, you might continue
to deceive were I not the first to disengage. And as for you,
Mademoiselle," he turned to me: "Nothing more natural than
your objective should be the same. No bonds to keep you here;   20
you wish to return to your country with equal determination.
However legitimate your intentions, accomplishing them depends upon me. I may or may not permit your departure, as I
wish or as the interests of my court oppose it or not; but love
will not be considered, I assure you. I renounce, Clémentine,   25
all my feelings for you; and as for you, Mademoiselle, your
charms never seduced. Take up the bold project I'm about to
suggest. Once accomplished, a vessel will await you, money
as well, and inside three months you'll be in Lisbon."

"Can it be? Monsieur, tell us what we must do!" I ex-   30
claimed. "For my part, I'll do anything to obtain what you
offer!"

"I'll take the same oath," said Clémentine. "You found me
out, Dom Lopès. I'm eager to return to my country. Give the
order and I'll do as Léonore does."

"Then listen," said the Portuguese. "We're busy with plans
for unification with Benguela and intend to build a series of
inland forts that will reach from the border of Monomotapa
to Saint Mary Bay. But the people whom we require as allies
for success in this venture is one of the most cruel and ferocious in all Africa; small in number but the most warlike. We
are weaker than they and despair of victory by force of arms.
That leaves diplomacy and ruse. Ben Mâacoro is the name of
their chieftain and his passion for women is beyond belief.
White women, most especially, have decisive power over him
and any woman of that color is sure to make him do what she
wants. To this monarch I assign you. You are the perfect ones
to gain control over him. I will spread false information that
will prompt him to attack my fort. I'm certain I can recapture
it at will. I'll let him succeed. He will take you both prisoner
and you'll be brought to his court where you'll captivate his
heart, arouse him, and give yourself up to his passions. By this
means you'll acquire the necessary power to press him into
the alliance my sovereign desires.

"But to succeed you must foreswear any thought of jealousy between yourselves. That would only compromise the
plan and put an end to the project. Let the one less desired
serve the other with fervor; let she who is triumphant turn
the myrtles of Venus into laurels by achieving our goal. Be
always united, help and support one another; your mutual interest requires it and our plan demands it. When the alliance
is prepared and authorization to build forts in the Kingdom of
Butua will be granted, you'll urge the monarch to inform me.
I'll arrive post-haste, my troops reinforced by detachments
from neighboring colonies. Once at the monarch's court I'll

find a way to take you both back. Knowing I'm close by and
invigorated by the courage that inspires, you'll manage to flee
and I'll guard your escape without revealing my own involve-
ment. Back in Benguela you will find money and a waiting vessel. If escape this way turns out to be impossible, I'll demand
your freedom as the first clause of the alliance. And if he were
to refuse, we'd wait a few months more while I build my forts,
then enlist troops from all over. Benguela will unite under me
and, while we imperceptibly become masters of the country,
we will gain by arms what was denied by negotiation.

"As I said, you must respond here and now. Understand
the risk, but it's your only way back to Europe."

"Have you considered, Monsieur," I said to the Portuguese
as he finished, "how atrocious your proposition? I'd like to
know by what title and right you lay claim to the use of two
free women."

"Free women," replied Dom Lopès haughtily. "You are
quite wrong. You're no longer free. The moment I revealed
my project your enslavement began. Just try to leave this very
room."

At those words Clémentine rushed to the door only to
step back in fright and dread. Soldiers were everywhere.

"Monster!" she cried in despair. "Is this my reward for
having loved you! Must you repay my tenderness by delivering me up to a cannibal? And what about this poor girl?
Why should she be involved in this diabolical scheme? She's
not from your country. Does she belong to you? Did not your
friend entrust her to your care?"

"All such vulgar feelings you ascribe to me, Clémentine,"
calmly replied Dom Lopès, "have no value when faced with
the power of the state. Love — gratitude — the rights of man
— all such relations disappear when duty calls, when my obligation is to serve the country. States are established and secured

at the expense of the weak, who count for nothing when the rights of the powerful are at stake."

"Terrible injustice."

"So it is. When you know a little more of politics, you'll be convinced that injustice and violence underpin all monarchies, and the rights they arrogate to themselves are rooted in abrogating those of the people. Besides, you may choose. Nothing obliges you to prefer my offer to the other, which would be to spend the rest of your life here in chains."

"Dom Lopès!" I cried. "You do away with all restraints but must you disregard those of your religion? 'Twas before the altar of the God you serve that I swore fidelity to my husband and now you want me to be unfaithful."

"I take the crime on my conscience," answered the Portuguese with a scornful smile. "Only in the minds of people does heaven make kings. At the tribunal of personal conscience there's no God but the one that serves their purpose, no sacred interest but their own, and no divine law outside their ambition and pride."

"So!" I replied vehemently: "What's to happen to his subjects if a king disregards what's just and fair and has no god besides his own passions!"

"The fate of his subjects leaves the monarch indifferent," said the Portuguese. "His own grandeur and that of his state are what interests him. When the loss of one serves the other, there's no doubt who pays the price."

"You describe tyrants."

"So are all kings, more or less. Their crimes differ only as to their interests. You fear attacks because you may be hurt — but how do they contest Nature? Study shows that sacrifice of the weak for the sake of the strong is first among her laws. Leafy branches of the oak deprive the plants beneath it of sun, so they languish and die. The wolf devours the lamb, the rich

exhaust the poor, and everywhere force crushes whatever sur-   o
rounds it without the slightest claim from Nature in favor of
the oppressed. She neither avenges on their behalf nor gives
comfort; she neither protects the human heart nor saves it
from despotism and its power to destroy."

"So tyranny in no way is an outrage to Nature?"   5

"It serves her. Tyranny is the image of Nature, imprinted
in the heart of civilized and natural man alike. It rules the lives
of plants and animals, and it makes the rivers run. It is master
of the heavens. There is not a single operation of Nature that
has not tyranny at its base; her every action is an act of tyranny."   10

"And humanity?"

"Reason belongs to the weak, a shield to oppose the fetters that bend and enslave him. Circumstance counts. Should
he change places, he'd become the same barbarous tyrant.
Does the sophism of inferiority break the law of Nature? Ever   15
selfish, humanity is born in the heart of the slave. If he sheds
tears over the torments he witnesses, it is only because he
fears them for himself. That's why the state is so cruel. The
government never fears the subject while the subject has
everything to fear from the state."   20

"Well, then," I said to my companion. "Let's dare be as
courageous as this monster is cruel. Let's go ahead with it."

"But what about the promise you're making?" asked
Clémentine.

"I shall keep it," said Dom Lopès. "It concerns only me. In   25
acting on behalf of my prince, I commit wrongs that would
surely afflict my conscience if I acted alone. I promise to save
you and will do everything possible to succeed. I give you my
word and shall keep it. As a statesman I bring you misfortune;
as a friend, I shall serve you well."   30

"I've decided," I said firmly to Clémentine: "I trust him.
He won't abandon us."

"So then!" said Clémentine. "I join my fate to yours." Addressing Dom Lopès:

"Shall I be allowed to take my servants?"

"Of course. They will be captured with you. Ben Mâacoro will learn that the fort harboring white women is poorly defended. He will march on it, I will flee and you'll be his prisoners. You'll succeed — with the only kind of success that can secure your freedom. There's no way to enter the kingdom of this prince if you don't open the door."

"It is absolutely clear," I answered. "I understand and am not afraid; I've courted dangers equal to this. With heaven's help I'll triumph over these as well. When do we leave?"

At these words, Dom Lopès, surprised by my courage, condescended to praise it.

"Emulate such valor," he said to Clémentine. "Assist her, remain united, no jealousy; the one who is less desired must yield and offer counsel to the other. I guarantee you will succeed."

I asked Dom Lopès if the monarch might already know something of the plans.

"I don't believe it possible," he said. "For a long while he's kept in his court a refugee from my country, a well-known rascal who works for him. If you find him still there, avoid him; he'd betray us. The only good thing about him is that he taught the monarch Portuguese. You can use that language to convince Ben Mâacoro of the advantages to the alliance we propose."

There the conversation ended. We retired to our rooms and were kept under close watch.

The operation began the very next day and a week later the fort was attacked. Although informed and prepared to flee, the Portuguese forces lost two men. With terrible screams, the savages barged into the rooms in which we were locked away.

They immediately captured us — myself, Clémentine, and her
two servants. Because they greatly wanted to present us to the
monarch, we were well cared for during the four-day journey,
all needs provided. But within, fear constantly fought hope
in my heart, keeping me in a tumultuous state, and I must
confess Clémentine's cheerfulness was a welcome distraction.

"I'm infinitely less afraid," she told me one night, "of serving this monster's pleasures than being his main course at
dinner."

"Not me! I'd prefer a thousand times to be eaten than satisfy his disgraceful lust."

"Don't you think that's taking virtue too far?"

"No, it's only to cherish the man I love."

"When things calm down a little, you'll explain to me
such *délicatesse*. I still don't understand it."

"Why can't you understand that death is preferable to
betrayal?"

"But rape isn't betrayal."

"No matter. Death is less awful."

"So I must be lucky not to have a lover. If I adopted your
philosophy, my custom of taking everything to extremes
would have me begging Ben Mâacoro to roast me on a spit
instead of thrust me in his bed. Thank god I love nobody and if
he chooses me I shall be his — whatever repugnance his pro-
clivities might cause me. For in addition to his custom of con-
signing women to flames — not exactly a cause for celebration
— he also uses men for his pleasures. That quite disgusts me."

"What! Those are the things that stop you? Terror of how
we're to be made victims? Horror of some crime awakened in
your soul?"

"Well, I can't think of anything else."

"It's a strange principle that abhors crime owing to the
infamy of the perpetrator but not the pain of being defiled."

"And so you see me, wholly without moral refinements. If I become your student, it will be either to improve myself or sin more voluptuously."

"*More* voluptuously?"

"Well, certainly. It's essential to be intimately familiar with the force of the offence in order to be more deliciously aroused. When I lived in Madrid, devout by appearance like all the women in Spain, I went to confession for that alone. I wanted to know about all the gradations of evil. To be told of all their dangers — if only you knew the pleasure it gave me to then go out and commit them!"

"Scamp and miscreant!" I cried. "Let the emperor go and eat you! Enough! You're perverting me."

We finally reached the capital. There we were veiled and blindfolded, our ears plugged with cotton, and taken off to the palace. We were not warned about the preliminary formalities or the cruel inspection, which seemed to have little effect on my companion.

But for me it was a terrible blow that nearly killed me.

"I fought back against this barbarous fellow," *said Léonore, turning to Sainville and smiling.* "This cruel man — the same one I was so fearful of wounding —yet 'twas he who gave the order to outrage my modesty."

We were taken to the harem, once the examinations ended, where the monarch himself removed our veils. Clémentine's two servants were taken off to the most secluded apartments, assigned duties and ministrations, perhaps even providing peculiar pleasures of which we knew nothing — for we never saw them again. We were appraised and as our skin color

alone inflamed the King, who was already in a violent lust-   o
thirsty state that required no further investigation, he roughly
seized poor Clémentine.

Great God! What a scene! It was as if I was watching a
little lamb made prey to an enraged tiger. Could human beings
exist on the face of the earth that were so devoid of sensitivity   5
and decency as to wholly pervert the sweet pleasures of love?
To taste them only with expressions of bitter fury and sacrifice
to their solitary satisfaction all the faculties of the object they
destroy? Immediately I felt such violent disgust for the man
that I doubted I could muster the force by which I intended   10
to subdue him.

First fires quenched, he turned to me, no doubt intending
to rekindle them.

"Come here," he said. "Come and make yourself as happy
as your companion."   15

"Tyrant!" I replied. "If you think women are born to be
made happy by the caresses of a monster like you, you don't
know the country I'm from. Merit the favors you want and *I'll*
decide when you've shown yourself worthy."

Stunned, Ben Mâacoro, who until now had barely glanced   20
at me, took me by the hand and led me into broad daylight
where he contemplated me at length.

"Where do you come from?" he asked, "that you address
your master with such insolence?"

"From a country where pleasure accompanies love, where   25
men seduce by kindliness and kneel before women, and obtain their favors only as reward for their care."

"So the one who just obeyed me is not from your country?"

"No — but you've outraged her all the same. You had your
way with her and she detests you. You'll have to behave differ-   30
ently with me. Put off your brutal pleasures and learn some
delicate ones. They'll delight you in ways that last your whole

life long, unlike those you've just tasted, which she despises and you've already forgotten."

"And what are those pleasures you promise in place of those you refuse?"

"Pleasures of the soul, the sweetest a man can have, and the only ones to make him happy."

"Explain! I don't understand!"

"I will love you."

"Love me?"

"More, I shall esteem you."

"And what will that bring me? Is there anything voluptuous I'll gain from all that?"

"Purity of well-being the likes of which you've never known. It will transport your soul to a place of happiness sweeter and more intense than anything that ever touched it."

"You are beautiful," said the monarch, fixing me with his gaze. "It seems I already sense something of what you say. I enjoy looking at you; it gives me almost the same pleasure as when I fill my imagination with the thought of the god I worship. Perhaps you are this god, taking the form of a white woman."

"No, I'm no god; by no means. I'm the most ordinary of Nature's works. But if you listen to me, if you deserve my love, I'll bring you greater happiness than any god."

"You hint at pleasures unknown in these climes."

"Yes, but it will take time before you understand. You must cede, on your knees, your chimerical rights to all powers over me and let my fragility triumph. I shall command — you will obey. You'll see and satisfy my desires. You'll be my slave. I'll put you in chains and the cost of submission will bring you the happiness to which you aspire."

"Your voice wields power over my soul. Your eyes inflame it as words penetrate it. To even gaze upon you I must shield my eyes — as if braving astral fires. Your words are like honey soothing the wound inflicted by the poisoned arrow of a Jagas."

"Do you then see something of my ascendancy over you?"

"Like that of the moon over the stars in the heavens above. My power fails before your beauty's beams — like lightning that splits the proud soaring cedar."

"Well, then, leave me alone with my friend. Outrage her no more, and me, never."

"And if I obey?"

"I'll let you to do everything to serve me."

"But will you reward me?"

"Yes, when I can be sure of the sovereign influence you promise."

With these words he flung open the doors and ordered the most beautiful rooms in the palace be prepared for me. He asked if it would displease me to share a meal with him. I said I would like that. Fruits were brought. He ate them, then offered some to Clémentine and me. The meal over, I told him of my desire to retire to my apartment alone with my companion. He agreed on the first point but was more difficult as to the second. I had the feeling that by keeping us apart he was hoping for a faster conquest. Only with painful struggle and threats to never love him did I succeed in making him agree that Clémentine and I would not be separated. At last he agreed and we left, followed by two female slaves ordered to serve us.

"All this, my dear Sainville," *said Léonore, addressing her husband,* "explains the monarch's irritation that you noticed the next day, a change of attitude that made you fear disfavor and occasioned your flight."

"O! What a man," exclaimed Clémentine as soon as we were alone. "What gigantic proportions! I've never seen anything like it. There's not a woman in Europe who could become the wife of such a man. Yes — go ahead —," she saw me break out in laughter —: "If the same thing happened to you, you wouldn't look so gay."

"And what? A little thing like that brings you down?"

"*Little thing!* Nothing more frightful, I'm telling you. I would've a thousand times preferred fighting a bull at the Alcala Gate in Madrid to jousting with that cannibal. But patience: you're next and you can tell me all about it."

"Not likely. I'm confident of my power over him. You've nothing more to fear."

"God willing," said Clémentine.

We went to bed and early the next day the monarch came to see us. He wanted further liberties with my companion and seized her. That he apparently wished to vary his performance from the previous night frightened Clémentine all the more. But when I started to cry he immediately let her go and came to me.

"What's wrong, Proud Slave?" — calling me by the name he'd given me —: "What's the matter? Why are you upset?"

"Your infidelity. I thought you loved me. Now I see I was wrong."

"I'm not attacking you. You've refused me and so I press no further. Isn't that what you want?"

"My desire goes further. In hoping to win your heart I also want to be the only one. Sharing it is an outrage. How can you?"

"What are you saying! No pleasure with you whom I love, or anyone else, either! You demand too much, Slave! Too much!"

Fearing his depraved heart might slip from the hand that sought to capture it, I said: "What I'd like is proof of your affection.

You're free to give it or refuse; but you mustn't take it from
others if you want me to believe you love me."

"Well, once more I'll give you satisfaction and prove how
much I want from you the thing you price so high. As for you,"
he said, turning to my companion: "You'll no longer serve my
pleasures since they inflict you with such pain. As for her —
she whom I love more than life itself — she'll provide them
when she wants."

With those words, he left.

"You see," I said to Clémentine, "we're now mistresses
and have the tyrant at our feet. Am I dreaming or isn't that
the delicacy you deride as illusory? Will you finally admit its
power and agree there's no man a woman can't capture with
the art of resistance?"

Clémentine, delighted to be free from this monster,
showed her gratitude with all possible ardor.

We allowed a week to pass before opening negotiations,
during which time I did everything that could reinforce my
dominance; but as I only wished to carry out Dom Lopès'
plans, not (as you can well imagine) own the detestable satisfaction of making a submissive lover of this most unworthy
man, I lightened up on my stated desire to hold him captive.
My aim was less to master his caprices than to prevent him
from making me their object. So I ought not do too much to
impede his desires, for the more I prescribed limits the more
dangerous they became. I finally discovered an excellent way
to allow their expression while wholly conserving the appearances of sweet sensitivity I'd first ordained.

One day, when he took me into the most secret apartments of his harem and made all the women appear before me,
he also offered to show me his catamites. I went along in order
to please him. After he proudly demonstrated the intemperate
way that obscene homage was paid to him, no sooner inside

this place of horror and corruption than the evildoer dared ask me if I would let him engage in this sort of pleasure — if it would injure his love for me. With an air of contempt I immediately replied that it would not. I was sure that it could cool his ardor without loosening love's grip on his heart. Tolerating this weakness would mean less violence with just as much love, two objectives necessary to my plan to captivate but not fear him. The monster, much pleased with permission granted, and so little did he understand the language of true love, that he went on to spend three days and nights in horrifying debauches with the objects of his vile intemperance, something he hadn't permitted himself since falling in love with me.

"Some hearts by their very nature are impossible to explain," I said. "Could it be that false and contrived needs, and the acquired tastes of habit, no matter how criminal, might balance the soul's most refined sentiments and seem even to ally with them?"

"No doubt," replied Clémentine. "Aren't we always seeing tenderest love felt for the most despicable objects of public debauchery, and at the same time the most villainous excesses demanded by the best-loved mistress?"

"At that point it's depravity, not sentiment."

"You're wrong, Léonore. Men's passions are unfathomable and their tentacles are everywhere. Any excess you like can excite a libertine but also the most sensitive of men. For one debauched, what follows in the wake of such improprieties belongs merely to libertinage, I agree. But delicious refinements can also be found in a man animated by the flame of honesty, for whom all goes to the profit of sentiment that dictates and inspires even the most inconceivable excesses, necessary for such a soul, which serve as proofs of ardent love. Every man is born with a relative disposition to such quirks as may surprise you, in which everyone indulges differently

and more or less. Love, only establishing itself in the wake of
first received impressions, is shaped by the degree of activ-
ity it finds in them. If nourished by weak impressions, love
cannot become violent; it reigns with wisdom and expresses
itself gently. If, on the contrary, love is founded upon the excessive tenor of the passions, it sweeps away everything in its
path, like the impetuous North Wind that devours and tears
everything to pieces — a fierce all-consuming ardent flame
that consumes anything used to extinguish it.

"All these results owe to love. The mischievous child
breaks his rattle and takes pleasure in its destruction; soon he
sheds bitter tears over the wreckage his fury wrought. Such is
love and such are its effects: incredible excess by turns cruel
and impure but always born of Nature — unknown to the fool,
punished by the crude puritan, yet respected by the philosopher because only he knows the human heart, he alone holds
the key. All those who, unlike the wise man, are forever surprised by the conjoined effects of hearts and minds — and
nothing is more common than one of these be purely good,
the other wholly bad — and when both act at once, we often
see actions of the same being as a multitude of vices attached
to virtues. For this we blame contradictions natural to men
without seeing that what happens in no wise owes to foolishness but only to the joint effects of two principles that, inevitably divergent, must necessarily produce dissimilar effects.
Hadrian could love Antinous the way that Abelard could love
Heloise; the former had had an evil mind, the latter only a
good heart. Hadrian, both more sensitive and a libertine,
would have loved both Heloise and Antinous; while Abelard,
merely sensitive, would have only loved Heloise."

The monarch, in the end, had fallen in love. He took no
action except by my counsel and made no decision concerning governance without my advice. As soon as I sensed this, I

started negotiations. With helpful instruction from Clémentine, I made him see that he could gain from friendly relations with the Portuguese, and to understand the value of forging alliances with them for his ongoing wars with surrounding nations. The superiority of the people with whom I suggested he make alliance frightened him at first; he feared falling under their control. But I explained that this was far from what the Portuguese wanted, that they would be more burdened than enriched by his provinces and only wanted to facilitate commerce and establish passage for their compatriots on the western coast of the continent. When he asked if I was charged by the Europeans to negotiate this affair, I concealed nothing. I even told him that if he had not attacked the Portuguese garrison, I would have come to his court with my companion to discuss the plan.

After a moment of silence, the monarch indicated to me that he did not oppose my offer but feared that the Europeans, once within his borders, would take me away from him. I made him understand that this was far from their intention and that their own best interests were served if they had someone from their nation whom he trusted, who could maintain them in his good graces. He understood. When I pressed him more closely, he assented without difficulty, granting everything I asked.

But he added that this was the last time I would have any influence over him if I didn't determine to make him happy. He was unwilling to wait any longer. No woman had ever obtained from him what I had done; my power was like that of the serpent that created the earth. He made it clear that the day he signed the alliance with the Portuguese was also to be the day he triumphed over their emissary, and he told me so in a way that made me expect violence if I did not willingly assent.

Having obtained everything and been refused nothing, it was only a matter of taking the project to court. There came some opponents to the plan; I confronted them in council. I reasoned against them with arguments so strong that gradually I brought them around.

We immediately dispatched three warriors to invite the Portuguese into the country as friends. Less than a week later Dom Lopès arrived, at the head of two thousand men from the neighboring colonies; he quickly met with me privately.

"I demand you keep your word," I said to him in French, as soon as he entered.

"You may count on it," Dom Lopès replied. "A vessel awaits you in Benguela; six of my men, well-armed and passing familiar with the route, will escort you and Clémentine overland. A company official has been informed and expects you, but first you must flee. I can guard your escape but must not otherwise help. I cannot start out with a hostile act toward people whom I must treat with care."

"Why not demand our departure as a token of the alliance?" I asked.

"I will try, but how can you hope that the monarch will agree when he's in love? I repeat: escape is the only path. Decide upon it and I give my word: I'll do all I can to prevent pursuit."

However difficult or hazardous the compact, we had to take it. A man as determined as Dom Lopès would never change his mind. Everything went well during the audience with the King, and the treaty was signed without further hindrance. But when the Portuguese talked of returning the captive women to the garrison at Fort Tete, Ben Mâacoro trembled with rage and protested that he'd die first. Dom Lopès, fearing hostilities, and not about to imagine that a pair of women were worth spilling blood over, fell silent.

My situation grew more precarious by the minute. I no longer had a pretext to refuse; everything I wanted had been granted. Death itself would be sweeter than becoming a wife to this monster. Yet, how escape? Determined at all cost not to resign myself to the terrible fate that awaited, I told Clémentine to be ready the next evening and entreated the Portuguese to provide the six promised soldiers. Beneath the walls of a garden favored by the monarch stood a low enclosure of rough-hewn wood located along a path and covered by a parapet, no more than three feet high within and six feet round. With no choice left, I told the king I was at last ready to make him happy and, as I adored the garden, wanted nothing more than to give myself to him in that voluptuous setting. Ben Mâacoro understood: the garden was expressly forbidden to us; we could only see it from our windows. He could readily suppose that I might admire it.

"That's not all," I told him when he granted my first request. "My companion must be with us, too. You will see, Great Emperor, what powerful effect a second woman can have upon the singular pleasures I've promised you!"

He responded with cries of joy and I grew more confident that he could be better controlled by inflaming his head rather than winning his heart. Full of enthusiasm for the promised pleasures, he spent the whole day, as was usual, plunged in preliminary debauches that I tolerated because I was sure it would enfeeble strength and reason alike.

Shortly before our rendezvous, he requested my permission to bring a few of his women to witness the promised tutorials and to show them how much they had to learn in the art of providing real pleasure. I assured him that was impossible, that my companion and myself were adequate to the task of sensual exhilaration but, were there other witnesses, our modesty, natural to our native land, would prevent us from

sharing and inflaming his pleasure. At nightfall — I'd suggest-   o
ed that time of day, favorable to our plan, was best because
it was cool — the three of us went into the garden. As soon
as we entered the enclosure and could confirm that the six
promised soldiers awaited, I made Clémentine recline along
the parapet of the low wall and fully expose her charms to the   5
lascivious monarch.

"Shall we begin," said I with an air of submission. "Let one
inflame your desires while the other satisfies them."

Those words were the signal. As soon as Clémentine
heard them she let out a scream and jumped from the para-   10
pet onto the path. Seizing the moment and taking advantage
of the monarch's startled reaction and his move to restrain
my companion, I too bounded over the wall with the same
agility and tumbled to the ground beside her. We sprang up
and rushed across the grounds, our six guards at our back,   15
delighted to escape with so little sacrifice from that terrible
den of iniquity.

We heard him calling for help but by then were long gone.
As he saw others with us, he was hardly going to come after us
himself. He must have gone back deeply ashamed, I think, for   20
having been duped by two European females — a man who
daily made two thousand women tremble in his seraglio and
who, at the head of his army, was known as one of Africa's
bravest princes.

In Benguela we learned that his anger was first directed   25
at Dom Lopès, whom he accused of having facilitated our escape, and that was the reason — the presence of Portuguese
forces within his borders — that he didn't give chase.

Dom Lopès for his part protested innocence and had
even sent several of his men to make a show of chasing us,   30
in order not to compromise his alliance. The state of mutual peace was reinforced when the Portuguese promised the

emperor ten white women, among whom he swore the least beautiful of them would be infinitely worthier than either of the two just escaped.

But we were by no means out of danger. We had to pass through the land of the Jagas, a people just as dangerous as the one we'd just fled. It took a week to reach Benguela, eating only a few monkeys we managed to hunt down and kill, and sleeping at night in trees. Yet Clémentine and I came through without incident. Dame Fortune, who destined us to greater harm in our native land than we knew among the most savage people on earth, had only brought us under her wing to plunge us deeper into a frightening abyss that she was already preparing beneath our feet.

Thus it was we arrived without incident in the Portuguese colonies on the African coast. The Consul there expected and welcomed us lavishly. He sang our praises and after lodging us in his home to wait for a favorable wind, brought us personally to the merchant vessel that would take us to Lisbon. We solicited his concern on behalf of the two women who had been captured with us and told with what regret we were forced to abandon them; he gave his word he would try to help them. And we left.

While the sails, filled by the cool north wind, sent the vessel flying across the fluid plain, passengers rested and grew bored yet with sweet hopes of soon embracing their dearest beloved, the chaplain prayed, the sailors cursed, and the officers got drunk. Let me take a moment to tell you a little about the situation in which we each found ourselves.

That of Clémentine was just fine and promising. Although she possessed few belongings besides the flimsy dresses we'd worn in the country we just left, from Dom Lopès she had

about 60,000 francs which the chief of the Portuguese colony
in Tete had transferred to his correspondent in Benguela, and
which she'd receive when we arrived.

As for myself, I had little. When captured in the widow's
garden in Venice, I'd at most had seven or eight louis in my
purse, from small sums Sainville provided for little pleasures
and replaced as soon as they were spent. The privateer from
Tripoli had taken that money while Duval, who paid all expenses and did not trust me, never put one penny at my disposal. That was my state of poverty when Dom Gaspard took
me under his wing. You recall I declined his purse when he
offered it in the desert; later, at the fort, he begged me accept
a few doubloons and when he died he left me all his possessions. But that didn't suit Dom Lopès, who declared that the
young man was under his parents' authority and not at liberty
to give away his assets, which must be returned to Portugal.
That reasoning, I guessed, was based on his desire to use me
in implementing his plans and to entangle me by every means
possible, poverty included, and certainly the most efficient —
which judgment, I say, fair or foul, deprived me what little help
I might have counted on. When we arrived in Benguela I had a
small sum that I concealed in my hair; that sum was augment-
ed by a bonus of two hundred Spanish pistoles, to be shared
with my companion, for our services to the King of Portugal.
Before boarding ship we'd spent two-thirds of that on clothing,
with the result that I was left with a pittance.

All our possessions consisted of three trunks: two large
ones for Clémentine and a small shabby one for me. With singularly poor judgment, my companion advised me not to keep
my money with me during the voyage but like her to hide it
in my trunk. Fortunately, I didn't listen. On the crossing all
went well and seven weeks after leaving Benguela, we sailed
into Lisbon.

The largest vessels, as you may know, are able to enter the city thanks to the extreme breadth of the Tagus River. After customs formalities a great number of Galician porters offered their services. Clémentine cast an indifferent glance at the nearest of them and, our trunks having already been searched, ordered our luggage to be taken. In a trice our trunks were carried off on the backs of three of those fellows.

"Where to, my excellency?" asked one, staring at my companion.

"To the Strella, *chez* Boulnois," replied Clémentine, and she gave the address of an inn run by a Dutchman, recommended in Benguela.

At that, off trotted our porters and we followed. Along the quay they stayed a little ahead but always in view. But soon they hastened their pace and imperceptibly we lost sight of them in the crowd. At that moment there arose a prodigious commotion. It was the King, passing in a ceremonial carriage, on his way to visit a convent where a young woman of high society was about to take the veil. People squeezed around to contemplate this ridiculous scene. Like the others, Clémentine wanted to stop and watch. While we enjoyed that futile and vulgar entertainment, others were working to plunge us into despair. As the streets cleared, we moved forward and soon caught sight of the steeple of the convent of Sao Bento, facing the Boulnois residence where we were to stay. We arrived at last and Clementine imperiously addressed the doorman at the hotel:

"Take us to the apartment with our baggage left by three porters."

"What baggage?" he replied, staring.

Here I couldn't help but tremble, for misfortune threatened and the idea of it had already entered my mind.

"What are you talking about? I didn't ask for insolence!" snapped a fiery Clémentine. "I asked for my luggage and told

you to show us to the room where it must be with the porters   o
who brought it."

"There's nothing of the sort here."

"Is this not the Bon Repas?

"It surely is."

"The Dutch establishment in the Strella owned by Mon-   5
sieur and Dame Boulnois?"

"The same."

"Did not three Galician porters just bring in our trunks?"

"You must have given them wrong directions," said the
valet, turning away. "They did not arrive."   10

Clémentine grasped my hand. "We've been robbed." She
underscored as much with a revolting blasphemy, as was her
custom at every vexation, then: "Robbed — but say nothing
for we must not go without dinner and shan't spend the night
in the street." She called to the valet: "Give us a room, *Came-*   15
rieros, and pray watch for those three men. Send them along
immediately when they arrive."

"Maybe your people made a mistake, Madame," said the
valet. "They must have gone to Buenos Ciaires, the English
hotel owned by Sir William."*   20

"Certainly. Go there and be back straightaway."

We were conducted to a vast apartment, obviously more
comfortable than we could afford, and the valet left to inquire.

Those first moments were not so awful as they might
have been. Hope remained. But we were fiercely agitated.   25
Clémentine paced the room while I collapsed on the sofa; we
exchanged a few sharp words, nothing more. The least noise
upset us. We listened and plunged into sorrowful reflection.

---

* This establishment, like the Bon Repas, was at the time this was written the best
in Lisbon.

o   Finally, the valet returned to announce that nothing like we
were expecting had arrived at Sir Williams' Inn.

"It doesn't matter," said Clémentine with a constrained
tranquility that revealed her character better than ever since
we'd met. "We'll have dinner. They'll arrive. Impossible they
5   won't come." But to me, as soon as the valet left: "We shall
never find our belongings. We're ruined, Léonore."

She watched as I burst into tears.

"Don't be upset," she continued. "Think of all the dangers
we've been through. We'll come out of this one, too. Don't for-
10   get, my child, that with spirit and froth two beautiful women
need never starve."

"Oh, heavens! Don't expect me to take part in the sort of
infamy I hear you suggesting."

"I don't want to engage in debauchery any more than you.
15   I hate that sort of life, though not because I think it offends
God — far from it. Nor do I suppose that the corruption of
women harms society but rather serves it by multiplying the
objects of pleasure it harbors. But I hate and fear prostitution
because it both diminishes us in the eyes of men and makes
20   us scorn the sex that (were we to do it justice) merely deserves
our disdain. Inconsiderate as men are, they force us into an
abyss and dare punish us for a frailty of which they're the prin-
cipal cause. But we must live, Léonore. It is Nature's first aim,
this imperious law that prevails over all social conventions,
25   which were only established to better serve that law. Secondary considerations deserve only contempt when they fail to
heed Nature's first imperative."

"But surely not every means to reach that goal is permitted."

"Any and all. Nature forbids not a one. When it's a ques-
30   tion of self-preservation, does Nature punish one who lives
in the world and employs whatever means she can to procure nourishment? Would she act more cruelly toward us?

Conventions that oppose this way of life when no others are
open to us owe not to her. Why should I respect them? They
contravene the only voice that genuinely speaks to my heart.
But no matter. In order that we have nothing to reproach ourselves for — you being so delicate in such matters — let's start
with honest steps to recover our possessions."

We went downstairs.

"No need to take the key to our room," the foolish creature said as we left. "Can we agree that God's mercy insures no
one touches our belongings?"

Less determined than my companion to overcome our
misfortune with the help of crime, and so even more upset, I
didn't reply to her little joke. But the young woman's merry
composure, I confess, even when in deep trouble, revived my
courage and I followed her, filled with hope. It was still daylight; we returned to the harbor but came across none who
bore any resemblance to the men who'd taken our baggage.
We looked for the vessel we'd disembarked, for perhaps there
might find some help; but after leaving the passengers, once
his documents were examined, the captain had sailed immediately on to Cadiz, called there by affairs of great importance.
He'd left an hour earlier.

We walked back to the city, inquired as to the address of
the Alcaide, or chief constable of the district where our hotel
was located, and went to lodge a complaint and ask his advice.

Dom Laurent du Pardénos was one of those men whose
sweet and smirking physiognomy conceals a terrible corrupt
soul, one among the many liars who view their post only as a
means to swiftly assuage rapacity and lust by any means necessary so long as whomever is caught in their web offers up
something to serve their passions. In short, he was a great
hypocrite and profound evildoer, deceitful, cunning, hardened against pity for another's misfortunes, offering no relief

and help only if there was hope of getting what he wanted as an unrestrained libertine.

It was to just this respectable magistrate's office that we went to complain about the rascals who had reduced us to beggary.*

Dom Laurent showed us into his office as soon as we were announced, welcoming us in the mildest and most inoffensive manner. He asked what he might do for us and cast soothing glances; before we said a word, he seemed to encourage and commend us with kindly gestures of hand and head. We told our story, detailing our services on behalf of Portugal. He expressed compassion and told that our biggest mistake was not to have solicited a letter of recommendation from the leaders of the colony, which would have been far more useful than money, and with which we might have found help at the Chamber of Commerce of Africa.

"If you go there without such a letter," continued this hypocrite, "two honest women might be taken as adventuresses. I cannot advise it."

"What can we do then, Monsieur," I asked bitterly. "What will become of us?"

"Before you despair," the magistrate went on, "let me undertake my inquiries. Until then wait and above all behave yourselves." He gently patted our cheeks. "Be sure not to succumb to any of the numerous traps that crime, ever on the lookout, sets for innocence. For my part, I have hope. God's goodness is abundant. Has His helping hand ever abandoned the unfortunate? Tell me, my lovely young ladies" — and here he lightly ran a hand across Clémentine's bosom and she let

---

* The portrait here is not imaginary; perhaps in place of the one in Lisbon we might suggest the original. In any dictionary of grand rascals, look up the word "Sartine."

it remain—: "Did you choose a confessor when you arrived in   o
the city? You lived among barbarians, after all. It so happens
that I can recommend a deeply honest man."

At this juncture, Clémentine was outraged and brushed
away the hand — which had been making immense progress.

"No, Monsieur," she said. "We chose no confessor. Our   5
want of dinner was more urgent than a trip to confession, and
we don't have the wherewithal to satisfy that imperious need."

"Ah, too bad! How unfortunate!" replied the sainted fellow. "In truth —"

At just that moment the Angelus bell tolled and Dom   10
Pardénos immediately stopped talking to kneel at the base of
a tall crucifix. He invited us to so join him and spent the next
quarter hour in prayer.

"I say it again," he continued when he rose: "all hope re-
sides in the goodness of heaven! I will take action and tomor-   15
row shall tell you what I find."

"All that's well and good, Monsieur," said Clémentine in-
solently. "But I repeat: we have not even a single *réis* for food.*
At least loan us a dobra.† A devout man like you must love
performing good deeds. They serve heaven better than pater-   20
nosters and you're sure to be rewarded."

"I never loan money," said the good magistrate. "However,"
— he returned a hand to my companion's breast — "because of
you and this dear child," — hoping to treat me the same way —
"yes, because you both inspire me with true compassion, take   25
this half-dobra. But if by tomorrow I don't bring you good news,
fair warning. It's a loan. You must repay me, one way or another."

                                                                       30

* The least valued coin in Portugal; 6400 réis are equivalent to 42 livres 13 solidi 6
  denarii.

† A half-dobra is equivalent to about 20 livres.

Having said this, he showed us the door.

"One moment, Monsieur," said Clémentine. "Can you further explain? How do you expect us to repay you if we don't find our belongings?"

"The way some women do," said Dom Laurent. "Don't they always find a way?" He placed a hand on Clémentine's rump. "To reimburse me, don't we find more than enough right here?"

"We'd be unworthy of your loan if that's how we agreed to repay you," I replied angrily. "Your contempt ought to stop you from helping us."

"I understand nothing of that," said the magistrate, his composure ruffled. "I've given what you asked. Either repay or I'll require satisfaction in whatever coin I fancy."

"Very well," said Clémentine. "You spare us any particular obligation. We were afraid you'd scorn us but, on the contrary, you're the one to merit that very sentiment in all its splendor. You put me and my friend at ease."

Returning to the inn, our first concern was to know if there was news of our trunks. We were assured there was not. Without belongings, now a little mistrusted, as is common in such establishments, if we wanted to be served we were asked to pay for our supper in advance.

"See that," said Clémentine, looking first to me: "*Pity*, the sublime sentiment. You see how men respond when they hear the word. No sooner are we suspected of being destitute than we're insulted right and left. One who might help us makes our virtue the price of what little service he offers; and the next, with gold aplenty, asks us to pay in advance for a miserable supper." Turning to the valet, Clémentine tossed him the gold coin. "Take that, fool. But make it good and be quick about it."

The meal was served straightaway.

"Is that all we get for our money?"

"No, Madame, here: I owe you two cruzados."   o

"For that sum, some Setuval wine. I want to toast the scoundrels who robbed us. Those who've got nothing can afford to raise a glass without insulting a soul."

The wine was bought and Clémentine demanded we be left alone unless there arrived news of our luggage.   5

"*Bon appétit,*" she said. "As you see, we're not yet without resources. There will be plenty of time for despair when misfortune is certain."

My companion's stoicism rekindled my spirits; I ate almost as much as she but drank much less. Determined to   10
drown her sorrows in the delicate juice from the vines of Setuval, she downed two bottles the way I might a tumbler of lemonade and soon after was seized by a state of madness that made her more foolish, livelier, and more joyful than a pretty woman ought to be. Her beautiful black hair floated across her   15
alabaster breasts, her superb eyes flamed now with scorn, next with pain. Sometimes tears moistened from some memory she could not suppress. The frothy disorder of a gauzy chimmar, the only garment the heat permitted, and the touching expression that a little lassitude brought to her features — it   20
all rendered her so beautiful and voluptuous that no man on earth could have resisted her, and I myself needed all power of love and reason to remind myself I was of the same sex as she.

We went to bed with her putting out a hundred ideas, each one more extravagant than the last, and all this on the   25
evening before the day that might oblige us to seek charity or do worse just to live.

But drunkenness is like opium, soothing the pain only to make it more vivid on awakening. Opening her eyes next morning, Clémentine dissolved into tears.   30

"How I wish I died in my sleep! One must never wake with misfortune the only prospect. Wouldn't fate have been kinder, my friend, if I'd passed from the last night's intoxication into death's embrace?"

"No," I replied. "We've come away from situations more dangerous than this. Let's hope for heaven's kindness."

"Heaven's kindness? Never count on that. Hope founded on illusion is only for stupid minds."

"O Clémentine! Illusory or not, it's a port of call in case of misfortune. Let's not destroy the idea in our hearts, for it can at least console us."

"Let lightning strike me the moment I'll be consoled by such nonsense. Stop talking to me about a Great Being indifferent to the fate of His creatures, who creates them only to make them unhappy and keeps them from harm only to drown them in sorrow, who prolongs life only to better exercise His rage by burdening them with calamities whilst in the end they await flames and execution. Death be damned! My utmost satisfaction is being sure and certain such a tyrant never existed; let me go down in fury and frenzy before I believe in Him a single instant!"

"You've poorly portrayed the one you insult, Clémentine. Misrepresented by the cults, to you He seems odious. Vanquish such foolishness and you'll soon come to love Him. You'll see in this divine essence none but a loving and compassionate father who, even if He subjects us at times to misfortune, has artfully located the beams of sweet soothing hope in the deepest reaches in our souls, just so we don't grow discouraged. The more terrible our reverses on earth, the sweeter and more divine will be the recompense He proposes. Afflicted by so much struggle, the eternal happiness to which we lay claim will be so much more pleasant! Listen to your heart, even at this cruel moment of abandonment when your sense of injustice flouts the Eternal One and, still, you'll hear His comforting voice. O my friend! It's a consoling being I offer

you, the one who opens His arms to you. Let us implore Him
by our actions; let me spare you speeches and affectations,
cults and altars. But let our hearts, created in His image, serve
him through virtue."

"I don't believe in virtue any more than I do in your God,"
said Clémentine, shedding bitter tears. "I'll embrace virtues
when I've got the wherewithal to live; I'll believe in God when
I see nothing but goodness on earth."

At that moment someone knocked sharply. As we were
still in bed, we asked time to get ready. When at last we opened
the door, it was Dom Laurent de Pardenos.

"No hope," he told us as he entered. "Your thieves belong
to a large band that has long infested the city and surrounding
precincts. To find where they keep their goods is impossible.
It is simplest to forget about it."

Here all courage dissipated and I began to weep. Clémentine, with more confidence, replied that this news was
still more upsetting because while waiting she'd written her
mother in Madrid for help that would certainly arrive with
dispatch; yet she found herself obliged once more to take advantage of the kindness of Dom Laurent to request another
loan.

"You quite misunderstand, ladies," said the magistrate,
closing the door to the bedroom. "Far from ready to give you
more, I come to ask you either to return my money or provide
the necessary favors."

And approaching me: "Come now, my love, make up your
mind. First you, then the other. And be quick about it, I beg
you. I'm not without practice — thanks be to God — and while
I'm talking to you, another awaits to perform the same chore."

Wholly absorbed by pain, my back turned to this monster,
my head in my hands, half lying on a couch. I didn't see him
coming. Suddenly the viper grabbed me, pinning me down

with one hand while with the other pushing aside everything in his way and exposing me nearly naked to his gaze while I was unable to defend myself. But his victory was short. Bounding up faster than he'd brought me down, I knocked him away with a vigorous fist to the chest.

"Begone, coward!" I exclaimed. "Since you're vile enough to refuse us any help — begone. You're not going to outrage us one bit."

At the altercation Clémentine had rushed to the door and called for the proprietress.

"Our story is short, Madame," said my companion. "Kindly sit and listen. This man" — she pointed to a very confused Dom Laurent — "this ignoble man knows of our misfortune and has taken advantage of it. We've come from the colonies; we've added to Portugal more than three hundred leagues of African land even though we're not native Portuguese, for I'm from Spain and my friend is from France. For our services we were praised and rewarded. Yesterday we arrived with three trunks filled with clothes and money. We entrusted them to some *galègues* to carry them here. They stole them. We asked for help and counsel from this miserable wretch who, because we were impoverished, having lost everything and unable to pay back the little he'd done for us, demands we take part in his despicable pleasures. Is that right, Madame? Must we? Is your establishment a place where two honest women who hoped for shelter are treated this way? Answer and we'll do as you order."

Madame Boulnois looked to Dom Laurent and asked if it was true that a man honored with the public trust would permit himself such things.

"These women are lying," answered the hypocrite, recovering his ingratiating manner, "Don't let yourself be duped. I gladly make them a gift of the money they've swindled. A little charity from time to time never hurts."

At these insulting words, he left us with the hostess.

"Madame," I said, "the monster's embarrassment proves his crime. I beg your pity. We told you the truth; you can be sure we didn't lie. You can see to what extremes two young women would be reduced should you refuse us your help. Abandoning us now would bring a crime on your conscience. We're about to write to friends and relatives; we'll do everything to repay the sum we beg you advance us; while awaiting a response we'll be your hostages and not leave your establishment. Have pity, Madame, and heaven will reward your kindness."

"In truth, my pretty friends," said the hostess, "I've no desire to feed two women for free. I wouldn't lack for your sort if I wanted but — praise God — my inn has never sheltered such. However, if you decide to stay — it's up to you — my servants quit me yesterday. I offer you their place. The conditions aren't bad."

"A fine day in hell!" exclaimed Clémentine. Furious, she rushed at the woman, fists raised. "We should take the place of your servants? I'll teach you, you dirty slattern. My own mother has servants worth more than you."

"Don't listen to her, Madame," I said, stepping between them. "Misfortune inflames her. Be so kind as to keep us another day and I'll ask no more favors. And here —," I unfastened a little necklace with a gold cross I was wearing — "take this in return."

"Very well, then!" As she took the necklace and went out: "You'll be fed for the price of this object. After which, you're on your own."

Furious, Clémentine flung herself down. "My mind is made up. Either that — or let this be the last day of my life."

"Mother of God, decide nothing from despair."

"And what do you expect us to do?"

"Poor and modest, we shall work."

"I'm good at nothing."

"Well, as for myself, I know how to sew and embroider; I will work for both of us and earn enough for us to live on. I'll never leave you: I only ask you behave decently and not give in to despair."

"O Léonore!" replied my companion, burying her head in my breast and flooding it with pain's bitter tears. "'Tis you I love more than life itself — I'd never abandon you either — but let me take care of you. Less delicate, I have better means. Preserve that fancied virtue from which arises your wraith of glory; I shall offend it to earn a living for you; and should ever remorse come tearing at my soul, I shall stifle it in the name of friendship."

"Do you imagine I could be happy living on the wages of your crimes?"

"Listen," said Clémentine, now a little calmer, "I don't want to prostitute myself any more than you do. I've got to be in desperate straits to throw myself into such an abyss; but I don't see any other way out of this odious country. You know our plan: Madrid. Once there, I promise that if my mother and the Duke of Medinaceli are still alive, I'll give you all you need to return to France. But we must get there first. Consider the possibilities: Either we earn enough by prostituting ourselves, or beg by the side of the road, or else we steal. Which of those three is the most honest? Work for a living? How far will a few cents for a day's labor — twelve hours at a stretch — take us? Write to ask for money to be sent? Feeble resource there. Sometimes you get something by asking directly but almost never by post. Many on principle never even reply to those taken by misfortune. If our letters brought nothing, we'd have to vegetate here in some attic, far from where we want to go. So forget about everything that can get us nowhere and think about what might really work — at whatever price and sacrifice it entails."

"Ah! But how can you think," I responded, "that I could ever accept any of the means you propose! Among the three, begging still seems the least awful."

"My dear friend," continued Clémentine, "even then we couldn't avoid what so frightens you. In this century of horror and depravation, men don't give alms to young women like us — not without charging interest. Charity is never free, my dear: pride and intemperance give rise to it. Anyone who bestows charity either wants to be known for it or else profit from it. Gone is the idea that good deeds get you to heaven. We've seen the powerful interests of those who preach that doctrine. We understand that religion, first embraced by the poor, should make alms-giving a virtue; and a persecuted religion must call for charity and scatter gold upon the altars of a base-born God. But philosophy has improved the mind of man only by toughening his heart. In order to purify the one he must mistrust the deceit of the other; we couldn't discover *truth* without abandoning the illusion of *goodness*. And furthermore, for many among the depraved, does not this sorry state of affairs make it still more attractive? Follow with me the thread that leads through the twisted and impenetrable detours of a libertine's heart. Don't you know that he wants to dominate the object offered up to his passions? That force and violence alone please one whose soul has been hardened and enervated by debauchery? Equality, in denying him the despotic pleasures that nourish his lust, leaves him to find victims, best he can, among those whose misery bends them to his brutality. To become pitied, we wouldn't escape the least pitfall and our moral ignominy would force us to run all the dangers of misfortune and inflame men's lust without so much as touching their humanity. We'd cause much crime yet nothing in the way of virtue."

I was about to reply when dinner was brought, interrupting our conversation.

"A light meal," said the server, "but Madame asked me to tell you that she prefers offering reduced fare while letting you to stay a bit longer; she'll feed you three days in recompense for the object you gave her but, as you see, with reduced fare."

"So be it — we're pleased. Close the door when you leave." Clémentine invited me to share the bad boiled meat and a few figs. "Come receive from the hand of the Portuguese nation the price of our services. Learn how to serve kings."

"Alas!" I replied. "The one who rules the nation in which we find ourselves is unaware of what we've done for him. Let's hope he'd be generous enough if he knew."

"Gratitude! Such a virtue in the soul of a king! Don't count on it. Nature, in forming all such scoundrels, molded their souls with vice and as a warning locked ingratitude within."

No sooner had we finished our dinner than the valet reappeared, asking permission to introduce a messenger charged with delivery of an important letter.

"Show him in," I replied. "In our situation we neglect nothing. The faintest glimmer can bring a new dawn."

A lackey without livery appeared, but only to drop a letter on the table and rush out without a word. I opened the letter and read:

> *The Duke of Cortéreal has news and can provide sure and certain information concerning your stolen possessions. The same man who brought this note will return with a carriage at sunset; he will drive you to a country estate several miles outside the suburb of Belem, owned by a lord who seems interested in you. Once there, for the price of unlimited obedience, your trunks will be returned plus one-third of their value.*

Our first reaction was mute surprise that kept us staring at   o
each other open-mouthed, holding our breath. Clémentine,
always more alert to misfortune than me, called to the servant.

"Who is the man who just brought this letter?"

"In truth, I don't know. He never before set foot here."

LÉONORE: "He said he belongs to the Duke of Cortéreal.   5
Do you know of this man?"

THE VALET: "Of course. One of the wealthiest lords in
Lisbon."

CLÉMENTINE: "A great libertine?"

THE VALET: "He likes women and pays them well."   10

CLÉMENTINE: "How old?"

THE VALET: "Fifty years."

CLÉMENTINE: "Tell us, my friend — you seem an honest
fellow. How can the Duke possibly know anything about our
trunks?"   15

THE VALET: "Does he?"

LÉONORE: "Yes."

"Listen," said the fellow, shutting the door for fear of being overheard: "I'm going to reveal part of the mystery — but,
for the love of Saint Jacques, don't betray me."   20

"Fear nothing, serve us, and be sure that a good action is
always rewarded."

"Have no doubt: he's got the trunks. But you'll never get
them back unless you gratify the desires of the Duke and his
friends — three of them. They've been companions for 30   25
years. All are about the same age. They partake their pleasures
together. Of their prodigious fortunes they spend two-thirds
on women. They and their agents invent every kind of stratagem to trap their prey like birds in a net. Money, seduction,
low schemes and lawsuits, prison, thievery, stupration, and   30
maybe worse. Nothing costs them much and, as one of them
serves as director general of domains, their favorite method is

to send hired rascals to the customs rooms where the baggage is searched, to observe travelers arriving by land or sea. They do what was done to you when they find quarry they like. If you go see these lords, you'll have your possessions returned; if instead you use this note to lodge a complaint, they'll deny they wrote it. They'll claim your trunks were seized because they were full of contraband; and if you persist, they'll use their powerful reputations to have you arrested on some pretext, and thrown in a prison for debauched women. There they'll abuse you all the same and never let you out of their grasp."

"Leave us, my friend," said Clémentine. "Sincere thanks for your clarifications; be sure that once we're able, you'll be rewarded."

Once alone, she said to me:

"Did you ever in your life hear tell of crime more odious? With men forever setting traps to innocence, aren't women right to deceive them! But this isn't the time to waste words. We must act. What do you say?"

"We must flee Lisbon."

"What? When we're down to nothing?"

"What difference if virtue's intact?"

"So we should play dupes to these scoundrels?"

"Only if we give in. If we don't fall into their traps, *they'll* be the dupes."

"No! You're not showing enough courage," insisted Clémentine. "We'll go there to get our trunks back. By resistance and reproach we'll grind them down and crush them!"

"Vice accomplished laughs at virtue. It means nothing. We'd brave certain perils to come away with nothing."

"She who fears hath no courage!"

"She who confronts, too much pride!"

"Let's ask our hostess. Maybe she'll want to join us."

"We can try but she'll refuse."

We invited Madame Boulnois upstairs. We showed her   o
the letter just received and, without compromising the valet's
confidence, asked what she thought. What would she do in
our place?

"If I were you, I'd go," she answered boldly, not concealing
from us what might happen. "In fact, considering your situa-   5
tion, would it be so tragic?"

From that moment we were convinced the woman was
bought and paid for. I was inclined to dismiss her. Clémentine, with more pluck, replied disdainfully that such advice
surprised her. Now she realized how wrong she was to believe,   10
as an honest woman, that she could feel secure at the inn.

"What we had in mind was much different, Madame," she
continued: "We wanted to lay claim to possessions that the
Duke's shamefully stolen. We were asking you to come along
to help protect us."   15

"Me? I ought enter such a place?"

"But didn't you tell us to go?"

"'Tis your trade, not mine," said the woman as she went
out. "Do as you will but know that in 24 hours I shan't be able
to keep you."   20

"Great God! Hell itself conspires against us!" said Clémentine once we were alone. "Your damnable virtue is going
to be the end of us." Furious, she headed for the door. "Stay
here. I'm going to confront those imagined dangers head-on."

"No!" I seized and held her tight. "I shan't tolerate prosti-   25
tution. I won't live off the fruits of dishonor. And what would
become of me in this awful place? My anguish over what
would happen to you and fear that the same could happen to
me would mean you'd return to find me dead."

"So take courage. We'll go together, afraid of nothing.   30
Take these weapons." From the table she seized one knife and
handed me another. "We won't be gentle with cowards who
want to sacrifice us to their shameful passions."

"All right," I agreed. "I'm with you."

It seemed best. We might go recover our belongings and escape crime or else be consigned to utter poverty from which only crime could free us. We agreed on a plan, rehearsed what we'd say, and awaited the cruel hour that would decide our fate. The valet returned. Had we made up our minds?

"Yes," I said, "We're ready. Is the carriage waiting?"

"Nearby. We'll meet it on foot, if you don't mind."

We went out. At the corner we entered a vis-á-vis and the valet jumped on behind. The coachman drove fast.

I can hardly describe my state of mind. My circulation seem stilled as if only the palpitations of my heart kept me alive — fewer of them and I would've succumbed. Clémentine, either bolder or more determined, was silent and somber. From time to time she squeezed my hand and said not a word. The route was long and poorly explained to us. After leaving Lisbon we followed the banks of the Tage for about two leagues, turned sharply left toward Leivia, then suddenly veered off the main road and passed along a wooded leaf-covered path, finally to arrive at the grand entrance to a beautiful but wholly isolated estate. Entering the courtyard, the gates shut behind us. The valet jumped down and opened the coach door. He led the way in the dark and showed us into a second anteroom, also without light. He asked us to wait.

I placed a hand on the heart of my companion. It beat as strong as mine.

"Courage," I told her now in turn. "So you exhorted this afternoon, let me do the same now. I'm ready for anything. Heaven fills my soul with strength always lent to virtue when vice must be crushed."

We looked around. The house seemed almost uninhabited. Too much effort to enshroud crime can sometimes turn against it. At last an old duenna appeared, illumined by a candle she held aloft.

"My beautiful children," she said, "be kind enough to com-   o
ply with the rules of the house. None but undressed women
may enter the apartments where my respectable lords await.
I'm going to help you if you don't mind."

She had already removed the pins from Clémentine's
corset, but the latter gently stopped her.   5

"My dear lady," she said, "we are repelled, my companion
and I, by this degrading ceremony. We won't submit. Be good
enough to tell your masters that we insist they exempt us from
the practice."

The duenna went out, leaving us in the dark.   10

"No doubt about it," I said to Clémentine. "In truth, it's
foolish to go further."

"Let's see what they say."

When the old woman returned, it was to assure us that
our reluctance was absurd, that sooner or later it must be   15
done. Why not now?

"At least these," she continued, designating our clothes
from the waist down, "in return for which perhaps they'll
spare you the rest."

"Not in the slightest, Madame," said Clémentine, "yet we   20
beg you, once within we will fully comply."

"So you must," said the old woman. "They'll make you do
as they say, all right. But since you're as stubborn as Galician
mules — come with me."

And so we did. We passed through three more rooms,   25
each cloaked in darkness.

At last a bright-lit drawing room opened at the far end.
The old woman entered, we followed. Four men, aged 50 to
55, were attired in loose flowing taffeta robes that left them
half naked. They were all pacing the room nervously when the   30
door opened. Just as we laid eyes on them, we were astounded
to see our baggage, all three trunks, set out on a table.

"Why these difficulties?" asked one of them while the other three stopped to gaze at us attentively. "Does it not seem," he continued, "that it would be a fine mysterious thing to see two naked wh---s! Did they think they were coming here to lay down the law?"

"No," said another. "Perhaps they're virgins — afraid of coming down with a cold."

"Not at all," said a third. "They want us to admire their magnificent finery."

"Dona Ruffina," said the last, addressing the old woman, "grab one of these vestals and strip her clean in a trice."

The old woman approached.

"Stop, Madame," I spoke her with such prideful resolve that she gasped. "We didn't come for that. Tell me, messieurs," I said, addressing them all, "which of you is the Duke of Cortéreal?"

"What on earth does she mean?" asked the one who had spoken first. "And why does she come here looking here for the Duke of Cortéreal?"

"Is this not his house?"

"Credulous innocents," said the second. "How readily misled. You happen to be at the home of the First Magistrate of Lisbon. Here he is" — he pointed to the oldest among them — "gathered here with his three friends, like himself men of justice, intent on amusing themselves with little imbeciles like yourselves who, from time to time, fall into our hands."

"Those trunks belong to us," said Clémentine. "How can men charged with maintaining order so meddle with it!"

"Dom Carles," said the one introduced as First Magistrate, "I'm hoping here's where we'll learn about the law from a veritable bachelor of Salamanca. She'll instruct us as to our duty."

"Be patient," replied Dom Carles, "we'll send them to our own school soon enough."

"Monsieur," I said to the chief, cutting him short, "they're stolen and we want them back."

"So you shall have them," said the first magistrate, "but you must understand that there are some preliminaries. Would it have been worth taking them if we didn't want you to earn their return?"

"Earn back what belongs to us!" Haughtily I replied: "A magistrate dares talk like that? How can you impose conditions? Just give back what's ours."

"That's not got a logic we share," said one of these eminent scoundrels. "The one who's stronger is ever master of the law. A glance shows you've nothing. Alone and abandoned, pray tell: how wise to refuse our offer to help?"

"What's help got to do with giving back what's ours? To dare take it in the first place is a cruel insult."

"Dom Carles, you were right," said the first magistrate. "Yesterday I should have had these creatures thrown into the dungeon. They'd be more flexible today. Dona Ruffina, if I need ask you again, tomorrow I'll send you to a house with which you're familiar, and you'll never again see the sun shine."

At these words, that impudent broker seized me by my dress and dragged me toward the settee. But I twisted out from under, escaped her grip and took firm hold of the knife I was armed with.

"Miserable witch!" I cried. "One step more and you'll be dead!"

At that moment the four friends thrust themselves upon Clémentine and me. But my valorous companion, armed just like me, knocked down one with a free hand and brought the blade point to the chest of the other. I did the same with the other two.

fig. 9   "May our distinguished rascals," she exclaimed as we rushed for the door, "see how innocence and virtue triumph over villainy!"

o   She fled with me right behind. We thundered through
the apartments and made the courtyard. Whether because
they were cowards or weakened by vice, none had the courage
or strength to come after us,

     "Open the gate!" Clémentine demanded of the same valet
5   who'd brought us. "Try and stop us, it'll cost your life."

     The no-good knave, frightened at the sight of the knives,
complied. We escaped. Not stopping to look back, we ran
on through the thick dark night, passing through woods and
emerging onto an open field.

10   "And so!" Clémentine threw herself down from fatigue
and exhaustion beside a nearby hovel. "You see, my friend,
how we escaped without shedding a drop of blood or giving
up that precious flower of modesty you so value. But it's expensive to do good. Truly, vice gives less pain. Had we cut the
15   throat of one of those wretches, it's a sure bet we'd have been
sorry of your fine plan to stay chaste! Vice can be found in the
same breast as virtue and the best actions might not be right
if crime wins in the end."

     "By God!" I exclaimed, equally out of breath and exhaust-
20   ed. "Vile prostitution on one side, foolish imprudence on the
other!"

     "At least," continued Clémentine, "we know where our
possessions are."

     "And know too there are countries on earth where abuse
25   of all that's respectable is so rampant that the first to break the
law is the one who's supposed to enforce it!"

     "No secret there. Impunity encourages it. Elevate one
man and you place within him eagerness to do wrong the moment he has a chance."

30   "Should then no man be superior to another?"

     "Not kept so for long. Fear of being treated as weaker,
of being done to just like one's done to others is always a re-

ſtraint on passion.* But all that aside: what's to become of us?   0
Our ruin is more certain than ever. What refuge would wel-
come our poverty and what resources do we have left? And I
don't think we'll be returning to Lisbon."

"Agreed," I said. "Let's get to Madrid. Maybe we'll find
souls less corrupt than in Portugal. Maybe —"   5

"*God almighty!*" exclaimed Clémentine suddenly. She
jumped up and recoiled in fright. "*I've been sitting next to a
dead man!*"

"*No, not dead.*"

A tall and well-built fellow ſtood up.   10

"My beautiful angel," he continued, taking my companion
by the arm, "you weren't sitting beside a dead man — but one
asleep. A horseman of upright diſpoſition who means you no
harm."

"But who are you?" said Clémentine, ſtill in his graſp.   15

"Who am I?" Replied the swashbuckler: "Someone surely
enigmatic to the likes of you. If I were I to tell you, you'd know
scarce more."

"Do tell us then," I came forward, heartened by his ap-
pearance and voice.   20

"My good friends," our ſtranger said, "*I am an enemy of
God, servant of the Devil, friend to my fellows and devoted
to their well-being.*"

                                                                                   25

---

* Some readers will say: "Here's a fine contradiction. We were told earlier that ministers should not often be replaced and now we're told the opposite." But may such
fastidious readers observe that this epistolary compendium is in no way a coherent
moral treatise in which all parties must agree. Created by different persons, this work
offers in each letter the correspondent's own way of thinking or that of the persons
involved and to whom he offers his ideas. Thus, instead of attempting to disentangle
the contradictions or restate them, which would be inevitable in another kind of work,
here it remains for the wise reader to enjoy and pay attention to the different systems
on offer, whether for or against them, and to adopt those that fit best with his own
ideas and inclinations.

"Well, that says it all," said Clémentine. "By great Saint Christopher. I don't understand. Say what you mean."

"Hush," said the stranger. "Start by telling me about you yourselves. In my trade we've the habit of never confiding in the fox. So speak, you, before I answer."

The more we examined this comic character, the more surprised we were. As much as we could make out by the feeble light of a rising moon, he wore a green doublet beneath a yellow coat. He sported a huge handlebar mustache and his hat was decorated with feathers five feet high. Taking him for a harmless charlatan, Clémentine innocently recounted our adventure and concealed nothing of our difficult situation.

"Ah! Young maidens then!" our man exclaimed. "Which is to say: empty stomachs by dint of virtue. Come, come, follow me. Rascals they were who owed you hospitality. Hypocrisy, debauchery, infamy among high chiefs of justice and everywhere hearts of stone. Come, I say — you shall find friends among a troupe of Bohemians."

We followed our man in confused silence. He went around the mean dwelling against which we'd been resting and knocked on the door. It opened. We entered to find a dozen people around a fire, several speaking in low tones whilst others slept.

"Comrades," said our man. "Here are two poor lost young women who don't know where to lay their heads. When the rich abandon the poor, when justice sacrifices innocence, it's up to us to stand up for their rights and our first duty to restore them. Come, tablecloth, be spread!"

We wept in spite of ourselves.

"O Clémentine!" I exclaimed, "so this is the way men are! We found only vice and horror in the offices of power, yet virtue awaits us amongst people that the public scorns."

Those who'd been asleep awoke and the table was set. Six women were among these Bohemians, four of them quite

pretty. They came around to caress and praise and pity. They   0
asked us to sit next to them and, though they'd already supped,
invited us to taste their fare. We were served roast capon, two
thick pâtés, ham, and leftovers of two fowls reheated in rice.
They brought out bottles of excellent Madeira and exhorted
us to chase away all sorrow. The men among them swore to   5
one another that they would die before they'd abandon us. We
wept still more, so moved that we were almost robbed of the
ability to enjoy the kindness of these good people. Over and
over to each other we exclaimed:

"What people think — dread opinion — how often we're   10
fooled and how unjust the world."

Once we'd recovered a bit of strength, the sweet and
charming young women pleaded that we be kind enough to
tell our stories. We satisfied them immediately as they sat
around us in a circle, listening with rapt attention.*   15

"It is time for you to rest," said the man who'd brought
us there. "Dona Cortillia" — he addressed the oldest among
the women — "provide these young ladies with as much comfort as you can. Tomorrow is another day and they can decide what they'll do once they honor us again by sharing a few   20
flasks of wine."

Dona Cortillia showed us to her appointed corner, where
she scattered leaves to make our rest easier, placed rags beneath our heads to protect us from humidity, and kissed us,
saying: 25

"I wish the palace of the King of Spain was mine, for I
would offer it to you happily."

---

* Another virtue unknown to ordinary people, who pay scarce attention to stories of
trouble and travail; rare is he who opens his heart to such laments. Depiction of another's misfortunes irritates the happy man; it proves that the same could happen
to him and offends his pride so much that he responds with cold disinterest.

We fell deep asleep. It had been a long time since we had spent a night so calm; we'd been constantly on edge when among what pass for honest people. Among *Bohemians* we were at peace.

At daybreak our charming hostess and her companions, having made a fire, heated wine and bouillon. They offered us some and asked if we'd passed a peaceful night; we responded to their caresses and thanked them for being so kind. The chief, Brigandos, returning from his vigils and receiving a toasted slice of sweetened bread, asked how he could help us.

"If you'll allow me" said Clémentine, "I'll consult briefly with my friend before answering."

To give us privacy, they stepped away.

"Have you any doubt," said Clémentine, "that heaven in whose help you so trust brought us here with any plan besides a chance to nurse our wounds? After all their fine deeds, do you wish to leave them?"

"Whatever my repugnance in finding myself in such company," I answered, "it's sure that if they're on their way to Madrid, best we follow. If not, I confess I'd not like it."

"I certainly long to see Madrid again as much as you," added Clémentine. "And look forward to seeing my mother and people I know. And I'd be pleased to help you."

"So we agree as to intentions. We must ask these people about their plans and decide accordingly."

We returned.

"Sensitive and generous people," I said, "you've deigned to welcome us though we're penniless, and we thankfully found with you what an unjust society, which so condemns you, has cruelly denied us. Would you forgive us for asking in what direction your next steps take you?"

"To Spain," answered the Chief, "We're no longer safe in Portugal. We must move onto another kingdom."

"Very well!" I said. "Would it be an imposition to ask your
protection as far as Madrid, where we haves hopes of finding
help?"

"Young lady," he replied, "as we wish to constrain neither
your morals nor your prejudices, we must disclose our customs before granting your request. As with anyone, we consent only if those who solicit our help agree to join us, to
follow the same calling and religion and agree to the same
laws — in a word, to comply with our habits and customs.
Under these conditions we'll take you to Madrid. But when
we part company there, if that is still your intention, we warn
you that if you act against us, you will no longer be safe even
with the whole city on your side. If, however, you leave us and
never talk about us or seek to harm us, wherever and whenever in the world you find our people, you'll receive aid and
assistance. If you find these terms unsuitable, we will raise
40 livres now and send you on your way."

Clémentine replied immediately: "We've made up our
minds and will stay with you until Madrid. We're prepared to
join your troupe if you'll accept us."

I didn't contradict my companion and my gestures
showed that, to the contrary, I agreed. I don't know why, but
I felt confident. These Bohemians in no way frightened. With
their respect for the few laws they impose, conscience among
rascals is sometimes better than that of the honest man, who
contends with too many laws to obey them all and when he
lets one go, all restraints fall away.

"Dear and brave companion," I said to the Chief, "only one
thing bothers me. Do your principles and customs include
bloodshed? If they do, neither she nor I may associate with you."

"By Lucifer," said the Chief. He was annoyed. "You may
be sure, *daughters of the Lord*, that we never destroy Nature's
handiwork. We leave such atrocious crimes to priests, to men

of justice and to sovereigns. Our hatred of them owes in part to their cold-bloodedness in daily carrying out such horrors. We give you permission to shed our blood should you see us spill any except that of the animals we use for food."

"Well, then — my hand," I said. "We're with you, friend. Look upon us as your sisters and accept us as you will. We're prepared for anything on condition we retain our virtue and don't soil our hands with blood."

"*Agreed!*" the whole troupe exclaimed in unison.

"One moment," said the Chief. "Have you considered what you must abjure under oath? We worship the *Devil* and don't believe in *God*. We serve one, we insult the other. There are powerful ceremonies from which we won't exempt you."

"Do they offend modesty?" I asked.

"They only eradicate prejudice and attack illusions. They leave the virtues in peace."

"We accept it all — all of it," said Clémentine, turning to me. "I'm going to answer for you, Léonore and shall stop being your friend if you make me take a false oath. Let's not reject what fortune brings for fear of offending a few miserable dogmas that failed even to feed us when we were stupid enough to proclaim them."

"Go ahead," I told my friend. "You've convinced me."

How is it that crime borrows charity's charm to seduce and fascinate? *O you! — Society I abandon! Why when I served you with virtue did you offer me only shackles? Stones in my pathway force me to part from you. Your ingratitude opens upon an abyss into which despair plunges me and if I offend laws human and divine, it was abandonment by God and men's malice that dragged me into error.*

The next day, the troupe of eight women and six men departed. Let me quickly sketch for you some of the most striking characters. Dona Cortillia, whom I already mentioned, was the doyenne. She appeared to be 40 years old, still fresh and beautiful, with extraordinary lively eyes, not tall but fine of figure. The prettiest of all was Castellina, 16, with a wasp's waist and skin white enough to resist the perpetual swarthiness threatened by the sun, with beautiful brown hair, dark and lively eyes, a gaze at once arresting and innocent, surely emblematic of her heart. She was the daughter of Brigandos. She had a brother, about 20, built like Hercules, with most pleasant and lively features, named Rompa-Testa; he was one of our best and bravest soldiers — the one we'd come across sleeping and who introduced us into the troupe's lair.

A young dark-haired girl of 13, named Florentina, was mischievous, witty, and lively; after Castellina, she was the prettiest woman of the group. She had been taken near Coïmbre at age four from a priest who was probably not raising her for work as sacred as that she was doing now. Training every day with the troop, she possessed such agility and intelligence that she needed no more than two seconds to filch a jewel from the pocket of the most vigilant. Passing through a village, there wasn't a mongrel alive who could seize a fowl with such speed. She could grab it, break its neck, and conceal it in the blink of an eye beneath her petticoat, all while pleasantly jabbering away so that the pleasure you took in listening kept you from seeing what she was up to. She was at once the student and favorite of Dona Cortillia.

The other men and women I will not describe, but they were from 20 to 30 years old — all about the same size, vigorous, adroit, and in good health.

We walked together until daylight, when the Chief approached Clémentine and me. He told us:

"We'll follow the course of the Tage to the gates of Madrid. A longer route, but less travelled. At night we'll enter the small dense forests along the banks, or else there are islands in the middle of the river that provide safe hideaways. We'll start out separately at sunrise, but my son will always be just 20 paces ahead of you; you only have to follow him. Call to him when you need to rest and wave when you're ready to continue. He'll lead you directly to the place where we'll bed down for tonight — a cavern deep in a forest, right by the river, known only to us and the wild animals. My companions and I will leave the road one league further on and arrive at the same refuge by another route. There you'll be initiated."

With those words, he disappeared.

Everything took place as planned. We walked about six leagues and at night found Brigandos at the appointed cavern, giving orders as to our reception. We were warned about some of the ceremonials we would have to observe. Clémentine, already a declared enemy of all Christian dogma, looked forward to a festive occasion to condemn them all with heartfelt disdain. I didn't exactly share the same views, though my credulity was no greater; I've already made for you my confession of faith, but I retained a measure of partiality that I feared not being able to overcome. Almost insurmountable prejudice, far more than imagined, favors women's modesty when it comes to religious belief. Men's ridiculous habit of judging a woman's morality based upon it insures that nearly all who are good, albeit philosophical, don't dare acknowledge the progress of their minds. But what do morality and forthrightness in one's opinion have in common? Should we be tarred as libertines because we can't accept a multitude of unreasonable fables? If you'll permit me, the distance that separates debauchery from impiety is far greater than that between debauchery and religious superstition. One does what one likes when safe from

reproach under the mantle of religion; but the woman who   0
loves virtue for its own sake and serves it because it inflames
her heart, who's brazen and bares her soul — she'll be seen
rushing headlong to commit errors she can't hide.

Will you then object: what of the fires of Hell? Who
knows better how to avoid them than the woman who is de-   5
vout, you ask, able to calm them and brave them without a
single thought as how to behave? But so, too, with her opposite, whose habit of sinning in all tranquility leads her to
make every mistake that passion dictates. It is the former, so
constrained by laws of the heart and dictates of reason, who   10
permits herself nothing.

The ceremonies began. At this juncture I must ask you to exempt me from providing certain details. We were first sub-   15
jected to a practice not unlike the Dutch in Japan when they
wished to enter the cities — and it didn't end there. First a
symbol respected by Catholics and then another proof of
faith, for which esteem is essentially local, were both presented to us. Soon offered simultaneously, we had to exhibit for   20
them the most outrageous scorn, the sort of excessive disdain
from which there's no going back. You cannot imagine the
bold, icy contempt that the women of our troupe set out as
examples. With confidence Clémentine followed in their wake.
I confess that at first I trembled; I was mocked. They told me   25
that crude objects could not contain an immaterial being,
that God could not be represented as an image, nor contained
in a mere wafer; and that nothing material could deserve
homage without turning a faith into a cult of idol worship.

In the end I grew bold, did as asked — and never felt   30
remorse. What followed I found more frightful. At the outset
we'd only had to act; but now we had to speak. You understand

it involved abjuration: the words themselves were frightening
— the meaning of which was to swear that we belonged to the
infernal being, body and soul.

As soon as we finished, a pit was opened in the middle
of the cavern. We all prostrated ourselves around it and repeated the words of the Chief, which was a form of Devil
worship. When the prayer ended, Brigandos asked us: 1) if
we swore to be faithful to the doctrine we had just adopted;
2) if we promised to not reveal what we had done or would do;
3) if we agreed never to return to the cult we had just abjured;
4) if we had annihilated any idea of a Supreme Being deep in
our hearts in order to revere the Devil; 5) if we fully agreed to
appropriate the assets of others whenever we had the opportunity; and, finally — what most surprised — 6) if we would
always solemnly consent to help the weak against the powerful and lighten the burden of all unhappy people that chance
might send our way. We agreed to it all.

A splendid meal followed our reception during which
honest cheerfulness prevailed without the slightest word or
least gesture, with respect to us, that could have caused the
least concern as to decency.

The next day we decamped and walked as we had the day
before. Brigandos promised to soon instruct us concerning
the Bohemians' morality, customs, and religious ethic. We
stopped that night in the woods on a small inaccessible island
in the middle of a river. Here, while supper was prepared, the
Chief, to keep his promise, spoke to us as follows:

"When Bulgarians flooded the East and conquered Con-
stantinople, not all of them settled in the various provinces
that they might have found to their liking. Many preferred
the vagabond life and they moved north and dispersed in the
forests of the Gauls. Some flocked to the banks of the Rhine

and Weser while another swarm moved south to populate the
banks of the Tagus and as far as the Pillars of Hercules. Almost all were imbued with the principles of Manicheanism,
which they spread through the provinces where they settled
or through which they traveled. These were the people to
whom we owe our existence; their religion is essentially the
one we embrace. We believe that there is one Being in Nature
that rules over all existence; but because we regard this Being
as the sovereign mover of the universe and we see Him doing
more evil than good, we can only view Him as cruel and mean.
You call this Being the Devil; we do the same to accommodate ourselves to your principles. The ruling idea is at bottom
the same; you believe He is good, we believe He is malicious.
From frailty you think everything is the work of an intelligent
God, full of majesty and virtue. On this matter we are the
wiser. Although constrained like you to acknowledge an ac-
tive Being as creator of all that exists, inasmuch as everything
we see is vice and imperfection, we can only attribute it to one
who is false, treacherous, and cruel — one who must be ap-
peased by prayer and to whom we owe no act of grace for the
good things we have, which are solely due to our own labor
while, from Him, the only issue is evil. Thus, it is not God that
we require you to abjure but only the perfectly improbable
qualities of a just God and the Catholic superstitions too far
opposed to reason to be believed for an instant. What you
did yesterday concerned just that; thus, you did not deny God
as we are accused of doing in our catechumens. Rather, you
merely agreed that an imperfect world can only be the work of
an imperfect being, and that a perfect being is an impossible
illusion amidst imperfection.

"Moving on to our customs, we permit theft and incest.
They are the only two offences we tolerate, although we are
suspected of many more that we never even contemplate.

"Are we wrong to permit theft? Are the laws that govern property not found in Nature? Nature created us equal, equipped with same senses and same needs. By what divine or natural right ought one man be richer than another? Is it not clear that property is only a wrong inflicted by the powerful upon the weak, who must seize such reparations as they can? What crime do we commit in restoring the order established by Nature? Our ancestors, coming from the Palus Méotides and appropriating neighboring provinces as they liked, were thieves like us; and like us, their intentions were simply to establish equality and give him who has less a bit more, taken from those who have too much. Recognizing, however, the mistake we made in depriving ourselves of power by dispersing into small troupes, the injustice of employing violence to steal from others while fully convinced that shedding human blood is a bad thing, we content ourselves with knavery and employ only cunning and sleight of hand to rectify the whims of fortune.*

"We permit incest. What alternative is there for a dispersed people who only wish or are allowed to forge alliances amongst themselves? We take women from our own families because who would give them to us otherwise? We would have to abduct them and isn't that a far more serious offense?

"Incest is a human and divine institution. The first men necessarily formed alliances within their families. Laws and constitutions of certain governments must forbid incest just as others must tolerate it. By itself it is of no importance and

---

* In Syria, wiser laws more severely punished the person who, by carelessness, exposed his possessions to temptation rather than one who stole them. He who lacked for everything and took what he found was acting much as he ought; this was far from the case with one who neglected his possessions and consequently deserved more punishment than the other. So reasoned the Assyrians.

only offends the body politic; as to the social contract, it does   o
no harm. It strengthens families and reinforces bonds among
members, perhaps better than the laws of Nature.

"But do not think that libertinism enters into our moti-
vations in tolerating unions that you find illicit even though
authorized in ancient law. Whatever the extent of that law, we   5
restrict it among ourselves. We allow unions in which equal-
ity of age seems proof of Nature's consent. Never can a father
marry his daughter nor a son soil the bed of his mother. *

"We do still commit, I confess, other bad actions. We em-
ploy dangerous potions as a matter of commerce, our way of   10
obtaining goods that we surely would not otherwise have; and
when dealing with the wicked one must be wicked oneself. It's
too risky to be the only good heart in a depraved century. Our
secret crafts consist first of all in promulgating the diseases
of animals. When a company of tax gatherers bribes us, for   15
example, to increase the price of some livestock by rarefying
its breed, we make the greedster's fortune while earning our
keep. We only aspire to live, that is the first law. We don't want
more than we need; when we have enough, we rest. We provide charity when we have too much.   20

"The second bad action we tolerate, with our knowledge
of potions, is the production of a powerful narcotic. From
stramonium and poppy we obtain a powder the somniferous
effect of which puts at our disposal the owner of possessions

---

* Saint Thomas objects only to the type of incest under discussion. Brothers allied
with sisters would make for too passionate love that would, by its very intensity, be
contrary to chastity. It takes little to refute this refuge in sophistry; thus, according to
Saint Thomas, incest is vicious because it gives birth to what makes the most perfect
marriage. Let us agree that it is absolutely impossible to find a legitimate argument
against these kinds of unions but, on the contrary, it is easy to prove that there result
a multitude of virtues.

we wish to steal. But we never poison anybody, we never provide abortions; we do not cast spells or incantations. We tell fortunes, but that skill is harmless. With necromancy we evoke the souls of the dead: among all ways to reveal the future to men, the most accredited. All nations believed that we could evoke the *di Manes,* owing to the system of immortality of the soul.*

The 11ᵗʰ book of Homer has as its title *Nekyia* because Ulysses descends into hell to consult the souls of the dead. When, in *The Persians,* the tragedy by the poet Aeschylus, the ghost of Darius, the father of Xerxes, is invoked, he tells Queen Atossa of incipient misfortune. You're familiar with other such evocations in the *Æneid* and in holy scripture. *Geomancy* gives us the skill of divination through interpreting signs provided by the earth; the secret comes from the Arabs. *Hydromancy* teaches us to divine by means of water; *acromancy,* by air; *pyromancy,* by fire; *lecanomancy,* by use of a basin; *chiromancy,* by studying the palm of the hand; *metoposcopy,* by observing the lines on the forehead; *crystallomancy,* with a glass or a mirror. Cyril of Jerusalem, in his mediations on adoration and belief, says that in his time, ghosts were also invoked. *Cleromancy* uses sortition alone; *bibliomancy* is the skill of divination by the use of books; *cephalomancy,* by the skull of an ass; *capnomancy,* by smoke; *botanomancy,* by herbs and plants; *ichthyomancy,* by fish; *dactylomancy,* by rings.

---

* We read in the fourth book of *The Æneid*:

> *Nocturnosque sciet manes mugire videbis*
> *Sub pedibus erram.*

And in Horace, Satire VIII, first Book:

> *Cruor in fossam confusus ut inde*
> *Manes alicerent animas responsa daturas*

"Whatever superstition in all this, my friends, are we not   o
often right? We'll convince you of these arts, by practice or
through study, when you judge the time is right.

"People accuse us of abducting children who later become
victims by prostitution. That is true. But what sort of children
do we steal? Either abandoned orphans or poor children who   5
can only gain on the exchange; we often keep them with us, in
which case their lot is certainly better than it would have been
in the paternal home. That's what happened with Florentina;
with us she does what she wants and is our doyenne's favorite;
she'd probably be dead by now had she stayed with her father,   10
who was the poorest peasant of Biscay, could not feed her, and
could only be happy at losing her. Our conscience is clear for
we are quite sure that a small offence is always permitted if it
is a question of a greater good.*

"At all events, our métier certainly forces us to engage   15
in a great many irregularities but the attractions of virtue go
no less respected in our hearts; they inflame us and we act
upon them as much as we're able. We have often returned to
poor people the goods we stole from then; we've bought back
prisoners jailed for debt; we've relieved widows and helped   20
orphans, and eased the lot of the unfortunate. We make you
swear to do the same and will often set out examples."

As Brigandos concluded his talk, Dona Cortilla told him
supper was ready and we sat down to table. The next day we
departed, coming together for dinner in a large market town   25
where our people sold herbal belts made with monkshood for
the heart, orchis for impotence, Palma Christi for pain in the
joints; dentaria for afflictions of the mouth; and colutea for

---

* On this point Brigandos is mistaken. A better logician said so in this same volume:
never commit a wrong to make a right. Perhaps in what follows we will see our Bohemian better in both reason and act.

the bladder. Dona Cortillia told everyone's fortune. Clémentine, lent a guitar, strummed and played nicely while Castellina
and I danced and played the tambourine. Our men meanwhile
wandered through the barns and lofts and came away with
what they could — and the day's haul was so good that when
we reunited in the evening they displayed provisions enough
for four bands as large as our own. Florentina, who had not
danced, turned out her pockets filled with rings, handkerchiefs,
and other things skillfully lifted, winning praise from all.

Clémentine and I were to be engaged in peddling and not
thievery — she offered the powder of sympathy composed
of vitriol, Arabic, and tragacanth gum mixed with vulnerar-
ies and astringents; myself, the somniferous powder I mentioned earlier. We sold many of those drugs the next day when
we stopped in a small town where the sickly approached
my friend whilst women in love came to me. I gave them the
stuff to put their chaperones to sleep and we brought in an
immense sum. Rompa-Testa, bustling about the plaza, was
asked whether he possessed the candle of Cardan, made from
human flesh and used to hunt for treasure.

"The purest." As he handed out goods just stolen from a
nearby house, he shouted: "Light it and you have only to follow. It will lead you without fail to treasures hidden in the
bowels of the earth!"

Another of our people sold an abundance of powdered
mandrake root and the day was one of our best.*

---

* Mandrake root, with its shape resembling a man, is credited by some with the power
of numbing the senses; others say that, like the ginseng plant, it arouses love. Circe
used it to cast her spells, and it was said to be the secret of Joan of Arc; some allege
it is produced *ex semine hominis suspensi vel quovis alio supplicto morte mulctati.*
To be useful it must be harvested in the spring, when the moon is in conjunction with
either Jupiter or Venus. That the Bohemians sold this powder seems to contradict
what was said previously concerning abortions, for we know that this root produces
that criminal effect; they probably sold it with more than one purpose.

By the 10th day of our journey, ready to cross the Por- o
tuguese border, walking as a group along the main road, we
came upon a little horse-drawn wagon in which a man and
woman were bound together back-to-back. They were guarded by two officers on horseback.

"Stop now!" said Brigandos to the driver. Addressing the   5
guards, he cried out: "Where are you taking these people, my
good men?"

"Where you'll soon find yourself, scoundrel," answered
one of the officers. "I'd take you too in a trice if I had more men."

"My brother," replied our hero. "That's no way to talk."   10
He grabbed the cavalryman by the leg and flung him to the
ground ten feet from his horse. "Think it over there in the
ditch. Next time don't lead with your chin."

Meanwhile, Rompa-Testa unhorsed the second officer
with a sharp blow to the chest. He and his comrades untied   15
both prisoners and bade them escape. That accomplished, our
people grabbed both officers as they lay half-crumpled on the
ground and bound them upon the cart in the same position
as the two fugitives. Rompa-Testa and Brigandos jumped on
their horses.   20

"Drive on," said Brigandos to the wagoner. "You were
asked to carry two rascals and I can see you were mixed up
as to who was who. And you, my fine friends," he continued,
addressing the officers: "How do you find it up there?"

"Not so good," one answered.   25

"You lorded it over men no different from yourselves — by
Beelzebub's beard, a pair of rapscallions who want to meddle
with Justice and violate the holiest laws of Nature."

Continuing on our way, we soon caught up with our two
fugitives.   30

"Take them," said the Chief, making them a gift of the two
horses. "Fly faster, my friends. When you tell your story, be

o   sure to say that honest people brought you to the brink of
death and a bunch of scamps returned you to life. *Adieu.*"

More vices were to be found in our troupe besides those to
5   which the Chief had confessed, some unacknowledged and
others simply accorded so little importance that he hadn't
mentioned them. One was the singular tendency of women
to take as much if not more pleasure in their own sex, which
made them seek, among their female friends, companions in
10   debauchery. It is assuredly a sad and lonely penchant but one
in no way damaging, a small depravity that does society no
harm; the act itself is less dangerous than the disorder that
arises from the mingling of sexes and which, though it returns
nothing to Nature, at least takes away very little.
15   Among the women so inclined was Dona Cortillia and
unhappily I became the object of her passion. She couldn't
help but reveal as much and was ready, she said, to give up Florentina, whom she loved madly. She would do anything for me.
Her delicacy in the matter is impossible to describe; Sappho
20   never showed as much with Damophyle. Any flower I touched
she cherished and kissed a thousand times and it withered in
her bosom. Letting her take care of me afforded her pleasure
and tears flowed if I denied such innocent gratification.
    "I ask nothing in return," she told me with the sensitive
25   warmth that so characterizes women like herself, "but only
beg you let yourself be loved. Don't refuse sentiments that
come from my heart and, at the very least, if you won't make
me happy, don't humiliate me."
    She cast herself at my feet and kissed them. Her tears
30   flooded the ground I walked on; if something I said inflamed
guilt-limned hope, her complexion would bloom anew, her
lips would ripen with delight. But when, determined to be

firm and not satisfy her, as I was often forced to do — I would   o
beg her to talk no more of these things — then the hot south
wind that shrivels the calyx of the carnation could not afflict
her more. Confused and hurt, she would leave. If I called her
back? She would fall again at my feet. Whenever our senti-
ments did not conform one to the other, matters were most   5
delicate.*

But my invincible resistance eventually compelled her
to seek revenge. She sought victory by stinging my pride and
pursuing Clémentine, who was more welcoming than me. But
that only made me feel sorry for them both. My passionate   10
and hot-blooded companion, without principles and lacking
in virtue, only avoided corruption owing to my friendship
and counsel, but couldn't resist the Bohemian's solicitation.
Their affair took torrid flight and brought me all the anguish
of friendship but also other worries. I was angry to see my   15
companion engaged in this kind of disordered behavior. I
knew she was hot-headed enough that I was afraid such intrigue, which delighted both her temperament and her heart,
would keep her forever among these thieves. If that happened,
would she keep her promises to me? Would she and I leave the   20
troupe together once we reached Madrid? Would she help me
as she'd promised?

Clémentine soon recognized the pain all this caused me.
She asked me to remain calm and swore that the affair in-
volved only her head and in no way afflicted the sentiments of   25
her heart. That reassured me but the society in which I found
myself now seemed only more frightful. I couldn't stand the
idea of being so completely isolated and often shed silent tears.

---

* A good name for this deviation is yet to be found. The one used by loose women is
awful. In that Sappho achieved immortality owing more to her disorder than to her
poems, why not refer to this singular sort of female libertinism as *sapphotism*?

My friend, who couldn't bear the torment she inflicted, slowly separated from Cortilla. She returned to me more tender and faithful than ever.

I've told you about the beginning and the end of this affair so we need not return to it. Let us once more take up the thread of our journey.

Soon after entering Spain, at four leagues from Alcántara, we were walking along a path on the banks of the Tage on the way to shelter for the night. Castellina, at the front of the group, heard moans coming from a ditch to the left of the path. She rushed over and called back to us. It was a man in a terrible state. We saw he was stabbed in several places and all but drowning in his own blood. To the poor girl I must do justice, for she alone should be praised for her good deed while some of us turned away with horror and others, less prone to be sensitive, walked past with indifference. But by herself Castellina lifted up the wounded man and propped him against a tree. She tore pieces of clothing from her own garment, coated them with a powerful ointment, and bound his wounds. She revived the dying man, bringing him back to consciousness, and saved his life.

"Rest here, my friend," she told him when she finished. "Don't go looking for help. Half a league from here I'll fetch strong men who'll take you to our camp, where we'll take care of you."

So saying, she rushed off to inform companions far ahead of us.

Acting the way she did, it seems to me, does the young woman honor. And when virtue emerges so powerfully from a soul so corrupt, either we must pity her lot in life or believe that such corruption, which unites so many other qualities, may in and of itself be chimeric.

An assembly took place once we arrived. The chief's
daughter was highly praised for what she'd done and two men
were immediately dispatched to return with the injured man.
The women meanwhile made up a bed for him in our shelter. But Brigandos, although he gave the order to help, was
worried.

"I'm acting more out of pity than good sense," he told
us. "If this fellow is the victim of some crime for which the
perpetrators are wanted men, what if he dies in our hands?
Foreboding that never deceives tells me I'm wrong to accord
him such care. That said," continued Brigandos as the man
was brought in, "just the sight of him interests me enough to
put aside those fears. Let's just respond to the fine pleasure we
take in giving relief to our brothers."

The wounded man had every sort of care we could provide; and the next day, when we saw he was a little better, we
asked about his misadventure.

"My enfeebled state," he answered, "does not enable me
to relate every detail of my terrible misfortune. My name is
Don Pèdre; I am a man of law and justice, a knight of the Holy
Brotherhood, sent forth into Portugal by the Court of the Inquisition in Madrid, of which I'm a proud member, to secretly
arrest a distinguished scoundrel accused of the capital crime
of being a Judaizer in his own home — not only of himself but
his family, too. Imagine the infamy! A man who still believes
in the god of Moses deserves only to be burned at the stake.
After some remarkably clever ruses I at last took the circum-
cised party into custody. But I relied too much on my own
strength. While I was bringing him back to the Holy Office on
horseback he cleverly got his hand in my pocket, grabbed my
dagger, and stabbed me while I was unable to defend myself. I
fell from my horse, stunned. He jumped down and was ready
to finish me off in the ravine but rode away and left me for
dead where your women found me."

"Brave knight," said Brigandos to our guest as he finished his story: "With a little more philosophy you might have avoided such misfortunes. Why the devil did you care if the man was a Jew or a Turk? Why didn't you leave him in peace?"*

"What are you talking about? Don't you think it's a queer fellow who refuses to eat pork?"

"Imbecile! You're crazy if you think God punishes or rewards a man for the kind of meat he eats. The Eternal One demands virtues, not such foolishness as to shock common sense. Friend, let me tell you that the man who does good is sure to be saved, whatever his faith; and it would far better to reject God altogether than to imagine one who'd damn men for embracing this religion instead of that. All religions are equal in the eyes of God. He sees only right and wrong."

"But in the end we have our job to do!"

"Take up a decent occupation or make honest one that's not."

"The harsh task has got to be done."

"What's got to be done is to be honest. So I'm telling you to let people live in peace. Arrest nobody. Take away nobody's life and liberty. Except for the executioner, the trade you exercise is the most repugnant and deserving of public execration. I'm a Chief. Like you, I have a nasty trade; but if I worked dishonestly, I would've buried you instead of rescuing you, for your occupation makes you one of our greatest enemies. If your profession mixed a little virtue with vice, you would have left the Jew in peace and today not been at death's door."

"You're surely right, my good friends. I beg you: care for me, please, and I'll quit my shameful profession. I swear I will."

---

* The reader should not be surprised, in this passage and elsewhere, to see Brigandos set aside his religion's principles. Each time he talks with people who are unfamiliar with them, he simply accommodates himself to their beliefs. We will see him revert to Manichaeism when he talks with his women and his fellows.

Brigandos, touched by the scoundrel's profession of re-   o
morse, real or feigned, heard only the voice of Nature and
stifled his intuition despite the risk entailed by staying put
in order to tend to a situation that could lead to trouble. We
didn't move for four days.

"*Adieu*, my brother," said Brigandos to the man of justice   5
on the morning of the fifth day. We parted company, with the
fellow taking the main road while we followed the paths along
the Tage. "*Adieu*, and don't forget the good turn we did you. If
ever you take up arms against us, know you're as good as dead."

Don Pèdre left us, eyes brimming with tears, swearing to   10
either give up his profession or, if not, to remain always our
friend and protector.

We moved on and that evening entered a vast grotto
where we were to pass the night. Our chief still had several
lessons to teach Clémentine and I concerning the art of divi-   15
nation; here is most of what he told us:

"Man's credulity in wanting to know his future and learn
of hidden things is nothing new," he told us, "Joshua invoked a
holy curse to learn who had betrayed the Lord God. With his
science he thereby discovered who had purloined a robe, a bar   20
of gold, and 200 shekels. Using the medium of pythonism, Saul
consulted Samuel's ghost. Stories both sacred and profane are
filled with such things — sibyls, augurs, prophets — all used
just as we Bohemians use them, with the sole aim of drawing
upon the best notions, past and present, to foretell the future.   25
Such is the foundation of our art. When a man wishes to be
told his destiny, we do everything to learn about his tastes,
habits, character, and prejudices; we find out what concerns
him now and in the past. The most reliable sorts of induc-
tions may be drawn from such knowledge: what a man does   30
and what he did, he will do; man is a kind of machine whose
actions are almost always rooted in habit. Most importantly,

do your best to make a multitude of prophecies, presented always with double meaning; in this way, one of them will succeed or else can be easily applied when things transpire differently — and thereby you'll win a reputation.

"Understand I'm not saying that the sciences I talked about the other day are wholly chimeric, but without the time to thoroughly instruct you, I'm offering succinct but superficial knowledge, which is all you could find useful. In telling someone's fortune, be careful to avoid anything that might be displeasing; that way at least you'll charm if you don't succeed. Not a man alive, even one destined to die on the morrow, wouldn't be pleased to hear you give him 20 years more; there's no cuckold who wouldn't love to hear you praise his wife's virtue; no miser whose ear would not be titillated by your homage to his charity — add to which if you point to some treasure to come, you'll delight him to high heaven. There is a kind of art in lying to men and that's what you must learn; let your masquerade flatter and you'll never be reproached.

"Just a word concerning talismans. Arab philosophers invented them, as you know, made of stone or sympathetic metals, responsive to certain constellations.* The Palladium at Athens, the Colossi of Memnon, Sejanus' Statue of Fortune's, the stone storks of Apollonius, Virgil's brass fly and golden leech, the staff of Moses, and various serpents enshrined in cities — all these were nothing if not talismans. We know them well, reflect on

---

* According to the author of *Talismans Justifiés*, the seal, shape, character, and representation of a celestial figure, planet, or constellation is engraved by a craftsman committed to his work. He uses a sympathetic stone or metal corresponding to a star and sees to its completion with no distraction whatever on a particular day and time with the planet in an auspicious position in a serene sky amid beautiful weather, the better to attract heaven's influence by an effect dependent upon the same power and by virtue of such influence.

them, and sell them; but we don't believe in them because   o
there's nothing supernatural in the world and no effect has a
supernatural cause. The contradictions that embarrass us are
only the whims of the evil and malicious Being who invents
torments only to take advantage of men's credulity and little
by little lead them to their fall. That is why we fear this Being,   5
implore Him, soften Him if we can — but in our hearts we
sovereignly despise Him."

This discourse done, we ate dinner and left early the next
morning as usual.

We'd walked about two hours when the sun began to rise   10
and we watched with delight as its first rays bathed the splendid undulating wheat across the field whose borders we were
following — when we suddenly we came upon two women.
Both were weeping, arms raised to the sky.

"O friends, fly to't!" said Brigandos. "An opportunity to   15
do *good* while we so often engage in *evil*."

No sooner said than done. We descended upon the two
women, importuning them not to be afraid and asking why
they were aggrieved.

Too upset to answer, still in tears, they pointed to three   20
horsemen galloping through the beautiful fields of harvest
wheat, breaking the stems and scattering the spikes. In a moment they destroyed the work and source of hope of an entire
family.

"Noble *Caballero*," one of the women, still sobbing, finally   25
said to our Chief, "This is my elderly father's field and 15 of us
must live a whole year on what it produces. This past season,
with favorable weather, that good and dear man hoped to put
aside money for the marriage of my little sister, whom you
see beside me. But now he won't have the satisfaction. The   30
men you see galloping about our property have been doing
the same thing for three days. It's the parish priest with his

vicar and his sexton; they've done more damage than four thunderstorms in a summer."

"But what for?" asked Brigandos.

"One of the parishioners," the women continued, "whose house you can see from here, has been unwell. He asked for the priest, who rushed to the side of the moribund, from whom he expects a large bequest, crossing our field instead of taking the main road. He doesn't want his penitent to die without receiving the sacrament, so riding as the crow flies, says he, gains him 45 minutes. The day before yesterday, he came to exhort; yesterday, it was the holy oils; today, I don't know why. But he's ruining us, noble *Caballero*."

Both women again set to weeping. Meanwhile, slicing through the air, the priest was riding our way when Brigandos let loose his thunderous voice, ordering him to stop immediately or die. But the holy man, still galloping, quickly drew from a gusset on his dress a small white metal box. The vicar doffed his hat and recited few paternosters while the sexton rang a bell. None stopped but all three continued to trample the crops.*

"*By Lucifer's beard,*" exclaimed Brigandos, rage inflaming his brain. "*Stop, you shameless scoundrels, or I'll bury all three of you beneath those spikes of wheat.*"

"Unbeliever!" cried the priest. "Can't you see I'm bearing witness before God?"

"Bear witness to the devil," answered the Chief. "Keep it up and I'll slice you open like a pig."

Together we moved toward the three horsemen, forcing them to stop. The two women watched without the slightest idea as to what Brigandos might do.

---

* This is the indecent way that many priests, in Spain and even in some provinces in France, perform last rights in the countryside.

"Tell me, good fellow," said the Bohemian, deftly dehorsing the priest, "who told you that in bringing the Lord to a dying man you ought to destroy the legacy of one in good health? Are there no roads hereabouts? Why not use them?"

"Should a man go to hell for a few grains of wheat?"

"Can't you see, fool," thundered Brigandos, grabbing the priest by the collar, "that the puniest stand of wheat that Nature provides these poor people is worth more than all those idolatrous bits of watery dough you carry in your disgusting culottes. Besides, wheat is the staff of life and when you destroy it, their divine species cannot reproduce."

"Horrible blasphemer!"

"No need of compliments! I didn't interrupt your priestly duties to hear your praises but to right the wrongs you've done these people three days running. See them shed tears for your crimes, then dare tell me you serve God?"

"*I* should make reparations?"

"You'll pay in the name of the devil himself."

"And how much would you have me pay?"

"For the three of you, the sum of 100 piasters — my estimation of the damage you've done."

"In the whole parish you couldn't find such a sum."

"We shall see."

Our Chief signaled his people to follow his lead as he assaulted the pontifical robes and came away with the holy box.

"For this jewel," he said, flinging it 40 feet above his head, "I wouldn't give a sou."

Stripping the priest of his robes, he found an old leather purse. The priest cowered and covered his privates. Brigandos turned to his comrades:

"Children," he said, "See if your hunt proves as good as mine. We'll add them together."

Three purses emptied, their contents brought a total of 10 piasters more than the Chief had estimated.

"Come, good women," he continued, calling forth the plaintiffs. "Take what the Bohemian Court awards you as reparations."

"O! Monsieur! Monsieur!" They shed tears over the hands of their King Solomon. "You make us but happy — alas! — so vicious is the man of God you've just condemned that no sooner you'll leave than he'll be back to reclaim your fair restitution."

"Reclaim it? My troupe won't leave the vicinity for a fort-night." Brigandos turned to the priest: "If you even think of committing such infamy, scoundrel, I'll have your b---s on a skewer. Here, take back the rest. I'm not like men of justice. That's not the way I take my wages. Pick up and take back your God. Hop on your horse and stop thinking that what you did was right and worth the wrongs your stupidity allowed. Your good was imaginary, the wrong incontestable. Remember, my friend, what we call good is useful. Nothing useful causes the indigent to weep."

The priest was badly confused. Perhaps no sermon of his own had ever been so philosophical. He hurried to retrieve his holy box but while the case was being deliberated and the verdict handed down, something peculiar had transpired. One of our women, with an *urgent need* to satisfy Nature's call, had ventured into the wheatfield to be hidden from view so she could at once relieve herself and obey the strictures of modesty. The unfortunate box was lying open after falling to the ground and, whether by chance or with malice afore-thought, it ended by receiving within its own entrails the sub-stance evacuated from those of our companion; and it was in this pitiful state of augmentation that the reliquary now presented itself to the priest. Too battered to dare complain, he simply crossed himself three times and took back the wa-fers of God, now well-seasoned He mounted his broodmare and took leave even as our Chief promised nothing less than friendship if he behaved.

We got ready to leave. The two young peasants, enchanted by their adjudicator, begged him and his troupe to stay at least a few days.

"We cannot," answered Brigandos. "But I won't lose sight of you. Should that rascal come back, so will I. But if I took up your kind offer, what could we make of my intervention? The honest man must find virtue's reward in his heart. How can he take pleasure if it's bought and paid for? *Adieu.*"

And so we departed.

We decided to leave the vicinity. With plenty of narrow-minded people in the world, too many might fail to see actions of our Chief as laudable. We left quickly and spent the night some seven leagues distant in an impenetrable refuge, then continued on early the next morning without incident.

We had to pass through a large forest before reaching Coria. There our Chief wished to spend a couple of days. But about eight o'clock in the morning, as we were all walking together through the woods, we came upon a Knight of Alcántara. A servant followed aboard a horse quite as good as his master's.

"Commander," signaled Brigandos: "Your Excellency must surely have come a long way today."

"Very far," answered the knight, irritated at the encounter.

"By Satan's horns!" exclaimed our Chief. "That's a long journey without a drink. Honor us as a guest, Commander, and you'll have fine wine served by pretty girls."

"I'm neither hungry nor thirsty," replied the knight. "I ask you to let me continue my trip."

"Pearl of the Two Spains," said Brigandos, frowning. "Don't you know that friendly offers from people like us are much like orders? Be kind enough to dismount and don't force us to be disrespectful."

"Really — what a way to act —"

"More honest than you think, Cavalier. You'll find only kindness and honesty among us."

Recognizing resistance was out of the question and noting his valet had already been stopped while he himself was disarmed, the knight complied. He came off his horse and asked what we wanted.

"I already told you, Cavalier," replied our Chief. "To share a meal and enjoy the privilege of a moment's conversation, then to part on best of terms after customary niceties, in the course of which we'll show you as much courtesy as we hope won't displease you."

Meanwhile, as the Chief ordered, we spread a tablecloth on the grass and began to serve a midday repast. The cavalier, thinking that the fastest way out would be to make the best of things, made himself ready to eat and drink as if at home. He sat down and sliced himself some ham.

"Tell us what's happening in the world, Commander," said Brigandos, delighted by his guest's comfortable demeanor. "Spending our lives like bears in the woods, we're only too happy when an amiable traveler such as yourself can bring us the news."

"We've just seized Mahon," answered the Cavalier.* "The British are defeated, abandoned by their colonies — perhaps soon, too, by Ireland and Scotland — ruined by their nation's debt and crushed by internal discord. I see the crown kingdom itself on the brink of falling apart."

---

* These events had just taken place.

"Hold on there, my good knight." said Brigandos, taking
gulps from two glasses of wine, one in each hand, as was his
custom. "There we don't see eye to eye. The British have more
resources than you suppose. The difference between you and
them is that with your constitution the government would've
collapsed 20 times had you experienced half their misfortunes.
The force of theirs will preserve them from turbulence."

"And the colonies?"

"The British can do without them while you can't live
without yours — you who once supplied the whole world
with gold.* English colonial settlers are only children of the
motherland while your colonialists are her fathers. The capi-
tals of Spain are Lima and Mexico, not Madrid. Were there a
hundred Bostons and just as many Philadelphias, London will
always be England's capital. While you're miserably weakened.
What would happen if your colonialists abandoned you? Accustomed to gold, no longer mined in your own country, what
would become of you without America? I don't know if you
did yourself any good with the *Pacte de Famille*; there might
have been a wiser course to take with the British.

"Yes, my good Knight, you're looking at a prophet. Do
you want my prophecy? France is about to undergo a terrible
revolution that will throw off the yoke of despotism; the English will follow and as allies the two will finish by bringing
down your country. We must judge men by their ingenuity;
it's the best way to understand them. If you observe the inhabitants of London and Paris, you'll see the same pride, the same
interest in freedom, the same taste in the arts and sciences,

* Gold and silver were found in Spain in such abundance, wrote Strabo, that people
sometimes came upon masses of the metal while farming; streams swept them along,
and rare was the excavation that didn't come upon underground mineshafts. These
mines were responsible for the wealth of the Assyrians and Phoenicians.

and philosophy in the same key — everything they need, in a word, to do battle with one another one moment and afterwards become good friends. If this alliance comes about, you may be sure it'll turn against you. You're in scarce shape to fight. Gone are the glorious days when the universal monarchy elaborated plans in the cabinet of Madrid; and nothing can bring them back. Crushed and more debased than ever by your Inquisition and your priests, in Spain we find constables and knights of the Crusades and Santa Hermandad. But Beelzebub throttle me now if there's a soldier anywhere to be met, much less a General!"

"What are you talking about?" replied the Chevalier. "Is this the time to disparage? Today, Spain is reborn. Never have its fields been so teeming, its workshops so busy. Look at the commerce in Catalonia and the multitude of products made there, and cast a glance to our highways. Within 50 years they'll be as good as those in France. The academies bring forth men of importance; the arts flourish and the sciences advance; administrative services are growing vigorous and versatile. As for the revolution, it shan't happen, why even think about it? All Europe would oppose it."

"Europe would be delighted to see your country crushed and defeated," said Brigandos. "It would no more protect you from invasion than it kept Poland from being divided; and despite the faint glimmer of dawn, you are today and will long remain the laughingstock of every other nation on the continent. Your charades and holy processions, fraud and sluggishness, will always make you despised. Every one of those countries would lend a hand to your dismemberment. By Jove, Commander, since we're talking politics, let me share with you my plan to remake Europe. I aim to reduce it to just four republics: North, East, South, and West."

"Republics? What on earth for? Ridiculous."

"A republic is the best of all."

"Which is why people will never go for it. They've labored centuries under the yoke of monarchy. You could go from good government to bad — degradation is Nature's way. But the reverse will never work."

"Look at Rome, which started with kings," said Brigandos, "and only turned to a republic after recognizing the dangers of monarchy."

"Yes, but it wasn't long before that republic failed. And shackles the Cæsars imposed were more burdensome than those of the Tarquin kings. In the history of the world you'll find not a single republic without some sort of aristocracy causing it to rot from within. If an aristocratic government is the worst of all, don't wish it upon all of Europe. Once again: a republic is always at greater risk for despotism than a monarchy."

"True, if nobles head the government as they do in Venice, the result will be total oppression of the people. But a government that frees them from their shackles and, toppling the monarchy, establishes a foundation for itself up on the rights and imprescriptible duties of men — such a government would be a model for all and that's what I want. Don't cross me here, Commander. The republican government I describe is the one that I intend for all of Europe. Accordingly, let me tell you how I'd divide it because I find this multitude of small states to be hopeless. Our continent should be divided as I just said into four republics — North, South, East, and West. To shape the Western Republic, I join to France: Spain, Portugal, the islands of Majorca and Minorca, Gibraltar, Corsica, and Sardinia — all with the proviso that they rid themselves of monks, inquisitors, and priests. Let all such holy windbags be sent to chant mass in deepest Africa. The Northern Republic will be comprised of the Swedish states together with England and its satellites, the Netherlands and the United Provinces, Westphalia, Pomerania, Denmark, Ireland and Lapland. Russia will form the Eastern Republic, ceding to the Turks (which I exclude from Europe) all her Asian possessions, which can only be useful for overland trade with China, which it does not do and will never contemplate. To compensate I add Poland, Tartary, and all land ceded by the Turks. The Southern Republic will include all of Germany, Hungary, and Italy — from which the Pope will be exiled, for no one is more useless to my plan than a *sodomite* priest with twelve million in income and nothing to do except hand out indulgences, for which we care not a whit, or *Agnus deis,* which we trample underfoot. Also included will be Sicily and the islands between it and the coast of Africa.

"Such is my division, Cavalier, and I want eternal peace to reign among these four governments. I want them to leave America alone altogether, for it can only bring them ruin. Let them trade only among themselves and keep to a single religion, a simple pure cult, devoid of idolatry and monstrous dogma — a religion that people can follow without any need for arrogant vermin that they elevate to mediate between heaven and their own frailty, who only deceive without improving them. In my plan, the Senate will be headquartered in the free city of Danzig. There all discussion will be conducted in a friendly way with judgments by arbitration that become law; and if the proposed compromises do not suit, 10 deputies from each republic will be assigned to do battle in person so as not to have millions of men slaughtering one another for interests that are rarely their own."

"Long ago," said the Chevalier, "at the turn of this century, your plan was the dream of the Frenchman, Abbé de Saint-Pierre."

"Not at all, Cavalier. I'm familiar with the book you cite.   o
The good father didn't divide Europe but left in place all the
petty sovereigns who undermine and destroy it. He didn't reunite the powers as I do by attacking the root of the problem.
In a word, Saint-Pierre gave up on systematic equilibrium in
favor of unification; but I establish unification by strengthen-   5
ing equilibrium, which makes my plan better by far."

"It wouldn't guarantee perpetual peace."

"As long as it equalizes, it'll reduce the motivation for war."

"Ambition will be always there. That's what poisons men's
hearts and is stilled only by death."   10

"That's passion without a motive. What makes one country declare war upon another is the desire to recover territory or to invade; it wants as much or more than the nation
it attacks. But with my system, we have three nations against
one. An aggressor, aware of that fact, would remain at peace.   15
It's very difficult to establish equilibrium with a multitude of
unequal powers, while nothing is simpler when each of four
powers brings to bear the same weight."

"But you must at least have a patriarch. If you're going to
expel the Pope, a religion must have a leader."   20

"A good religion, Cavalier, needs only a god; and we can
start by unanimously agreeing on the essence of it, the attri-
butes of the one you venerate, by admitting that He needs only
our hearts, that everything else is dangerous and superfluous.
Because we need no longer cut one another's throats to serve   25
God, a leader would be perfectly useless. In wars of religion,
it's almost always the leader who's the cause. Without his disorder and debaucheries, Luther would never have separated
from the church; but just consider the rivers of blood that division entailed. As to the idea of a Pope: no. One god is more   30
than enough. I must count you as very wise to allow it, for it's
a system most dangerous to bestow upon fools."

"I take it you're an atheist, my friend."

"You're not drinking, Cavalier. Don't you like the wine?"

"It's excellent, young bachelor."

"Ye gods! Brave fellow — do you mean to tease me by that title?

"On my honor — no."

"You should know then, my friend, that I hold a master's degree, obtained after five years' study in Salamanca. And were it not for some youthful escapades that brought me face-to-face with the law," said Brigandos, twirling his mustaches, "I might today be Rector of the University of Compostela."

"So you're from Galicia?"

"In truth, Cavalier, I'd be hard-pressed to tell you from what land I hail. All I know is that my mother was the great granddaughter of a bastard born to the mistress of an abandoned child in Barcelona. So there's some reason to think I'm from Catalonia. If my days end badly, at least I'll have the decided satisfaction and consolation to be treated by the executioner as a first-class noble."*

"But still, you must have been born *someplace*?"

"Atop the crow's nest, Commander, in which my mother, returning from Lima, took shelter so as to foment less scandal by bringing into the world a child clearly the fruit of indiscretion with a common sailor. No matter, for my father confessed it to me and married my mother. I was made to study and can tell you I would by now be at the very least a Holy Canon were it not for *dreadful inclinations*."

"Ah, then you're a scoundrel!" The cavalier stood up. "Now I've got to go confess to a priest how I raised a glass with the likes of you —"

---

* This is the conceit by which all Catalan nobles describe themselves.

"Halt right there, Commander," said our Chief, who like-   o
wise rose to his feet. "I told you: the final moments would be
hardest. The time has come: *Rabelais' quarter hour*. Where
are you off to, Your Excellency? If you don't mind my asking?"

"To Lisbon."

"I know it well. Has your Majesty, pray tell, acquaintances   5
in that Portuguese metropolis?"

"I shall be with my family."

"Ah! Well, Commander, 25 cruzados* should be enough
to send you happily on your way — you, your valet, and two
horses. You'll find that sum in this purse. Just be so kind as to   10
give me your own in exchange."

"By what right have you —?"

"Nature herself, Commander, whose law proscribes in-
equality. It's unfair that one has all the wealth while the other
has none. You just learned I favor an equilibrated system. Pray   15
let's establish it. All you need do is join our union and once
the deed's done, nowhere in the Two Spains will you find a
servant more loyal than me."

The Cavalier, seeing he was surrounded, wisely judged
resistance to be vain. He handed his purse to Brigandos, took   20
our Chief's in exchange, and went to mount his horse.

"One moment, Commander," the Bohemian said. "What
you have given thus far is only what is *due*. We await your
gratitude."

"You have everything, I swear."   25

"And that magnificent cross of cut diamonds? Is that of
the same sort upon which Pilate hoisted your god? Such luxury is a genuine wrong for a religion that requires a vow of poverty. Give it here, brave servant of Christ, so it may adorn our
women, who will regale you with a *sarabande* or a *fandango*."   30

* About 25 écus.

"Go to the Devil — you and your wh---s!" The Cavalier flung down the cross and he and his valet mounted their steeds. "Let's be off, Gabriel! And rue the moment we fell among such miscreants."

"Great God Almighty!" exclaimed Brigandos. "There goes what you might call a man in a foul mood. Let him find anybody who'll steal from him more politely than us and I'll surrender three times my profit. Let's move on, children, for time is short and we've work to do."

Nothing else happened the rest of the day, spent mainly in Coria, where we handed out love potions, ointments, and talismans; we danced and capered hither and yon, and told fortunes for good or ill.

In the days that followed we passed through the province of Estremadura, still skirting the river after leaving Coria, and nothing of consequence held up or distracted us. We turned in the direction of Toledo and were about to enter New Castile when, while cutting through the middle of a forest located on the border of Estremada, we heard a cry for help from a distant thicket. We hurried to see what it was and discovered a young girl, 13 or 14 years old, lying pitiful and stark naked on the ground, her splayed arms lashed to two trees. She was fallen prey to a tall young man, strong and vigorous, whose mule was tied up nearby.

"What's all this, my brother!" exclaimed Brigandos. "What did this poor girl do that you treat her so harshly?"

"Ah! Seigneur," sobbed the young woman, "I've done nothing to him, I swear. He met me three leagues distant while I watched over my father's herd. He asked me the way to Toledo and I showed him. He told me he was afraid of getting lost and asked if I'd be kind enough to walk ahead to guide him.

To be nice, I did so, yet when I wanted to leave he promised o
me money if I'd lead him clear of the forest. When we reached
here, thinking no one could hear us, he got off his mule and
attacked me. Pistol in hand, he threatened to blow my brains
out if I resisted. All I wanted was to escape. He kicked me in
the ribs, wounded and knocked me down. Seeing how I was 5
defenseless, he dragged me through the woods and stripped
me to the state you see me in now. He was ready to do his
worst when Heaven and my patron saint sent you to help."

"Baron," said our Chief, staring down the rapscallion, "what
have you to say about all this?" 10

"Nothing. And why do you ask? Aren't the roads free?"

"By the very flesh of Astaroth!" said Brigandos. "You're
clearly no more civil than gallant. Tell me, thickhead scoundrel: have you ever fought a bull in Toledo?"

"Wise sire," responded the traveler, moving to mount his 15
mule, "be so kind as to let me leave and spare me anything to
do with you."

"Not so fast," said Brigandos. "We can't just leave things
like that. Here's an affair that must be judged." He ordered the
women: "Untie this girl and keep her with you. Turning to 20
the men, he said: "And you, my boys. Watch over this bawdy
sprite, keep him close. He's a nasty colt that needs taming."

Our Chief by these arrangements found himself between
the groups of women guarding the shepherdess on one side,
men holding the captive on the other. Hiking up his breeches, 25
he said:

"Let us adjudicate."

He came first to the young woman.

"Tell me, Maiden. If the young man who mistreated you
had spoken of love instead of acting as he did — proposing 30
to pay for your virginity, what would have been your price?"

"Alas! Monsieur," said the child, "I know that a girl must
one day lose what's dearest to her, that these things can't be

kept forever. Had he spoken politely and offered one dou-
bloon, just for the pleasure of having it, he might have done
to me as he liked."

"Very good." Brigandos said to us: "So she's certainly a
wh--e. Now it's only a question of the price."

Then he turned to the young man:

"Fruit-for-the-Noose: you understand you've committed a nefarious act. Were the Corregidor to judge, he would
sentence you to the gallows as surely as he'd hang a litigant's
fattened chicken in his pantry. Tell me what made you act as
you did?"

"Torch of the Two Castiles," responded the prisoner in
a low, fearful voice, for he knew he was trapped, "I'm but a
young law student whose aim is to one day wear the robes
of justice. My family, always of that profession, is about to
purchase for me a high seat in the magistracy of Seville. I'm
returning to my homeland from Salamanca, where I studied
six years. Naturally I'm inclined to love women. So I found
myself astride a mule, my brain fried seven long hours by the
sun's ardent rays when nature spoke — and imperiously, once
I came across this young tail. I listened only to desire."

"All very well. But why mistreat her!"

"Sir Cavalier, wrathful Nature is not always at her most
delicate. The more violently she speaks the more completely
she effaces within us all such lawful considerations. Have you
ever seen the Tagus overflow? Does a floodtide respect the
beautiful olive orchards whose careful cultivation so nicely
spreads shade along the riverbanks? If we proposed slowing
the river, would that not just make it still more impetuous?
Star of Estremadura, the allegory tells the tale. The young
woman resisted and that excited me still more. There are moments when Nature, to which we must pay heed, is quite ir-
responsible. The law would have it I was about to commit a
crime. Yet I protest that I only obeyed Nature."

"Friend, nobody knows this cruel mother and her disor-   o
ders better than I; yet the point here is not philosophy but
an arrangement. Tell me, what would you have done for this
young woman had she willingly granted what you wished to
forcibly ravage?"

"I would have given her what she asked."   5

"How much?"

"On my honor, a piece of tail like this one would be worth
ten piasters to an inflamed traveler. I would've gone to 15 in
Madrid."

"Comrade, you condemn yourself and I pass judgment   10
by your words alone. Ten piasters for this child's maidenhead,
five more for mistreating her. That equals the 15 in Madrid.*
Is that too much, my man?"

"Not at all."

"Then give her the money and the child is yours."   15

The traveler counted it out and Brigandos turned to the
young woman:

"My young Christian," he said, handing her the 15 piasters,
"you confessed to me that if this fellow had behaved as he
ought, you would have given yourself for two pistoles. Here's   20
double that sum. Now give yourself to the man and deny him
none of your charms."

Then to his troupe:

"Step away, children, yet we won't lose sight of them until
the transaction is complete. We owe them our protection. Ad-   25
dressing the young man: "Rising Star of Seville, you and your
damsel must come have a drink with us once your operation
is ended."

In mounting his conquest, one of Andalusia's fiery stal-
lions servicing a bay mare from the hidden valleys of Cordoba   30

*   15 piasters is equal to about 84 livres.

would not have been so nimble as the student from Salamanca. They went off while we held the mule hostage. An hour later they rejoined us.

"We come to thank you, your Lordship," said the young man to Brigandos. "No case was ever better decided. My adversary and I both came away victorious."

"My good fellow," said our Chief, "since Heaven mandates you shall one day become a judge of other men, let this be a lesson. A judge's duty is not to punish but to make each of the two parties as happy as can be with the verdict. The process is not difficult, and if each opponent cedes a little ground, prompt agreement may be reached. It is only a question of knowing whether the act, in and of itself, is right or wrong, irrespective of its effect on either party. If good for only one or the other, it can only be viewed as bad in the public square — a vain opinion to be despised by a judge. Which means that almost everybody is wrong owing to the illusion that accords everything to the law and nothing whatever to humanity. Consideration and tolerance would bring about an amicable conclusion; but that requires care and the study of man, and Nature proves too much for such people as judges. Intending to do better than they in a case like this, I don't imitate them, and the result is that here you are, both content. Show me a still better way and I'd snap to it."

"O! Monsieur," exclaimed the girl, "'tis true you've made me happy and I'm so taken with this young man that if he'll have me I'll follow him to Seville."

"What of your father?" said our Chief.

"A ploughman, crippled and poor."

"Does he have other children?"

"Yes, Monsieur, my older sister won't leave him."

"That's not important. You're useful to him and can work while your sister takes care of him. In old age he would miss you.

Return home. Say nothing of what you've done, not because   o
it's bad, but because idiots will see it that way. Give your father
half the money you've earned here and tell him it came from
charity." Our Chief turned to the young man from Seville:
"Do you agree with me, young fellow?"

"With heart and soul, Seigneur Cavalier," he answered, "I   5
would not wish to harm a poor man. And how could I bring
this child into my family?"

"So she shall return home. As you need not meet again,
take this route, Comrade, the road to Seville. And you, my
child," added Brigandos, addressing the young girl, "the way   10
must lead back to your father's house."

They embraced and separated. We ourselves left only
after ascertaining that they were far enough apart not to rejoin one another.

"Fair and equitable," I said to our Chief as we resumed   15
our journey. "Let me ask you a question. If this young girl had
been more concerned by her virtue than money, how would
you have decided?"

"An imperious and uncontrollable need incited this young
man to commit a crime despite himself," answered our Cap-   20
tain. "A violent need that had to be satisfied and any object
would do. So I would've given him two hours with one of the
women of my troupe. Whether here or in the city, there's a way
to make a man happy. A hungry man ought not be beaten or
hanged; he need only be fed. No matter when and where, he   25
comes away content whilst the young woman, unbound and
holding to her honor, returned safe and sound to her father's
house, should be equally satisfied. Deviate from the rule and
mock the law: if you only respect the human being and Nature, you'll resolve the toughest case. But if you hew to rigor,   30
cite Cujas and Bartole, adhere to prejudice, seek vengeance, or
tend to your own interests, claiming like fools *I do not judge,*

the law does — then you'll make everybody unhappy, provide nothing but platitudes, and eventually you and your laws will inspire horror in every living thing."

Having heard Sainville talk about a multitude of moral disorders like this one, in which the libertine, blinded by passion, seeks a victim to serve him rather than a companion in voluptuousness, and knowing too that just this kind of vice filled the heads of French magistrates with imbecility and indecency, I asked our Lycurgus what he thought of their extreme severity.

"It's much to blame," he quickly replied. "Laws and punishments are not required to eliminate such excesses. The disgust they inspire in some and the fractious sorrows they provoke in others are enough to eradicate them among a people. Let those who act and those who submit mutually punish one another and be careful not to turn such base acts into noisy scandals that disgrace the magistrate and impugn innocence whilst villainy laughs. Recognize above all the danger in protecting objects of public intemperance — protection that your magistrates grant in exchange for stinking favors from poor women, unforgivably and foolishly endowing those creatures with rights that disgrace then deprive them. That's only to return to society the same vermin it works hard to eliminate, opening the door to every vice, fostering moral corruption, and seducing an endless number of reticent young women who, without the danger of protection, would be subject to scorn and shame. With such fatal protection on offer, why wouldn't the daughter of a bourgeois or craftsman rush to embrace the kind of life which, with its many satisfactions, ensures they're protected from the laws they break but that honest women fear and respect? Let those lying judges convince themselves (if the cutthroat lure of those sirens will let their souls embrace the flame of impartiality that intemper-

ance extinguishes) that there's nothing more dangerous than
protecting that sort of woman.* The true spirit of morality
requires that women who accommodate the libertine's licentious desires find just and genuine punishment in acquiesc-
ing to those same desires, and do fair and actual penance
for their despicable compliance. At that price, what woman
would embrace the profession? Without magistrates casting
so much as a glance upon such dishonorable villainy, is that
not punishment in and of itself? The courtesan would bear
upon her wounded body the pain of her shameful prostitution
and the libertine, who no longer cared for it, would temper his
behavior or go without. But to persuade your pulpiters of Themis that they ought to be so wise as to renounce the ghastly
dross that provide them with sweetened pots and high esteem
would be to preach the virtues of a good diet to a greedy gour-
mand or sing the praises of luxury to a miser."†

---

* Only in London and Paris are such despicable creatures protected. In Rome, Venice,
Naples, Warsaw, and St. Petersburg, they are asked, when they appear in court, if they
were paid for their services. If not, they must be, for it's only fair. If they have been
paid and complain only of mistreatment, they are threatened with imprisonment
should they harass the judges with such absurd rot. Find another line of work, they
are told; or else, if it suits you, endure it despite the pricks. All these cities contain,
proportionately, a third fewer such women than Paris and London.

† It is quite extraordinary that some magistrate got into his head the idea that some
good can come from bringing to light and publishing the secret horrors that libertinage entails. Whoever he is, or might have been, how could he have reconciled his
system with religion and decency whose laws so clearly oppose such public airing?
It is the miserable prostitute, on the contrary, who ought to be severely punished for
being stupid enough to reveal her depravity, which harms not only herself but also
soils the judge who delights in such disgraceful confidences and all those who learn
of them from his grand revelations. Take a moment to compare the danger that may
arise from turning a blind eye to such base acts with all that results from their scandalous proclamation. Would it not be better for a city to secretly harbor 100 libertines
than bring to light 10,000 by revealing their iniquities? Before the reign of Louis XV,
we knew nothing of the infamous art of corrupting youth that brings about so little ☞

₀   As we continued our discussion, we approached Toledo.

We could make out the mountains between which that splendid city is situated, spotted the ruins of the aqueduct of the Moors, and could distinguish the castle tower in which Philippe IV long imprisoned the Duke of Lorraine. But here ₅ Brigandos called a halt before entering the city, saying he didn't want to spend the night there and had important orders to issue.

"Close by are the ruins of the enchanted tower," he said, pointing between two steep rocks a half-league east of Toledo. ₁₀ "We'll hold our meeting there despite a few snakes. In the city there's much money to be made, but we also have many enemies. We must make sure our sheep can graze without the wolf coming to devour them, for within are *God worshipers* who, for people like us, are more dangerous than demons. ₁₅ Come, let us enter, friends. Here we'll spend the night. While waiting for supper I'll tell you the story of the tower — a worthy anecdote."

---

good and so much evil; there were neither spies bent on entrapment nor diaries in the homes of courtesans, and everything went on quite as well as today. It is to Sartine we owe those inquisitorial absurdities. Ever since the days of that grand magistrate, a man knows today at age 15 what in the past he would still be ignorant of at age 40. That despicable Spaniard was ordered to keep track of all base acts the better to amuse an indolent sovereign. The imbecile imagined that his dishonorable task must be burnished with a spirit of equity, and with love of morals and decency as excuse for these vexations. By these means you — the unfortunate French — were duped and deceived. Here was how, while you were out celebrating and chasing harlots, your freedom was curtailed and your simplest pleasures and fantasies penalized. Your most natural needs were thwarted and your children corrupted — all this under the specious pretext of having an excellent police force. The Romans conquered the world without spies among courtesans. For the famous magistrate in question, one clever project that was intended to humiliate the citizen involved the manner in which he voided urine. The plan was adopted and might have gone forward but unfortunately it provided no obscene detail, no list that might amuse the King at supper, so Sartine rejected it.

We gathered around our chief as usual when he intended   o
to hold forth, and he started as follows:

"What I'm going to tell you concerning this monument,
my friends, harkens to the invasion of Spain by the Moors
and King Roderick who, after searching the tower in hopes
of finding treasure, disappeared into thin air. The details are   5
important, so listen closely.

"Don Roderick, the most skillful of princes in the art of
lending variety to his debauchery was also the least scrupulous in obtaining his victims —"

"*O! My friend!*" cried Dona. She rushed up to him, fright-   10
ened. *"Let's leave! Flee! It's not safe here!"*

"What's wrong, little lamb?" replied our Chief. He stood up.

"The body of a woman — see there, just where I was going
to build a fire for supper."

"A corpse?"   15

"In truth."

We all got up to see and soon established that our doyenne was only too right. A young woman, about 20 years old,
had been stabbed twice in the chest. She was of such perfect
beauty and her death so recent that her features were yet   20
unaltered.

"It might be safer to leave," said the Chief. "But all the
judges in Toledo couldn't make me budge — the devil take
them. We'll dig a grave for this poor girl, stay calm, patrol and
keep watch. Whoever killed her won't say where he left her   25
body, though it would surely be unfortunate if we were accused of the crime. But she'll be in the ground and out of sight.
What the earth hides it hides well. Be brave, my friends, don't
be upset. One must admit that there are people in this world
worse than us, even if they're not the first to be arrested. So   30
fair and just is Providence that the unfortunate victim who
falls into a trap is always the one who, by hewing to virtue,

has not systematically followed the criminal path; kindness brings him down instead of one who's malicious and takes care never to fall into the perilous paths of virtue. A cruel reflection, my friends, but real and true. I can't be quiet about it. At all events, let's all go to bed. I don't feel like talking. Besides, we must be up tomorrow before dawn."

We went to asleep and passed a peaceful night.

"Friends," said the Chief next morning before we started out: "if we had less important dealings in this dangerous city I wouldn't stay; but I'm long expected and can't put them off. An old Mozarab canon* expects me to reawaken his vigor with cordial love potions the secret to which only I possess. One of his nieces is coming to see him and plans to stay six months. Despite his 60 years he hopes to welcome her as if he was 20. Too, the Duke of Médoc has sent me letter after letter asking if I'd protect him from an abduction, while the Grand Vicar of the Archbishop had the misfortune of getting his patron's niece with child and now wants his handiwork destroyed. Of course I'll do nothing of the sort. I won't be involved in such infamies. But the festival season is here and my work in the shadows will provide cover for your own.

"Rompa-Testa," he added, turning to his son, "and you, Brise-Idoles, listen closely. There's work to be done at the cathedral, where you'll find in the chapel of Notre Dame a statue of the Virgin in a silken dress embroidered with diamonds, rubies, and emeralds. Never would Mary, mother of Jesus and a poor carpenter's mistress, dress so magnificently. We won't tolerate it. Art must not allow it and we oppose such luxury. You'll slip into the church and fleece the Virgin, whose

---

* Under this name Cardinal Ximenes had founded a chapel for a dozen clerics, thus to be called New Christians, that is, converted Moors.

naked body of solid silver is beautiful enough. I'd take her as   o
well but if you can't take the beast, be content with the halter.
Bring me the precious rags. If you succeed, I'll make you both
lieutenants.

"As for the rest of you," he continued, addressing the other
men," you'll scour the streets and sneak amongst crowds.   5
Search one pocket in a *juste-au-corps* but stick a hand in the
other lest the difference in weight might alarm.

"And you, Mesdemoiselles, pair off and stay near the Vega-
il-Rio,* a quarter that's especially good for us. As for you,
Clémentine and Léonore: I'm giving you an address near the   10
Cordeliers, where you'll be just fine. I'll send orders daily and
you'll meet with various people to whom I steer you. Tell their
fortunes and, if you like, pick up a little on the side. That I
leave to you. Each of you should have some soporific; its effects are sure, to be used as needed. For you, Dona Cortilla,   15
here's some hippomane. But be careful not to love it overmuch,
for it's incredibly rare."†

Orders taken, we set about entering the city in small groups.

When finally alone and on our way to the appointed lodgings, I told Clémentine that I wanted to leave the insalubrious   20
group with which we'd the misfortune to become so attached.

"The Chief's a brave man," I told my companion. "He's
got sound principles and I like his philosophy. He'd be a fit
commander anywhere and you can only praise his leader-
ship. But he's leading a band of rascals. We must quit these   25
people."

---

* Promenade in Toledo.

† Considered by the credulous to be the most efficient of all talismans. It is the fleshy
growth found on the forehead of newborn foals; rare, because the mother bites it
off as soon as she gives birth. Its effect is to make one beloved by the woman made
to ingest it.

She objected, pointing out we had no money. Brigandos was providing us with lodging and made us welcome and we wanted for nothing — but he also kept us penniless. We'd expressly agreed to hand over every penny we'd earned to his messenger, who was to come by every day with orders.

"Besides," Clémentine objected, "these good people welcomed us when we didn't have the slightest idea where to turn. Wouldn't it be ungrateful to quit them when we can be useful?"

This sudden surge of gratitude from the dear girl astonished me; virtue rarely guided her and I began to think she wasn't unhappy with our situation and it would be hard to convince her to leave.

"A third reason," added Clémentine, "are the dangers we'd run if we decide to escape. They could recapture us at will. Despite the appearance of honesty so long as we obey them, they'd be sure to treat us badly if we misbehaved."

"But won't it be the same in Madrid?"

"No. Once we arrive I'll introduce you to friends of mine whose protection would counter any of these people's dishonest schemes. Besides, they know we're going to leave them there."

"All right," I said. "Follow them we will. But we risk more adventure ahead."

Clémentine stared at me with the inescapable embarrassment of vice that knows it's in for a fight. She asked after my own plans, now that we were in Toledo.

"To stay as pure as always after being separated from my husband. Nothing could change that, not even death itself."

"I can't promise the same. Being good is starting to bore me. I'm a free woman and don't need to be faithful to anybody. The life we're leading weighs upon me, physically. I've had it. What do I gain from so much prudery? I'm nothing less than a fallen woman by trade and, circumstances what they are, we'd

be fools to care about reputation. What consoled me after my
first mistake compelled me to a second — and then tranquility. The most foolish woman of all is the one disgraced by one
mistake and stupid enough to resist a second. Isn't the damage
done? At first fall, a little pain and much pleasure; after the
second, all roses and no thorns."

"What are you saying? When our possessions were on
offer if we complied, virtue held you back. You resisted. Now
when it's a matter of a little profit and some mad hope for
pleasure, here you are ready to throw yourself away!"

"How little you know a woman's heart. None of that matters. When the blood's hot, it's the moment that counts. We
stay chaste for a fortune but turn harlot for a handsome man."

"O Heavens! Again — you've been seduced."

"I must confess. One of our companions gave me the address of a gentleman here in the city. He's passionate about
women like us. And regardless of the physical pleasures I
might expect, given his age and appearance, if I want he'll lavish me with gifts."

"And if our Chief obliges you to give it all to him?"

"I'll do it and he'll give it back when we reach Madrid —
that's part of our agreement. How count on the help we're
hoping for in the capital? The people on whom I'm relying
might be dead. What I can earn will help us both."

"But whatever happens in Madrid, we'll leave the troupe?"

Some of what Clémentine told me, as you can see, was
contradictory and made me doubt I could much count on
her. Best for me was to resolve to follow these people to their
destination in Pamplona, and from there escape into France,
where in the first city I came to I'd throw myself upon the
courts for help and protection enough to let me return to my
native province.

But Heaven, as you soon shall see, destroyed all such fine
intentions without my lifting a finger, and put an end to my

misgivings. Still, before reaching Toledo, I did all I could to divert my companion from her dreadful plans. But when a woman is headed for a fall, the more you try to stop her, the closer you push her to the edge. Desire only increases when danger incites fear, and were hell itself to open beneath her feet she'd only plunge into it faster. I tried everything to hold her back while she did all she could to oppose me and justify her descent. Never was eloquence so animated. She had bad intentions, a robust constitution, and no lack of energy.

When she saw I'd given up trying to persuade her, in fact, Clémentine decided to cajole me in turn. She used some of her same arguments to prove she was right in giving in to weakness. I'd been unable to convert her, so she thought she'd be quite able to corrupt me. There was another address she could give me, she said, where I'd find at least as much pleasure and perhaps greater profits than at the place she'd reserved for herself. What satisfaction could I obtain from my rectitude? How could I expect to impose it on anybody after the freedom I'd enjoyed and the life I'd led? I'd only regret not having enjoyed myself while unable to convince anybody of my virtue.

"Come now, dear friend," continued the siren. "Men accord far more merit to our person than our goodness; today their hearts are so depraved that the modesty you take to be so precious means nothing to them. They see us worthless if we retain what a woman always gives up for something she wants; if we've never succumbed, they call it the fault of a weak attack rather than fierce resistance. Just suppose the husband for whom you keep yourself pure doesn't care what it costs you. You'll be the only one to reap its rewards and will you then have known great pleasure? Do you think that kind of vanity offers the real flavor of it? In exchange for the feeble titillation pride provides, won't those illusory pleasures have deprived you of inexpressible delight? Further, if nobody

divulges your lapses to the husband you respect, and if it's   o
certain he'll remain forever in the dark — thus, you stay ide-
ally as pure in his eyes — the lapse itself cannot affect you for
it's left no trace. His grief would only come from knowing and
so, if he doesn't, he'll know no pain. He'd be infinitely unhap-
pier if he believed you'd done it even if you hadn't, so still bet-   5
ter to ignore it even if it happened. You're not the guardian
of his happiness. His happiness will owe to received opinion,
which you should work to make good even if your conduct
is bad. Wrap yourself in mystery and operate in the shadows,
if you like, to become far worse than Theodora or Messalina.   10
You'll make him happier than you would by good conduct
athwart unfavorable opinion.*

"How foolish to feel constrained! Why become a slave for
the pleasure of carrying your chains? Why refuse to free yourself when even right reason allows it? All things considered,   15
to remain in chains is only for your personal satisfaction —
and is that interior pleasure anything besides irrationality and
stubbornness? Must you see yourself as less worthy for having
been worthy in the eyes of others? Will you deprecate yourself in proportion to the esteem you inspire? Would you con-   20
sider yourself vile for having succumbed to Nature's sweetest
penchants? Do you believe the inclinations she inspires are
somehow less sweet than the sorry satisfactions for which you
sacrifice them?

"Think about it. Your husband loves you or loves you not.   25
If he loves you, why fear that something of which he knows
nothing might turn him cold? Why think something that only
affronts common prejudice could make you less virtuous?

---

* Theodora was Justinian's wife; her disorders are chronicled by Procopius. Some of
the laws we still follow are the work of those lovers. She hid what she did herself while
amusing her husband with the atrocious codes. So it was that the imbecile Justinian
complied whilst his wife lay back.

Even if he knew about it, if he loves you there are many reasons to forgive — your age, abandonment owing to circumstance, irresistible physical urges and, if he's a sensitive soul,
the pleasure that the lapse itself procured for you. A truly just
and loving husband enjoys his wife's pleasures more than her
sacrifices for him; is it not gentler to permit them than to demand shackles? Where is the barbaric soul who would delight
in privations? Must you obey the moment he asks? Is it not
a more delicate thing to imagine that we make the one we
love happy by granting freedom in purchasing pride's triumph
at the price of sensations sacrificed for vain glory? So there
are no obstacles to pleasure and no inconvenience even when
your husband knows about it — if he really loves you. And if
he no longer loves you, why be sorry you're no longer the victim of an extinct sentiment? Either he loves you or loves you
not, but you will always have been wrong not to give it up and
always repent for having not done so while you could, with
impunity. I don't take issue with religion, for I know how your
kindness and sense of fairness put you above those ridiculous
restraints. I confront only your pride and foolishness, stubbornness and prejudice; I seek to destroy them, certain that
it's only for them that you abjure the most delightful pleasures
on earth. Enjoy — enjoy, Léonore! At our age we're made
for pleasure, and it's as brief as roses in bloom. When we're
stripped of our petals, will pride's cold pleasures compensate?

"As far as I'm concerned," continued Clémentine, "there's
nothing to hide. I'd rather die than not give myself away —
and not just to the man whose name I bear but to many more,
to all those who want me, to all whom my charms might seduce. Why should such charms exist if we don't yield them
up? Didn't Nature make us pretty so as to please? If it was
a crime to cede, would she have given us the allure that inevitably brings about our fall? That must be what she wants,

for she gives us all it takes. She who resists renders her gifts   o
useless and offends Nature far more grievously than one who,
knowing their value, intends to use them often. To live and die
without pleasure, curled next to your phantom virtue — for
myself, I live only to let it go at the first opportunity."

"O Clémentine!" I cried. "I'm afraid of losing you. Seduced   5
by a multitude of new pleasures, you'll give up those of friendship. I'll have loved you only to pity you and known you only
to weep for you."

"Don't toy with my sentiments," said Clémentine. "You
can be sure I'll always love you; but don't try drilling into my   10
soul in hopes of changing it. I'd harden it rather than let you.
Don't play tricks on my heart, for my mind is made up. And
don't fear a love affair will take me away from you as a friend;
the misdeeds I contemplate leave no place for delicacy of mind
but only of need. I don't want love but only to accommodate   15
my desire for pleasure."

"And without the heart, what does that amount to?"

"Everything. True enjoyment comes only when we're not
in love. In love our pleasure is for the other; only when sentiment counts for nothing is it for oneself. I don't wish to stir my   20
heart but only amuse my senses. Calm detachment is delight-
ful for analyzing sensations, exclusively absorbed by oneself
yet with sovereign contempt for those who think only of us
while uncurious about their own experience. Sacrificing all to
one's own self is pure philosophical enjoyment. Ah! Léonore,   25
if only you knew how sweet it is when we don't love but know
that we're beloved! That's the sort of cunning that spices the
mind's apprehension of sensual pleasure."

I opposed these discourses but in vain, for unfortunately
the heart in conflict with the mind almost always comes up   30
short. Her wrongheaded arguments, unconvincing but alarming, brought us to the gates of Toledo; and we crossed the

whole city to reach our appointed district. Hardly had we entered the Plaza des los Carmelitas than our singular appearance and dress attracted every gaze. Clémentine, her guitar slung over her shoulder, countenanced the insulting curiosity with such effrontery as to reveal her morals. One effect of corruption is to destroy the painful feeling of shame, for once you decide everything is permitted, nothing can make you blush. In the presence of the seductive charms of vice, the modesty of restraint evaporates. Here we see how seduction works to destroy decency within the corrupted soul; it is possible to do anything with a young woman who's convinced that it's foolish to be alarmed when Nature takes its course. Constraints made to seem ridiculous are far sooner shattered than those attacked outright.* For myself, I lowered my gaze, wishing I were anyplace else.

We at last arrived at the home of a woman about 55 years of age. Her house, located in a narrow street behind the Franciscan monastery, seemed to me highly suspect; but there was no going back. With the way we were dressed, we'd scarcely be welcome elsewhere. The owner, whose name was Dona Laurentia, readily admitted us. After we gave her news about her friend Brigandos, she showed us to a room with two beds. With no further preliminaries, she asked if we wished to receive men. Clémentine was ready and willing to say yes — but she quickly saw that I opposed any such thing and decided to keep quiet.

---

* The reason is simple. We can resist the arguments vice employs to triumph with a mind of wit and intelligence. Thus, all opposition flatters and succeeds because it evokes qualities that do us proud. But if we are shown that our conduct and opinions are truly ridiculous, pride comes away compromised and the whole picture changes. Ridicule wounds vanity so much that were it possible to persuade the wisest man that virtue is ridiculous, he would immediately give it up.

"As you wish," said Dona Laurentia. "My house is as secure   0
as the residence of the chief magistrate himself. Only honest
people come here and to avoid any unpleasantness I receive
priests only if they're elderly; with them, there's no danger.
Just listen — listen and tell me if you hear any noises but those
you might expect. Yet I've six of them in the bedrooms right   5
now with an equal number of borders. They'll come down as
soon as they're done, more will go up, and that'll be the end of it."

"O! Great God," I said to Clémentine, "where are we?"

"Don't worry," the foolish girl replied, bursting into laugher.
"Didn't you hear Madame say that we may do here as we wish?"   10

"Most certainly," continued the duenna. "No obligations;
you've got complete freedom. If the *demoiselles* I mentioned
receive men, it's only because they want to. You can be sure
nobody will force your door. But I advise you to enjoy yourselves. The carnival season is on. You're pretty and won't lack   15
for opportunity. I say it again: My house is safe. Why, even
daughters of the wealthiest bourgeois families in the city come
here. Young chicks veiled in black mantillas tell their parents
they're off to confession and as the churches are damp within,
I welcome them here. The confessor arrives and the ceremony   20
takes place without a fuss. Penance is sometimes a bit rude,
but at least they're always certain of absolution."

"Madame," said I to our hostess, "we're still novices. We'll
be happy to execute Brigandos's orders and go wherever he
sends us. But most assuredly we won't be receiving anyone."   25

We made arrangements concerning meals. Laurentia told
us that with women sent to her by our Chief, she took care of
everything and would see we lacked for nothing. She left and
ordered up all we needed while we had the rest of the day to
ourselves.   30

The next morning, opening our windows, we were greet-
ed by a grim spectacle: an unfortunate man being led to torture

and execution. A huge crowd followed. In every country in the world, perhaps moreso in Spain than elsewhere, the people are rife with such morbid curiosity.

"What was the man's crime?" Clémentine asked Laurentia.

"A frightful incident, the day before yesterday. The man who committed it, unable to bear the horror of his crime, came forward to confess. He's one of the most important men of the city. I'm surprised you didn't hear of it, for it took place just half a league from here and along the route you traveled."

"Great heavens!" I said, "I'll wager we saw the victim... and the poor girl."

"She was assassinated — you saw her?"

"Yes."

"Well, then, the story will make your blood run cold — but wait! What's that? Hide, my dears, for here come two Franciscans. Here we are talking and they're gesturing to me that they want to slip inside. Go enjoy a peaceful meal. I'll join you for dessert to recount the bloody tale."

The duenna went out and the monks arrived. We'd just finished dinner when Laurentia reappeared.

"Listen," she said, "and I shall recall for you the tragic tale by which the gentleman you saw pass by just now died a saint."

———

Here Léonore, having asked whether the assembled wished her to tell the story, and receiving assent from all, continued as follows:

The Crime of Passion or, Love's Delirium
A SPANISH STORY

No family in Toledo was wealthier than that of Count Flora-Mella, and no Lord in the two Spains joined that advantage to greater privileges or a more illustrious line; but fortune does

not abide equally amongst those she thus favors; her incon-   o
stant hand often takes them to the peaks of grandeur only to
precipitate their dramatic fall.

The Count married quite young and just three years later
he lost his wife. Having only a daughter, he determined to
wed once again. Such second unions rarely succeed, and the   5
Count was living proof. A young demoiselle from the House
of Brajados, beautiful and rich, became the object of his fasci-
nation, but her virtues hardly conformed to her precious en-
dowments. Nothing was more scandalous than her conduct,
in fact, nothing more perverted than her morals.   10

The Duke of Medina-Sidonia at the time was a prominent young man in Toledo. Even though married himself, he
was the terror of husbands and the idol of all their wives. The
Countess Flora-Mella was too vain and possessed of too sharp
an eye not to desire to add that celebrated lover of all pretty   15
women to her train of conquests. To meet and seduce him
proved the work of a single day, and their intrigue quickly won
such public attention that Count Flora-Mella could scarcely
stand the shame of it.

Whatever his tribulations, however, the Count's desire for   20
a male heir compelled him to dissemble. He stifled his pain,
tried to silence rumor, and continued to share with his wife the
intimacies of marriage. His wish was fulfilled: the Countess
became with child and gave birth to a son, Don Juan — he to
become the unhappy hero of this bloody tale. For now the   25
Count let down his mask. He decided to delay vengeance no
longer and relegated the young Countess to her own land, deep
in Andalusia. She was to quit her husband and Toledo forever.

Meanwhile, the two offspring of Count Flora-Mella's two
marriages grew up together in his palace, and the unhappy   30
father seemed to find in the qualities of his two beautiful
children at least some compensation for the grief occasioned

by the death of the mother of his daughter and the frightful
conduct of the mother of his son. Nothing was neglected regarding the cherished pupils' education; with both no care
was spared to unite their talents with the gifts that Nature be-
stowed on each. Don Juan had just reached his 20th year when
Leontine, his sister, turned 22. If Don Juan evinced pride, nobility, and male charm in great profusion, for her part, Leontine shone more beautiful than the sun and fresher than flowers blooming beneath its rays — she possessed everything to
make her a woman of deserved admiration: the loveliest skin,
fine and delicate features, a gaze most lively and spirited. Her
hair flowed free from a flowery tiara. Doubly slender was her
enchanting figure, like that of the Graces.

But if Nature outdid herself to settle beauty upon these
two young people, if she provided each with features of equal
charm, how extreme the contrast she produced in temperament. Don Juan was as violent and as impetuous as Leontine
was sensitive and reserved. One listened only to the music of
passion; the other took reason and duty as her only guides.
In no way did Leontine's charms escape Don Juan. He knew
obstacles stood in his path but Nature, more powerful than
social convention, and of such masculine vigor as to destroy
instead of strengthening them, raised a tumult in his heart
which he found impossible to silence. So he set mad hope to
the side of love. The honest freedom he enjoyed with his sister
often gave him occasion to explain himself to her. Long he disguised his angst and held himself captive to cruel constraint,
preferring to do himself violence rather than show the guilty
sentiments that burned within. But so much of it became
difficult to bear. Not with the fiery soul of a Don Juan does
one love intensely without professing as much. For her own
part — perhaps — Leontine had noticed and been moved by
the graces of the charming young man she was permitted to

love as a brother; but as her excessive modesty tolerated no   o
irregularity, if her sentiments were more fervent than kinship
could allow, she would silence them, for Nature no more re-
linquishes her rights to a soul like Leontine's than it does to
a heart such as Don Juan's. But virtue, more readily obeyed
in one, knows at least how to restrain her power, to hide pain   5
and suffer in silence.

One day, as they wandered together in the fresh blos-
soming valleys through which flows the Tagus near Toledo,
far from the merciless eyes and ears of chaperones and duen-
nas, Don Juan could no longer suppress his passion. He dared   10
throw himself at the feet of his sister. "O, you whom I worship!"
he cried, pressing burning lips upon the hand of the beautiful
young woman. "You whom I wish to love without transgression.
O Leontine! Is it yet true I will lose you? These happy days of our
childhood are destined to be forgotten forever, and their blasted   15
memories shall serve only to torment me the rest of my life.
Yes, Leontine, my love for you must be withdrawn — furious,
impetuous love I never dared reveal. Barely does it flare that
its flame must be smothered, and the heart that fed it must be
broken the instant it shines forth. For I'm losing you, Leontine.   20
Learn the frightful news from the one whom it plunges into despair. The Count intends you to marry Don Diegue. You will be
his spouse and belong, one month from today, to that unworthy
rival. As for myself — confused, desperate, dying — I will have
your image with me to the ends of the earth, or else immolated   25
in the temple in which it was placed by the hand of love."

"O Great God!" cried Leontine. "What are you saying,
Don Juan? What have you just revealed to your poor sister?
To what kind of love have you just confessed? What sorry fate
did you just portend?"   30

"Ah! that you might be as little surprised by one as alarmed by the other. What I tell you is true, Leontine: I love you.

But how say it? Inadequate words do battle with my passion. You whom I worship, I shall lose. Cruel girl. Did you think I might be insensitive to your many charms, or see them without cherishing them? Can Leontine exist without all rendering homage? Like God of the universe who gives life to all that breathes beneath His feet, does she not deserve a universal cult?"

"But what of the bond that unites us?"

"Nothing my love can't dissolve; none with which it cannot do battle if threatened with destruction. Do you really think a heart such as Don Juan's can be restrained by frivolous conventions? O how I despise them, those arbitrary conventions that cruelly separate what Nature unites! At your feet I listen only to Nature and she tells me to adore you. So I do and want to live only for you or to die, by your arrows speared."

"Don Juan! What are you saying!"

"What I feel and what you inspire. I dare speak to you of my love. I dare implore you to listen to this alone: may heaven be my witness, I shall never have another wife but you."

A kiss from Don Juan upon the rosy lips of the object of his passion sealed his oath. Leontine, trembling and blushing, did not refuse it. Others approached and our two young people were quickly surrounded by attendants.

They pretended nonchalance, continuing their walk back to Toledo.

The fateful news Don Juan revealed to his sister that day proved only too true. The next day Count Flora-Mella announced to his daughter his arrangements for her marriage and, a few days later, he introduced her to Don Diegue. To everyone, just as to the aforewarned, Don Diegue would be an object of horror. Joining to the most unpleasant temperament every one of Nature's flaws, no one could imagine why the Count dared propose such a union. Circumstances of fortune justified it, to be sure; but how feeble such motives

for any kind and sensitive soul, ready to sacrifice everything   o
for bonds of affection, unable to imagine living without those
forged by love.

Leontine dared tell her father how little inclined she felt
toward the proposed union and the Count, who loved his
daughter, was distressed to displease her. On the other hand,   5
he could not break his commitments and so beseeched her.
He knew he had to convince her. She would respond neither to harsh invective nor tender imprecation. But friendly
eloquence persuaded. An honest soul never resists attacks
mounted by sentiment whilst duplicity, secrecy, and violence   10
— all those odious weapons that imbecility dictates to paternal tyranny — strip from their iron yoke the heart to be
subdued whilst kindness and trust achieve the desired end
without remorse occasioned by antagonistic measures.

So Leontine gave her word. Fully prepared for sacrifice,   15
she declared she would submit. The virtuous young woman,
forgetting her brother's love, which she could only view as
criminal, also lost sight of the repugnance inspired by Don
Diegue. She preferred the pain of the impending union to the
cruel heartache of inflicting the slightest chagrin upon the   20
one who had brought her into the world.

Don Juan, who was at once too agonized, violent, and in
love to abandon the object that held him in thrall, soon learned
of all that had happened. With every expression of such a soul
bound to be rude or violent, he overwhelmed his unhappy   25
sister with reproaches most bitter; he condemned her weakness in no uncertain terms and dared intemperance to the
point of saying, with pride, that after having declared his feelings for her, he couldn't imagine she would so betray him.

"Betray you!" responded Leontine, nonplussed. "What   30
did I promise? What could I have promised? How might I
deserve such uncalled-for accusations? Have you forgotten

the bonds which constrain us? Would you force me to detest them when I wish to cherish them?"

"Abhor them, fatal bonds — loathe them. O Leontine! How could I not detest what so inclines your loss of affection for me? To your eyes they will never be so dreadful as they are to mine."

"But you must at least respect them."

"Ah! Never imagine they are without force within the heart that loves you. But ought they not also, within your own, if moved by my torments?"

"I feel them. Don't believe I'm indifferent. But it's all I can do."

"But who can guarantee these bonds are real? We don't share the same two parents and you know about the conduct of my mother."

"Is it possible that your love for me be so blind as to prefer shame and dishonor to the certainty of a criminal passion that shall never be fulfilled and must lead to your downfall?"

"Dishonor and shame! What do I care for those illusions! What importance the blood in my veins if you're forbidden to me! In the whole universe I know only you and respect and cherish only you; and this very moment, if you won't pledge to break the fatal forced promise, I stand ready to pierce the heart of the traitor who is taking you from me."

"Do you want to make me utterly and perfectly unhappy? Do you want to rob from me the innocent pleasure I enjoy in loving you as a brother? Do you want to put eternal barriers between us?"

"I want to possess you or die; I want to take you away and flee to avenge every obstacle to love."

"You're cruel!"

"You don't know the vehemence of the heart you set ablaze, Leontine. All its sentiments are passions that can be stilled by death alone; and if the least among them can be stirred to such a point, what about the one your gaze set afire?

Let us flee our tyrants, Leontine, and live forever at the ends of the earth. But — what I am saying? Alas! How dare I? One must be loved to obtain what one demands. And your cold indifferent soul doesn't share the ardor that devours me. Go, unfaithful lover. Languish like a coward in the odious chains that await. Sacrifice the one who worships you to the vile interests of a father in the clutches of greed."

"Unjust! The tender father whom you offend doesn't deserve your reproaches. I merit them even less in obeying him, for your own fortunes shall surely increase thanks to the fetters I take upon myself. Don't condemn me when so clearly I deserve your gratitude."

"How awful to allege! Would that you hate me rather than love me like this! What do I care about fortune? What would be the value of honors earned at the expense of the one dearest to me on earth? Must I become the unhappiest of men when I always believed I would be the most fortunate — were I loved by Leontine? Nothing matters besides her love; it's all I need; felicity is her hand alone; it is the only prosperity to which I aspire, all that I wish to possess, even were it to cost a thousand lives."

Leontine was moved by such ardor and no matter how hard she tried, she could not keep from tender glances. That was too much for Don Juan. No sooner had he come to believe her to be indifferent than he saw how he might soon find himself beloved. He took Leontine's resistance as owing to her virtue rather than the sentiments of her heart. He imagined all sorts of ways to save her from the impending marriage. Hiding his real plans by feigning honest and sweet attention, he first proposed that Leontine allow him to at least do his best to convince the Count to delay the wedding he so feared. She consented. He dared ask for a sign of favor — and received neither rejection nor wrath. But when he sought more,

0   Leontine stopped him. Several months passed in that way with
the impetuous lover obtaining nothing but pity and deferral.

Yet he kept up his efforts and meanwhile the role he
played vis-à-vis Count Flora-Mella, although inspired by
the same principles, was quite different. In spite of his fiery
5   temperament, he was able to insure flexibility and persuaded
his father that the delay solicited by Leontine was for a good
reason. Her heart was already taken, he hinted, and he alone
was in a position to tease out the fateful secret; he had already
broached the issue, although he could not be certain with-
10   out making himself suspect. He added that the Count must
help him in his efforts to probe the recesses of his sister's soul:
he could not easily operate constantly surrounded by all the
many servants; it was essential to be away from them. Privacy
was required before he could speak on behalf of Don Diegue
15   if he were to defeat the reserve Leontine was beginning to
manifest, and now that she had noticed his efforts to fathom
her thoughts.

The Count, fully the dupe to his son's scheme, far from
suspecting his intimate motives, provided all the help he could.
20   Leontine was looked after less and chaperones disappeared
when she went off with Don Juan. The Count himself encouraged her to listen to the counsel of a brother who thought
only of her happiness.

Leontine was not long in recognizing love's subterfuges;
25   but she was careful not to reveal them and only tried not to
become their victim. For his part, Don Juan obviously had
no intention to serve the interests of Don Diegue in the short
time left him. He depicted his own inflamed passion, proposed a thousand ways it might triumph and they might flee
30   together. Thus passed moments so precious to his heart — yet
then so cruel when he saw with what inflexibility his sister
opposed and rebuffed him.

Once convinced that her resistance was insurmountable, nothing could stop him. As long as he had hope, he'd contained himself; but once that vanished, the only voice he heard insisted on his initial plan. He resolved to use force, for no other method could succeed. Using the freedom he'd been permitted, he intended to lead his poor sister to a place where reliable men would be waiting to abduct her. Taking every possible precaution, he further arranged in advance for a post carriage that could take them to Portugal, where he planned to seek refuge; this carriage, lightly fitted out and escorted by faithful valets, was to stand ready and waiting near the monument known as the Enchanted Tower.

On the appointed day, under the pretext of a simple promenade, the impetuous Don Juan proposed a visit to those ancient ruins. Once there he could not contain himself.

"O Leontine! All awaits us — everything is ready — everything. We shall never again see Toledo. We must flee your imminent union. Further delay is impossible."

"What do you dare propose?"

"Our happiness."

"Good God! At the expense of my father's? He'll surely die when he learns of the depths to which we've fallen. Think of the misfortunes that already overwhelm him. Consider that in all the world only we can comfort him. From us and us alone can he expect blossoms in the autumn of his life. Should we destroy that decent hope? Shall the hands that ought to wipe away his tears instead cast him into the grave?"

"O Leontine! I listen to love alone. Duty, honor, respect, virtue, and religion are all effaced from my heart. Passion is the only flame I recognize and I go where it leads me. You must follow; my people await. Six months I labored in vain, using any means that might destroy your scruples. What came of such zeal? What did I gain from such passion? I've succeeded only in convincing myself of your indifference. That is what I must overcome or die!"

"Cruel man! Pity me — and my father — and yourself. Don't plunge us into an abyss of despair from which no measure of human felicity could ever rescue us. Today in Toledo nothing rivals the success of our family. To that your deeds will put an end tomorrow and you will plunge it forever into grief and pain.

"Is that how you want to prove your love to me? If you were as sensitive as you seek to persuade me, would my honor not move you? Would you defile it for a shameful and criminal moment of pleasure that will bring us sorrow and remorse forever!"

"Do you think I brought you here," replied Don Juan furiously, "to listen to sophisms about hatred and constraint? I shan't respond to them. I'm convinced that my mind wields little power over yours, that your rigor blunts my weapons. My love falls victim to despair and to it alone I surrender."

He seized her and took her in his arms.

"You must come with me, Leontine. Don't try to escape; don't try to defend yourself. My derangement would be fearsome. I'd no longer know you and you can't imagine the lengths I'd go to exact revenge for your disdain. You know how impetuous my fiery, unstillable heart. Don't exacerbate it, Leontine, at the risk of both our lives."

"Then pierce this one, this heart that refuses to be soiled by crime! Split it open, I tell you: I'll not parry your cuts. I prefer death a hundred times to the awful torments that would rip my life asunder." And her tears flowed: "For the life your furor would take from me, Don Juan, I shall regret it only for my father's sake. I wished to devote myself to him, to bring him happiness and long life. You brutal beast! I might've loved you but you don't want that. Don't hesitate, Don Juan.

This the heart that you made throb — and saying that, I'm not ⁰
fit to live. Stab me. Take me, I'm ready. But never imagine you
could make me share your iniquity."

"You will share it. Or answer with your life."

"Great God! Your cruelty outrages me. After what I've
confessed, your disgraceful soul is unworthy of me." ₅

Escaping his arms: "Begone, traitor! Flee forever from
the one whose heart harbors for you only hate. I won't reveal
your reckless plans nor reproach myself as your accomplice."

With those words she attempted to flee the captivity of
the ruins. But Don Juan, fierce and blinded by passion that ₁₀
overwhelmed his soul, chased after and captured her.

Dagger in hand, he thrust himself upon her and she fell
dead at his feet.

"Great heavens!" he cried at the sight of his sorry victim.
ⓢ *fig.* 10 "Can it be? Have I cut short the life of the one to whom I was ₁₅
to sacrifice my own? And now my own hand refuses to avenge
my lover! Armed for villainy alone, it recoils from punishing
the murderer. I must flee."

But he tried in vain, held back by an invincible force, the
power of which he had not foreseen. Acting like a madman, he ₂₀
furiously threw himself upon the bloody corpse of the woman
whom he idolized. He covered her with ardent kisses. He
addressed to his heart's divinity expressions of his ferocious
love. With sighs and bitter tears, he hoped to bring her back
to life and — there, all alone, brought low by despair amidst ₂₅
the silence and darkness of rock and ruin, consumed by love
and by pain — the poor man dared consummate his crime.
He ravished the honor of the woman he had just shorn of life.

Soon, senses calmed, he descried the double horror of
what he'd done and defiled. He possessed neither the strength ₃₀
to bear the weight of his infamy nor the courage to punish
its author. He wanted justice to avenge his execrable crime.

He was free to flee, with horses and his people waiting nearby. But he did not. Paralyzed by terror, he stood stock still, trembling, and gazed at the lifeless body. For a moment he thought he was mistaken and he saw in his arms the woman he loved, and called her name. Come round from his frightful act, his despair precipitated him once more upon the misshapen corpse.

"O Leontine! You will be avenged!" he cried. "You will be avenged, Leontine. With torrents of my guilty blood, if anything can compensate for all that my furor spilled."

He rushed to Toledo and gave himself up. But the city magistrate, who was quite taken aback, wanted to return him to his father. So he did — but what a scene — and still more remorse awaited! For Count de Flora-Mella had just learned not only of the recent death of his perfidious spouse — and now of a still greater catastrophe.

Talking with the Count was the Duke of Medina-Sidonia, who turned to Don Juan and said: "O my son! Dear boy! What have you done? Must you to be taken from me no sooner you are mine! Must you flee happiness just when it comes to enrich your life! Must you add dishonor to my remorse? *For 'twas I who gave you life, Don Juan. You are not the son of the Count de Flora-Mella.* Here I have irrefutable proof that you belong only to me. Read the dying words of your poor mother. Your unhappiness would have ended. But quake now before the abyss that shall engulf you."

Don Juan seized the letter. His hand trembling, tears flowing, his eyes could barely make out what was written there. Finally he read out the words of his mother the Countess:

> *There remains to me only time enough to confess my crime and set it to rights. Don Juan does not belong to Count de Flora-Mella. He is the son of the Duke of Medina-Sidonia. It is my dying wish that, in the*

hope of making amends, that the Duke implore his   0
forgiveness and reclaim his son. He must recognize
him as the issue of past love, and he must designate
and declare this child his universal heir. I expose
nothing by this request. My shameful conduct with
the Duke was too well known for this to reveal any-   5
thing secret. I strive to make reparations but need
divulge nothing to thereby relieve my conscience of a
terrible tormenting burden, the horror of knowing my
husband embraces a son who does not belong to him.
Imprudent women, take heed! You who might fol-   10
low in my twisted footsteps: remember that no hon-
est soul could stand the tumult. Let the dread that
might tear you apart keep you from the precipice. To
my preceding requests I add a further wish, and it is
up to my husband to grant it. Having learned of the   15
intimate feelings of Leontine and Don Juan, I beg
Count Flora-Mella to give consent to their union, my
confession destroying impediments that contravene
their desire. I dare note that my husband's daughter
could scarcely expect a more advantageous mar-   20
riage; such a union, bringing together two former
rivals, making them friends again, will help allay my
regrets and bring tranquility to my final days.

"God Almighty!" said Don Juan as he finished the terrible   25
letter "So happiness could have been mine!"

"'Twas yours!" cried the Count. "I've given my word and
signed my consent. There it is, just look."

"Monsieur," said Don Juan to the magistrate with the
greatest resolve. "You can see the many crimes with which   30
I have bespoiled myself. I slaughtered my mistress, the respectable daughter of a man who took care of me as a youth.

You see, too, how I aimed a dagger at the heart of a father who can acknowledge me only to weep. Take me, Monsieur. I wish to die in public. Give me what I deserve. You, Count, must disown me. This letter authorizes you to do so. And you, father, never recognize me. Thus shall my death dishonor no one."

They wanted to soothe his despair and save the illustrious malefactor. All efforts made, none succeeded.

"My crime is too atrocious," said Don Juan. "My head must pay the price." He seized the hand of the magistrate: "Let us go now. Or I shall confess to other judges, should pity prevail over duty."

At these words he rushed into the street, resolved to mount the gallows to which his crimes had led him. The magistrate no longer dared resist. Don Juan was deposed the same evening in prison, confessed to everything without being tortured, and promptly paid with his life for the invidious crime he had committed by dint of reason in turmoil and impetuous temperament.

Yet the whole city wept for him, with greatest sorrow extended to the two unhappy fathers, each of whom rendered tribute in sorrow and tears that could never efface from their souls the terrible losses come upon them.

"Such a tragic story," said Madame de Blamont. "The fatal result of women's misconduct. To what terrible misfortune such behavior can expose a family! I should not be surprised if the law punished their failings more severely than those of men."

"As for myself, I'm always amazed," replied Madame de Senneval, "that the men who seduce us take advantage of our weakness and their superiority; they're the primary cause of the wrongs we do. They alone deserved to be punished."

"All this might best be discussed at leisure," said the Count o
of Beaulé. "There is some fault on both sides. Yet in great measure each is right; neither the men who attack them nor the
women who surrender to them are wrong. What is wrong at
root owes to the impossibility of divorce. Let a young man
marry the woman he loves, and when they tire of one another, 5
let them change partners by mutual consent; then you won't
see adultery — a truth Sainville put forth to you in his description of Tamoé. But let's leave that aside for now. I confess I'm
curious to learn how our pretty adventuress will escape the
dangers it seems she faced in Toledo and whether our dear 10
Clémentine will find such pleasure she expects from the *faux
pas* she contemplates."

Léonore, seeing that she commanded everyone's full attention, returned to the story of her adventures as follows:

15

The Story of Léonore (Continued)

Dona Laurentia had no sooner finished recounting her story
than Brigandos arrived. He asked how we were, commended
us to her, and provided money enough to buy two outfits complete with feathers, finery, and fashionable ornaments — one 20
for Clémentine, the other for me. He told Clémentine to go the
next day to the home of an old courtier in Toledo, who wanted
to learn how long he had to live. Unaware she had renounced
virtue, he assured her that she ran no risk.

"He's a pious and superstitious old man who believes 25
he'll burn in hell if he dares even think about what aroused
him in the past. Such are the sorry effects of devotion to the
Lord." Our Chief continued: "It fills men with confusion and
fear as they grow old; it embitters temperaments, upends their
mood, makes them feel hopeless and worried; they grow tor- 30
mented, anxious, upset, severe, and cruel. Filled with remorse
for the past, devotion makes them unable to enjoy the present

or imagine anything in the future. Maybe I'd have been a believer myself if I thought it was good for anything. But for all the pleasures it denies, it adds nothing. Is it worth believing in useless illusions?"

"Go easy there," I said to our philosopher. "You describe a superstitious man. But one who's truly attached to his faith, who follows and believes in it with simplicity of heart, who adopts virtue because religion inspires and rewards it, who despises vice because religion condemns and punishes it, who is perpetually in awe of the Supreme Being, consoled for the torments of the world in hopes of soon returning to the bosom of the Creator and so lives in fear of displeasing Him and dies trying to imitate Him — does such a man not seem to you a worthy model?"

"Certainly," replied our Chief. "I don't dismiss the figment you sketch and in which you believe no more than me. But if such a man exists, I feel sorry for him. He's worked his whole life for illusions that won't repay the sacrifices; and he was virtuous only out of fear — a negligible merit more difficult to achieve than you think, Léonore. I want a man to do good for its own sake, with fervor and others' happiness his sole concern. If heaven and hell form part of his motivation, I say to myself: 'Here is an idiot' — but not an honest man."

Too much on the side of our Chief to contest him further, I let the discussion drop. Clémentine, who from a woman in the troupe had secretly received the address of the gentleman from whom she hoped so much pleasure, kept quiet and accepted the order.

Brigandos turned to me:

"As for you, Léonore," he said, "you'll betake yourself to the home of Don Flascos de Benda-Molla, doyen of the canons of Toledo, where you'll fulfill the same duties as your friend and provide the same sort of assurances. Examine his

eyes, read his palms, and promise him he'll live 20 years more, ○
although physicians of every stripe have given up on him. Sell
him the expensive love potion I call *Balm of Life*, though it
won't prolong it for even an hour. Once you're done, I'll send
new instructions."

Our dresses were delivered the next day and we did ev- 5
erything we could to adorn them and make them elegant and
charming; then we set off to our separate destinations.

The doyen's poor health, as Brigandos had described it,
and the potion he was supposed to require, made me imagine
a septuagenarian. But Don Flascos was only about 50 years 10
old. While his slight frame and red cheeks suggested weak
lungs, his demeanor was nonchalant and his eyes blazed with
sensuality. A very pretty servant, stirring a cup of hot chocolate when I arrived, withdrew by command as soon as he cast
me a glance. 15

He made me sit beside him, asked my age, and told me to
guess his own; I lopped off 10 years. He offered his forehead
and gave me his hand so I could tell his fortune. With the help
of what I'd learned from Brigandos, I told him what he'd done
for the past 20 years and assured him he had 30 years more, 20
at the same time revealing details of his family that seemed
impossible for me to know. Amazed, he blindly believed everything I said. His answers to my clever questions cast light
on an infinite number of things that lent astonishing support
to my predictions, and in the end he was so satisfied and con- 25
vinced of the truth of it all that he embraced me with fervor
and gave me 20 pistoles.*

But the joy I'd just instilled in his soul, heating his blood
and provoking his lust, made him curious to see whether I
could give him pleasure in the present just as nicely as I'd 30

---

* About 240 livres.

predicted his future. He started with light caresses; his age-cooled passions demanded circumlocutions to reach the degree of vigor which he seemed intent upon; and he stammered that if I would lend myself to his every desire, he'd add six doubloons to the 20 pistoles; without awaiting my answer, he ventured a hand beneath the gauze veiling my bosom. When I recoiled in defense, my resistance produced a miracle that became altogether glorious. So long it must've been since Nature had been at his beck and call that he triumphantly dared display the effects of my charms. When I rose up intending to flee, he saw and pursued, throwing himself athwart the door and declaring it certain I wouldn't be leaving without giving satisfaction. His eyes gleamed and he stuttered words of love and libertinage. He finally threw off all restraint and, man of God that he was, in filthy terms he swore that when in such a state, which truly happened seldom, he was not to be resisted.

"Wait! But what's that I see, Monsieur?" I pushed my fierce assailant away from the door, pretending some sudden great fear: "Come, hurry! I must have a closer look. There's a sign on your forehead I hadn't noticed. Oh! Monsieur, it frightens me."

"What is it?" He stopped, alarmed, no longer barring my path. "Tell me what you see, my little minion. You're scaring me. And look, shrunk before Nature — I thought today — imagined I could — but what's that you see?"

"How long is it, Monsieur, since you've been with a woman?"

"More than six months."

"Oh! Then you must be careful. Before I wasn't sure — but you're dead, Monsieur — DEAD, I'm telling you, if you consort with a woman before the sun enters Capricorn."

With these words I scampered out the door so nimbly that I was already in the street before he'd time to recover from the fright.

On returning I found Clémentine in a state of great deso-   o
lation. She'd undressed, and her body looked as if it had suffered as much as her spirit.

"What's wrong?" I asked. "What happened?"

"Nothing but suffering and sorrow for not having listened
to you. So quick to attend to pleasure rather than work for   5
our Chief, I went to see the man whose address I'd been given.
He expected me and I'd been told he was young. But I found
a terribly ugly man about 50 with a wicked mind and corrupt
soul. Léonore! You can't imagine the moral depravity of this
libertine, incredibly dissolute in the way he talked about his   10
fantasies and bizarre tastes. I've had two lovers in my life but
neither of them — no, nothing like that. However lascivious
you think I am, the details are too horrifying. Enough to tell
you he wanted to assault and ravage me. When I resisted, he
called for help and had me forcibly restrained. Then he had   15
his way awful way with me."

My friend broke down in tears as she told her odious tale.
I didn't console her for I thought now was the time not to
soothe her soul but to strike hard and penetrate it.

"And so!" I said: "Here you are, punished for your princi-   20
ples, crushed by experience. An adventure like that serves you
right, better than anything I could say to combat your sophisms. O Clémentine! could you really think that voluptuous
pleasure could be enlivened with no place for sentiment? Or
that anybody vile enough to pay for love could bring you enjoy-   25
ment? Let this be a lesson and may darts of remorse keep your
heart from total corruption. I've heard you excuse aberrations
and dare say that all these deviations come to profit love as
though gifts from Nature. Forgive me, but I thought you knew
what you were talking about. Your pain proves otherwise.*   30

---

* See p. 545 for Clementine's point here refuted. See also p. 536, where Brigandos says:
  "Let those who act and those who submit mutually punish one another...".

Stop giving yourself over to the paradoxes of an inflamed mind and the vain glory of showing spirit and wit by encouraging transgressions, much less defending those you know nothing about."

In tears, Clémentine kissed me. I didn't need make her promise to be good, for she took a heartfelt oath and didn't need me to remind her of the advantages of right conduct. Moved by her tears and regrets, I calmed her so she could at least pass a peaceful night.

The next day Florentina came to see us. She brought the companion who'd convinced Clémentine to see the man she'd visited the day before, and my friend could not help but reprove her. Here I could see the gulf that separated Clémentine, whose only fault was obstinacy, and a truly libertine creature.

"All very fine," replied Aldonza. "But we mustn't be difficult in our line of work. Did you think I was sending you to a house where love awaited? I believed the same as you when I was young, for that's what I was told. But what difference? Men who pay aren't looking to satisfy our whims, my dear; theirs alone concern them. I gave you a fine opportunity but you didn't take it. We come away with less difficulty than you; there's no need to be raped. One can become used to anything, my child, perhaps more readily than you think. He asked us to return and with it comes a profit of 25 pistoles. Do you think that's the price of simple pleasure? In our business, in which money is our only concern, the greatest irregularities, just because they've got the most value, become the bedrock of our work."

Aldonza was in truth the most corrupt woman in the troupe. We never heard anything like it from the others. Appalled by her words, Clémentine and I were about to put an end to the conversation, pretending to go about our business, when Dona Laurentia came to beg us to receive two Dominican

monks. They were anxious to meet us and, without waiting
for our reply, she herded them into our rooms.

"Wait a moment, Madame," I told the impudent broker.
"There's no need for two men to have four women. Allow me
and my friend to retire."

"As you wish," replied the duenna. Our Chief must have
forbade her to use force. "Two demoiselles will do quite well
by our reverend brothers. Wait in the salon, where you'll be
free and undisturbed while your room is being used."

We left and the despicable characters cavorted with our
companions to such an extent that only in the evening could
we return.

Clémentine had little interest in meeting the old gentleman whom she'd neglected while pursuing her own deceptive
pleasures; she feared traps and her newfound wisdom turned
to mistrust; she begged me to take her place. I accepted, for
the old man could pose no danger for me, and I shan't bore
you with the details of my visit.

Three or four more similar encounters brought our Chief
one hundred pistoles and our stay in Toledo came to an end
when, after several weeks, we were asked to leave the city. We
were told to wait at the entrance to a small forest on the left
side of the main road that led to Madrid. We went there after
taking leave of our duenna, who was considerably unhappy
we'd earned her so little.

"Perhaps you'll blame me," said Léonore, *addressing her mother*,
"for not having used what I earned to flee from such dishonest
people. I proposed as much to my companion, who shared
my desire but insisted we consider the greater peril of leaving
with stolen money. Clémentine, now surrendering not only to
virtue but to sincerity, admitted to me that far from relying on

hoped-for help in Madrid, she was now counting on me; she said she was far from able to present herself to acquaintances in her current state and, as for her mother, she confessed that she was dead. She could only join her fate to mine and consequently we decided to stand by the plan I suggested: to follow the troupe to the French border and from there to escape into whatever city from which the authorities would help us return to my province."

Once so resolved, we contented ourselves in pocketing some double pistoles, which we hid with the greatest care, a most necessary precaution because Brigandos searched the women whenever we regrouped. Several who failed to take the same precautions had come away with little; nothing escaped the Chief.

"I take care of you," he said. "You want for nothing. But the money belongs to me. I won't tolerate theft of a single réal."

We resumed walking. My friend stuck close beside me and the first night we slept beneath the walls of the Gardens of Aranjuez, the beautiful country estate built by Philippe III. We left in the morning, planning to spend the next night in a cavern half a league outside Madrid, near Manzanares, where our Chief was to give an oration with orders regarding our stay in the capital. We walked in a group beginning about seven in the morning. Brigandos seemed on edge and anxious; it was as if he harbored premonitions of some catastrophe. And suddenly, about four leagues outside the city, a detachment of 30 cavaliers burst out of a small wood and quickly surrounded us. They brandished carbines and threatened us if we didn't stop at once.

"You'll do what you want," said Brigandos. He seemed resigned. "We can't fight and we're in no condition to resist."

But to his surprise, hardly were the words out of his
mouth than we recognized the leader of the detachment: Don
Pèdre, the cavalier of Santa Hermandad, the man whose life
Castellina, our Chief's daughter, had saved not far from Alcan-
tara and whom the troupe had taken care of, fed, and helped
over the course of four days, despite every risk.

"Scoundrel!" cried Brigandos. "Don't you remember us?
You owe us your life!"

"Friend," replied that infamous villain, "gratitude is unknown in our land. Duty alone counts. We'd slit our father's
throat to serve the Holy Tribunal to which we're proud to belong.* 'Twas I who denounced you and 'tis I who arrest you.
All social bonds count for nothing when it comes to criminals.
They deserve only the lash."

And so saying, the monster bound tight Castellina's hands
— the very same that a few weeks ago had stanched the traitor's
blood and returned him to life.

"*O Justice!*" Our Chief watched in disconsolate horror:
"*How can anybody call you heaven's envoy when your breth-
ren soil themselves with such infamies!* If there's a God that
governs men, how can anybody call Him just when He toler-
ates such execrable behavior on earth, when doing good only
makes for terrible crimes! Let my example teach mankind that
the greatest stupidity of all is to listen to pity's feeble voice; it
makes only for ingrates. We'd be better off never doing good
instead of laying ourselves open to remorse when men's ingratitude returns to penetrate our hearts. *You — judges, sovereigns, magistrates — all those who tender forth the scales of
justice — wouldn't it be better to change your laws and trample*

---

* Thanks be to heaven that such terrible maxims were found only in Spain and never
besmirched our own history.

*your precepts underfoot rather than permit principles that
set remorse next to virtue and convince men that the greatest
danger abides in doing good?"*

All such declamations came to nothing. Without distinguishing innocence from crime, we were all tied up and
pitched like burlap sacks onto horses and brought to the Inquisition Palace in Madrid — taken into custody as Bohemians and vagabonds, guilty of every excess except bloodshed
— by virtue of which, instead of being imprisoned, we were
simply to be judged before the Holy Tribunal.

Wholesome Virtue! I said to myself, *is this my reward for
praising you? What did I gain from heartfelt reverence? Who
can now decide if I'm guilty or not? Who will protect my innocence and what right will I have to make it forthright known?*

We were delivered up to the judicial police, followed by a
crowd of people, and served up to their stupid curiosity. Then
we were taken off to different prisons.

"O Léonore! A thousand *adieux,*" cried Brigandos as we
separated. "If my dear child is fallen among you, I entrust her
to your care. Never forget, my virtuous girl, that if my faults
engulf you in disgrace, two things at least deserve your forgiveness: the first, to have helped you in need; the second,
loving you but never to have dared tell you."

The latter confession stunned me, and I was still in shock
when the poor man, whose tear-filled eyes met mine, was
brusquely hustled off.

Good Lord! I told myself — I've found men of the world
to be hard, ready to take advantage of my innocence and misfortune. But the leader of a band of thieves shows himself to
be honest and kind. *O Society! Either your laws are unjust or
your members corrupt!* This chief followed a dangerous path I
scarcely want to excuse but he was fair, his heart sensitive and
delicate — and so he was bound to succumb. With beings so

perverse, unthinking and unjust as men, one who opens his soul   o
to many virtues apart from a few faults will unfailingly perish.*

Fortunately for me, the room in which I was kept was close
to that of Clémentine — a consolation.

We were all interrogated separately the next day. I followed Clémentine, who told me that she thought the other   5
women had gone before us. She'd seen two of them but was
unable to talk with them. She had no time to tell me more.
They came for me and I was taken to the audience.

The Grand Inquisitor was alone when I entered. This was
not the same man as had interrogated Sainville but, rather,   10
the superior officer and Chief Prosecutor. Tall and haughty,
with a ferocious brow and somber gaze, about 45 years old, he
was built like Hercules and conveyed an air of power, health,
and vigor. His voice was raucous and threatening. He looked
much more like an executioner than a fair and humble min-   15
ister charged with honorably dispensing justice. Don Crispe
Brutaldi Barbaribos de Torturentia — such was his name —
ordered me to kneel and make an act of contrition before the
crucifix while he stood watching me with a stern and severe
gaze that was at the same time infused with a sort of malicious   20
delight and lubricious curiosity. After pretending to obey him,
I stood up as he sat down and bade me approach. Regarding
me impudently and addressing me familiarly, he asked my age.

---

* If sometimes we wonder about the reason for such discordance, we should look to
the human heart itself. It's not the bad qualities of others that humble us, rather, their
perfections — in consequence of which we pay no attention to one who is wholly bad
because we have no affinity for him. But our pride makes us look down on a person
of mixed qualities. Dismayed to find goodness in someone like that, we want to see
what wrong he does and in so doing reveal his vices the better to take revenge upon
his virtues. The inevitable conclusion can't be avoided: true wisdom comes from con-
ducting oneself as others wish; it's the only way to be happy. However, by those lights,
a man who's not absolutely good would be far better off being absolutely bad rather
than only partly so; he would be wrong by dint of virtue but largely right in the eyes
of men; and they're the ones who determine his fate. A sorry reflection — but true.

"Almost 18."

"Are you a woman or still a maiden?"

"A woman. I was abducted in Italy and taken from my husband. I am searching the world over to find him: By chance I fell into the hands of these Bohemians with whom I was arrested."

"You do not belong to their troupe?"

"I came to it by accident."

"Who are you then?"

At this point I briefly recounted where I was from and the story of my misfortunes.

"Very good. A nice tale that. You're an adventuress and a harlot."

"I'm telling the truth."

"Those Bohemians abused you. Did they rape you?"

"I've no complaint with them. I owe them thanks and hope I might enjoy as much good fortune with you."

"You'll get what you deserve. We know you profaned the holy sacraments, for which you will be slowly roasted alive, 12 hours amidst the flames and plunged into the fire only in death's agony."

"Great God! Whatever our faith in sacrament, do we deserve death for not believing? Does the God of Peace want men's blood? Must his ministers spill it?"

"You don't believe in these ceremonies?"

"I believe there exists a God and He is good and despises murder."

"You're wrong, God demands all those who have no faith to be put to death. He commands his people to slaughter whole nations that worship idols. His son said: '*I did not come to bring peace, but a sword.*'"

"That being the case I've got no belief in His son."

"Which is why you'll be set amidst flames, pulled away and returned to them, time after time, so that your torture will continue for 12 to 15 hours."

"I'll invoke the one and only God in whom I believe. He will rescue me from the hands of my executioners. Daniel implored Him in the lion's den and he was heard."

Here I began to weep despite myself. Observing my tears, the Inquisitor gazed at me. His expression changed in a way that made my blood run cold. He uttered a deep moan, pressed his lips together, and asked if my tears were a sign of repentance. I replied that I'd done nothing wrong and therefore knew no remorse. He continued staring, groaned again, and touched himself in a surprising and frightening way. I saw he was growing intensely agitated, fidgeting in his chair, repeating the same offensive gesture while stifling his moans. A hand he put forth as if to draw me closer encircled my waist and settled firmly but as if by chance at the small of my back, then followed with a lively exploration of what it found there. Scarcely can you imagine the power of virtue in the face of unrestrained vice. Proudly I stared at him, wiping away my tears. He took away his hand and asked me to kneel before him. I complied, trying as best I could to keep my distance, but now he thrust his hand between my breasts and, with me still on my knees, forced me between his legs. He enclosed my hands in his, pressed them on his thighs, and ordered me to declaim the Lord's Prayer. I told him I'd forgotten it. He asked for other prayers. I said that since I started traveling the world, they'd all slipped my mind, that I only invoked God in the depths of my soul and to protect myself from those who worked to ruin me.

"Impious woman," he said, putting his hand to my breast as if as if to cover it but in fact running his fingers across it. I thrust it away.

And now his face grew contorted with a prodigious show of wrath and lust. His agitation redoubled and again he touched himself with the same obscene gesture as before.

He let fly two or three insults and announced that I was to be tortured.

"Why?"

"To reveal your crimes."

"I didn't commit any."

"Your blasphemed."

"I worship God."

"And your accomplices?"

"I have none. "

"You'll name them on the rack." He breathed hard and fast, his chest heaved, and he stammered: "I'll torture you and drag out the truth."

Again his hands attacked my breasts, seizing them by the flesh, causing me terrible pain, and he drew me still closer. With me between his legs, he stripped away the veil covering my bosom and when I begged him to let me loose he told me to take off all my clothes.

"'Tis against modesty," I said. "You just rebuked me for having offended it."

"What is done in the name of God is never an insult to modesty."

I tried to calm him but dared not stop his wandering hands and their brutality made me tremble. He ripped my corset and freed my shoulders from the sleeves of my dress, so now my whole bosom was naked before his eyes. Now he told me to free both my arms, letting down my dress completely, and when I refused he threatened with a frightening grimace to call for help. So I obeyed, one arm, then the other. Still on my knees, my clothing fell away to my waist. His hands continued to grope my breasts, drifted across my shoulders and arms and all the exposed parts of my body. He took one of my hands in his and applied it to himself but I snatched it away so quickly that he failed to reach his goal. He asked if I

did not bear signs of the devil and in consequence he went   o
about inspecting my body as best he could. He made me stand
up straight and holding me tight between his legs said that
for the same reason he must examine me all over. I strongly
protested but he threatened me again and ordered me to un-
lace the straps of my dress and let it fall away completely. And   5
as I kept refusing he sought for himself the laces he wanted
undone. Not finding them, he forced me turn around, seized
them at the small of my back, and furiously pulled them apart.

My dress fell to my feet. I don't know and couldn't see
what he was doing to himself, only that he stared long and his   10
hands went roaming across all he had uncovered. His moans
grew louder and more agitated, there came incoherent words
mingling praise with menace and — suddenly it was over. He
ordered me to get dressed.

I told him that inasmuch as the state in which I found my-   15
self owed to his doings, I intended to go back the way I came
and repair to my cell in the same disarray. At these words he
came closer to me, his expression showing no sign of anger.
There was even a smile on his lips. He touched my chin and
told me I was a very stubborn little girl — very naughty — that   20
I didn't know what it could mean to be in his good graces. In
saying all that, in the kindest possible manner, he helped me
to straighten myself, rang a bell when I was ready, and sent
me back, telling me I ought to make known to him anything I
might need, that he intended I lack for nothing. I took advan-   25
tage of the moment to commend my companion to him but
he replied that he wanted nothing to do with anybody but me.

The first thing I did was to tell Clémentine everything. I
asked her if the Inquisitor had acted the same way with her.

"I would've told you all if I'd had time before you were   30
taken away," said my companion. "But it was impossible for
me to warn you. I wasn't as patient as you and didn't let him
get that far. Guessing his intention from the start, I asked him

either to send me back to my cell or interrogate me in front of witnesses. My determination raised his fury and he swore he wouldn't spare me."

"Alas!" I said to my friend. "I'm sorry for not showing the same courage as you. But there were two reasons why. For one thing I'm afraid. But I also hope to inspire tenderness, the better to escape great dangers by braving small ones. His first movements were brutal, but some little love might come to inspire him. If I believed such a sentiment could ever arise in that soul, I wouldn't refuse it so that his heart, softened by a generous God, might give us both a chance to escape."

For fear of being overheard we could not continue and I gave myself up to my own reflections.

Great God! Was this the tomb to which I was to be confined by fidelity purchased so dear and so gladly preserved? For I'd escaped the traps of a Venetian nobleman; a barbarous privateer had not dared assault my modesty; I'd not given in when pursued by a French consul. On the verge of being impaled in Sennar, only able to save my life at the price of honor, yet I found a way to preserve both. I'd brought a cannibal king to his knees. From the hands of a young Portuguese I came away intact; so, too, from an old magistrate and four of Lisbon's most renowned debauchees. Don Flascos de Benda-Molla did not triumph over me; nor a Bohemian woman; nor two monks; not even a chief of thieves who fruitlessly longed for me. After all that — was I to meet my end as prey to an Inquisitor! Everywhere I'd come upon resources — everywhere but here. Either I must perish or God must work a miracle — and I hadn't seen Him working any in favor of women's virtue since the Annunciation of the Blessed Virgin.

A week thus passed without the slightest hint of what was to happen or any alleviation of our situation, leaving Clémentine and I with nothing to discuss besides our catastrophic predicament.

"This was the time you were brought in," *said Léonore to her* °
husband, "and my friend implored you on our behalf. We were
afraid of you and while your prudence proved harsh indeed, I
don't reproach you for it. It was the right thing to do. Sometimes commiseration is impossible, not even natural, a second-
order dictum owing to selfishness. Had we been convinced of 5
the truth of as much when we saved the life of that scoundrel
Don Pèdre, we wouldn't have later so cruelly become his victims. But at all events you alone escaped. It caused an uproar
and brought harsh discipline and exasperated the guards.
There wasn't a single prisoner not made to suffer. 10

"Two days after your escape came the fatal confrontation."

We were instructed one morning, *continued Léonore*, to be
ready for an interrogation with *obligatory* formalities. I didn't
dwell on the word but Clémentine, either more fearful or 15
clairvoyant, asked if I'd noticed.

"No," I answered.

"You can be sure that *obligatory* can only mean torture."

"You're frightening me!"

We both wept. 20

At the stroke of nine o'clock, as we'd been warned, the Alcaide arrived. The guard who opened my door took me aside.
Out of earshot of the others, he confirmed Clémentine's fears.

"You will be subjected to interrogation," he said. "But
you'll go last. That will give you time to reflect. If you ask our 25
revered Father Inquisitor for a second, private interrogation,
he'll grant it and you won't be tormented."

I confess that when he started to talk I was so badly shak-
en that I barely understood what he was saying. Seeing my
confusion, he repeated himself. 30

We went out. Clémentine, taken away by our jailers, was
ahead of me and I couldn't talk to her. After being led through
the whole place, we went down a great staircase beneath a

vaulted ceiling, and a hundred steps more brought us to a door in a corridor so dark we could barely make our way. At the end of that long passage a narrow iron door led to another staircase, spiral this time. Another hundred steps and I felt sunk into the bowels of the earth.*

Silence was observed during our procession past effigies of saints and virgins, representations of torture covering the walls, and lugubrious sounds of a multitude of iron doors opening and shutting behind us as we went. The profound subterranean darkness save a few torches illuminating the paintings, the dampness beneath high vaulted ceilings, and occasional screams and dull moans emanating from the deepest dungeons — all of it conspired to inflict the soul with a kind of sinister terror that made my blood run cold. I lost the strength even to follow my jailers. We finally arrived at a door where a guard gently turned a key in the lock and it swung open. As we passed inside, the guards withdrew and we entered alone.

At the center of a vaulted rectangular room, lighted only by wall torches, was a long table around which were seated the Grand Inquisitor, the Grand Vicar of the Archbishop — duty-bound to attend the proceedings — and the clerk. In each of three corners of the dreadful place could be seen one of the methods of torture used by the Inquisition — rope, water, and fire.† Two executioners assisted with each apparatus, dressed in black tunics and hoods with eye holes. A most impressive silence prevailed in the assembly.

---

* All details are from observations made at the scene. The reader may be sure of their accuracy.

† The rope torture, or strappado, is applied by tying criminal's arms behind his back, with the rope running through a pulley and the victim raised from 20 to 30 feet; after being left to hang for some time, he is brutally dropped to half a foot off the ground; the jerks dislocate his joints and often puncture his stomach, causing him to let out horrible screams. The water torture consists in forcing the subject to ☞

Castellina, the sweet charming daughter of Brigandos, was waiting at the door and brought into the room with us. Fearful as I was, my courage didn't fail me. I kept in mind the magistrate's words and the small hope and consolation they offered, though sure to be costly because I could imagine no reason for such lenience besides an outcome crueler than death itself. Yet that was trouble I might at least be able to escape; not so, the frightening instruments of torture on display.

First, we all three were ordered to kneel around the table and in this posture the Inquisitor asked why we had profaned the sacraments of the Church. We answered that we never did. The Grand Vicar now spoke and declared it was pointless to deny what our companions had already confessed to.

Asked if she did not have criminal and incestuous relations with her father, Castellina swore she did not. She explained that marriage between sisters and brothers was part of

☞ swallow a quantity of water, then installing him on a hollow bench, in which position he can be squeezed at will. A wooden stick suspends the body in a way that breaks the spine, provoking incredible pain. Most severe of all is the use of fire. A brazier is set to blazing while the soles of the criminal's feet are rubbed with a penetrating and combustible substance. He is made to lie down with his feet toward the fire and they are burned until he confesses. These three tortures last an hour, often longer. Not just men are subjected to them, but women and girls of all ages, sometimes draped in a rough gown, often naked. But they are always brought undressed before their judge. In this way — according to the author whose account we have transcribed word for word in this note — most women, shattered by their indecent appearance, say whatever they are asked to say to avoid torments. Neither age nor sex makes any difference, according to this author; everybody is treated with the same severity — with all subject to torture, naked or nearly so depending upon the perversity of the Inquisitors, who more vigorously mistreat women and girls who refuse to give in to their desires. Yet those who do obey come off no better. Inquisitors incite them to surrender and give them hope they will be saved, but no sooner do they take their pleasure than they condemn them to death in order to conceal their crimes. Their excesses were so frequent that Clément VI established a special commission to combat such infamies, led by Bernard, Cardinal of Saint Mar. See Part Two of the second volume of *Histoire des Cérémonies religieuses des peuples du monde* and *l'Histoire des inquisitions*.

their customs and her union had been arranged but, as she was not yet his wife, they had not had any licentious contacts and, as she wished to remain virtuous for him, she never engaged in prostitution like her companions; she swore that she was a virgin and it could be proved by examination. She added that Clémentine and I had remained absolutely virtuous since being accepted among them.

Asked if she believed in the Catholic religion, she said she did not. To the same question we gave the same answer. Asked why she did not have faith, she replied she could not and to that question, my companion and I replied we were convinced that Catholicism was undeniably a sovereign offense to divinity and for that reason we had abjured it from childhood.

"A dangerous answer!" exclaimed Madame de Blamont. "O Léonore! Could you not have been more prudent?"

"Not even the most frightful tortures could make me lie about that, Madame."

"Great Heavens!" cried Madame de Blamont, in tears, her kind and tender soul alarmed by all that seemed to violate the pious feelings to which she was so inviolably attached.

"Ever respectable," said Count de Beaulé, taking the hands of his friend in his own, "and so pure that even a story can offend. But please, let your daughter go on. Léonore, what was the next question?"

"We were asked," *continued Sainville's amiable spouse,* "if we were Jews. We said assuredly not. We said we were deists and there existed no kind of torment that could change our minds. Asked whether we helped the men steal, we answered we did not. Finally, we were asked if we had given ourselves to the Devil. We objected: No.

Our answers were all taken down in writing, then they ₀
demanded we stand. The clerk remained seated at the table,
with Clémentine and I placed on stools nearby. The Grand
Vicar and the Inquisitor occupied two chairs in the corner of
the room not taken up with instruments of torture. They called
upon Castellina to undress and she recoiled in horror, protest- ₅
ing she had never done such a thing in front of a man. The Inquisitor said it must be done, that it was necessary to examine
her body, and what was viewed as a crime by ordinary people
was not so deemed by the servants of God. When she still
refused, on orders of Don Crispe, two torturers approached. ₁₀
They seized her, stripped her, and stepped away. One of them
picked up a knife and held it to the fire, awaiting instructions.

"It is a question," said the Inquisitor to the beautiful and
unlucky young woman, her chastity offended and cheeks wet
with tears, "of examining every part of your body to see whether ₁₅
it bears signs of the Devil. Come closer."

As she obeyed, Don Crispe moved his chair in a way
that placed her between the Grand Vicar and himself, and
both commenced to carefully inspect every part of the young
woman's body. After a long while she was made to turn round ₂₀
and offer to one what she had just presented to the other. The
silence was profound; the observation close and scrupulous.
Fingers verified what the eyes could not discern, facilitating
the examination and imposing postures. The inspection lasted more than an hour, with every part of her scrutinized three ₂₅
times by each of her judges, without a single word. At last,
when the Inquisitor noticed a vague and almost imperceptible
blemish on her left breast, he immediately showed it to his confrere and both demanded the clerk to record the discovery of
stigmata, clearly demonic. They also enjoined him to observe ₃₀
and write down a description of how this child of the Devil
reacted when the hot iron was applied to the sign of impiety.

If it owed to Satan, the victim would not feel pain. Seeing the torturer approach, Brigandos' poor daughter begged not to be burned, protesting that the blemish came from her mother. But without success. Don Crispe grabbed her breast and pointed to the place. He himself would restrain her. The red-hot iron was pressed to the flesh and the victim screamed.

"Well, then," said the Inquisitor, "this method failed, so we shall try something else. The creature is certainly devoted to the Devil. But as she does not confess we must employ torture."

With that, she was seized and her feet forced to the fire — the first torture she had to endure. As soon as the acid and piercing spikes penetrated the soles of her feet, which were soaked in combustible material, she howled in pain, then confessed: she'd indeed been devoted to the Devil since childhood. Asked why her parents acted thus, she said that she did not know and so received another application to extract a second confession. After suffering a long while and not knowing what might put an end to the pain, she said she was devoted to the Devil because she hoped to make a fortune — and that in compliance with her religion's dogmas. Finally, they asked her for the names of her father's accomplices outside the troupe. When she replied she didn't know, once more the fire, but brought closer. She let out horrible screams and although tightly bound, recoiled with such violence that her body jerked back some two feet in spite of being restrained. Her features contorted; her hair started up wildly on her head, her convulsed muscles writhing in a thousand directions. The poor girl inspired as much pity as horror. I recalled when she helped the villain who caused the awful torments she now endured. It brought to mind her goodness and candor, and I asked myself: *Is it possible that such fine qualities do not counter imaginary vices? And how can Heaven abandon virtue to dreadful torments?* But if the infamies I witnessed compelled

🖑 *fig.* 11

me to declaim against God and men, what came next only   o
intensified my disgust with the whole world!

Upon the third application, Castellina, who was young
and strong, vigorously fought back against her torturers. One
of them, as he struggled to constrain her, lost the hood that
concealed his face — and revealed none other than Don   5
Pèdre — yes, the execrable Don Pèdre — the unbelievable
scoundrel, not satisfied with the work of denunciation and
arrest of the young woman who'd saved his life. Here he was
among her tormentors — and still more! He was the only one
to carry on with it, the only one to force her to submit yet   10
again. She recognized him and looked away, horrified, while
the monster, quickly adjusting his hood, scorched her feet,
burning them to a crisp.

*O! You who put to work your fame and felicity in helping
to heal the evils of misfortune — you who seek out the poor*   15
man beneath a humble roof — you who dry tears and return
such people to life — such an abomination mustn't stop you!
Not all beautiful souls are as ill-starred as Castellina, nor does
everybody in receipt of help act like Don Pèdre.

The sorry victim of such a band of villains, at last van-   20
quished by pain and suffering, confessed to everything they
wanted. But she continued to say that Clémentine and I had
only come among them by chance, and we were in no way
culpable. They released her and declared her guilty based on
her confession of impiety, of having commerce with the Devil,   25
and public thievery. After giving her a moment to recover,
the Inquisitor ordered her back to her cell, where she would
prepare to die. She turned to us, round languorous eyes filled
with tears, let out a sigh and seemed to address us with a final
goodbye — and she was taken away.   30

Thus was treated a young woman of 16, of excellent character, modest and virtuous, as lovely as an angel — one who

a few days earlier had deprived herself to save the same man who became her torturer — and wrong only to have been born to parents who led her astray while still a child.

Even though Castellina's confession should have spared us if justice reigned in such a gruesome court, we were told we must prepare to suffer the same torments and torture.

They called upon me and as I stood right before the monsters I observed them. Fire shot from their eyes and each of them showed prodigious ardor but the cause of their irritation was hard to discern. Suppose for a moment they were reasonable beings: should they have experienced anything but rigor modulated by considerable pity? But those sentiments don't move souls such as these, or cast them into a state of savage agitation, or make them froth and spew imprecations, or create a look of tenebrous rage nearly impossible to define. There had to be something else in those perverted hearts besides what was born there naturally. What was this wild and tumultuous passion which, while making a game of inflicting torture, extinguished the genuine emotions that ought to have moved them?

O! You who tolerate such tribunals — reflect on this harsh analysis and decide if the good you receive from these dangerous institutions is worth all the secret crimes that ensue!

The Inquisitor stammered, breathing with difficulty, and harshly demanded if the scenes I'd just witnessed sufficiently impressed me. Now I recalled what I'd been told and, judging this not the moment to anger him, said that I was so severely shaken that I'd resolved to confess to powerful secret things of a sort that could only be heard by him alone. I implored his kindness to permit a private interrogation. The Grand Vicar refused and said I ought to have taken advantage the first time it was offered, that he could not accord a second interrogation; I was to make my confession after inspection of my body.

While telling me this, his physiognomy grew distorted and he   o
cast his eyes upon me like a lion ready to devour its prey. I
threw myself at the judge's feet and demanded with great insistence they hear what I had to say in a place less frightening.

"This is never done!" exclaimed the Grand Vicar, and he
gestured for the torturers to approach.   5

Now fully prostrate, my face pressed to the ground, I renewed my entreaties with such insistence that Dom Crispe, as
I expected, had to respond. He said to his confrere: "All right.
Tomorrow I'll know what all this is about and in the morning
we can meet again to finish our task."   10

The Grand Vicar was clearly unhappy but he agreed and
sent me away. When I left, they were together with my unfortunate friend — and Clémentine would not return. She disappeared from my sight and side.

Instead of Clementine, at dinner hour the door to her   15
room was opened and another woman brought in. When
I called out, a stranger's voice replied and, although I reproached myself for being careless, we started a conversation.
I quickly realized the woman was only there to make me accept the propositions that were to be on offer. To recount all   20
the provocations and seductive ruses of this emissary would
be long and tedious. You need only know that she advised
me to accept whatever the Inquisitor proposed. I was lucky
enough to have been granted a second interview, which was
clear proof he was favorably disposed to me. I would be mad   25
to resist when he could readily obtain what he wanted by force.
"Besides," continued the woman, swearing me to secrecy,
"what happened to me will happen to you. Although my crime
was less serious than yours, I was about to lose my life. He
showed me kindness and, after giving in, I immediately won   30
my freedom. Don't let his appearance frighten you. That harsh
gaze is common to the trade but in the end he is the kindest

man on earth and with women the friendliest. Believe me and seize the chance; refusal could cost you dearly. Consider that the man is more powerful than the King himself. Even at a hundred leagues from here he could absolve or condemn you at will."[*]

Hoping to obtain everything from the sentiments I wished to inspire in the Inquisitor, I carefully didn't reject the offers of his emissary; I said I'd count myself happy to please the eminent judge and only hoped to be worthy of his kindness. My responses were passed on to him the same night, and next day Don Crispe, clearly impatient for the deed to be done, made it known that he honored me with an invitation to drink chocolate in his lodgings. I dressed as best I could, neglecting nothing that could enhance some feature that might spare my life or set me free, but without any intention of making this suitor more fortunate than any of the others from whom, until now, I'd been lucky enough to flee.

Near 10 o'clock they came for me and I was secretly brought to His Eminence's apartments. He immediately gave orders to lock all the doors and forbade that we be disturbed for any reason whatsoever. The place was quite warm and the Monseigneur, still in bedclothes, wore only a brown silk Gros de Tours gown that barely covered him. Sitting sprawled and inert in a cushioned armchair, he gestured me to take a seat close by and facing him.

"My child," he said, "I am doing something for you that I permit myself only rarely and with very few women; but

---

[*] What more solid proof of the inquisitorial powers than the tragic death of Don Carlos? Philippe II, father to that unfortunate prince, led him cruelly to his death only at the instigation of these rascals.

I shan't conceal the fact that I like you. Your fate is in your   o
own hands. Yesterday you saw what happened to one of your
companions. The same torments await you and by this time
tomorrow I won't be able to save you. Moreover, all this goes
further than you think. To be subjected to torture most often
means you will be sentenced to death. Your life is at stake and   5
I warn you that you can save yourself only at the price of blind
submission to all my caprices," — he stared at me impudently
— "even if they're not the sort that please you. You must understand that men such as I are not like common mortals. Our
use of women is fatal to veneration: there is the despotism   10
and impunity we enjoy; the immense resources we control;
our right to confer death on any subject of the empire; the
multitude of slaves who revere us; and our desires, fulfilled no
sooner then they are conceived. All this corrupts morality and
depraves taste. But whatever you are compelled to undergo   15
here will always be better than torture. I need not demean myself by requesting what my simplest command could instantly
obtain without the slightest possibility of resistance. Consider
how fragile your situation. You're French and far from your
native land, in trouble with your parents. Had you a thousand   20
lives, feeble creature, if I wished to take one of them every day,
not a living soul on this earth would ask why. Faced with my
power, let your frailty bring you to your knees and endure humiliation without delay. This morning I will proceed to some
preliminaries that will test your submission. If I am pleased,   25
I will see you again in the evening and you'll spend the night
with me."

    "O! Monseigneur!" I threw myself at the monster's feet,
for it was best if I took him to be my master. "Look closer. See
how intensely your power lays claim to me. Its true strength   30
arises from deep in my heart. You needn't compel me to do
what you so richly deserve. No reason to command what you

were born to obtain. Aren't acts of sublime power one of love's worthy rights? No woman will talk to you as I do because they're all abject slaves to your caprices and they satisfy them. But they despise you. In me you provoke movements of a quite different sort. Let me enjoy their delicate nature and don't disrupt the pleasure I can take in describing them for you. Don't freeze the heart in which you reign, or snatch and break it from the hand that offers it. Let love prepare your pleasure."

"How can it be?" Astonished, the old monk brought me to sit beside him. You're saying I inspire in you some sort of affection?"

I looked down and blushed.

"Is it true, my child, that you love me?"

"Truth to tell," I said, and cast him passionate looks, "I've never met a mortal man with whom I dared to hope for such happiness. If I could only incite in you half of what I feel, the fate of no woman on earth could compare to mine."

Wiping away tears that seemed to come straight from the heart:

"It's hopeless, I know. How turn my gaze upon the world's most powerful sovereign? How dare I? That he would deign to step away from his grandeur, to forget the titles by which he bends before him the whole universe, and think of himself as simply a man to be loved. Would he but allow an unfortunate woman to adore and find in him the thing that makes him worthy of the world's great princesses."

Nothing works like *amour-propre*. His holiness Father Don Crispe Brutaldi Barbaribos of Torturentia, the most frightening of men, suddenly believed himself more beautiful than Adonis; his depraved morality, tempered by pride's illusions, persuaded him he was loved and, indeed, made for love.

"In truth, my child," he said, "if I ever imagined you could feel such passion for me, I would have spared you all the pain

you've endured. Here we're accustomed to using women for   o
pleasure with no consideration for love. It's a sentiment about
which I know very little. But to learn about it with you! I've
seen few creatures more lovable and none more beautiful. But
this won't change our plans. I will still see you this evening
and we will spend a delicious night together."   5

"Great God! What are you saying!" I responded with horror: "Love's delights amidst executioners! Fragrant roses whilst
being stung by slavery's thorns? Surrounded by such horrors,
how could I hear my soul speak? In that shackled soul, how
could you discern the feeling you've inspired? You'd have in   10
your arms you a false idol and not a delicate woman inflamed
by your charms! You don't know the lively and ardent imagination of a French woman. It takes little to excite her, still less
to offend her. Yet no matter how fine, the lover who doesn't
know how to inflame an imagination whose dreams are to   15
be worshiped shan't get what he wants; he'll be just another
would-be seducer. Let's flee this cesspool of infamy. You must
have a house in the country — let's seek happiness there and
rekindle desire by the dove's own sweet songs. Come now, you
whom I love and adore; come replace the knots that bind my   20
hands with a garland of flowers we'll pick together and spread
upon the throne where victory will be yours. Zephyr and Flore
will embellish our games of love. There everything will enliven
our pleasure, and amidst her gifts, Nature will seem to exist
for us alone."   25

"Enchanting siren," said Don Crispe, drawing me close.
"Let me kiss the lips that speak such tender words."

Pulling away:

"No!" I exclaimed; "Why would I grant a kiss when you
promise me nothing? You ask for one of love's most precious   30
gifts. My heart wants to assent but reason opposes. Everything I see here troubles my mind; these surroundings turn

my blood to ice. Let's quit this place forthwith and what a change you'll see in my wicked soul!"

"Go then, little villain!" The monk was on fire. "Your words and the look in your eyes cause a change in me; I'm no more myself. When night falls, a man you can trust will come for you. Follow him and we'll go to the place you crave for thrills and delights. But once there you won't leave me. And if ever your perfidious soul —"

"Great God!" With a half-hearted scream: "Enough of your threats. What do you fear when my heart is yours? I love you — what more do you want? These chains fasten tighter than any that hold me here — and only because of you."

I went out, leaving my monk in love and all enraptured. As soon as I was back in my cell, the woman nearby wanted to ask questions but I feigned fatigue and she left me alone. When the hour struck, laying claim to my good fortune, I left the infernal prison, just as determined never to return as I was not to accord the thing that had legitimately or, rather, *illegitimately* set me free.

"Monseigneur is ahead of us," said the lackey who'd fetched me, "and the carriage here is for us. I answer for your safety with my life until we reach the home of His Eminence."

I said nary a word. We went off together and not two hours later a trio of superb mules brought us to a country house more than six leagues from Madrid. Despite the darkness, I observed the surroundings with greatest care — to what end you'll soon see.

Entering a delightful drawing room, I found the monk impatient and burning with desire. He was attired as a French country gentleman, which made him appear gigantic and even more fearsome.

"Are you pleased?" He rushed upon me and kissed me. In ecstasy: "Shall I now receive the prize I've done everything to deserve?"

"But of course!" I replied. "You force me to add the liveli- 0
est gratitude to all the other sentiments you've aroused in me.
I can't control myself and couldn't refuse."

To gain time I begged him to show me through the house.
A hundred candles were lit and he took me everywhere. Finally, entering a charming room designed to inspire sensuality 5
and abandon, in which a prodigious number of mirrors would
multiply positions and everywhere the softest couches serve
as so many thrones of love — there Don Crispe's overwhelming urgency spoke louder than delicacy allowed. He ardently
took me in his arms and told me he could not go further 10
without receiving proof of my sentiments. His libertine hands
wandered in every direction.

"Stop it," I told him, evading his grasp. "You know nothing
about the art of love and I'll have to teach you. Most delightful
pleasures await but why rush? Wouldn't a bed be better suited 15
than all these silly luxuries that do nothing but satisfy vanity?"

But my wayward student, little made for such reasoning
and far from understanding the spirit behind it, pressed me
with still greater violence.

"Just offer yourself like yesterday," he told me. "Don't hide 20
your treasures. See and understand, Léonore: I must discharge
and you must help. Show me those enchanting charms; the
sooner I see them and impress my lips upon them, the sooner
I'll be plunged into that excess of delirium that will restore me
to the calm you desire." 25

"What? What a proposition!" I replied. "You want yours
at my expense? Such excessive compliance would deprive me,
would it not? Don't recoil before the sacrifices love demands.
Let's flee these deadly surroundings where vanquishing my
dignity would spoil my pleasure." 30

I rushed into the adjoining apartments and he followed
in uncontrolled agitation, unable to restrain himself yet so

enslaved by love that its voice was the only one he heard. His countenance flared with rough lust, bewildered by the delicate sentiments with which I tried to contain him. His confusion was so great he no longer knew what he was doing or saying. We found dinner ready when we arrived.

"Let's be seated," I said, eyeing the table setting. "The pleasures of a fine meal will bank the flames and spice the pleasures that await."

Don Crispe, still in a delirium, touching and squeezing me everywhere, had a hard time renouncing his main intention; but I kept away from him, took my place at table, and he did the same. The charming dining room, small and excessively warm, gave onto a garden; everything was set out nearby and the servants were ordered away. He had the liveliest desire that we rid ourselves of our clothing. Unaccustomed to our notion of love's voluptuous refinements, the revered father salted his every thought with the debauchery to which he was accustomed. However difficult to turn down his invitation to undress, I was determined not to grant something that would so interfere with my plans. I told him that being in *such a state* would be bad for my health.

"Well, then! *Your breasts.* At least: *your breasts.*"

There was nothing I could do! He'd already seen them using force, so no crime to let it happen again. In some situations we give a little to gain far more. My part was no easy task. I had at once to excite and quell his desire, to contain it within bounds of decency yet prevent it from fading. As soon as I obliged him, though I tried to shield myself, I couldn't stop his fingers. And now he proved to me how coarse his desires and how little I'd refined his sentiments. He peeled off his clothes and approached me naked and tried to direct my hands — but they refused to grasp what he wanted. I pushed him away. He horrified me. Inflamed with wine, you can't imagine his

daring words. Deranged! God in heaven! What would become   o
of me if I fell victim to such depravity! Over dinner I tried to
talk to him about Clémentine but he silenced and forced me
to change the subject.

At last it's time for me to tell you of the way I planned to
deliver myself from the villainous monk and how I came away   5
just as happily as I'd escaped previous dangers. In prison I'd
managed to keep with me, carefully concealed, the precious
sleeping potion that Brigandos had entrusted to me. A fair
amount was left, and if the quarter portion I thought enough
to put my persecutor to sleep didn't succeed, my intention   10
was to swallow the rest and fall into the slumber that would
end all my troubles. The powder, together with a little money
that fortunately went undiscovered during the searches done
when one is entered into such places, were now my best hope.
Adroitly hidden in my hand was the dose destined for Don   15
Crispe, and once we sat down to table I sought a way to drop
it into his glass. Dizzied by wine and drunk with love, halfway through dinner he dissolved into my arms, covering my
breasts with kisses. Instead of pushing him away as usual, my
left hand clasped his head captive to my bosom while behind   20
his back, with my right hand, I carefully poured the powder.
His glass was full and it dissolved at once. Operation complete, I gently pushed him away. Filling my own glass, I drank
and invited him to do the same. He imbibed and the juice
swirling in his veins worked so promptly that 10 minutes later   25
his eyes dimmed, senses froze, and he fell into a kind of stupor
that would have frightened me if he or the situation were any
different. But when it's a question of life and honor, I wonder
if all means aren't legitimate to contend with an adversary.

As soon as I saw Don Crispe in such happy repose, my   30
first and only thought was to flee. The risks were clear in all
their glory. If recaptured, my days would be numbered — but

if I stayed I'd lose what was dearest to me in all the world. And for me wouldn't that be the cruelest tragedy of all?

"*Courage!*" I told myself: "*Dame Fortune has never deserted you in situations as perilous as this. She'll continue to serve you now.*"

With that, I dashed into the garden, leaving my man entombed in deepest slumber. The weather was superb on a beautiful evening; the moon shone bright as day. High stone walls enclosed the house, as by necessity with all such sanctums of pleasure. Whatever the motive, whether dictated by need or enjoyment, crime requires cover of darkness. Climbing the walls here or there was the same all around. The only door was clearly locked. But I was able to use a narrow trellis to reach the top and decided that, however high, I would blindly jump.

Without a choice, so I did.

My fall was so bad that it almost knocked me senseless. But a thousand sharp sentiments brought me to my feet and I started dashing across the fields like a mad woman. An hour later I stopped for breath at the edge of a small stream. I thought it best to find my bearings and avoid falling into the trap of blindly running off. Using the position of the moon, I located north and walked in that direction, convinced that by this means I'd be leaving Spain and heading for the Pyrenees. I sought a road leading that way and soon came upon one I could follow. I'd been walking half an hour when I heard galloping horses on the road behind.

"Great God!" I told myself. "It's me they're after."

I took refuge in the deepest part of a nearby hedge, hoping not to be seen. Imagine my distress as I heard one passing cavalier telling the other: "We've got to find her before daybreak. She escaped not half an hour before His Lordship called us to mount up."

The one who'd pronounced those words now dismounted and stood just in front of me as he took the opportunity to relieve himself. His fellow solider asked:

"What do you think His Lordship will do with her if we find her?"

"Kill her, I'm sure. His rage is like nothing you've ever seen." As he remounted his horse: "But I'm not feeling sorry for her. It was a bloody inexcusable trick."

They rode away.

I can't describe how those words afflicted me. My blood seized up and mortal cold took hold. I almost fainted. As the anxiety passed, I was left unsure whether to continue along the same road or retrace my steps. Either way was dangerous and I couldn't decide. For the time being I was tempted just to stay put — and then, listening carefully, made out the distant sound of the two cavaliers returning. This time I thought I really must be finished. Huddling by the hedge, I crouched down and must've taken up no more space than a rabbit.

This time the soldiers rode more slowly, and when I heard a woman weeping I realized they must have caught their prey. That revived my courage. As I listened and looked out more boldly through the leaves, by the light of the moon and to my great surprise, I could make out the figure and features of Florentina, the pretty 14-year-old from our troupe. At first I thought I must be mistaken. But the awful scene that took place before my eyes soon convinced me.

"Well, of course!" exclaimed one of the men. "We'd be fools to bring back the girl without some merrymaking. Chance offers, why not accept?"

"So let's to it," said the cavalier, who gripped her astride his horse. "You're closed-mouth and I trust you. His Lordship doesn't care about her anymore and only wants revenge for the little trick she played on him. Besides, if she talks, we'll just deny it."

"They'd believe us, not her," said the other.

Together they judged the foot of the hedge a suitable place to consummate their terrible crime. They lay the poor little girl on the grass so close to me that I couldn't fail to recognize her and — but how describe what happened? Easier for you to guess than honest for me to recount. The two brutes took turns satisfying their abominable passions and three hours of gross and vicious lust left the girl nearly dead.

When daybreak finally neared, seeing they'd not yet gone, I trembled at the thought of being discovered.

"By Blessed Saint Christopher and all the saints of heaven," said one of the wretches, tired of his vicious assaults yet now ready to commit another that was worse. "Wouldn't it be best to cut the throat of this minx rather than take her back to His Lordship? If she talks, we're in trouble. Tell me whether one woman more or less on this earth is worth us risking our posts. We've done everything we wanted with her. Now we're finished, so let's cut her 18 different ways and hide the parts in the hedge. We'll say we didn't find her and no murder could ever be more safe or sure."

These cruel words reawakened the barbarians' sorry victim.

"O! Good sirs!" She threw herself at their feet. "I swear on all I hold sacred that I'll never say a word. Hold me prisoner and I'm yours forever, here as at the home of His Lordship. You could kill me if I ever so much as opened my mouth."

The one who first suggested rape was by far the more ferocious. With one hand he seized the poor young woman by the hair and with the other he pointed a dagger at her heart.

"No — no quarter. No mercy. You'll talk less dead than alive." Still holding the girl under the blade, he turned to his comrade: "My friend, two options to weigh carefully. One, the death of this harlot; the other, loss of our livelihood.

The first affects only this vile creature; the second concerns our mutual interests. Can we hesitate even a moment?"

"Wait," replied the other. "I see how you're thinking. But one crime is enough, let's not commit another. She promises not to talk, let's believe her. If she breaks her word, we'll know how to punish her. Let's leave. Soon it's daybreak. They're waiting for us. Hurry up."

"You'll regret it." He released the little Bohemian. "You're forgetting that a crime ought not be done halfway. Those who don't finish are always punished."

"A principle not always sure." The soldier lifted the girl onto the back of his horse then mounted it himself while his friend did the same. "But true or not, there's always conscience and that inner voice to console us for not having committed every possible evil."

With that, away they galloped.

Drained dry within and dejected, before even thinking about what had happened, I made off from that deadly spot and continued sadly on my way, seized with fright by the least noise. I could only wonder how the little girl had fallen into the hands of those men. We hadn't seen her at the Inquisition, although we were sure she'd been with us. How did she escape? Why was she on the same road as us? It was all a puzzle and hard to grasp. I could only conclude that the Grand Vicar, Don Crispe's companion in crime and debauchery, must have also owned a house nearby; that these libertines shared some of the women from our troupe; and this one had fled from his place just as I'd escaped the Inquisitor. But why run away? She wouldn't have had the same motive. What looked like a dreadful prospect for me would have been for her a welcome opportunity.

Whatever happened, I never learned more or saw the poor girl ever again.

Continuing along my route, before noon I sighted El Escorial and would've passed through that town if I were on the main road, but I was not. It was enough to know I was making my way toward the Pyrenees. I walked the whole day, with brief rests beneath trees, avoiding inhabited places, and living on roots and water. By evening I found myself so far from the usual roads that, though headed in the right direction, I was lost. Gazing at the high mountains which divide old and new Castile, I knew I must cross them to reach San Ildefonso, where I could take the road to the Pyrenees; but as it was now too late to start, I sought shelter to await daybreak. To this end I took a bush-lined path, commonly found in this part of Spain, and came upon an isolated house with a sign on the door. I approached a woman seated on a nearby bench and asked if she knew why an inn was to be found along such a road.

"True," said the woman, "the road is not much traveled and you can see it's no good for coaches. But merchants who evade the royal tax while smuggling silk from Castile to Estremadura feel safer along this little frequented route and so they lodge here. We've a nice room for you, my sweet. It's vacant tonight. If you can pay, it's yours."

Delighted to have come upon what seemed to offer a safe and restful night, I gave the woman a *quadruple* and asked for dinner and a night's lodging. The woman, who seemed decent enough, gave honest change without the slightest whiff of swindle. I went up to the room, which was much cleaner than I would have expected, settled down, and in three-quarters of an hour was brought a nice supper. All this seemed to establish trust and after finishing my meal I looked forward to a calm night. With more delicacy than was called for — yet fortunately for me — when I examined the bed and bed linen, I noticed blood stains. That led me to suspect it had harbored

someone sick. Not to wonder, I decided not to lie within the
curtained bed but instead placed the mattress on the floor
so that I could better look forward to a peaceful night and
refreshing sleep. But scarce chance that! After falling into a
deep slumber, at about three in the morning, a terrible noise
jolted me awake. I'd taken care to keep some light and cast
a glance at the bed only to see — great heavens! — that I
might've been crushed. The tester of the canopy concealed an
enormous millstone that was fixed by a spring to drop down
and crush anybody foolish enough to be sleeping there. You
can readily imagine my fright. Presence of mind did not abandon me, though, and I dressed, sure that the cutthroat rascals
who ran the place would soon come to verify the results of
their perfidious stratagem. I decided to flee straightaway. Very
quietly I opened the window, glimpsed the path I'd come by,
and rushed out the back. I walked rapidly until the house was
entirely lost to view.

"Lord Almighty!" I thought when I could slow my pace
and think a little about where the least foolishness can lead!
So many calamities since I'd unhappily quit my family! This
is mankind? Can we find among people anything besides deception, debauchery, nastiness, betrayal and violence? Could
that be the work of a good Lord in heaven? Is that the way
He dares lay claim to our devotion? As for Brigandos: *Your
principles aren't far wrong. With nothing but infamy on earth,
only a malicious being unworthy of worship could have created
the world around us. Whether it's your system or atheism, good
sense finds no alternative.**

---

* If we look now to the school of misfortune, we find it is not as fine a thing as idiots
believe. Captain Cook observed that when the members of his crew were unhappy,
the more cruel they became and, he said, the more they committed senseless murders.
The more that misfortune oppressed, the more insensitive their souls and the more ☞

0   These philosophical reflections brought me to the foot of the mountains, to a place where they opened onto what I believe was a way to San Il Defonso. I was not mistaken and through the narrow passage known as *el Puerte del Frante Frio*, I arrived before the moon reached its zenith. But I didn't

5   enter the town of the royal palace, content as usual to follow paths parallel to the main road leading through the Pyrenees.

     Exhausted, still lost in thought after my nocturnal catastrophe, I walked only a little further before stopping to spend the rest of the night at the foot of a tree, preferring it to the

10   risks of again finding myself someplace unsafe.

     The next day's plan was to reach Segovia, but after wandering too far west, I became completely lost. At nightfall I could neither see the road nor any house nearby. Distressed, I was dismally making my way along a half-cleared little path

15   when I heard the sound of a church bell. I veered off in that direction and after half an hour arrived near a small, isolated monastery of Capuchin friars. I didn't want to ask for shelter, as you can readily imagine; in their retreat I'd be a too tasty treat. But the church was open and I went inside, thinking

20   that at least I might pass a peaceful night in feigned prayer. I huddled in a confessional and shortly after heard the doors closing. In this dark peaceful place, worn out by hunger and fatigue, I couldn't help but fall asleep.

     Not more than two hours could have passed before I

25   heard the choir door open. It led from the convent and first I

☞   ferocious and cold-hearted they became. The effect of unhappiness on the heart of man is to harden it; that is why the lowly are always crueler than people who receive a good education. And if that's so and, indeed, it's not in doubt, misfortune is good for nothing; anything that harms the soul and whatever extinguishes sensitivity can lead only to crime. Only when man is happy can he seek to bring happiness to those around him. And if adversity befalls him? He becomes prey to moodiness and bitterness, corrupt and hardened by grief, and soon impelled to commit horrors.

thought the friars must be coming for morning prayers. That
unforeseen prospect was enough to make me tremble but
what really transpired was far worse.

Two brothers, by feeble lamplight, entered slowly. They
carried the body of a woman, just murdered. One held her by
the head, the other by the feet.

"Let's put her down here," one said, settling his end of the
corpse on the balustrade of the choir, "and be quick to open
a vault."

"Beautiful creature!" said the other. "If it weren't for the
damned searches, she would've served us six months more."

"That makes *twenty-one* who've fallen into our hands over
the last four years. We're depopulating the province."

"Our damned institutions are the cause of it all. We're
men like any other and so we need women. If we had them
as we wanted and didn't need to hide our natural desires, we
wouldn't resort to crime and be forced to kill our objects of
pleasure for fear of betrayal. That's the dreadful thing, unforeseen by law! Just as a young girl, tender naive, becomes guilty
of infanticide to hide her sins; or a libertine must conceal his
caprices, so, too, the unbridled monk must become a murderer. If only they'd turn a blind eye to imaginary wrongs, to
weaknesses that don't harm society, a man wouldn't need to
become twice a criminal in order to avoid being branded one
in the first place."

"If her parents come tomorrow as we've been warned,
we'll tell them they've been misled. *Duplicity, treachery, deception.* Nothing matters after the crimes we're forced to commit. That's the way a man becomes depraved — how by trying
to make him good they force him to do still worse."

One of the monks advanced toward the confessional to
open a vault less than six feet away from where I lay hidden.

"Come on," he said to his brother, "let's put the poor thing
in her final resting place."

They picked up her body and placed her on the edge of the vault, then paused again.

"If anybody ever caught us doing this," said one, "we'd go damned hard on him. We'd end up burying two instead of one. Twenty of them and we'd stuff them all in the vault."

"Fortunately, we're so isolated that surprises like that are impossible."

"Impossible? You're wrong. A traveler might stop down here, let himself be locked at night to escape the next day, only to betray and bring us down."

"True. We should always search the place first."

Imagine how I trembled.

"Anyway, let's put her down. Nothing to fear today. Nobody comes by on Saturday. Next time we'll be more careful."

They entered the corpse into the vault and after a few moments re-emerged, closed it, and went back to the monastery.

Never had I experienced anything that caused me such fright, even during the incident with Florentina, for at least then I'd been unconfined. Completely shattered, I wondered if I hadn't been dreaming.

"Tell me, Dame Fortune!" I said under my breath: *"How in the deuce are you going to get me out of this? It's impossible I won't be seen when the church opens in the morning. And when that happens, I'm dead."*

You can't imagine and I can't depict my torment, anxiety, and fear that night. At times the fatal vault seemed to swing open before my eyes and swallow me alive. I saw myself being dragged inside after being stabbed a thousand times — that frightful livelong night!

Finally, daybreak. A monk arrived to open the doors and a dozen women and peasants entered to attend early mass. I decided it would be far safer to mingle instead of trying to flee. I quickly left my hiding place and joined the villagers;

they kneeled and so did I. Sometimes one has no choice but to pretend. An outsider is readily noticed in such remote places as this; many cast a glance but nobody said a word.

The priest appeared — one of the same monks who'd just defiled himself with crime. His impure and bloodied hands went about offering the divine sacrifice. Watching such revolting idolatry made me feel as if I was committing a crime myself.

Great heavens! I told myself as he raised the Host. *How could the miracle they talk about take place in the mouth of this monster?* Disgusted, I looked away.

Ever since that moment my hatred for Holy Communion is such that I'd find it easier to watch a man be tortured.

The impiety concluded, I went out with the people. Soon they came around me and started asking questions. I told them I was a French pilgrim returning to my country. Joining them was the monk who during the night had helped the brother who'd just celebrated mass. He looked me over carefully and I saw lust in his gaze. He asked where I'd slept.

"Under a tree, a league distant," I answered, "finding nowhere else to lay my weary head."

He bade me enter the monastery, assuring me that pilgrims were allowed. As I'd not eaten dinner the night before, I could have used a meal. Yet even starving, I'd have been wary. He insisted and I refused still more firmly. Asking a villager the way to Segovia, I quickly went off in the direction he pointed without looking back. Barely two leagues distant, I came upon a house and went inside, hoping for some food. It was not an inn but a large farmhouse belonging to good people, and they welcomed me. Immediately I was struck by a young woman, weeping beside the fire in the kitchen. I asked the cause of her chagrin.

"My dear daughter," said an old man who seemed head of the household, "has been inconsolable these past two months."

"What happened?" I asked.

"She had a little girl, 15 years old, beautiful as can be, who disappeared. Impossible to find out what happened to her — well-behaved like her mother, devout as an angel, a child we all adored. She was to be the hope and consolation of my old age."

The good man's eyes brimmed with tears.

I'd no doubt about the dire connection. But I said: "You've left no stone unturned?"

"None," said the old man. "Some malicious people came to tell us she was locked away in the little monastery of the Capuchin Friars, which you must have passed on your way here. Could you even imagine such honest saintly people doing a thing like that? Only three of them live there and they all deserve to be canonized. One of them came again yesterday morning to console us — the holy fellow. He said that God must love us since he so cruelly chastises us, that we must bear this tragedy as one of the crosses upon which the Son of God was mortified, and that she whom we mourn may now be in heaven. How can anyone cast suspicion on such devout people? They would surely have brought her back to us had she sinned, not caused us sorrow by taking her away — poor thing. They've known her since she was a child, and one of them took her confession and showed us all the way. 'Twas with them she learned to read and from them last year that she received first communion. They came here daily to give us counsel. They cherish us. Only evildoers would want to blame such upstanding people for our dear little girl's disappearance."

Here I forced myself to maintain the sharpest silence. However horrible the crime committed by the monks — and even though I'd no doubt the lost girl and the one I'd seen dead and buried in the convent were one and the same — nothing could make me risk denouncing them. Incrimination couldn't save the poor girl's life. In Nature's machinations there's

something dubious and obscure. If it's a crime to cause an
individual's death, wouldn't I be committing one if I brought
about the death of these monks? And if it's not an individual's
loss that establishes a crime, and if death conforms to Nature's
laws, which is how she maintains herself, is there any way to
prove that three monks deserved to die? Because my denunciation would kill them all — yet is one human life worth three?
Can a murderer's death prevent other crimes, or compensate
for ones already committed? Can it restore the blood that was
shed? Even though they'd confessed to still more crimes, it
was not up to me to hang them — without no evidence of
several but only one and barely — I say *barely* since I didn't
see it happen. So I couldn't denounce them. I would've done
anything to grant monks anywhere in the universe public permission to commit some small crime so as to avoid a greater
one; but I wouldn't raise a finger to condemn those unfortu-
nates who are compelled to become criminals, constrained by
absurd laws of which I'd be wrong to make use in order to see
them executed. So I said nothing yet felt sorry for these good
people, and paid them an ample sum for their help, then followed the road they assured me would take me to Segovia that
same evening.

Although the path was narrow, when I reached the main road
three leagues further, as I'd been told, I decided not to take
it, still afraid I might be hounded as a fugitive from the Inquisition. I walked along the side trails, always in the direction of my destination; but after going the whole day without
seeing anyone, again I got lost. With no shelter nearby and
black night falling, I'd no hope of finding my way. Overcome
with misfortune and shaken by so many sinister events, I was
seized by sudden fright. Exhausted and helpless, I collapsed

at the foot of an oak tree. Hardly a moment passed before a man — armed with a rifle in a sling and a belt replete with daggers and pistols, jumped down from a tall tree and landed at my feet.

"What are you doing here, wh--e?" He spoke harshly. "Looking for something roundabout — are you?"

"Alas! Monsieur!" I immediately stood up. "I'm not what you think. I'm an unhappy woman, brought out of France by a lover whom I married and from whom I was abducted. I've searched for him the world over and now shall seek him in my own country."

Those explanations didn't satisfy the rascal.

"You're French," he said, using our language. "So am I. Show me a little kindness."

Pressing me up against the tree, he was ready to give no quarter despite our common bond. One hand kept me from screaming while the other went to facilitate an enterprise of which I was assuredly to soon fall victim — and would have, too, if it hadn't been for the whole troupe of his fellow thieves. Suddenly they surrounded us. They were eight in all, armed and sinister-looking.

"Stop now!" said one, violently thwarting my adversary's assault. "A moment, if you please. Each of us must have a slice and it's not fair if the newest recruit goes first."

"Captain," he said, turning to another who'd just arrived: "settle the question."

That surly fellow — "Who's this harlot?" — dragged me away from the tree to inspect me in better light. "Not bad, my friends. Give the devil his due. Let's take her back to our cavern. You know we don't have a proper cook. When we come back from the hunt we've always got to prepare dinner for ourselves. For that sort of thing this little wh--e will do nicely — and for the rest: whenever it strikes our fancy. Let's be off, it's late.

Tomorrow at dawn the carriage from Madrid will pass by this   o
corner of the woods and I aim to take every écu and neglect
not a single traveler. Today I'm sorry as can be that we missed
the Duke of Albuquerque's coach. Tomorrow I'm going to
make up for it."

 We commenced walking during this charming conversa-   5
tion which, as you can see, left me not doubting my bad luck
in finding myself among a band of thieves — nay, of dedicated
assassins who showed no mercy, living invisibly in old Castille,
saturating it for the past six months with the most atrocious
crimes. I won't tell you my own thoughts except to say I was so   10
distraught that I could barely breathe. Several times I begged
them to have mercy and let me continue on my journey. But
they only laughed and threatened me; I had to do as they said.
After half an hour we arrived in a densely wooded copse with
branches so thick that it was almost impossible to walk in   15
single file.

 Midway through this small forest the chief, who was
ahead, lifted a scrub-covered stone, revealing a staircase. We
went down in silence and at nearly a hundred feet reached a
vast cavern, illuminated by a distant torch. When they lighted   20
several candles I could make out the shape of the place. It
seemed to be an abandoned underground quarry. Several tun-
nels led to a large cavern in which small rooms were carved
into the thick stone.

 As the thieves took off their weapons, the captain looked   25
me over carefully and asked who I was. When I answered him,
just as I had before, the terrible brute grabbed his rifle, paying
no attention to the misfortunes I described, and after some
execrable blasphemy, he said to a comrade:

 "Bras-de-fer: I've the urge to use this young virgin for tar-   30
get practice. I've never murdered a woman in my life and want
to see if it's better than taking apart a man."

"Very well put, Captain," replied Bras-de-fer. "I itch to do the same. I never get a good night's sleep without killing somebody. Let's strip her naked and set her down, legs spread. The first to put a ball in the bush will have to himself all the loot we take tomorrow."

But seeing me turn pale as a ghost and ready to faint, the Captain laid down his weapon and told me to calm down — that this was only to show me my fate in store if I tried to run away or failed in my duties.

I was shown cooking utensils, bade to start a fire, handed some game meat and ordered to cook it. Judging that total obedience and a little skill might soften my new masters, although I'd never done it before, I was so eager to succeed that I managed to make a decent meal. They were so satisfied that they invited me to a place at their table, which I took with far more fear than hunger. While preparing dinner, I couldn't help but think of the sleeping potion that had worked so well with the Inquisitor. How useful it would've been right now! But climbing the walls when escaping from Don Crispe, I'd unfortunately lost it. I never imagined needing it again so soon.

When the brigands had eaten their supper and drunk a great many bottles of wine, their gaze turned to me with more than a little interest but neither love nor gallantry in their sights. Every kind of brutality was considered. One deviation leads to another; the enemy of virtue is equally so of decency; accustomed to breaking down all restraints in favor of inclinations to which crime portends, you can hardly suppose it would respect them when it comes to debauchery. How can I tell you everything they said? Yet to pass over it in silence would paint a poor picture, so I'll use figures of speech to cast a veil. Only dishonest expressions truly shock.

First, they told me I must place myself amidst them, naked, and blow out the candles whilst like wolves on a sheep

they would come upon me, each to his own satisfaction. But
then they changed their minds and said that the best must
be reserved for tomorrow; tonight they'd content themselves
with judging my skills, and the one best-served or made happiest by reaching the goal in the shortest time, would be tomorrow the first whose ardor I'd reward. A third suggested
something different. The fortress, he said, must offer lively
resistance and in order to be ready for the next day's attack,
skirmishes must take place outside the demi-lunes and the
redoubt seized before entry into the interior. Still others said
things yet more obscene; they were inflamed by every kind
of obnoxious plot and crapulous, barbaric invention. Finally,
the Captain calmed everybody down and said that, because
they had to leave in an hour, nobody must lay a hand on me
before returning. But for this next hour to be a pleasant one,
they were to roll dice and let chance decide the order in which
they'd become my lover. This plan was immediately executed,
the results written down.

"Listen, boys," said the Captain when they finished, "We've
said it all. Now let's go; essential tasks await. Don't forget that
what we've just done was only a game, for I wanted to keep
you happy and awake. That this poor woman serve us and we
need her — all very well — but if any of you take advantage
of her weakness and misfortune to obtain by force what she
must confer upon the one who'll please her the most, I warn
you: that man I'd take for a coward, dishonest, and likely to
betray us. Nothing would stop me from getting rid of him immediately. Not against the weak and poor must we brandish
our weapons; we target only the rich and strong. Our occupation, as noble as that of Alexander the Great, aims only at
establishing among ourselves the kind of compensation disrupted by civilization and its laws. We've got nothing and get
help from nobody. Without taking reparations we'd be lost.

We can do anything we want to redress the misdeeds of fortune and the ferocity of the rich; but when it comes to crime,
that sort of thing's forbidden. Bad enough we must commit
crimes to survive, but never for no reason. Anyone who wants
can contradict me; I'll show him the light in a way he won't
forget."

The speech won unanimous applause. All took up arms
and went, leaving me instructions to ready things for their
return.

"Great God," I told myself, confused by what I'd just heard.
"Once more — virtue amidst infamy!"

These wayward fellows said awful things but did me no
wrong and even talked of their desire not to harm me. They
hadn't delivered me up for the good of the state to a barbaric
king who might've literally devoured me. Unlike in Lisbon,
they didn't want to take advantage of my misery to satisfy their
lust or rob me so I'd give myself up to them. They didn't scorch
me or break me on the rack to obtain confessions to imaginary
crimes; they didn't make me choose between dishonor and
death so as to triumph over frailty; and they didn't kill me
to stop me from revealing their crimes. Would it be always
among society's outcasts that I'd find solace and charity whilst
those assigned to keep peace and insure order, and make piety
and religion prevail, were invariably seduced by despotism or,
trembling themselves under the yoke of fraud and deception,
offered up only horrors and crimes! Is civilization thus to be
counted as something good? And if most crimes are committed under the mantle of authority, are not the constraints that
it imposes the instruments of its passions rather than virtue?"

These thoughts so powerfully troubled me that I spent a
solitary two hours, crushed and shattered, sitting and staring
by the fire. Finally, curious about the place, I got up. Since
sunlight never entered, guided only by the dim glow of a lamp,

I thoroughly explored the redoubt's every corner — and imagine my astonishment when I could make out low voices coming from an obscure vault that seemed to contain several lugubrious abodes. Entering it I came upon a door and realized that the sounds could only be coming from within. I listened carefully.

"O my dear Angélique!" A man's voice spoke in French: "Our ruse won't work for long. Once they stop believing us, death will be the price we pay. This terrible cavern will be our tomb forever."

Those words emboldened me. They could only come from companions in misfortune, sent my way by fate. I would talk to them.

"You in there!" I said softly. "You who lament as I do this horrible place. I think I've more freedom than you. Tell me how I can help you."

"Who are you?" The man who'd just spoke asked from behind the door. "Will not your semblance of pity deceive us?"

"Don't be frightened!" I exclaimed. "Like you, I'm a victim of the villainous masters of this awful place, though until now with little reason to complain. I'm just as eager as you to escape."

I recounted my adventures and Monsieur de Bersac — the name of my comrade in misfortune — told me of theirs — he and his wife. They were French actors on their way home from Cadiz when the public coach in which they were traveling was robbed. The other voyagers had either fled or were killed. He and his wife had survived the murderers' rage only by promising to reveal some important secret.

Their ploy had no other aim than to buy time to find a means to escape. They told the thieves that in three days' time the French ambassador's carriage, loaded with gold and jewels, would pass along the same road. For telling the truth, they begged mercy.

Their stratagem had succeeded but it was based on a soon to be discovered deceit. How could they hope to escape?

"We must get out of here," I said to the poor man. "We must flee together; I've courage enough and skills; I've escaped many a great peril. Don't worry. Your freedom becomes as dear to me as my own. I'll manage for all of us."

The good people shed tears as they listened and swore to devote their lives to me if I succeeded in setting them free. I left them to seek a way to do it.

It seemed unlikely that the thieves would have taken the key to the room; it must be somewhere and I had only to find it. I searched everywhere, neglecting no corner of the gloomy place. At last I discovered it concealed beneath two huge bags of raiments. Grabbing it, I rushed back to open the door and warmly greet my companions:

"A fine thing, it augurs well," I said. "We're halfway. Let's work fast on the rest."

Monsieur de Bersac was a strikingly handsome man of 45; his wife, also in her forties, retained a pleasant appearance. Onstage she portrayed famous coquettes and he, the noble father.

The couple offered most tender marks of gratitude while I pressed them to make haste.

"Time to leave," I told them. "That's all that matters. Once free we can share the mutual feelings such encounters inspire. For now, let's work to escape."

They remembered as well as I the way to the staircase; we reached it and quickly went upstairs. But what then, when we found the trap door blocked shut? Bersac didn't despair but saw a gap and shouldered hard against it. A huge shrub-covered rock yielded to his efforts. We all helped him, the rock rolled back, and we got out.

To know what it's like to break free from captivity, you've got to have done it. The sensation and very air you breathe

seem new. An enormous weight seems lifted from your   o
shoulders.

Before going further, we couldn't resist the pleasure of
kissing and encouraging one another.

"Let's get going," I said, and all agreed. We'd be lost and
hopeless if the criminals came back."   5

It was then about seven o'clock in the morning and we
prepared for a long day ahead. We walked 10 leagues without
incident until sunset, toward Valladolid, reaching that city the
next day. My companions had no money and only with a tiny
sum the thieves had not thought to take from me did we man-   10
age to get that far. Those honest sensitive souls would soon
repay my frugal subsidy; for once in Valladolid, Bersac and his
wife found friends from whom came help as they'd hoped.

"Here is what belongs to you, Madame," my good friend
told me, setting before me all the money he'd just received.   15
"Please, accept this as a small mark of our gratitude. Take it and
take charge. All we ask is that you lead us to Bayonne."

"What an insult!" I told these good friends: "Would you
deprive me the pleasure of serving you? Does a soul like mine
know of any reward for good deeds besides having done them?"   20
I embraced Bersac. "Protect me in my youth like a good father
and keep me from further pitfalls. That's all I ask for my feeble
help you so esteem."

From my soulful burst of enthusiasm, which Bersac took
to heart with all possible sensitivity, he told me that, consider- 25
ing my misfortunes, my situation with my family, my desire to
find my husband, and the little money I possessed, he saw no
future for me except on the stage.

And when he saw my reluctance and fear of still new
dangers: 30

"You're wrong," he told me. "No profession in the world
better protects a woman's virtue. If her talent exposes her,

it also safeguards her; she always can use it as a reason not to engage in vice. Her voice, her figure, her health — all provide motives that serve modesty, and she can always cite them in opposing those who want to corrupt her. A woman with no such recourse must in her work risk a thousand invitations to be seduced. Our métier does not present those dangers; one is almost always paid a little more than what's necessary to live on; rarely are we exposed to the sad inconvenience of being in need. A woman with transcendent talent is respected and rarely attacked. If mediocre, modesty grants her the consideration that art deprives and she is revered in the same way. No, Léonore, don't think of the stage as a pitfall to virtue; duty delivers you from persecution and you're rewarded for it. Besides, we stick together and support one another as comrades, wholly safe from poverty and insults; and what makes our work superior to simple manual labor is that, as to the latter, virtue if you're poor is quite ridiculous while for us it improves your reputation — splendiferously. We pronounce the names Gaussin, Doligny, and Préville with respect; they'll always inspire us as to both talent and virtue. Consider too the professional amenities, so much fragrance of roses yet so few thorns. What could more gratify pride than to be idolized on stage, acclaimed by thunderous applause, as though inhaling incense at the altar, your name flying from mouth to mouth, mentioned only to praise. Men love and desire you and seek your company; women envy, imitate, and lavish you with attention. You set the tone of both fashion and style. In a word, you never make an appearance without calling forth your every sensation of pride. With good conduct the most prominent homes will open their doors and you will be welcomed with pleasure — and befriended, respected, and everywhere praised."

"You tempt me, Father." Moved, my mind was almost made   o
up. "But I have no talent and barely know French after speaking Italian, Portuguese, and Spanish for so long. My words
come out all wrong."

"That will all come back easily," said Madame de Bersac.
"Avoid those foreign tongues and accustom yourself again to   5
the rules of grammar; keep your pronunciation pure and pre-
cise as we travel together, and I assure you that by the time we
cross the Pyrenees, nobody will believe you ever left France.
Your voice is delicate and delectable, with fine pitch and broad
range, your higher register tender and harmonious higher,   10
your lower without harshness. Tears become you. You're slender and pleasant-waisted with fine shoulders, pride in your
gaze, and grace of movement. The way you talk is warm and
truthful and it's only a question of a little work for precision
and aplomb. You'll learn how to act with a little study and I'd   15
wager that, inside two months, you'd be ready for the stage."

I was convinced, I confess. The care and protection Madame de Bersac and her husband promised me, and also the
hope, while traveling from one city to the next, for news of the
one dearest to me — for all these reasons I decided to accept.   20
Straightaway they bought me books.

After dinner the next day, Madame de Bersac told her
husband that he must file complaints against the rascals from
whom we'd escaped, and to have them arrested immediately.
To me his response seemed so wise, was quite in line with my   25
own thinking, and so clearly justified my own reluctance to
denounce the inn with the collapsing bed or the Capuchin
brothers for hiding the victims of their debauchery. I always
remember his words — and hope you'll let me to repeat them:

"I forgive," he said to his wife, "your slight movements of   30
rigor and severity; you come from Spain and must retain something of the heinous and rigorist morals of the half-civilized

Moors; but understand, my dearest, that I would find it dishonorable to lead those poor men to the scaffold. They attacked me and robbed me and put me in shackles — and that's more than enough to stop me from denouncing them. That I could never do without remorse. It would be retaliation, a despicable sentiment for a sensitive soul. To be unable to endure harm is a weakness; to dismiss it is to be strong. Among men I've made the singular observation that only ignoble souls ever seek revenge; they are infinitely more susceptible to insults because they lack the strength to endure them. Owed little, they always think they can never be repaid. By contrast, the man who's gifted with a strong soul cannot imagine being touched by insult, and either pays it no attention or disdains it; vengeance would require he acknowledge something he prefers not to suspect — that arming himself against those who would harm him would mean it was possible he could be offended.

"Let vile minions for hire, entrusted with the despicable task of sending unfortunate people to their death, discover their hiding place, but I'll never show them the way. It is vile and odious to denounce those who've wronged us, a way of acting that stifles remorse and regret for the grief they caused us in a society that perforce contains such wicked people. Let others vex them; if we're victims, show forgiveness. Vengeance makes us just as guilty because, like them, we've done wrong and become equally low and base. If we forgive, our superiority remains intact. We tremble and weep at the power of *Atrée et Thyeste*; and then, too, when Guzman tells Zamor: *Observe / The difference, Zamor, 'twixt thy God and mine: / Thine teaches thee to revenge an injury / Mine to forgive and pity thee.*

"The more we know of men," continued this sweet sensitive man, "the more tolerant we should become. If these dishonest people had to mend their ways, perhaps I'd try to cure them;

but I know that's impossible and I dare say, as does a man of
great wit: *that we have no right to confer unhappiness upon
those whom we cannot make good.** Do you think that if these
people were rich that they'd exercise what you've seen is a
dreadful profession? Need alone determines it while ambition
and pride, sentiments much less to be excused, lead to the
same horrors we find done by heroes whom we glorify. Are
Bras-de-fer and his companions, who band together to rob a
coach any different from two sovereigns who form an alliance
to fleece a third? Yet, these latter expect plaudits and immortality for needless crimes while others are despised, shamed,
and tortured for crimes authorized by hunger, the most pressing need of all. Let us not interfere with evil on earth; let
us avoid being hurt by it but not engage in repression. The
famines, wars, and diseases with which Nature overwhelms
us — don't they prove that destruction is necessary and in-
herent in her principles, and only through it can she create?
If such destruction is so useful to her, if she achieves it only
through crimes that she herself commits every day — if, in a
word, crime is one of her laws — have we the right to banish it
from earth? Who authorizes us to seek revenge? Bras-de-fer's
unhappy companions, who serve Nature's intentions just like
the plague and famine — are they any guiltier than the hand
that sends us these afflictions? Why do we dare not insult one
but condemn the other? Is it only a matter of force? We tolerate evils we can't prevent but punish the authors of those we
can. Is that justice?†

---

*   Marquis de Vauvenargues.

†   The interests of society are not at issue here. Answering Bersac's objections would be
    puerile: it is a question of knowing why we punish. Certainly, the plague harms soci-
    ety as much or more than the highwayman. But we do not take revenge on the hand
    that sends the plague while we punish the thief. Why? Reply, evil partisan of laws that
    sanction murder — reply. For that is the only way to frame the question.

"Let us rely on the prudence of the wise mother who governs us all; she will always maintain an equal number of vices and virtues in proportion to her need for one or the other. When she needs virtue, she will give birth to an Augustus, Antonius, or Trajan. When murders are called for, she will send us Nero, Tiberius, Alexander, Tamerlane, famines and plagues, Grand Inquisitors and parlements. But woe to the sophist who might conclude he must take up vice or find consolation in not being virtuous in order to follow Nature's law. A man who would say: 'Because war is a necessary evil, I will start one throughout Europe' — wouldn't he be a tyrant? Similarly, a man who said: 'I must catch a fever because it is an affliction of Nature?' — wouldn't he be an idiot? Just as ridiculous is one who'd say: 'I'll plunge into crime for crime is in Nature.' What a fool! Nature to whom you blindly give yourself also produces poisons but you avoid them; take the same attitude toward crime. Flee from it and loathe it, for it will never bring you happiness. Too many eyes are watching. Too many interests keep you from acting as you wish; so, too, the interests of society that weigh upon the selfishness that leads to crime and keeps you from committing it or punishes you if you do."

Such was the reasoning of this wise friend, who didn't content himself with teaching me acting or encouraging a taste for it; he also educated my heart and fortified my reason. From him I learned the worth of my adventures; he showed me the yield I could harvest from my misfortunes. And as his distinguished spouse improved my feeble talents, by the time we'd crossed the Pyrenees I could play eight roles and was ready to make my debut.

But this is to get ahead of my story. Before we arrived in France there occurred a quite singular event, very much worth recounting.

During our journey, I was afraid of staying in cities and
especially wary of traveling the main roads. When I told Bersac of my concern, telling him about my misadventure in Madrid, he assured me that the Inquisitor would be too ashamed
of what I might say, and so would make no effort to pursue me
— that my fears were chimeric. I believed him. Consequently,
after leaving Valladolid, we spent the night in Burgos, the old
city in Castille.

Inns in Spain are both few and shabby, and one often
lacks for comfort unless wholly provisioned. Unable to procure some necessities, we made do as best we could, fortunate
to have a roof over our heads — and, indeed, to be alive after
all we'd been through. Although Burgos is the largest city in
the Two Spains, our lodgings were far worse than in Valladolid; we had to content ourselves with a dismal hotel outside
the city, consisting of a few sinister and badly partitioned little
rooms that opened one onto the other. Forgive such small details, but they're essential to understand what happened in
this miserable place.

"Who's coming to sleep here?" I asked the hostess as I
watched her making up a bed in a small room that opened
onto ours, with no separation.

"You can rest easy, good lady," she answered. "Your neighbors are as honest as yourselves. He's an Alcaide from the
Inquisition in Madrid," — and hearing that, you can imagine
how I trembled — "just wed in the capital to one of Spain's
most beautiful young ladies. He's taking her to Biscay, where
he was born and where they intend to live."

Although upset, I kept powerfully composed but quickly
told my friends of my fears. They too were apprehensive at
first but Bersac offered a quick reflection:

"This officer's intentions," he said, "seem quite remote
from what worries you. You can readily see how he must be

entirely occupied by the early pleasures of marriage and so far from any concern about you. He has turned his back on the Inquisition and is on his way to settle down in Biscay. He's harmless; don't worry. I know enough about life to assure you that this happenstance portends not the least danger."

We sat down to table and, fully reassured, I enjoyed supper as usual. Nevertheless, when the hour came to retire, we were concerned when our neighbors did not return and asked the servant why.

"The lady's new spouse," she told us, "is traveling with an old comrade and lieutenant in the dragoons, a certain Monsieur Rodolphe. The two of them get on very well and so each night go gallivanting late. But the young woman, put off like you by such tardiness, will retire awaiting her husband's return. As soon as she's in bed, all will be quiet. We've asked Don Santillana, her husband, not to make noise when he returns, so as not to disturb you."

Indeed, soon after this explanation, the young lady came upstairs, followed by the hostess. As no door separated our rooms, to afford her privacy we merely looked the other away. She went to bed and so did we.

I'd been asleep not more than an hour when I felt the sudden press against my own flesh of a naked man moving with such unambiguous urgency that I sprang awake to find my virtue imperiled as never before. I wrenched free from his embrace, jumped to the floor and ran screaming. I took refuge in the bed where I expected Madame de Bersac — and once under the covers hugged tight the woman I took to be my protector's spouse. Thereupon more piercing screams broke out until lamps were brought to cast light on the different parties to a scene both startling and bizarre.

Picture for yourself, first of all, the actor Bersac: half-naked and trembling, clutching two torches that shed angry

light at the sight of another man, also naked, fulfilling with
Madame de Bersac the marital duties that properly belonged
to him alone. Whilst I — who thought myself tight in her embrace, found myself in reality hugging for dear life — who?

None other than Clémentine.

Poor Clémentine — companion of so many of my misfortunes and adventures, whom I'd left wailing laments in
the dank dark prisons of Madrid!

How can I depict for you the sentiment and shock all
around? What words could picture Bersac, enraged at the
sight of the all too real crime just brought to light as his wife,
realizing her mistake, screamed in despair — whilst the fellow
who'd embarrassed them both hastily slipped away into the
darkness, fleeing the woman he'd dishonored and the husband
he'd outraged. To complete the picture, imagine Clémentine
and I together again in the same bed, kissing and embracing,
excitedly plying one other with questions, too delighted to
wait for answers.

Let's not linger over this singular tableau or your attention would flag. Let me quickly explain.

Clémentine was in fact the young woman sleeping in the
adjacent room — and now the cherished spouse of the officer,
Santillana, with whom she was on her way to Biscay. We shall
return to the events that brought her here but for now let me
continue because, as to the debauchery of the two friends, the
second of them was none other than — Brigandos.

Yes: *Brigandos.*

Who, under the name of Rodolphe and with Clémentine's
help, as I'll soon explain, had managed to escape the Inquisition. Tonight's carousing with Santillana had lasted longer and
gone further than intended, and it was at once the reason for
their late return and the confusion that put Rodolphe in Clémentine's bed and the officer of the Inquisition in mine. But by
unbelievable chance, the double mistake was compounded

when Bersac answered Nature's call. He had just left his bed when Clémentine recognized that her husband was not the man beside her. Her screams caused Brigandos to take flight and he barged into the actor's path as he fled, knocking him down the stairs. Furious, Bersac had jumped to his feet, grabbed a pair of torches from the nearby dining room and courageously mounted the stairs to discover the why and wherefore. Only to find Santillana, who had first clambered into my bed, but scared out of it by my loud reception, beneath the covers with Madame de Bersac. And he'd been treating her as husband to his wife while I fled to the bed in which — it so happened — lay not the actor's wife but Clémentine.

Such were the causes for tumult and both Bersac's stunned astonishment and the young officer's flight as he jumped from bed to bed, not finding his own.

Unfortunately, the *faux pas* with Madame de Bersac caused distress even more dire. A single moment is enough to bring dishonor upon the most modest woman alive, and for the actor's good wife, that moment had come. On one side, a young and vigorous man in no mood to be patient and on the other, a woman half-asleep who thought she was receiving her spouse's proper embrace. That was all it took; the deed was done. Madame de Bersac was the first to tell all. She fell to her knees before her husband and demanded he avenge the revolting outrage she'd just suffered.

With her words the scene changed. Melpomene's somber tones took the place of Thalia's gracious shades. Clémentine and I saw gloom descend and I rushed to introduce my friend, who implored mercy for her husband. Honest Santillana kneeled before Madame de Bersac to beg forgiveness for a fortuitous mistake; then, turning to her husband, he pressed him to take reprisals and said he'd not defend himself. All grew still for a moment as we observed and reflected.

"O Bersac!" I cried. "My protector! You inspired me to   o
clemency and now you must set an example yourself. And
Madame," I continued, taking Angelique's hands in mine,
"don't darken one of the happiest days of my life — one that's
returned to my bosom a friend feared lost."

"Consider me, dear woman," coaxed Clémentine with the   5
grace and naiveté she could so capably muster, "as the first to
be offended and in truth the only one who should be angry.
Let's everyone forget all about it."

"I agree," said Bersac. "It would weigh too heavily on my
conscience if I troubled Léonore's happiness in any way." He   10
said to his wife: "Think it no more. If I didn't know you so well,
Madame, and if you'd ever committed a wrong your whole
life long, such an accident might have upset me; but a woman
who's been chaste for 20 years can't discredit herself in 15 minutes. Your innocence is intact." Turning to the officer: "And   15
you, Monsieur. Let me take you to be my friend if you're husband to the woman Léonore loves most in the whole world.
Let's forgive and forget."

"Charming, Monsieur, charming," said Clémentine, de-
lightfully vivacious, so pleasant with her pretty French accent.   20
"And gallant. But to prove worthy of your esteem and beg your
pardon, though it's late, let's spend the night together and
allow me to offer you something to eat. We'll laugh all of us
at an event that in the end has done nobody any harm. We'll
enjoy ourselves until the fatal hour strikes and we go our   25
separate ways."

Everyone agreed. Bersac accepted, his wife was consoled,
and we called back Brigandos, who'd been bruised by his
collision with the actor; they hugged one another less violently while I rushed to embrace my old Chief and confessed   30
my great pleasure in seeing him again. Throughout the inn
resounded with laughter and joy.

After onion soup and grilled toast soaked in Madeira wine, gay and mischievous and always lovely Clémentine recounted how she'd escaped the clutches of the Inquisition with the help of the young man beside her, from whom she assured me that, fugitive though I was, I'd nothing to fear. She was happy too for having freed our Chief thanks to her lover. It was the least she could do and deeply satisfying to be able to repay Brigandos for the help we'd received when we had no idea what would become of us after the disaster at Lisbon, when the honest Bohemian offered shelter and the hand of humanity.

After I'd been taken from the torture chamber, she explained, it had been too late for another interrogation, so the tribunal had dismissed her with orders that she be returned the next day for the rope torture. But meanwhile, the Inquisitor, as you know, wanted the room next to mine and so he had her brought to another part of the prison. It was there she fell under the authority of Santillana, in whom she inspired the liveliest passion; he opened his heart and she heard him out; she accepted with the proviso that required both Brigandos' freedom and her own — delightful, this young woman who at that critical moment was more concerned with others than for herself. Santillana promised and gave her the best possible advice, carefully protecting her, not only saving her from further interrogation but also working to help her and the Chief escape. He then resolved to quit his infamous profession, which he'd taken up during his troubled youth, and which was made possible thanks to a legacy provided by a wealthy uncle in Biscay who had recently died. Thus he decided to flee with his beloved, to marry her outside the gates of Madrid, and take her with him to collect the inheritance that would provide quite nicely for both of them.

All this proved successful and Brigandos, escaping with
Santillana's help, had waited for them 10 leagues outside Madrid. The young couple took up their journey, so in love and
more charmed than ever by one another that Clémentine
resolved to renounce her wayward youth and devote herself
to the felicity of the amiable young man who'd sacrificed everything for her. As to my companion's missteps in the past,
Santillana was well aware of them; however, when Brigandos
mentioned as much to the others, Madame de Bersac seemed
surprised:

"Look here, Madame," said our Chief, engaging in his in-
clination for philosophical dissertation, which always brought
forth erudition, "is it not a foolish prejudice to demand a
woman's fidelity even before her husband meets her? Must
she owe something to a spouse whose existence she doesn't
even suspect?"

"But one might fear," said Madame de Bersac, "that a woman
who's unchaste before marriage might remain so thereafter."

"Such reasoning is unjust, Madame," replied our Chief.
"Only the most illusory constraints require a young woman to
preserve her virginity. If she carefully guards it only because
of paternal domination, that's nothing but her own weakness
and ignorance. Nothing obliges her to do so and parental authority, to be fair, cannot go so far as to demand the chastity
of a daughter — that is to say, a state of affairs quite opposed
to Nature. She's free to dispose of her maidenhead; she's made
no pact or promise. She answers only to herself and the only
reason parents seem to hold some power about the matter is
based wholly on greed and ambition; they fear not being able
to marry off their daughters and so force them to respect the
flower of virginity; but their reasoning, motivated solely by
paternal interest, is null in the eyes of the child. If daughters
obey, they've served their fathers' passion at the expense of

their own; in other words, acted stupidly, giving far more than they receive, for the passions they relinquish are far more imperious than those to which they sacrifice themselves. If you object that prejudice nevertheless condemns them — that's an infamy, unthinking barbarism, and inane idiocy seen only in the rural districts of Europe. Let's quickly review the customs of peoples who do better."

"Although Brazilians, Scythians, and Lapps used to prostitute young women to foreigners who nevertheless later married them; a visitor to Pegu rents a woman for the length of his stay in that country, despite which the concubine can afterwards find a husband. Among the Tartars beyond Tibet, each of the men who has been with a woman presents her with finery that she always wears, and her ability to find a husband depends on such proofs of libertinage as she can display. Herodotus assured us that the women of Lydia had no other dowry than their earnings from prostitution. According to Justin, the women of Cyprus would acquire a dowry by going to the port to give themselves to visiting foreigners. When we say a Circassian woman has no lovers, we insult her. Among the young women of the cult of Astarte, in the temple of Byblos, were practiced the most extraordinary kinds of promiscuity, yet without it none could later have found a spouse. Just as no man would marry an Armenian woman if the priests of Tanais had not already abused her in every way — and I say *in every way* because it was a central custom of these people, and what by our lights would be moral infamy, the harlotry had to be so thorough and complete that every temple of love received its worshipers. As Herodotus and Strabon tell us, this was how the women of Babylon were obliged to offer up their virginity to the Temple of Venus and the associated cult of the Callipygian Venus in Greece confirms what I'm telling you: in all antiquity, no restriction. Quite simply,

Madame, all wise peoples thought that promiscuity ought in   o
no way constitute an obstacle for a young woman; and several
only valued women under these conditions, believing with
much wisdom that the woman who's more sought after is the
more deserving; and if she were ignored it was because she
was mediocre — and must we take such a woman for a wife?   5
If really wise, a man should unquestionably prefer a libertine
for a spouse than a woman who's only served modesty; and
he should stop thinking that such modesty, treasured only by
ugly women, is worth a whit to anybody else. Hesitant husbands needn't worry. The same woman who's immodest when   10
unattached will become honest once wedded; faults committed when unmarried are no reason to presume she will not
rigorously revere the bonds of marriage. Men who are sensitive on this account can go find a bride among widows. But to
condemn women, to abandon them, to constrain them to the   15
horrors of a convent or reduce them to celibacy because of
some fault committed in the passion of youth — almost never
due to their weakness but the result of seduction — is a fault
that only proves they have everything one wants in an excellent spouse. Such harshness, Madame, is horrible and only a   20
nation still mired in darkness could be guilty of disregarding
the most sacred laws of reason, Nature and humanity."

    Angélique capitulated. Monsieur de Bersac, who perhaps
took consolation in Brigandos' argument, appreciated his system of thought, eloquence, and erudition; and the conversa-   25
tion turned to other topics.

    As to what had happened to me, Clémentine said that it
was such a closely guarded secret in the prison that she could
learn no news whatever. She thought I must be dead and often
expressed her grief to Santillana who, although a house officer,   30
was similarly kept in the dark. With no clue as to the fate of
Brigandos' troupe, and so worried about me and our kindly

chief, she had little time to think about the others. Brigandos believed that his two children were victims of the Inquisition; he would have given his life to save them but, unable to do so, he made the best of what he had and, not turning his back on his métier, intended to form a new troupe in Biscay with plans to cross into Italy.

Monsieur and Madame de Bersac, who had developed a lively interest in Clémentine based on stories I'd told them, were delighted to meet her.

"The only thing that bothers me," said Bersac, smiling despite himself, "is that my honor was the price of getting to know her."

"Honor!" exclaimed Clémentine, trying to rekindle the gaiety she feared would dissipate with recollection of the sorry catastrophe. "You're terribly wrong, Monsieur, if you think men's honor owes to women's behavior. What do you care what we do? You're foolish to pay attention to it. Your twinge of pain at our promiscuity is all in your imagination. Change your way of thinking, it's of no account. Our husbands ought to be fair and not constrain us with a yoke you'd be loath to wear yourselves; far from being shocked by the pleasures we dare taste without you, you should be sufficiently refined to provide them yourselves. Our obligatory gratitude should appear voluptuous to your sensitive souls. You should understand that if we're occasionally moved by others, what is far more precious depends upon a soul that more than ever belongs to you alone, and you only bind us more closely when you loosen the fetters. I'm only telling you what I think but if I were a man, that's how I'd behave. If I were sure enough of the pleasures I provided yet afraid of not offering my wife enough of them, I'd urge her to find them with my friends and regard her acceptance of same as proof of her amity and trust; and I'd thank her a hundred times for the happiness she brought me by letting me facilitate her own.

"To observe her ecstasy, Monsieur, shows the sensitivity of a well-organized soul; it's not merely a question of being happy yourself, or of making your wife happy only when you're happy. Felicity must spread amongst them, even at your expense; and don't imagine that a woman ought to be pitied or dishonored because of some passing pleasure distant from the overwhelming constraints of marriage."

Bersac asked Clémentine's new husband if he had adopted this system himself.

"Most certainly, Monsieur," answered the kindly young man. "You'll see me share her without fail and with all those who make my wife happy."

The entire company applauded these principles. Not even grave Bersac himself could resist. Only chaste Angélique, with a sidelong glance at Santillana, whispered: *"Your wife is mad... and you're reckless... such things cannot be done... I don't understand how I could've been fooled for even a moment."*

A cheerful honest spirit reigned the rest of the night until the moment of departure, which drew sharp tears from Clémentine and myself with a thousand promises to write one another — as we've continued to do ever since, and I can assure you she lives happy, healthy, and wealthy with a husband who adores her and who considers it his daily duty to assure her felicity. Brigandos left with them; not without emotion did I separate from that true friend.

Our own journey continued untroubled as we crossed the mountains in good order and soon arrived in Bayonne. Although my friends' original destination was Bordeaux, their talents were so widely known and admired in France that they were asked to stay over. There they contracted with the director for 20 performances, but only on condition that I would make my stage debut in that city and my emerging talents be encouraged.

So it was that my first appearance came in *Iphigénia* by Racine and Lucinda in *The Oracle*. But I was so frightened that without the strong support of Monsieur and Madame de Bersac, I might've quit the stage no sooner I mounted it. Yet the next day, supported by my friends, I appeared as Junie in *Britannicus*, then in *Zénéide* with much more confidence and won enthusiastic applause. The third day things went still better as I played Rosalie in *Mélanide* and Betti in *La Jeune Indienne*. Finally, the fourth day I had the role of Sophie in *Père de Famille* and it became my capstone. My success was acknowledged, and in reprises of my debut roles, together with new ones I studied each day, I played nearly two months at Bayonne to generous applause. The day I played in *Zénéide*, that evening brought to the foyer some charming verses together with a most pressing invitation to dinner.

"Ah! Dreams fulfilled," I told myself, "but now come the pitfalls that could be my ruin. Courage! If they're all like this, I'll easily triumph. At least decency and good manners embellish them. I needn't fear violence."

Not wanting to make enemies and following Madame de Bersac's advice, I declined with equal measures of honesty and gratitude. When this became known the next day I was even more acclaimed.

In Bayonne I earned enough to repay my friends for their expense in bringing me to the stage with such success but they adamantly refused and I had to give up trying; only in Bordeaux did Madame de Bersac accept a little jewelry worth 50 or 60 louis.

At last we arrived in Bordeaux. My appearance in this city was expected and I daresay even desired. I was about to go onstage to perform when there befell me this great good fortune: to come upon the one whom I adore the best and for whom I'd searched so keenly and eagerly the whole world over.

"You know the rest, Madame," *said Léonore.* "Heaven made amends for enduring so much misfortune by joining unexpected prosperity to the pleasure of reuniting with my husband and the gift of a mother. O! Madame" — she added, flinging herself into the arms of the President — "How by such rewards may pain be forgotten!"

Here Sainville's beautiful spouse ended her story and, as it was late, after mutual expressions of tenderness and affection, all retired except Madame de Blamont and the Count de Beaulé, who spent the rest of the night discussing what must be done to complete the young couple's happiness. Their decisions, which they have kindly imparted to me, will be the subject of my next letter. Some of them are rather long and you'll deserve an apology if what they contain does not reward, as it seems to me they do, the time it takes to read them. I embrace you.

Letter XXXIX
Déterville to Valcour

Vertfeuille, 24 October

Now we are alone, my dear Valcour — no more pretending.
Our illustrious voyagers have left. We can judge them at our
leisure. But as these reflections may intrude upon the pleasure you take in knowing what has been decided for them,
I'll start by telling you: they departed yesterday with Count
Beaulé, with whom they are to stay in Paris until leaving for
Brittany. The first thing we must do is contend with the *lettre
de cachet* obtained by Sainville's father; the Count will take
care of it. The young couple will then present themselves at
court, which should work in their favor, in terms both of their
character and disposition and by the singularity of their adventures. The Count believes they are bound to have some
success and will excite much interest and curiosity. All other
arrangements, which I provided in detail in my letter of the
17th, will be hewn to irrevocably. We will tell the President
nothing concerning the birth of Léonore and continue to ignore the fact he demanded the legal abduction of one of these
young women in place of the other, an abomination about
which we'd best keep silent. The young people, escorted by
good counsel, will then leave for Rennes, where the plan I described will be executed to the letter. Furthermore, Monsieur
de Beaulé, wholly and infinitely committed to them, will convince the minister to write to Spain to obtain however much
as possible of the gold confiscated by the Inquisition; and if
he succeeds, legal course will follow for restitution of the assets of Mademoiselle de Kerneuil. You can see the kind of immense fortune that might come their way before a year is out.
Do they deserve it? For him, I'd say so. But as for her, I'll not

conceal how little she appeals to me. At first Léonore much   0
pleased Madame de Blamont, whose soul is made to love everybody without reflection and all who are unhappy; but that
charming woman, who initially harbored some illusions concerning this new daughter of hers, without losing the desire
to be useful, has begun to look upon her with far more clarity.   5

It's quite evident, so far as I can see, that reverses and
setbacks have shaped Léonore in head and heart. It is certain,
first of all, that she has lost any religious sentiments that she
may have been exposed to as a child; she says she had given
them up completely before her adventures; but I believe the   10
people she had to deal with in her voyages damaged her far
more than any reading she might have done. In this she dem-
onstrates a steadfastness very surprising for her age, and as her
husband allows her the greatest freedom of belief, she invokes
her principles with powers of reasoning unfortunately very   15
strong, blaming them for the impossibility of her now returning to be what she once was. It has been difficult to broach
the subject despite the consideration she owes everyone here
and the strong interest she ought to have, it seems to me, in
keeping up appearances. She has obstinately refused opportu-   20
nities for simple piety. The day before yesterday, for example,
a holiday, we went to advise her about mass; she crisply told
her lackey that she never goes to church and that Madame
de Blamont knew the reasons why. When we returned she
apologized nicely but nevertheless in a way to make it un-   25
derstood that her principles were unassailable. And this unfortunately I believe goes further than nonobservance of her
country's religion. It preoccupies her. Deep down I suppose
her to be an atheist; several of her arguments persuade me of
it. Her refutations of Clémentine's views and her confession   30
at the Inquisition, due to circumstance alone, don't fool me

for a minute.* I am quite sure, my friend, that she believes in nothing. She only explains herself with a laugh: the *servants of God* set such bad examples that they gave rise in her to a great many doubts about the real existence of *their master*. If one seeks to prove that her reasoning is weak, that flaws in the work prove nothing against the existence of the Maker, she jokes and says that she believes as much as one likes in *this existence* and that she will be better persuaded still, with no more unhappiness to fear, when she is rich. But nothing stops us from guessing with whom we must contend or from forming a judgment about her.

Let us examine her virtues. I don't see where she has even adopted those that the brigands she frequented provided as examples; and her soul, either not naturally sensitive or undermined by misfortune (no matter what we say, the most dangerous school of all) — her soul, I say, refuses to be moved and admits in no way the delights of doing good deeds. Pity, gratitude, generosity, the ability to love (except where her husband is concerned), all the sentiments of the soul, in a word, are in her more simply manners for show, not to be felt; and further analysis, in bringing out the self that her worldly polish conceals, may reveal all the faults of a woman of wit — and, we will see, perhaps much cruelty. Lack of sensitivity does not come naturally to such a soul.† Léonore cannot be indifferent and must possess great virtues and great vices;

---

* The reader will recall that on the two occasions cited, Léonore claimed to be a deist.

† An excess of sensitivity, says Marmontel, devolves into insensitivity. Would that not be the case with the character of Léonore? A great many offenses owe to such an excess and are the unique result of this stage; they can be controlled by the simplest and gentlest means but, instead, we punish them and so they propagate. *O! mass killers, jailers, imbeciles of every reign and government! When will you prefer the science of man to that of imprisonment and murder!*

and as her virtues owe to Nature while her vices are the work   o
of principles, she never adopts a single one without reason.
If before the age of eighteen she was stoic enough to extinguish in herself any form of pity, perhaps she will be more
extreme at age forty. Wisdom supported only by pride cedes
to passions stronger than that sentiment; and when principles   5
do not restrain but tend to be all-destructive, when lapses
of head meet no barrier in qualities of the heart but, to the
contrary, the firm apathy of the latter allows the former to
escape everything that irritates or delights it, a woman can
create trouble more serious than the misdeeds of Theodora   10
or Messalina; for those afflict only morality, unlike others that
lead, ineluctably, to crime.*

The other day, after watching Madame de Blamont help
the poor, as she is wont to do when they come begging, Léonore
jested about it with an unfeeling air that pleased no one. She   15
went so far as to refuse to emulate her mother. With a touch
of irritation, Madame de Blamont asked her the reason why.

"You have been unhappy yourself," said that tender and
compassionate woman. "How can you have undergone so
much without learning to allay the pain of the downtrodden?"   20

She replied that she did so by principle, just as with
every one of her actions in life; that there was nothing more
dangerous than giving alms to the poor; that this served to
foster poverty and sloth; that it helped the awful vermin in
this country multiply as beggars, soiling and dishonoring it;   25
that if all hearts were like hers, set against this kind of useless

---

* And to crimes all the more dangerous in that we disclose and punish them; it would
be a hundred times better to suppress them than make them known. The publicity
surrounding the trials of La Voisin and Madame de Brinvilliers generated crimes of
the same kind; better, in the interest of public morals, if certain crimes we never even
dare suspect.

pity, those poor people, now sure of being able to live at the expense of dupes, would never have abandoned their métiers, provinces, or their families, whom thereby they deprive of help. Such men, endowed with everything necessary to make excellent workers, grew lazy owing to the habitual aid they received without lifting a finger, and it became simpler to pretend afflictions than to put themselves in a state not to suffer from them, all with the result that what we take to be good works turn out to be something quite the opposite.

"Just because I myself have known misfortune," she continued, "I can see how you can succeed without help from others; and if I'd been refused such aid as sometimes came my way from those like Gaspard and Bersac, I'd only have had to do more and more cleverly to counter the blows of fortune and turn them in my favor. Do you know" — here she turned to address her mother — "what will become of the man to whom you gave alms? If ever your charity stops, he might well become a thief. Accustomed to idleness and money given to him for no effort other than to ask for it honestly, he'll demand it when you no longer provide, pistol in hand."

"All these are clever and witty sophisms," responded Madame de Blamont. "They may be true, but I dislike finding them in your heart. Let a man ask me, whether poor or no, if the alms I gave him are well or badly placed; he has greatly moved me by his request and made me experience palpable pleasure in helping him. For me that's enough. If he's an idler for whom work is apparently painful, he may get still more pleasure; but mine is a reflection of his, so I am not less happy. What I am I saying? In fact, I'm all the happier because my aid to the idler provided him more pleasure than if I had helped one who struggles. Suppose for a moment, as you do, that it isn't right to encourage laziness. Is it not a greater wrong to not help the less fortunate? I'd rather do a minor wrong to

prevent an enormous one than commit an enormous wrong   o
for fear of making a small one."

"It is no *enormous wrong* to not relieve misfortune, Madame," responded Léonore. "There is only the inconvenience
of seeing it fester alongside those very real dangers I just noted.
The enormous wrong you talk about is rather to nurture sloth   5
with the result that every day not a few end up on the gallows.
What could be worse? But however that may be, you will do it,
as you say, because you take pleasure in doing so.

"We can deny such pleasures, let's note, or at least not
feel them as you do; but what good have you done inasmuch   10
as you acted for yourself alone? Is selfishness a virtue? And
does it not become a very dangerous vice if it results in the
almost certain death of the unfortunate one that just gave you
such pleasure? Let's not stop there. Suppose you've one hundred louis you can just throw out the window. You've been of-   15
fered a jewel you might buy, on the one hand, and then there's
some downtrodden individual. After having considered for a
moment, you renounce the jewel and give the money to the
beggar. Do you think you've done something good? You've
certainly ceded to the most imperious movement, and been   20
more taken by the pleasure of helping someone out of poverty — and deserving his gratitude — instead of procuring a
jewel for yourself. You did what made you happier and you
worked only to satisfy yourself. In giving to charity, you've
thus done no good deed — intense pleasure but no clear vir-   25
tue. Yet what will become of this choice after it's proved to you
there's nothing good about it and you're made to see just how
it could prove disastrous? In buying the jewel, you support
industry and encourage the arts; in preferring alms, you've
only helped a slaggard, an ingrate or a libertine who, as I just   30
said, if he doesn't find a purse like yours tomorrow, will go the
next day to pry one open with a dagger. Refusal and resistance,

all those truly virtuous movements that you like to qualify
as harsh, provide the unfortunate with the energy that your
charity would deplete: turned down everywhere, he was going
to look for work so that what you call harshness would make
of him a productive fellow while your misplaced charity sends
him sooner or later to be hanged.

"But as to comparing charity dispensed with a jewel
bought, let's go further. Take the low and imbecilic pleasure
of skipping coins across water — indeed, in delivering yourself to such childishness, you would've done something less
wrong than caring for ne'er-do-wells because in any case the
money is lost to you — without inconvenience in the first instance, but considerably so in the other, despite your efforts
to conceal as much by using pompous names such as 'charity'
and 'humanity,' as if the spirit of those virtues did not consist
in being hard in order to save men rather than destroy them
with compassion."

"As you like," said Madame de Blamont. "But you contest
me concerning the sort of pleasure that we experience in caring
for the unfortunate, and I don't like it that you dispute me so."

"And why is that, Madame?" was Léonore's lively response.
"Are each of our souls made the same? Must they all feel the
same things? Pity acts upon them only by dint of their being
soft; the more vigorous an individual, the less susceptible to
that sort of affront. From this it would follow, and it speaks
in favor of my view, that the soul least open to pity would
incontestably be the best organized; but let's analyze the fashionable sentiment that goes today by many pretty names yet is
actually less frequently felt than ever. Proof that this pusillani-
mous sentiment acts upon us physically, and that the moral
shock it imprints is wholly subordinate to that of the senses,
comes clear when we feel sorrier for a bad action done before
our eyes than one that takes place a hundred leagues distant.

If you see Monsieur, for example," — and now Léonore point-   o
ed to me — "cutting his finger, the sight of blood will move
you far more just because you're witness to it than if you
learned Monsieur had broken his leg two hundred leagues
away. The latter event, only acting upon your soul at a distance, would affect it far less than would the finger sliced open   5
with a penknife beneath your eyes. You would complain more
about the latter, which amounts to nothing, than you would
of the other, undoubtedly more important. So it is with pity,
a weakness and not a virtue, for it acts upon us only by reason of the received impression, of the vibration it makes upon   10
the fibers of our soul in function of the distance to misfortune. Why do you not wish we be protected from a weakness
that's never good except for other people, and which brings us
nothing but trouble?"

　　"Such insensitivity is frightful!" said Madame de Blamont.   15

　　"Yes — to the ordinary soul," responded Léonore, "But
not for those who possess a certain mettle. Some souls appear hard due in fact to their susceptibility to emotions; they
themselves actually experience more intensely what some
take to be indifference or cruelty. There are sensations not   20
known by everyone, whose refinement comes only from *déli-*
catesse, making it possible for someone to possess a great deal
of it even while being stirred in ways that by appearance seem
to exclude it.* What am I saying? That final excess of refinement makes for the most irritated souls; and the result is pro-   25
nounced vexation, an apparent and surprising contradiction
between the sensations of a soul simply organized and one of
the sort I'm trying to depict. From such confusion can arise
an experience that would vividly affect the former in one way
and the latter completely differently. Such marked contrasts   30

---

*　See the footnote on p. 638.

in organization explain why systems of thought, such as those of morality, can be both the cause of vice and basis of virtue. Once admitted, it's also easy to see that I may be entirely insensitive to what moves you, yet extraordinarily tickled by what causes you pain. We are not less sensitive either of us; violent shocks equally unsettle our souls. But those that strike mine are not of a sort for yours. How often are our impressions due only to habit of prejudice? How could sensations in a soul accustomed to vanquishing prejudice and rattling the chains of habit be like those of a soul in thrall to the dictates of principle? Here it is only a matter of being sufficiently philosophical to be able to receive the *most singular* impressions and consequently to enable an extraordinary extension of the sphere of pleasure.

"One can scarcely imagine," Léonore concluded, "what might be found beneath the debris of all these vulgar restraints. So long as we constrain Nature to our petty views, as much as we chain her to vile prejudices, ever confounding them with her own voice, we shall never come to know her. Who knows but that we must go much further to understand what she wants to tell us? Could you understand the voice of one who speaks to you if you throttle the organ that produces it? Let us study Nature. Let us follow her to frontiers furthest from ourselves and work to extend but never prescribe them. Let nothing hide Nature from our gaze or obstruct her impressions. Whatever they might be, we must respect them all; it is not for us to analyze them; we are made but to follow them. Let us learn how to treat her as a coquette, this unintelligible Nature, and dare offend her to better enjoy her."

"My poor thing," said Madame de Blamont, tightly embracing Léonore, "stop adopting the errors of those who made you so unhappy. They were imbued with those systems, the very same that cast you into the abyss by not allowing you to

marry the one you cherished. Those maxims belong to the vil- ○
lains who wanted to sell you help in Lisbon at the price of your
honor; so too did they fill the hearts of those who dragged you
through Madrid's dark dungeons. If you detest these monsters
and are right to hate them, why do you want to be like them?

"O! Léonore! Prefer the morality of those who love you 5
and abjure those principles, the bitter sterile fruit of which
provides only frightful pleasures — frenzied for a moment,
soon fraught with remorse. What refuge could you find anywhere on earth if everybody was like those whom you depict?
Your foolish blindness concerning our religious dogma is only 10
the result of a perversity that insidiously established itself in
your heart. Let sentiment from deep within bring about what
persuasion cannot. Here you see me, your unhappy mother,
in tears, urging you to love the good because your happiness
depends upon it, begging you to let her enjoy the hope that it 15
will endure as long as she lives and beyond. Would you rob her
of that consolation! Overwhelmed by her miseries and with a
heavy heart that may soon send her to her grave, would you
have her suppose that tender sensitivity would be her only
share in exchange for the hopelessness of her sorry existence? 20
And that once freed from those bonds, such sentiment would
count for nothing? Offer me no such sad, sorry future. Let
me console myself and ease my sufferings with the certainty
that they will come to an end beside the God I worship. *Lord,
divine and consoling, penetrate the soul that refuses your rap-* 25
turous majesty; would that you not punish her for its harden-
ing that owes only to misfortune."

Then, pressing her to her breast:

"Come, daughter, by and through the tenderness of your
adoring mother, grasp the idea of a Supreme Being. You can 30
see within her soul, by your presence blossom'd, the image of
a God who beckons you. By love's sentiments, let that image

come clear. And since we're not destined to live together, at least don't extinguish the pleasant hope of reuniting with me one day, at the foot of His throne of glory."

Everything could be found in this discourse, at once sensitive, eloquent, and captivating. But it had no effect. Léonore coldly kissed her mother. She remarked more icily still that she would always try to adopt her virtues and that if she had any regrets in being unable to live with her, it was because she readily saw that her conversion could only be achieved at the side of such an amiable mother. When Madame de Blamont realized that the ardent sparks from her own heart had in no way kindled her daughter's, she seized Aline by the arm and wept, and the two of them went off together.

Oh my friend! What a gulf separates the two daughters! Where in Léonore do we find the virtues constantly reborn within the heart of your Aline! It is assuredly impossible for two sisters to resemble one another less. You may find that the impressions I offer concerning Léonore's character don't altogether agree with the way she talked with her companion Clémentine — whose wrongs she was always trying to right.

"But that," she said in reply when we brought it up, "was merely a matter of establishing with my good but imprudent friend some principles about prudent behavior. Those were the topics of our discussions; as to principles, I never wavered, but they required no further commitment or acquiescence to error. One can be, in a word, virtuous in thought, character, and temperament — without being obliged to adopt a thousand absurd systems that have nothing to do with virtue."

We brought her to see Sophie. Aline went with her and we told her the story of that unhappy creature so worthy of a better fate — and whose life, so singularly of a fabric like her own, ought for that reason alone have been of interest to her. But she listened coolly, and the entire time they were together

she spoke to her in a tone of haughty superiority. The immense o
fortune awaiting her might suggest she offer some help and
she could have skirmished over the honor of doing so with
Madame de Blamont; but the idea never even occurred to her.
Sainville made up for this harsh negligence. With his infinitely
more sensitive soul — sensitive, that is, in an entirely different 5
way — he rarely lets escape the occasion to do a good deed.
On many things he may think like his wife but he surely has
not the same heart. Madame de Blamont refused his offers;
she said that Sophie was still her dear daughter and she would
never abandon her; and the unhappy young woman, always so 10
fine, tearfully said to Aline, squeezing her hand:

"Oh, Mademoiselle. Is she then your sister? She's happier
than I. May felicity be hers!"

However that may be, in spite of what little satisfaction
Madame de Blamont has drawn from it all, she is firm in refus- 15
ing nothing to Léonore by way of helping her regain the assets
of Madame de Kerneuil; she will serve, she and her friends,
and use all her power even though she experiences a kind of
repugnance owing to what she believes to be something ille-
gitimate in the process. For Aline, in spite of the extreme dis- 20
tance that separates her temperament from that of Léonore,
nevertheless loves her no less tenderly. An honest soul never
finds, in the faults of those she must cherish, any reason to extinguish her feelings. She silently weeps and never grows cold.

I imagine that by the time you receive this letter you will 25
have already seen the subject in question and will have formed
your own judgment. *Adieu*, my dear Valcour, you ought to be
pleased with me this summer; I think it would have been impossible to conduct a correspondence more frequent or more
closely detailed. Expect nothing further, as we are leaving for 30
Paris and soon enough we will talk together *tête-à-tête*.

Letter XL
Valcour to Madame de Blamont

Paris, 30 November

After receiving so much interesting news from your chateau, Madame, it falls to me to provide you some from Paris. Yesterday I went to see Monsieur de Beaulé and while there had the honor to greet Monsieur and Madame the Countess of Karmeil. Both of them invited me to attend, early next morning, the religious formalities of their marriage; these brief ceremonies are to take place at St. Roch in the presence and with the approval of Monsieur de Karmeil, the young man's father. As secrecy was agreed to by all, you would not be involved in any way and your consent is requested only tacitly.

Rescinding the *lettre de cachet* took just 24 hours. The Count de Karmeil came around with the greatest of ease to share the opinions and counsels of Monsieur de Beaulé; together they sought out the minister and the affair was immediately concluded. Sainville, if you will permit me to continue to use that name, was delighted to embrace and restore relations with his father, whom he'd always cherished at the bottom of his heart; and it was not without tears that the latter received his son's sincere effusions of tenderness. The question of 100,000 écus abided in his memory; but Monsieur de Beaulé convinced him that Spanish ingots ought to make him forget that youthful folly; and in concert with the minister, they at once wrote a letter to attempt to recover them.

The assets of Mademoiselle de Kerneuil are many times divided. There are a great number of collateral heirs, and whatever else may come from the presence of this young lady, we fear litigation.

We've retained Bonneval, the lawyer you suggested, who   o
will accompany them to Brittany, where Monsieur de Karmeil
was intending a short visit when his son arrived in Paris; he
will return to the city with the young couple. The constraints
he'd placed on his son's choice of a spouse no longer apply
because the threat of litigation against him has ended. We   5
insist that you, Madame, shoulder absolutely no part of the
legal costs. Monsieur de Karmeil will take care of everything
and make arrangements with Sainville. These young people
may turn out to own a considerable fortune. The minister is
assured of returning with at least 2,000,000 in gold ingots.   10
That represents an annuity of 100,000 livres, with the estate
of Madame de Kerneuil bringing in about 50,000 and the
same amount from Monsieur de Karmeil. That makes at least
200,000 livres and still much more if all the ingots are recovered. Léonore watched us do the accounts the other day and   15
the way she trembled with joy proved to me she loves money.
    She has until now appeared only at the Opera, where
her adventures have become known by word of mouth and all
eyes are upon her. She is thought to be very pretty, knows that
people think so, and does not seem to mind. Her expression is   20
certainly lively and animated; she is graceful, has a delightful
figure, and possesses much wit and spirit. Perhaps a bit pre-
tentious, I might add, and affected; there are many sophisms
in the way she reasons. But you must excuse me, Madame, for
when I discuss one who belongs to you, though my head may   25
find fault, the hand that follows my heart must depict only
qualities.
    So I escorted her to the Opera. Monsieur de Beaulé
wants me to do the same in other venues. She would like to
see *Le Père de famille* at the Théâtre-Français and *Lucile* at the   30
Théâtre-Italien. She will enjoy herself. I like the motivation that
makes her want to see *Le Père de famille*; she cherishes every-

thing that recalls the happy moment when she was reunited with the man she loves. So, nevertheless, she is sensitive.

This letter, Madame, would never end if I set out to detail for you all the virtues I have discovered in Monsieur de Sainville. The Count de Beaulé wants me to be his friend; in truth it requires little effort. Kindness, affability, talent, wit, and intelligence — he has all one needs to be a friend to all men and beloved by all women.

Ah! Madame! Only I'm so unhappy, 'twixt fear and hope whilst I see the best days of my life darkened by tears and suffering! Might you at least allow me to pay my respects? Finding ourselves in the same city, will you permit me to throw myself at your feet? My happiness is in your hands alone. Who better than you would know if my sufferings deserve to be rewarded? But why should I complain when I still have your goodness and Aline's heart? Consoled by these gifts, I can only suppose that the greatest misfortunes would be not their cost but the inability to enjoy their benefits.

Adieu, Madame, I await and will transmit your orders despite the maelstrom; and I assure you that we shall make it our most pleasant duty to carry out your wishes.

Letter XLI
Madame de Blamont to Valcour

Vertfeuille, 5 December

If I didn't know that Déterville had fully apprised you, I would
wait to see you before unburdening my heart. What do you
say, first of all, about the detestable effort to abduct Aline?
How he abuses me, that viper. How he forever toys with me!
O my friend, more than ever we must remain on guard. But
let us stop thinking of these horrors. I must turn to examine
other things more closely. Best I take them up with you.

As to this new daughter of mine — so did she please you?
She has not made me as happy as I might have hoped. More
spirit than feeling, far more vanity than goodness; but great
love for her husband, I agree, going beyond human endur-
ance in preserving herself for him. But why must all this be the
work of pride? Why did I find nothing when I aimed to sound
out her heart? And why must I despair of ever seeing arise
within her those qualities I did not find? O my friend! One
who fashions insensitivity into a system, fancies atheism as a
principle and indifference as a way of reasoning — she might
avoid error but never evince virtue; and if this cruel young
woman's reason were to cede to example, to the fire of passion,
what a precipice would open beneath her feet! Is she who feels
no charm in doing good ready to commit evil? Aberrations
of the mind are less dangerous than those of the heart; age,
which becalms the former, nearly always aggravates the latter.
If reversals could not form the young woman's soul, it is yet to
be feared they have rendered her wicked; and the riches she is
to enjoy will end up by corrupting her.

But let us talk of you, my friend. I'll be coming along
soon; this will be my last letter from Vertfeuille. In what state

shall I find the affairs that interest us? What shall I do about my husband? After this new horror, if he continues these maneuvers of stealth — how will I find out? How will I obstruct or stop him? Whatever the case, I will see you. I must kiss and embrace you, whether here or there. Kindly inform Léonore that I shall be in Paris without fail on the 10th; I want to see her again before she leaves. I shall receive them like people who chanced upon my estate while returning from their adventures. The story of their arrest at my home has created too much excitement abroad for me not to acknowledge it. The only thing to conceal is that she is my daughter, and I assure you that my heart reveals nothing of the sort. We have wept much, your dear Aline and I; to her, all that is not tender and delicate seems monstrous. She loves Léonore nonetheless and views her heroic attachment to conjugal fidelity as laudable and enchanting. With that virtue, she points out, she might acquire all the others. You must be pleased with that — aren't you, Valcour? That's why I am telling you. How I adore her and how she requites my love! Sometimes my heart gives way to pride when I think of her — but then there is humiliation at the faults of the other. Ah! 'Tis heaven's will. It would make me too proud to have two children like Aline! God wished to diminish my triumph with one of them but redoubles my love for the other. For you, the one I love will be the most beautiful gift I can bestow on a friend, the sweetest bond between us. *Adieu.* Be worthy of her. Love us — and write me no more in the country.

Letter XLII
Aline to Valcour

Paris, 15 December

Here I've come at last — close to you — yet without permis- sion to see you. A consolation nonetheless, and I feel it. Tho' love unites souls no matter how far apart, and for them all distances are the same; still, it's sweet to breathe the same air as the object one adores. I am distressed to see, my dearest, how this may remain the situation throughout the winter. It inflicts pain, I know, but do you imagine it upsets me any less than you? Do you believe this cruel heartache is less mine than yours? If you do, you scarcely know how I feel.

When I again saw the house where you used to come and go so freely and recalled the charm of your visits, once more I experienced the delicious excitement of awaiting your arrival. I felt the divine agitation, the shock as our eyes met. I went from one armchair to the next and loved remembering when we sat in them. Seated in one, I imagined you in the other and sometimes talked as if you could hear me. Deceived by such sweet illusions, for a moment I believed myself happy — but let us turn to the details you request, which it's only fair I provide.

The President, forewarned, was waiting for my mother. He gave her a glorious welcome, replete with caresses and a show of great concern. As to me there was at first a little em- barrassment, but soon he came around and was calling me tender names, insisting he never saw enough of me. Sainville and Léonore were our first topics of conversation, for they're the talk of Paris. But he did not bring up or speak a word of his cunning schemes. He was careful not to acknowledge that he had intended to commit an appalling atrocity, to seize both Léonore and I; and my mother, seeing quite clearly that he would deny it and go raving mad if we brought it up, resolved not to say a word. He praised Léonore to the skies; she pleased him greatly, it seemed to me. Just think — without that fraud committed by the wet-nurse at Pré-Saint-Gervais, she would have been the very woman he turned into a prostitute for Dolbourg! Great heavens! How such treatment would have enraged Léonore, with all her pride!

O Valcour! Something most singular abides in all this; that first night he spent nearly all of it at his wife's side. Can you believe it? It was a renewal of tenderness — unless counterfeit — and, indeed quite inconceivable and astonishing. With me the next day, Mother was greatly embarrassed. She was dying to laugh and tell me about it but did not know how. It had been more than five years. She wanted to escape such things that, for her, hold so little attraction. A man who has never been anything but a tyrant and a libertine can only be an indelicate husband. She nonetheless had to submit — *submit*, my friend. Is that not the word? To *share* would not do, and if I used that word you'd cross it out. Mother took advantage of these moments to reproach him for his debauchery, and to insist he behave in ways more more conducive to good health and reputation. She recalled to him the story of Augustine; she made him feel how frightful it was for him to have come to Vertfeuille only to seduce a servant. "In truth," said the President, "I'm all the more sorry because the young woman is so truly respectable." He had tricked her, so he claimed, into leaving Vertfeuille, promising her a great fortune without running the least risk. But as soon as she saw what was required, she had mounted what could be called a Roman defense. Both he and Dolbourg were edified by the young woman's behavior and they installed her in a convent until my mother returned, and they pray that Mother will take her back. On this he insisted in every way possible and she — always good, always

credulous — marveled at such fine conduct. She not only o
consented but energetically desired that the young woman be
returned to her service.

  If Augustine really behaved in this way, she deserves our
kindness and forbearance; and Mother will assuredly welcome her back. For some reason, though, I have my doubts. 5
Why does my father want her to return if she had given herself
to him? Wouldn't he prefer to keep her elsewhere for the sake
of convenience? We will see what she has to say. She'll need
be very cunning to fool us.

  The next day the President did not fail to bring Dolbourg 10
out to see us. He did not conceal from my mother that he
holds more than ever to his previous intentions, and that he
would be much pleased if everything could be resolved before
summer. But at least his propositions no longer had the air of
menace. He desired but gave no orders. In truth, Valcour, I see 15
a change in his behavior. I do not know what occasioned it but
it is real and impossible to miss. A glimmer seems born of this
change. May we hope? So sweet to perceive the dawn of happiness. Ugly, thick Dolbourg approached me out of nowhere
and asked if I'd enjoyed life in the country. He found I'd put on 20
weight, which is false. He wanted to kiss my hand but never
managed to do so.

  Despite promising signs, we must be careful. Mother
warns you under no circumstances to come see us. She will
see you at the Count de Beaulé's; as you know, he gives din- 25
ner parties two or three times a week. It is understood I shall
never attend. Yet here's how we can manage to see one another and exchange letters. You will without fail attend noon
mass every Sunday at the convent of the Capucines. I shall
be on the right side, just as you saw me several times this 30
past year. However awful and evil it might be, and however
terrible I may feel in permitting myself this slight indecency,

we will steal a few minutes from the devotions we owe the
Supreme Being. We will have a few words. We will exchange
letters — and never leave without swearing our love to one
another, or without asking God's forgiveness. The Good Lord
can see to the bottom of our hearts. He knows that if we wish
to be united, it is in order to love Him, to serve Him, and together to glorify Him. You know that for us to give thanks
together to the Eternal One is something I rank among our
most exquisite devotions. It seems to me our two hearts, with
religion emanating from them and burning with love, must
necessarily grow more tender and pure. It is not by indifferent souls that the most holy of beings wishes to be served; an
honest and legitimate love can only make hearts more worthy
of their offerings.

Apropos this, if I were jealous, what would I make of all
the attention and goings-on involving my sister? You know
they have gone to Brittany. My mother had them to dinner
twice before they left; and each time Dolbourg and my father
came, too. I made some singular reflections at the time. When
Léonore saw Monsieur de Blamont, she came up to me and
said in her sprightly voice:

"So that's my father the President?"

"Yes, it's him."

"Well, then! Nature deceives once again, telling me
nothing of the sort."

Inasmuch as it also deceived with respect to her mother,
such coolness did not surprise me. In general, I think Léonore,
proud and haughty, would not be much pleased if she were
obliged to renounce being the daughter of a countess to become child of the President. Returning to France, she would
quite prefer to find herself Elizabeth de Kerneuil and *not*
Claire de Blamont. I do love my dear sister, but in truth she
has many faults — all, unfortunately, of the heart. Her person

clearly contradicts her words when she dares to say that the   o
greatest virtues are allied to impiousness. If such virtues
manifest themselves in her in some ways, considerable flaws
obscure them.

Although unable to see you in my mother's home, I am
no less enchanted to be back. Yet I don't know but a certain   5
darkness tinged with sadness pervades my joy. A tumultuous
voice within seems to tell me I'm acting like sailors who rejoice whilst storm clouds gather. *Adieu*, let us not flinch in the
face of any reversals but unite our forces to love each other
and suffer together.   10

Letter XLIII

Aline to Valcour *

Paris, 17 December

Your complete obedience, as always, pleases and touches me greatly. That is the way of love, Valcour. Others less delicate or unaccustomed to sacrifice would find it hard to persuade themselves of that, but what do we care about opinions of cold indifferent people so long as our souls, more ardent and elevated than theirs, know how to enjoy what others cannot fathom? One of the things that bothers me most is to see how few the world over speak the same language as us. Why did Nature, once she destined people to live together, not endow everyone with the same soul? Why do we all not feel in the same way? Certain people inspire and move the humors within me and I don't know but that I prefer those who, like my dear sister, go well beyond the usual bounds by too great sensitivity of the organs, to those who feel nothing. The first sort at least compensates for fickleness of heart by a lively and extraordinary spirit, while others have nothing to make amends for their ponderous apathy. The latter are automatons who, it seems to me, affect us just like brutal weather on certain summer days when all our faculties, numbed by the thick air, lose all sense of organization. Is my comparison not apt? Has a fool never made you experience physical pain? Have you not felt, at his approach or from his discourse, a commotion similar to the one I'm talking about?

---

* There exists Valcour's response to the preceding letter but we suppress it here, not wishing to offer the public what could only lengthen the thread of the narrative without disentangling it and put off the denouement without adding further interest. *Editor's note.*

O my friend! — by the time you read these words I'll have
seen you. The hand that shall offer this missive in exchange
will feel the pleasure of your own. Our eyes will have spoken,
our souls understood. Let our innocent way of being together
not be disturbed, this coming winter!

The President is acting just as before; my mother doesn't
know how to understand his extraordinary attentions. He
stays with her some nights and I can tell you that his dear wife
is no happier for it. She would much prefer the most profound
indifference to those emotions which are the fruit of an un-
disciplined mind, almost always more chaotic than any sentiments of the heart, and which always place her in a position of
inferiority and humiliation that no longer leaves her with any
but the sorry role of a dove beneath a vulture's sharp claw. But
she must be both politic and artful; if by force of kindness and
civility she could chain him up and vanquish him for the sake
of her dear Aline, there would be nothing, she says, that she
would not undertake with more delight.

With Augustine, reconciliation. She threw herself at the
feet of Madame de Blamont, asked forgiveness for her misconduct, and begged her to think of it no more. Judge for
yourself whether my mother's tender sweet soul could resist.
She kissed the girl tenderly; she brought her to her feet and
renewed her confidence and protection. For his part the President was almost touched; he shows singular restraint as if he
never had anything to do with her.

But as to Sophie, my mother is embarrassed and has absolutely no idea what tone to take with the President. The last
time they discussed her, at Vertfeuille, my father insisted Sophie was not his daughter. Whether she wanted to or not, my
mother was far from believing he was telling the truth. Now
that she's sure that Sophie is definitely not his, it seems best
to say nothing and let him think she believes him. Besides,

the interest she takes in the unfortunate young woman can no longer be as great as when she believed Sophie was actually her daughter. She has two real children whom she won't sacrifice, she says, to one she's attached to only by the sentiment of pity. Thus, best be silent and leave her husband in the dark. She will continue to conceal from him what's happened to Sophie while still providing for her care. Isn't that the best way to do as she ought?

Letter XLIV
President Blamont to Dolbourg*

Paris, 10 January 1779

Sophie is ours. The business was carried out with nimblest dispatch. The Abbess clamored for Madame de Blamont but there was a *lettre de cachet* and she was forced to give way. Now that I think about it, such injunctions can be quite convenient. What a variety of passions they serve! Love, hate, vengeance, ambition, cruelty, jealousy, avarice, tyranny, adultery, libertinage, incest — these charming missives satisfy them all. Rid yourself of an annoying spouse, feared rival, mistress no longer desired, an inconvenient relation. I'll never finish if I detail all the uses to which they might be put. I've yet to understand how my colleagues can possibly complain about them, and I'm perplexed when they dare assert that they contravene the laws of the State, as if the State ought to have anything more sacred than the happiness of its lords and masters, as if there existed anything sweeter this side of the Asiatic method of strangulation. To be sure, I know those who oppose such delicious use of it treat the thing like some sort of tyrannical *abuse*. To bolster their case, they claim it weakens the sovereign by diluting his power, diminishing while seeming to expand it through despotism, and debasing it by concealing crimes — a dangerous tool that might be used judiciously once or twice a century but when used 500 times corrupts

---

* There were two more letters from Valcour but as they reflected no change we pass immediately to this one, which however frightful it is, seemed to us too useful to suppress but, rather, essential, both for its depiction of character and understanding the impending catastrophe. But many readers, women especially, will do well to not read it. *Editor's note.*

the roots of the tree by hacking off its branches. But that's all sophistry from those who've suffered from it. The weak complain from time immemorial; that's their lot in life, just as it's ours not to listen to them. I ask you: What would authority come to if its beneficent beams did not lend support to the throne? Only tyrants carry their own swords; good and just kings share the weight. Why carry one at all if you're not going to use it from time to time?

Was it not indecent that your mistress and my daughter* — just because it pleased her to escape from us by forcing us to throw her out — went off to live at my wife's expense? But, indeed, shouldn't she be paying for these sorts of things? For myself, I like propriety — amazing how I insist on it. Yes, I want honesty to reign even in the heart of chaos. When as to Sophie all this comes out, Madame will sulk. God knows but my attentions — *my so very close attentions* — will surprise her. "Is it not frightful," I shall be told, "to seek pleasures with the self-same one you have so burdened with grief?" My wife can't conceive the connection in that. She can't understand how grief and sorrow can shock the nerves with an immediate effect upon voluptuousness via the atoms of the electric fluid, and that a woman is never more desirable than when captive to tears. That alone would make it excusable for an old husband like myself, with his tender spouse, to use every possible conceivable way to attain what vigor alone can no longer provide. That is the physical side of things. But a little malice aimed at causing sorrow has its moral pleasures as well. And that your sluggish mind does not comprehend. Tell me — confess. Do you understand what you're really saying to a woman when subjecting her to these fires? It's like this:

---

* We must not forget that the President still believes himself to be Sophie's father.

If you only knew how your misapprehension and simple nature   o
nourish the piquant charm of deception and the pleasure I seek,
not to mention the way I finally make you my dupe. In those
fiery salts I find the voluptuousness that intoxicates — and it
would be nothing for me without darts of perfidy. Well, Dolbourg: is that all Greek to you? Are you like some ass grazing   5
in the green meadow without distinguishing the *wild rushes*
from the *precious herbs*, but devouring indifferently all that
finds its way to your mouth, without analyzing or examining it, without forming or acting upon principles? Am I not
happier than thou in refining *everything* the way I do, never   10
giving into *physical* pleasure without some little *moral* disorder? Whatever variety I may put in play in my love for the
President, however pretty she is still, however *bizarre* might
be my pleasures — what would become of them, I ask you, if
to inflame them I did not have ideas born of my well-known   15
treacherous *intentions?* And to *them* we must return, for our
plan at Lyon worked no success. Then, too, since formulating
those *intentions* — now that they're foolproof — the sensations are those of violence! What amuses me is that the fine
lady supposes it's all due to her good looks. She ought to know   20
that looks no longer count for anything with respect to my
intoxication. It seems impossible that she fails to see that I
have something else in mind. Sometimes I am not even master of my own words. During those moments of babble and
claptrap — he who talks the most nonsense is nearly always   25
the one with the liveliest mind — there escape from my lips
some very telling things. When there used to be a little more
honesty on my part, there was far less enthusiasm; she ought
to remember. What then the source of this new delirium? The
indecency of the act? I've long engaged in *singularities* — as   30
she must know. Seeing that's not the sort of thing setting me
afire now, she ought to ask herself what's going on, begin to

0 wonder and even tremble. But a woman's sense of security is
a strange thing.

You fancy yourself a bit of a *naturalist* and so should be
able to tell me: is there not some kind of ferocious animal
that with a female never roars but when it's ready to *devour*?
5 I just mentioned security — how it astonishes me —, but now
it's their pride I don't understand. They have it when they get
back the one they've lost and always imagine it's thanks to
their art and magic — they've effected a miracle! Innocents,
deceived by the cult of self-sacrifice, they place themselves
10 on the altar as *goddesses* when in fact they're only *victims*.

In any event, Sophie has been snatched by order of the
King from the convent of the Ursulines of Orléans. She was
spirited off to the Chateau de Blamont, where my concierge
received her and shut her away in a safe and secluded apart-
15 ment; he will guard her with his life. I have been told that the
dear little person wept prodigiously; she has more tears yet
to shed. With the way she toyed with us, we deserve to make
sure of it. But as she is indeed safely put away and we have
much to do at present, I shall be content just to stop down
20 in order to prepare her to receive us in the spring. Until then,
other affairs keep us too busy in Paris.

Nothing meanwhile has worked so well as the rehabili-
tation of our young lady, Augustine. I was witness to it and
occasionally allowed my eyes to brim with tears, to make it
25 seem I have a heart — I was believed. Once more, my friend,
what goodness these women possess! Here is this young girl,
beautifully placed; and you may well understand how sure of
that we had to be, for it's essential not to lose sight of the very
soul of our plan. You must admit: I'm a fine physiognomist.
30 As soon as I espied her at Vertfeuille, I knew it was so *in every
way*: She's what we need. Here's what fate put in our hands to
execute its caprices. And you see how after fulfilling our first

requests with docile compliance, to our second she cooper- ates with intelligence.

In truth, we needed something like her to compensate us for the very real loss of Léonore. Ah! That charming little woman is worthy of us, my friend! This Count de Beaulé, who's been getting in the way for some time, is beginning to try my patience. If he were not in such favor, I and some of my friends would soon have him in criminal court. I know the dear fellow dines occasionally with young women — so, in times like ours, all the more necessary he be sent directly to the gallows. It is only a question of suspicion and invention — of bribing a few complainants, a few spies and arresting officers — and then you have a broken man. For 30 years we've seen this sort of thing, over and over. I'd almost like it better today[*] if I were accused of conspiracy against the government rather than ir- regularities with dirty whores. And in truth this manner of going about things is respectable — it does honor to the na- tion. If we had to wait for a man to commit a crime against the state in order to get rid of him, there would be no end to it; but there are few mortals alive who don't break bread with prostitutes. So we've done well to set traps. This kind of inquisition with respect to the practices of a citizen who clos- ets himself with a young woman, together with the obligation by which we make these creatures render an exact account of the fellow's lustful acts, is assuredly one of our country's most beautiful institutions. It immortalizes forever the illustrious *archon* who put it to use in Paris.[†] And see that these laws, gentle yet prudent, must never be allowed to fall into disuse;

---

[*] No, not today, happily for humanity. Wiser laws shall govern in France; and the atrocities described by this rascal exist no longer.

[†] An archon was a Greek magistrate — though it must be said Sire Sartine was no Greek. See the relevant note on p. 474.

we cannot do enough to encourage denunciations by these priestesses of Venus; it is extremely useful to government and society to know how a man conducts himself in such circumstances. A thousand conclusions, each more certain than the next, may be drawn concerning his character; the result, I'm happy to say, is a collection of impurities that tickles the ears of a judge. It does not serve morality — so say the system's enemies — to spy on the libertine actions of Pierre in order to stimulate the intemperance of Jacques, but these are chains upon the citizen, the means to subjugate and do away with him when one wants — and that's what's essential.

Adieu. My better half the wears me out; no one has ever treated his wife so diligently. I'll charge you see to my pleasures whilst I sacrifice myself for yours. For the repast you're preparing, recall I must have hot and tasty dishes; so warn love's children that they'll need to reawaken sensations made extinct by the holy disorders of matrimony.

Letter XLV
Madame de Blamont to Valcour

Paris, 12 January

Today I was looking forward with pleasure to dining at the home of our dear count, and planned see you there, as well as Déterville. But I shan't be leaving home. What I've just learned has destroyed me. Every faculty of my soul has been shattered, not a single feeling untouched. The cunning monster — I was duped by his caresses! I'd hoped to bring him around with the force of art, to move him to tenderness by my care and attention; and just when I believed he was in my grasp and I thought he was mine — in fact *I* was the one crushed by the imperious yoke of this perfidious man. Nothing is sacred any more, nothing either of law or virtue; today all constraints may be undone with impunity. What a century! I blush with the misfortune of being born into it.

We've learned of the order, received by Madame the Abbess of the Ursulines at Orléans on January 6th at 9 o'clock in the morning, which enjoined her to immediately give up to the bearer of that order a young woman named Sophie, whom she was keeping at my behest. Having been warned by me, suspecting horrors, she at first said she did not know the young woman, who in fact was not residing there under that name. The subterfuge proved unconvincing; she was told that the cloister would be breeched if she continued to procrastinate. Seized with fear, the good woman dared not refuse and the unfortunate child was taken away to be delivered back into the arms of libertinage — by order of those who proclaim their decency. Show me depravity more complete or more devastating and I shall complain no more.*

---

* Here it is more than ever necessary to observe that these letters were written before the Revolution; such atrocities would be impossible under the present government.

Thus was Sophie taken off to the Chateau de Blamont, where she is being held under guard by the concierge, unable to see or talk with anyone.

Reasons the President gave for his startling and despicable action: he stated that I had long opposed a highly advantageous marriage for his daughter; that by my perfidious counsels I was preventing her from obeying him; further, joining ruse to overt maneuvers, I'd unearthed a creature with which the same friend to whom he destined his daughter had lived, to tell the truth, for only a few months. He claimed that I brought this lady-love into my home and, after instruction, made her pretend to be my daughter, who I said was robbed from me while with the wet nurse and raised in secret with the abominable design of prostituting her to his friend. And because said friend was the self-same Dolbourg who was about to become her son-in-law, now that couldn't happen because he would find himself intimate with both sisters. An execrable fable, he added, which could only have been suggested to his wife by some diabolical mind that wanted to get rid of him and his family. That evil mind, my dear Valcour, is supposed to be none other than yourself. Such are the so kindly impressions he bears toward you, undoubtedly with the idea of coming up with something more serious in the future. We must be vigilant. I fear everything. Now, to lend authority to his words, to convince people of my impostures, he has produced the certificate you learned about that registered the supposed death of Claire de Blamont.

"So it is," he adds, "that if my daughter Claire is truly dead, as this extract from the parish register proves, she ought no longer be identified as the person known as Sophie — and so I stake my judicial claim. The woman who called herself Claire de Blamont and dared offer herself as such, is nothing more than an adventuress instructed by my wife, who has turned

her against me — a scheme that merits attention in court if I
wanted to make it known and intended to become embroiled
in a scandal with the woman I still love and respect despite her
weakness for a man to whom, obstinately, and at odds with my
intention, she wishes to hand off her daughter."

In consequence, he demanded Sophie remanded to his
charge and now I shall never be able see her again; he obtained the right to have her secretly put away wherever he
liked, with the simple agreement that he pay a sufficient pension to take care of her. His chateau is only a stopping place.
He will confound me further, he told me, and place her in a
convent in some remote part of France.

Such are the lies the false-hearted cheat used to avenge
himself upon that poor girl, to punish her for following the
hapless star that brought her into my home, to make her submit anew to his odious intemperance. Just consider the frightful character of the man — persuaded at one and the same
time, though fortunately I know it's not the case, that Sophie
is indeed his daughter. And he overwhelms me with caresses
and passes whole nights with me, telling me that his feelings
for me are reawakened and that he still finds in his heart everything he felt for me in the first days of our marriage.

Such is the man I have to deal with; such is the dangerous mortal upon whom my fate depends. *O father! When you
wrought the bonds of matrimony, you promised happiness!
See what they've done to me.*

Cares more pressing nevertheless oblige me to continue
dissembling; I am resolved to change nothing in my conduct
with him; he must be left to his mistake and not even think of
looking into it; for Aline and Léonore are more precious to
me than Sophie. The fact is, he has in his hands nothing more
than a peasant's daughter but if I were to take her away, he
would fall upon my own.

What probity imposes upon me at present consists only in making the minister aware of the whole truth. Of that, Count de Beaulé is in charge. On many points, truth will seem in accord with what the President has said: she is an adventuress who does not in any way belong to him; I would have to say the same. I will only explain why I'd hoped to have her pass as his daughter. If I'd believed it, if I said so at one time, I will provide everything needed to show my mistake was clearly made in good faith; and that as soon as Claire de Blamont was dead, as he proved, I had no further claim and will leave him with his illusion intact in order that he discover nothing concerning the birth of Léonore and never know that his child Claire de Blamont, whom he actually believes to be Sophie, is actually now young Lady Kerneuil; for it would entirely be within the character with which heaven endowed him to tamper with all we've done to provide Léonore with the assets of the woman that she and everybody else must suppose to be her mother.

Yet my repugnance is not less for having accepted this arrangement with Count de Beaulé; for in the end, by this maneuver we dispossess the secondary relatives of Madame de Kerneuil; you cannot imagine, Valcour, how much this offends my sensibilities. It is illegal and it revolts me; but if I don't pass over this consideration, if I reveal the facts of Léonore's birth, what new wickedness, what more terrible complications will not come my way? And though she may be Sainville's wife, the Marquise de Karmeil, to what secret persecutions would the President not resort? If he could not attack her, his vengeance might target Aline — and I would find myself in a bottomless pit of misfortune. Acting as I do, I prefer a minor wrong to a major one — yet wrong nonetheless and I am exercised and angry. My conscience is alarmed.

Another still more powerful affront to my sensibility, which makes me shed bitter tears in private, is that in Sophie I

abandon an honest and sweet creature, full of virtue and reli- o
gion, in favor of another who is far from having the same qualities. But the one is my daughter while the other is nothing to
me. Yet now — how can we save Sophie from the hands of this
man, how is it possible? By what right can we undertake to do
so? We agree to give the house of Kerneuil to a beneficiary 5
who, as it happens, is not actually one at all so that I may do
the same for the President — provide him with a daughter
he never had. When it's a question of saving the unfortunate
from the hands of cruelty and injustice, can we not permit a
bit of subterfuge? Besides, if I continued to press my claim 10
that Sophie is my daughter, I'd only help arm the enemy and
further the plans of my husband's horrible friend. I am taking
nothing from Léonore and will never acknowledge her as my
daughter; she has no need of it. I will try to procure freedom
for Sophie and aim to insure happiness for Aline. More than 15
that would be in vain; he would bring to bear the death certificate from the parish and if I contested its authenticity, that
could only harm my Léonore. What mortification! For all that
I rejoiced on those days of my life when I brought children
into the world, I must now qualify them as the most grievous 20
and unhappy of my life.

No: I shall cede the ground. I must abandon Sophie. No
matter what I think, I cannot do otherwise. I can't help the
unfortunate child without afflicting the happiness of my two
daughters; I must renounce her — I must. Is it possible that 25
Heaven sometimes so little favors virtue that it's impossible to
rescue it from wickedness? Would that we forever remain unaware of such fatal truths, for too many young women would
conclude that the thorny road onto which education places
them is hopeless, for they shall only fall sooner or later into 30
traps set by intemperance and vice.

If I resolve not to be angry about all that's happened, con-
ceding everything to the man who deceives me, continuing

just as before, will I succeed in moving him? Perhaps my absolute devotion will put a stop to his shameful designs upon
Aline. But on the other hand, will he believe I'd so readily give
up on the young woman whom I so clearly believed to be my
daughter? Well — let my sweet disposition explain my complete resignation. I will say: *She touches me as person but you
are now her master. I commend her to you and beg you to make
her happy.*

It almost makes me angry not to have given Sophie over
to her good nurse at Berseuil, for now she'd be married. But
what am I saying! With the maneuverings of a man like the
President, by the intrigues of that vile snake who uses influence, spares no expense, and makes no move unless it serves
his passions, would everything not come down to the same?
There would be just one more crime — *wait, someone interrupts. I will finish my letter tomorrow.*

---

13 January

Can you believe it? He came to me last night as if it was nothing unusual, to obtain, as he said good-naturedly, the gift of
marriage from the hands of love. As he noted a slight change
in my expression, no matter my efforts to contain myself, he
set out a warning. What he has done is assuredly for the better
— although, in fact, he said he's done little. It was Dolbourg,
seeking my accord for his intended and embarrassed to learn
that one of his former mistresses was with me, who wished
to take her back.

"I did nothing wrong," he continued, "except fail to warn
you. But you were imbued with the mad idea that Sophie is
your daughter and so you would oppose it. I carefully put
aside anything that could give rise to trouble between us.

I've the liveliest desire to repent of my old ways; you must   o
forgive this little lapse in favor of my extreme desire to retain
your esteem. Nothing concerns me more, for in so few women
are united so many graces — such divine features, such rare
virtues. I should fall out with you? Confront and contest?
How could I?"   5

"But Sophie is now in your custody," I said, interrupting
his simpering flattery.

"Yes," he replied, astonished that I knew. "Yes, indeed, she
is at the Chateau de Blamont. I could not refuse Dolbourg,
who wanted to see her briefly."   10

"And what will he do with her?"

"She will be sent away," he replied, adopting that mysterious tone by which imposters give lies the color of truth. "She
will be taken to a convent deep in Gascony. She will be well.
He will provide her with an honest pension. You don't know   15
Dolbourg and never do him justice. His morality is the simplest possible, and he possesses rare honesty, a truthful nature,
and precious innocence. Believe me, he's the only man to really make our Aline happy. Aren't you now persuaded that all
you believed about him are simple fabrications?" (Here I said   20
nothing.) "There are plenty of people who have the greatest
interest in deceiving you and, indeed, they do so. Consider
that fellow Valcour, for example. Mistrust him, I tell you. He's
a most clever rascal."

"One moment, Monsieur," I said, not able to counte-   25
nance such falsity but also curious to see how far he would
go. "While you're explaining yourself, pray tell the reason for
that secret order to arrest Léonore at Vertfeuille? Why did
the arresting officer come armed with a letter — from you —
with a description that would have taken away Aline instead   30
of Sainville's wife?"

At this, my friend, the art of imposture thoroughly suf-
fused the features of that odious face.

"*From me?* An order to take away our daughter in place of Léonore? You should know, I dare say, that only from public knowledge did I learn that Sainville was at Vertfeuille — a circumstance that greatly embarrassed me and even made me bristle with anger at you for not having warned me, as I had no idea about how to reply to all the questions put to me on just this subject."

"So you deny the accusation?" I demanded and rose up with growing furor.

"Come now," he said, smiling. "Now I see you're joking; but if you continue, I shall become angry. I've certainly committed enough wrongs; don't invent new ones. As concerns Aline, don't worry. I shall not take her from you. Rather, I only *ask* for what I want and may hope that after some reflection, you will no longer refuse me."

I sat down again, feeling I'd been wrong to break silence on a subject about which I'd promised myself never to speak and which was useless to bring up because it was clear he would deny everything.

"I believe you," I said with pretended calm. "Yes, I believe you. But if you accuse me of having enemies, assuredly you must have them yourself. The evil deed of which I suspected you has been openly attributed to you. And I —"

"Enemies! Who doesn't have enemies? Only fools don't make them! But all these calumnies — I so perfectly despise them that I don't even try to discover who fabricates malevolence in my name."

He grew lively and heated, not giving me time to respond. He renewed his adulation only to end by asking for what I'd resolved to continue to accord him. I was determined to dissemble. Never before had I had seen him so ardent — or I should say, so depraved. Love and sentiment in such souls are never anything but an excess of disorder. The man's mind is

dark, even in the midst of the sweetest pleasures. Listen to   o
his words: *

"How beautiful you are!" Examining me when I was un-
clothed: "Not even death will damage this great work. You are
not like other mortals. This fine flesh will never fail. Nothing
can despoil or tarnish it and even at Nature's final sleep, as   5
a model you will serve her still."

In thrall to that idea, his pleasure reached its apogee;
that idea, *delicately horrible*, intoxicated his senses.

O my friend! I don't know but all this alarms me, this
sudden change in his behavior and eagerness for things that   10
ought no longer inflame! Even in the first years of our marriage, he did not lavish attention on me with such assiduity.
What does it mean? If he truly loved me, if he desired to right
his wrongs, would he aggravate them the way he does? He
flatters yet deceives; he caresses yet he torments. I can only   15
tremble! What does he want? What's the need for such a ruse?
Is he not the more powerful? We deceive only those whom we
fear; trickery is the weapon of the slave, permitted the weak
but it dishonors the strong. Whether he elevates me or batters
me down, praises or degrades me, I shall always be his victim.   20
Nothing can stop it. And what of Aline! With me not there
to wrest her from their cruel grasp, will she fall victim? I tell
you, Valcour: tears flow despite myself. My mind grows dark.
My soul overwhelmed by misfortune chafes hard by the danger of more on the way. Time comes when we can no longer   25
withstand the terrible weight of our chains, when we would
prefer a thousand times that our existence come to an end
rather than more misfortune. O Valcour, if I were to be taken
and was no more, and if Aline fell into misery — let blood

---

* See p. 663, where the President says, "Sometimes I am not master of my own words."

be shed if it must, my friend, to rescue her from the horrors menacing her very existence. Keep forever in your mind's eye the mother who gave her to you. Tell yourself from time to time: *She loved me. She desired my happiness, and that of her daughter. Providence opposed it. But I owe her both my love and my regrets. I must cherish them beyond the grave or else, with them, perish myself.*

Adieu — I am too sad to continue tonight. We are not the mistress of our thoughts — some of which, you can be certain, Nature puts forth as warnings for all that awaits. Try to come to dinner Thursday at the Count's; I will do everything in my power to see you there.

Letter XLVI
Valcour to Madame de Blamont

Paris, 20 January

I have just had a singular visit, Madame. What transpired
seems to me so essential that I believe you will permit me
to immediately share it with you. The arrival of Monsieur le
President de Blamont was announced to me at about 10 o'clock
this morning, just as I was getting ready to go out.

"If you please, Monsieur," I said, "to what do I owe the
honor of your presence?"

"You must know."

"I do not. But if you would like to be seated, I invite you
to explain."

"I'm not here to engage in small talk."

"Well, then, remain standing. But explain yourself promptly, for business elsewhere summons me."

"I shall take my time and you will be so good as to listen. You've no more pressing affair than the one I've come to
discuss."

"Well, then! What is it? Explain yourself."

"I've come to give you some advice."

"Not something I much like."

"A wise man must take it when it's good."

"The wiser man doesn't give it."

"Your safety depends upon it."

"Good conduct keeps an honest man safe."

"Change your conduct, then, if you want to stay that way."

"That doesn't sound like advice, Monsieur."

"Insistence does not always come modulated in the friendliest of tones."

"Insistence?"

"Would you like it better if I said *force*?"

"Neither. You are the most ill-bred of men, Monsieur, and have about you an air most feeble."

"My profession — "

"One of the most mediocre, a sorry station in life and nation, and little esteemed. If my valet had 100 sacks each filled with 1,000 francs each, he'd be your equal."

Flinging himself into an armchair:

"Monsieur de Valcour, your conduct serves you badly and you would do well to change it."

Seating myself across from him:

"How exactly does my conduct offend you or anyone else?"

"To seduce my daughter offends. To meet with her in church is a public affront."

"Your reproach is false in two respects. I don't seek to seduce your daughter nor did I ever make an appointment to meet her anywhere. Know too that between a young man and woman, love alone seduces. If I met her several times in church, 'twas by chance."

"Easy to say, talk is cheap."

"I only want to reply truthfully."

"Fine! Such being the case, what are your sentiments with respect to my daughter?"

"Profound respect and inviolable love."

"You are forbidden to love her."

"What law prevents me?"

"My will opposes it."

"We shall wait and see."

He rose up with fury: "*Wait and see!* For that, Monsieur, the foundation of your happiness depends upon the day I die."

"Not at all. It would please me to call you father. I would be honored to obtain Aline's hand from your own."

Pacing up and down the room: "Never dare imagine it."

"Have I been wrong to assure you we shall wait? A dis-   o
honest man would not say so."

"But that's as much as to tell me —"

"That you can make yourself beloved as a father, or at least
stop being an enemy."

"A fine thing when a man can't do what he wants with his   5
daughter."

"He can if his views accord with her happiness."

"Such constraints are mere sophisms. Not so the rights
of a father over his children."

"Some things are altogether unjust."   10

"That won't change the law."

"Nor will you extinguish my love."

"I shall put a stop to it."

"You'll end by making yourself hated by those who ought
to love you."   15

"We must ignore the sentiments of those whose wrongs
we punish."

"One thing that's not wrong is to love your daughter."

"Another is to cause her to be disgusted by the spouse for
whom I've destined her."   20

"Were she never to think of me, I would render a service
by keeping her from an alliance with a libertine."

"That's your interpretation! Such are the sentiments you
suggest to my wife."

"One may enlighten one's friends. Solicited by others be-   25
sides your wife and daughter to cast light on the conduct of
the monster with whom you want to unite her, I refused. But
Providence permitted his misdeeds to be discovered naturally.
You should be ashamed of intentions that dishonor you."

"Monsieur de Valcour, don't force me to extreme mea-   30
sures. It would displease me. Let us follow a friendlier path."

So saying, he placed on the table 10 rolls of coins.

"I know you're not a rich mean. Here are 500 louis. Now provide me a signed renunciation of your intent to marry."

Seizing the money, and flinging it to the floor of the antechamber: "VILE CREATURE. HAVE YOU FORGOTTEN WHOSE HOUSE YOU'VE ENTERED? Have you forgotten your ignoble existence, your lowly status, your abasement by vice — and all the rights that virtue and Nature give me over your despicable person?"

🅑 *fig.* 12

"You insult me, Monsieur."

"As you like. For the moment I must insist you leave my home."

"Such quick temper!"

"What did I do to deserve your cruel humiliation? What on earth makes you think I'd take money to renounce life's most precious sentiment? You're contemptible. Yes, I'm poor. But my ancestral blood runs pure. Less would I regret those faults that cost me my worldly assets than to acquire others that made me ashamed. Let them die a thousand deaths — those who compensate for the virtues they lack with bags of gold, the provenance of which they dare not avow. What little I have is mine alone. What your friend offers amounts to some widow's dowry, an orphan's patrimony, and the blood of the people. You ought to tremble at the thought of passing on to your grandchildren riches acquired at the price of honor. Someday those treasures may beget misfortune if fairness ever reigns in the vile tribunal of which you boast being a member."

"Then you won't give up your designs upon my daughter?"

"Only when she demands it and tells me I'm no longer worthy of her."

"You shall cause her to be unhappy. For I've given my word and cannot go back on it."

"And by what frightful injustice is your friend's happiness worth more to you than that of Aline?"

"Both are equally important, and I'd make them both   ○
happy if you hadn't turned my daughter's head."

"If your daughter's happiness were the sole consideration
before which all others must yield and someone must be sacrificed, should it not be Dolbourg — whom she does not love,
rather than he who worships her in the proud belief that she   5
cares for him?"

"Why Dolbourg? Sacrifice should come from the one
who really loves her."

"At the expense of her heart? It hardly makes sense."

"But Dolbourg makes no pretense in that regard. He will   10
leave her free to do as she pleases, glad only of the alliance and
fully aware that nobody his age captivates a young woman's
heart. He lays no claim to Aline's sentiments. He will marry
her and that's an end on it. Leave aside *this grotesque display
of chivalry.* One marries a woman for her social position, for   15
her wealth, to make use of her as needed. Willingly or not, a
woman owes obedience to her husband and must *blindly* submit; whether she loves him or not, whether it makes her happy
or not, whether it is legitimate or not. So long as we get what we
want, what does happiness have to do with it? You people with   20
your noble sentiments locate felicity among the metaphysical
chimeras that exist only in your empty brains. Analyze it all
and the result comes to naught. Provided one takes pleasure in
a woman, what good is her love? At the moment we take our
pleasure, what does love add to the physical sensation?"   25

"If your friend Dolbourg is despicable enough to think like
that, and your daughter was born sensitive, you'll do nothing
but make her unhappy."

"Why so — if we demand of her nothing she can't give?"

"Frightful, when not from the heart."   30

"Well, of course! A few difficult moments each day leaves
her the rest to do as she pleases."

o   "A virtuous woman is not only duty-bound in the moment
but at all times; and when the moment is cruel, her chains
grow all the heavier. And her honest soul does not permit the
use of dishonorable means to lighten their load."

       "All those are the principles of young men fresh out of
5   school. By the time you're my age, Monsieur de Valcour, instead of love's sophistry you'll prefer ideas less intellectual.
If the husband contents himself with the physical side alone,
his wife must make do without the moral."

       "And without a woman's heart, do you think a husband
10   can be happy?"

       "Happier, I'd say. Physical pleasure is the blossom while
love is only a thorn. What if I told you that the most intense
pleasures are best enjoyed with a woman who hates you than
with one who loves you. The latter gives freely while you must
15   snatch it from the other and what a difference in sensation!
Rape holds ever piquant charm, for we must do battle and win,
with the fruit of victory far more delicious. Do you realize that
in a man's life he has 20 years when he continues to want pleasure on a daily basis even while he's certain to inspire only
20   disgust? And how could he be happy, unable to provide love,
if only love makes for happiness? That he's nonetheless happy
shows that it is quite possible to not give pleasure, yet to
receive it."

       "A young woman's ideas at 18 are not the same as those
25   of a man of 50."

       "Does one have ideas at 18? Are you sure? Believe me,
the age when we listen only to the heart is never the age of
ideas. Misled by that ridiculous guide, we misjudge sensations
and want a sensibility that relishes things that are good only
30   if outraged and defiled. As for me, I confess, only in the past
decade has pleasure been mine; and so ten years I've wondered
what must be excluded, what must be stifled to improve it.

Remarkable how more acutely we feel when our prey is about
to escape; the less we're sure of getting it again, the more intense the flavor. We need experience to decide what's good and
at age 18, what do we know? Still ruminating over principles,
believing in virtue, and admitting of gods and illusions, still
cherishing all such prejudices — how then can we imagine the
divine aberrations that issue from disgust and depravation, or
have any idea of the delightful quests to be had from helpless-
ness? One must grow old, I tell you, to become voluptuous.
We are only lovers while young, and it's not always in the cult
of Cythera that one finds sensual pleasure. But let us put an
end to it, Monsieur de Valcour, for I preach without convincing you. What is your final decision?"

"I would rather die a thousand deaths than renounce my
Aline."

"You're asking for a world of trouble."

"With her love, I will brave it all."

"That's your final answer?"

"The only one you'll ever get from me."

Furious, he stood up:

"Well, Monsieur! Don't be surprised by the measures I
shall take or the forces I shall bring to bear."

"Should you behave dishonestly, you will give me the right
to despise you — and I shall do so most abundantly."

"Remember first of all, Monsieur, that you are forbidden
in my home. I shall put my daughter under surveillance and if
you persist in writing her and meeting with her, I shall resort
to the severity of the law and compel by its strictures the respect
you owe one of its ministers."

He went out, very angry, gathering up his rolls of coin,
promising me that I'd soon regret my stubbornness.

Such is what transpired, Madame. I should have liked a
more sociable visit and confess that I am sorry, out of respect

to you, for the bitterness I displayed. But I could not allow him to treat me as he did. To suggest I might barter my love for Aline! Every ounce of my blood, shed drop by drop, could not force me to renounce her; and were the throne of the universe to be mine for my sacrifice or else risk the most extreme torture, I would not hesitate a single minute.

I await your orders, Madame — but, like you, heartfelt disquietude and apprehension. 'Twas I who hoped to inspire you with courage. Alas! I have need of yours. Say not a word to Aline; it would add to her distress. Fortunate moments of quiet happiness — where are they? Nowhere to be seen.

Letter XLVII
Madame de Blamont to Valcour

Paris, 26 January

The President made no effort to conceal his visit to you.

    I waited and he told me about it the day before yesterday. As his tone was unchanged, I kept quiet; he omitted mention of the 500 louis and said nothing about the tenor of the conversation, except to say he asked you to renounce your intentions, but you proved impossible to convince. He has requested my help in this regard; and without harshness or anger, he said it was my duty to oppose certain meetings he was sure were taking place. I know of them, my friend — the fleeting encounters. You must realize I was not unaware; you wouldn't have liked it had Aline proposed them behind my back. They were harmless and I'd be disinclined to forbid them were your own interests not at stake. But we must do more, Valcour. You must avoid going out for any reason at all until the storm passes. I have no clear sign of wrath from the man we fear but with a character of such guile, even when he's calm we must not be deceived. Nothing he might do would surprise me. Time and again I've learned just where absence of all principles takes one with a heart like his. Once again he proved it to me with his caresses; if only they were merely *false*. He must know I accept them for the sake of *prudence* and would treat him as he really deserves were it not for my children.

    I can readily imagine how difficult it must have been for you to control yourself. Still, you were perhaps too heated. About that he said nothing — and it worries me. Yesterday he went off to the Chateau de Blamont, assuring me that Sophie was no longer there, even while knowing full well she was. A few days ago I received a letter from her, delivered to me in greatest secrecy, posted from where she's being held. I don't send it on because it contains only particulars you already know concerning her abduction. I've found a way to conduct secure correspondence with the poor girl, and learn in detail of everything that happens to her. She is there now and the President will soon be on his way — all the while denying it. Meanwhile his attentions toward me — undiminished. O my friend! His ruses and subterfuges and duplicity — aren't they obvious? We can only tremble! It simply inspires the most terrible fear.

Before posting this letter I must know: *Will Dolbourg go with him?... And now having asked*: No, I'm told. The President will go alone and Dolbourg will not leave Paris. What is his motive? *My poor Sophie! Will the kinship he imagines protect you from the furor of his debauchery? Does he repent having respected you as Dolbourg's mistress?* And now those bonds broken, will not the thought of the crime, though fortunately not genuine, inflame his perfidious imagination?

I must tell you of Aline, for my mind needs turn to virtue after having been forced to think of crime. She sends kisses. A little tormented even while knowing nothing of your confrontation. Like her mother, she perceives something more than dubious in all that goes on. She was comforted to see you for a moment each week and now is displeased this must stop. However, she exhorts you to take courage, just like her, and we both kiss and embrace you.

Letter XLVIII
Léonore to Madame de Blamont

Rennes, 22 January

I would fail my duty, dear Mother, if I did not bring you up
to date as to our efforts and their fortunate first results. My
return to Brittany surprised many and afflicted some. A horde
of distant little cousins who were carting away every bit of
the Countess de Kerneuil's legacy find it very nasty of me to
come and dispossess them. These poor country folk are all the
more bitterly bursting with despair for having nothing whatever to support their ridiculous claims. Nothing amuses me
more than to see my arrival put an end to their little fortunes,
much as if the North Wind doth blow and parasitic plants
born one day are destroyed the next. Call me hard-hearted
but, reproaches aside, you'll agree that misfortunes that befall
others can sometimes seem sweet indeed.* Can we not count
among them the one that makes us rich?

The Count de Beaulé sent us the response from Spain
that assures us of prompt restitution of a portion of the gold
ingots, which together with the rest will make our house one
of the wealthiest in Brittany. But we don't plan on spending
our fortune in the provinces; we'll settle in the capital. Pleasure's center suits wealth best; and once you're able to satisfy
all your desires, it's best to live where they can be fulfilled.
Besides which, this plan will bring us nearer to you. What's
more to decide? And as to my conversion? The glory of it shall

---

* It is said that Paolo Veronese, upon being asked for a monumental composition that
included two sisters in very distinct costumes, so artfully painted certain features of
each that one could distinguish them at a glance. Here is it not possible to recognize
Léonore as the daughter of Monsieur de Blamont?

belong to you. That will be quite the cure and I fear you'll fail! I shall call on my heart to help my head — but you say they're both bad. I shan't blame the first and my sensibility is always prepared to cherish you.

Fated as I am to chance encounters, I happened upon Monsieur and Madame de Bersac, now directors of a theater here in Rennes; they'd seen a little of my success and flattered my smidgen of pride. Our adventures together gave me an idea concerning young Sophie, to whom you'd introduced me in Orléans. Pretty as she is, my friends offered to take her on to train her. If you think it's a good idea, it seems to me better than a convent. With a face like hers, wouldn't it make infinitely more sense if she were useful to men rather than useless to God? If this plan shocks my lovely mother's fierce virtue, I could instead offer Sophie a place in my home as soon as we're settled. While we're young we must work; to disburse a pension so she can pray to God, blither and blather in the depths of a convent, is in truth money ill-spent. I don't wish to dampen your compassion, but if the girl doesn't want to do anything, I'd have no scruples in abandoning her. As I've said, there's nothing worse, as far as I'm concerned, than encouraging idleness. It's an offense to society's laws, and indeed an affront to all.

The decision will be yours, and please tell me what you want done. Whatever your instructions, I will be honored to follow them to the letter. Sainville and I both embrace tender sweet Aline, and to you we offer our respects.

Letter XLIX
Sophie to Madame de Blamont

Château de Blamont, 29 January

Why must I be doomed to recount infamies? O Madame! Why did Heaven grant me life only to make me forever the victim of misfortune? And how dare I talk to you of my tormentor when he is so close to you? You consented to read my first letter and from your answer, which I hold deep in my heart, I learned you shed tears for my suffering. Once more I take the liberty to confide in you and implore your protection, for I am threatened by afflictions even greater than those already endured. Madame, please — rescue me! I am not asking for still further generosity, knowing it is impossible for you, but I only ask and beg you to free me from this place. I will go live in some little corner of the world and nobody will ever hear of me again. I will work with my hands to feed and clothe myself and ask nothing more than the freedom to work. My poverty will be pitied, and my youth respected, for not all hearts are hard. I only ask for the fruits of my labor, which I shall deserve by what I do and how I act. Let me turn to the particulars, Madame, since you permit me to do so.*

Monsieur le President arrived by coach on the evening of the 25th. About eight o'clock he entered the house. A fire was laid and supper served in his rooms; he went up and soon sent for me to come and talk. A leaf shaking on a tree in a thunderstorm would have been calmer than I. His servant carefully locked all the doors on his way out, leaving open only the passage to my bedroom. My strength nearly failed me.

---

* We must warn the reader that decency obliges us to leave out many details; yet some too strong remain for we must not overmuch weaken the tenor and tone. *Editor's note.*

As I entered he was deep in the apartment, facing me, seated in a wingback chair.

"Come closer," he told me, "I understand your fear. You must be trembling to see me after all your foolishness. You are well aware, I hope, that I have come to make you pay, but for now let truth be your guide. What were your reasons for seeking shelter with my wife?"

"Chance alone, Monsieur. That's the only reason. I was making my way to Berseuil. Your friend had thrown me out and I thought to implore help from the woman who raised me. Madame de Blamont found me in the woods and brought me back to her chateau. I didn't know it was the home of one so close to you."

"But you told her everything that happened with me and my friend?"

"I didn't know who I was talking to."

"You were not to do that under any circumstances."

"After the cruel manner in which I was treated, I thought I might complain."

"You deserved what you got."

"No, Monsieur."

"You're impudent and you betrayed my friend."

"That's not true!"

"Don't lie to me. You're a strumpet. Worse, when you left you stole from us."

"Me? Stole from you, Monsieur? Great God in heaven!"

And throwing myself at his feet:

"O Monsieur! I'm poor and unhappy but indigence does not exclude sincerity or honesty. You must believe me when I swear I'm innocent."

"No time for that now — at the very moment I come to punish you severely for your bad deeds. You're not going to make me believe you didn't commit them."

He left his chair and began to pace the room. I rose to
my feet and stood silently, not daring to look at my judge and
trembling whenever he stopped. He came close and with one
hand cupped my chin as he forced my gaze:

"They flattered you. They told you you're pretty; it's impossible to be less so. They said you resemble Aline: too bad
for her if she were she as ugly as you. A few features in common. Perhaps. I was joking when I called you my daughter. I
hope you know you don't belong to me."

"O Yes! Now I know about my birth, Monsieur."

"You know?"

"Yes, Monsieur."

"What of your birth?"

Here, Madame, I didn't think it would be too imprudent
to confess that I knew I was the daughter of Claudine Dupuis
of Pré-Saint-Gervais.

With great surprise: "Who told you that?"

"Alas! Monsieur, I don't remember. But that's what I was
told at the chateau."

"They lied to you. Nobody knows better than I. You were
suckled for a time by that woman but don't belong to her."

Grabbing me by the throat with one hand, gripping my
head with the other, he examined me closely.

"It's enough that you know you're not my daughter and
even if you were I'd still have the right to punish and make you
submit and bow down before me. Now — undress."

He was already engaged in the task himself. But when he
saw me recoil and bow my head as if to implore him to stop,
he thrust himself at me furiously. After ripping off every stitch
of clothing he gave me the same treatment I'd had from his
friend before being thrown out of their house.* Neither tears
nor prayers could soften him; on the contrary, my efforts to
disarm instead seemed to excite.

*. See p. 67.

After these cruel preliminaries came actions still more indecent, and during half the night he subjected me to every irregularity his mind could imagine and every perversity his heart could suggest.

The next day he had me brought back to see him as soon as he awakened.

"All I did yesterday," he told me, "was to give you a slight sample of what my friend has in store. You betrayed him and thus upon you he will wreak vengeance. I will bring him around shortly; be ready to receive him and try above all to move him to tenderness, as you did last night with me, with the help of those big blue eyes streaming tears. The results, you must have noticed, were none too sure. We men of justice regrettably grow a little blasé about all such little tricks women convey. Might you say I pulverized you?"

His eyes devoured the vestiges of his intemperance and he contemplated them for a long while with ferocious curiosity. Then he started on me again: ....
....

After which he called on the man who served as the guard here and told him to watch over me more vigilantly than ever and above all to keep from me every means of communication, verbal or written, with anybody. He added that he would soon be back with his friend. Then he went off by coach.

If I've done anything foolish, Madame, deign tell me what it was so that I can make reparations as best I can; but I beg you not to abandon me. I have only heaven and you — and let me beseech both. Permit me a little surcease after all this misery! I dare throw myself at the feet of Mademoiselle Aline and offer my respects. Vanished the sweet illusion of those happy moments when I could call her my sister! Some are brought into the world for nothing but suffering and misfortune! What would become of them without the consoling hope of a righteous God to alleviate their torment?

But, alas! I'm frightened! Youth held no charm but only °
adversity for poor Sophie. How many more years must I suffer
on earth! Happy are those beside the coffin who, longing for
death yet yoked to life, can finally glimpse the Sister of the
Shears, ready to cut the thread and end their pain! With what
tranquility must they perceive the moment that will reunite   5
them with the Creator! Happy to be at peace in glory, reborn
at the side of His power! With what joy must they shed humanity's tattered rags! Why was I brought into the world and
to what end? Nameless, despised, a burden to the universe itself — was my birth even worth the pain? *Are these my trials?*   10
*O God! I offer them to You and in return for my submission ask
only for a quick end to the miserable existence of a creature
who yearns only to return to serve and worship You.*

Forgive me, Madame, for you must find my lamentations
tiresome. Alas! They might be the last I ever address to you.   15
For who knows what comes next! Who knows what will become of me! *Before she returns to you, Almighty God, spare
Sophie the pain of torture.**

---

* This and the previous letter were included in the next missive.

Letter L

Madame de Blamont to Valcour

Paris, 1 February

I forward two very different letters, just received. Both distress me but in distinct and contradictory ways: one is drenched with my tears and you too will certainly weep; as for the second — alas! I don't know what to say. Just go ahead and read it. Must we now not fear calamities gathering everywhere? How deceitful this man, and how cruel! You can see that he believes she *is* his daughter. He disabuses her of the notion using only her words; nothing indicates the truth of his own or destroys the first opinion he must have formed about her. He takes her for his daughter, yet, see how he treats her. Would that he be struck by lightning! I would've liked you to have seen how calm he was, returning from his lovely sojourn, how his usual habit of dissembling allowed him to appear quite composed. Not a false note in his words or the inflection of his voice. Crime was never so confident. The same caresses, the same attentions; he desired, as he has for some time, to spend two or three hours a night with me — and I was all the while unaware, knowing nothing of what those cruel hands had done. Alas! I allowed him to touch me and now tremble with horror. How will I play out to the end the role I've forced upon myself? How can I keep from trembling when he even so much as looks at me? But what to do? I'm without the strength to imagine much less to act.

It nevertheless seems essential that you meet with the priest at Pré-Saint-Gervais, first to learn from him whether the President has made inquiries concerning Sophie. Also, you should advise this churchman as to what we would like him to say in case anyone comes seeking to learn more.

I won't advise Sophie; she can say whatever she wants. What   o
am I to do with the poor girl? It's hard to abandon her — but
dangerous to help her. Since I've decided not to acknowledge
Léonore, perhaps I could continue to claim Sophie as my own.
But how do that now, after what she's told him? I need your
advice, my good friend, for the sentiments of my heart afflict   5
my ability to reason. I don't know what to do. I imagine a hundred ways to save the poor girl and some of them, if put into
action, seem dangerous. To have someone talk to Dolbourg
would grant him confidence he'd surely abuse. Meanwhile the
Count is engaged in such crucial negotiations on Léonore's   10
behalf that I can't ask him for more. What can I possibly do
for Sophie that won't incriminate my husband? I attack one by
protecting the other; I'm fond of one while the other means
nothing to me. Some crimes are woven so tight they can't be
undone.   15

And what do you think of Léonore calmly dispossess-
ing those poor relations? Truthfully, I regret our decision
more than ever. I've always felt something was wrong and
my conscience is deeply disturbed. I told you as much when
we determined she should claim her inheritance. The Count   20
wanted it and now it's too late. But why reduce poor people to
beggary? Could she not have contented herself with her husband's wealth? Or at least shown some mercy for the poorest
among them? And as to her indifference when she talked to
me about Sophie — the very idea of making her an actress or   25
a housemaid! — is that the way pity speaks from the bottom of
her heart? Quite like the man who's the cause of all our pain.

Good night — I close, too confused to write more. Advise me — enlighten me — and above all press forward with
what I've asked.   30

Letter LI
Valcour to Madame de Blamont

Paris, 4 February*

You were right to suspect, Madame, that the President would seek clarification, as if impatient to learn whether his crime was real, and unafraid to weight his conscience with this new horror. The first thing he did after returning from Chateau de Blamont was to rush to Pré-Saint-Gervais. He asked after Claudine Dupuis, but she was dead. He turned to the parish priest and that good man, recalling what we'd said and done, served us as well as if we were right beside him.

"Monsieur," he asked, "what do you want from me?"

The President replied: "To know what became of Claire de Blamont and the woman with whom she was put to nurse."

"The infant died. I provided you with the official death certificate."

"No, Monsieur. She did not die. I had my reasons for taking her away from my wife and made an agreement with the wet nurse to feign her death. I took the girl away with me under cover of night."

"If that be true," asked the priest, "what then do you want of me? Who better than you could know the child's fate?"

"Perhaps the nurse deceived me; I told her I envisaged the happiest life possible for that little girl. The woman may have wished the same fate for her own daughter, whom she might have substituted for mine while keeping the one I intended to take with me. As the result of which, I'd have her daughter and not my own."

* Here it is necessary to recall Letter XXIV (p. 124).

"Such things cannot be done."

"What then became of Claudine's daughter?"

Here the priest made clever use of what happened to Elisabeth de Kerneuil, assigning that child's death to Claudine's daughter — that is, Sophie. In this way he avoided mention of the third child with whom Claire de Blamont had been exchanged. He allowed the President to remain in error. He convinced him that Claudine's daughter was dead and that the person he knew as Sophie was indeed his own child.

If these facts could be supported in a court of law without incurring the scandal you wish to avoid, you'd have no way to save Sophie other than to claim her as your own. Léonore, with no interest in contesting the issue, certainly would not do so, and thus you would perhaps succeed. But that would mean a trial you don't want, and I am far from counseling you to take that path. Everything tells us you must listen less to your heart than see to your own interests. This past fall I very nearly said the opposite — but now the situation has changed. We must not cast matters so darkly. Isn't it simpler to suppose that the two friends, after a new round of debauchery, will place the girl in a provincial convent? Isn't that more reasonable than to suspect some purposeless and unlikely atrocity? There are gratuitous crimes too terrible to conceive, even allowing for excessive human perversity. The crime you fear would be of this type — and so you must not imagine it.

When he saw the priest, to be sure of his facts the President proposed that the supposed body of Claire be exhumed, assuring him they'd find no trace of the remains of an infant. The priest, who thoroughly knew what he was talking about, replied that such a search would serve no purpose; that, as he himself had given the order, he could be certain that the fraud was executed. It was bad enough to have abused the church in this way without adding to the indecency a request for exhumation.

"Besides," he added, "I cannot do it without permission from the archbishop. Would you like to confess to this fraud before him? Believe me, consign this child to the distant past, Monsieur. The child you took away is in your hands and beyond doubt she is your daughter."

"But once more," the President went on, desirous of any proof that could better establish his crime, "what became of Claudine Dupuis' daughter?"

The priest once more told him that she was dead. He finally convinced him by showing the death certificate of Elisabeth de Kerneuil, who was buried with the name of Claudine's daughter, as part of the nurse's scheme, just as you learned of it in the course of my previous inquiry. I repeat: the President is more certain than ever that Sophie is his daughter and all that might have been said to the contrary was nothing but servants' chatter, not to be taken seriously. At this juncture any honest man, recalling the indignities inflicted upon the poor girl in a moment of furious anger, now certain she was his daughter, would be dead from pain and regret. But the President, perfectly at ease with evil and desirous of information only to enjoy the certainty that he had committed this crime — the President, I say, went away as a man fulfilled, features glowing with the malicious pleasure seen in rascals convinced of their atrocities.

I thanked the priest a thousand times for having served us so nicely and we agreed that nothing he'd done compromised his duty; he did not lie but only guarded an entrusted secret, taking advantage of frauds committed upon himself.

Those are the facts, Madame. I have no need to repeat my advice that you should abandon Sophie to whatever Providence has in store; my heart would suffer too much to do so. But whatever interest she inspires in you, kindly consider that you have two daughters and one husband to contend with.

In a judicial investigation, if the priest were compelled to tes-　o
tify, you'd fail to save Sophie but have Léonore returned to
you. However clever that young lady — at present considered
dead in her crib — you'd thereby expose her to the dark deeds
of an atrocious father, able and willing to eliminate Sainville
as an obstacle to the infamies that his perfidious imagination　5
would undoubtedly conceive for this new daughter. If you sued
and lost, which seems certain, you'd have sacrificed Aline to
Dolbourg, with no way of saving her because Sophie would
no longer be considered her sister. And whether you won or
lost, the scandal would ensure that all eyes in Paris were upon　10
you — and all this for a young woman unrelated to you and
yet for whom you've already done everything that the most
extreme sentiments of pity might dictate.

The situation is an unhappy one, Madame, and you may
see in my example the worst possible case that supposes the　15
most unlikely atrocities. But who knows? It's unfortunate too
when a wise shepherd sacrifices a stray sheep rather than risk
the fate of the flock by saving the fugitive. The President uses
guile with you and so, you must use it with him. In every way
possible. I know his presence and attentions disgust you but　20
to refuse them could be dangerous. Follow your initial plan:
the more you draw him close, the more readily will you reveal
his maneuvers and parry his threats. If you distance yourself,
he will become more deceitful and his small schemes will go
undiscovered. Meanwhile, work vigorously to resolve Aline's　25
fate by calling for a family meeting. There you can lay out
the reasons to oppose the union your husband wishes; and
there, too, if your heart maintains for me some affection, you
will mention my name and defend Aline's sentiments thereto.
Restraint and delicacy forbear, I insist further as to this last.　30
O! How my cause will be well served if only you'll defend it!

As to the rest, I shall follow your advice. I will isolate myself; it's a small sacrifice to one who lives and breathes for the tender object he is not allowed to see or meet with. I will deprive myself of the joy of knowing she's nearby when I pray to the Good Lord who can put an end to our misery. So sweet it was to have her by my side in church! When in the fervor of her invocations I sometimes saw her beautiful cheeks flush with the fire of saintly ardor, and tears of pity and contrition flow — then, with much joy, I would say to myself: How could God who so enlivens her not fulfill her desires? He is deep within her and when she implores Him, He will grant her wish — and then, imagining myself prostrate before her, worshiping the same God in this most divine sanctuary, I would address to her and God alike all the sentiments of an inflamed soul. And yet! I will deprive myself of these delights even while my homage abides. Ever before my imagination, I shall adore her in silence, at rest and in solitude — and she and God, confounded as one in my soul, will become the selfsame object of the most violent sentiments of love, offered every moment.

Letter LII
President de Blamont to Dolbourg

Paris, 6 February

So how do we find you, Dolbourg? In truth, I think you're becoming well-behaved. If so, I'll say not a word, for I find nothing more touching than a conversion; I've seen them so seldom that one would be a pleasure to encounter. It certainly must happen. Recoil from them though we might, damned passions trouble and blind us: in youth, violent; at our age, depraved. The older we grow, the more they control us. Tastes are formed, habits developed, and by dint of outrage and abuse we succeed in putting the soul to sleep; we come to understand that the annoying and resurgent passions which sometimes torture it are extinguished by fulfillment, and that the surest way to eradicate them is to nourish them. So, instead of stopping, we redouble our efforts; yesterday's excesses fire today's desires and help invent new projects for the morrow, so we arrive at grave's edge without the slightest concern about falling in. But once there, what becomes of us? Prejudices reborn, we expire in despair.

Here's how it will end: I see you surrounded by priests proving that the Devil waits; and you, trembling and pale, crossing yourself, relinquishing your friends and abjuring what you relish, pass out of life like an imbecile. And why? Because you've no principles. I've told you before: you only listen to your passions without trying to understand them; you've never had enough philosophy to submit them to systematic understanding. You passed over all the prejudices without trying to destroy even one; you left them all behind and they'll be back to torment you when you'll no longer be able to fight back.

701

Infinitely wiser, I use reason to support my deviations. There's nothing to doubt; I've vanquished, uprooted, and destroyed in my heart everything that might disrupt my pleasures. Must I forego them in the end? Having so loved them, I'll be angry and feel at fault as I slip peacefully from life into Nature's bosom, to leave them behind. I've accomplished her will, I shall tell myself, and followed her inspirations. What I did surely must have pleased her for she aroused my desire, and what's there to fear in the end? Must I be frightened of punishment for having gone so pleasantly under the aegis of the laws that guided me? We may go in peace: everything ends when I die, all to be extinguished when my eyes close for the last time; the moments that followed my appearance on earth were just like those when my existence was null. I ought not tremble more for what would come after than I did for what came before. Nothing belongs to me, nothing comes from me. Always guided by blind force, what difference the things it made me do?

With such sentiments, my friend, the tranquility of my final days is not in doubt. Again I tell you: it's not a question of putting aside prejudices but of defeating, subjugating, and destroying them; a single one left behind is enough to give grief. Against every one, my friend, even those that seem the most respectable in the eyes of men, we must declare open warfare.

At any event, I had no business more pressing when I returned from the Chateau de Blamont than to investigate the young creature's own words — so flattered was I to belong to her in so many different ways. I should have fallen into despair, I confess, if one bond could not lend charm to the other. It was not you I feared; your claims were of no account. Only kinship mattered and — you know me, Dolbourg — I trembled from apprehension that my pleasures might be based on naught. But now all is confirmed. I most assuredly have the honor

of having brought Sophie into the world, which must make
memory of the pleasures you enjoyed with her all the more
delicious; she is most certainly legitimate and the sister of the
woman for whom you are destined.* As the happy husband
to my entire family, you shall yet taste the pleasures of the
gods.† There remains only my wife. You wouldn't believe how
much I'd like to see you wither the blossoms of conjugal virtue
of which that lofty spouse is so proud. Would you like me to
hazard a proposition? You play the role of a passionate lover
for twenty-four hours and if she doesn't surrender — as might
be expected — I'll come to your aid. Hah! Forgive me for
laughing, but this seems to me one of my maddest ideas in a
long while. But, yes, I'd like to see you become my wife's lover.

Meanwhile, prepare for the upcoming trip. For a thousand reasons, each better than the last, we must make a decision regarding Sophie as soon as possible; on the road together
we can discuss the best way to proceed with our *agreed-upon
plan.* I don't think that we ought to deviate from it. Madame
de Blamont is dangerous; we must be on guard. Although she
says nothing much for the moment, I won't be her dupe. The
wretched woman works best in silence, like a spider. We must
stop her, set aside any possibility that she might lay claim to
the girl and claim that it's impossible, because Sophie was your
mistress, for Aline to become your wife. You must understand
the necessity to nip in the bud any such calumnies, for any
number of bigots would recoil at the incestuous character of it.

---

* The reader should recall that the President first led Dolbourg to believe that Sophie
was the daughter of his mistress; and said mistress, in addition, was also the sister
of another dulcinea with whom Dolbourg lived; and that each man became father
about the same time to daughters they mutually promised to prostitute to one another when they reached a nubile age.

† The allusion here is to the multiple incestuous relations among the pagan divinities.

Evil-doers always lay blame on the wrongdoing of others, as if they hope by such pedantry to hide their own aberrations.

So, without fail, I shall wait for you on the morning of the 21st. I signal our meeting well in advance, so you'd better remember. All positions will hold during our voyage. I shall do as the great generals: attack the enemy on one flank while weakening the other so that, perhaps, at the conclusion of a successful operation, we'll come away on top, another enemy gone down. Above all, let no pleasure divert you from our essential business; I always fear some momentary distraction will cause you to desert when there's work to be done. Caesar, infinitely more amiable than you, much less mercurial, and more dependable, would lay everything aside for the battle. *Adieu.*

Letter LIII
Déterville to Valcour

13 February

Twice this morning I went to your home, my dear Valcour, but you were out. I decided to leave a letter at the door with instructions that you receive it immediately upon your return. For you must take precautions, remain alert, and from now on, and for some time to come, avoid being alone. The President has set traps; I've not yet learned what kinds of dangers you must fear, but with this kind of monster they are incontestably dreadful. Consider his motives, character, wealth, and the impunity that such vile scoundrels seem to enjoy — and tremble. I'll do everything possible to discover what kind of plot he's brewing. Meanwhile, you owe it to yourself and your friends to be cautious. The moment you need a comrade-in-arms, just launch the word and I'll be at your side.

Think of it! Rascals like him come down hard on the least offense. They dishonor, disgrace, and murder the nation's best citizens while they themselves, the scum of the state, enmeshed with but never serving it, constantly disrupt and betray it — secure against the sword they wield and yet, which they themselves so richly deserve.

When I think of the multitude of dangerous abuses and the intolerable foolishness — the extent of which, aside from comic opera and a few sharp songs, we can't even begin to suspect — how I'm tempted to go live amongst bears!

Letter LIV

Valcour to Madame de Blamont

From my bed, 23 February

There is no sweeter consolation, Madame, than your show of affection! I feel neither pain nor disquiet, for I know you and my dear Aline deign to shed tears for the sorrows that beset me. I've decided to write you myself to prove I'm as well as to be expected — for a man twice stabbed. Neither wound is dangerous. The one that penetrated the top of my left shoulder is the most painful; the other, which pierced the flesh in my right arm, I barely feel. In fact, I can use that hand to write with and recount what happened. Forgive the style and strokes of the pen; the head determining the former is out of sorts while the hand drawing the latter is still weak.*

Yesterday evening, after supper at the home of Countess des Barres, where I had gone to say farewell, following your advice to break off with all my friends, the weather was clear as I walked home. About midnight I turned onto rue de Buci, on my way to rue Mazarine. Four men, armed with swords, ⓑ *fig.* 13 crossed the street and came at me so swiftly that I received the first blow before I had time to defend myself. Backed against a house, I fended off the others; meanwhile, my valet, among the bravest young men I know, sprang at one of the men and with his knee gave a vigorous blow to the stomach that sent him into the gutter. He was about to grab another when I received my second wound. Realizing I was dealing with assassins, I thought only of battling to retreat and, though my arm

---

* The mistakes and repetitions in this letter are indicative of Valcour's condition and ought to convince the reader of the veracity of the correspondence.

was going numb from loss of blood, I protected myself as best   0
I could. I cried out for help and as I saw a police patrol come
running and the murderers fleeing, I quietly put away my
sword. My valet bound my wounds as best he could with handkerchiefs; this brave ally was himself slightly wounded. We
were not far from home and returned without further incident.   5
Without Déteterville's help, I probably would've been quite
worried; but that sweet and dear friend arrived with two of
his domestics and he did not leave my side for even a moment.

If I'd heeded his advice, this unfortunate event might
never have happened. He scolded me and cared for and con-   10
soled me. He talked to me of you — and so wouldn't any misfortune be forgot? All this gentle attention would not have
been mine to enjoy without this accident, and for such friendship I'm so very grateful. We both endlessly speculated about
the incident. Déterville insists on a provenance I cannot allow,   15
as too repugnant to my heart. I'm loath to attribute an act like
this, one I can't even imagine doing myself. A mistake or attack by some low rascal — anything, in a word, to contest my
friend's supposition — makes most sense to me. His affection
for me blinds him and I beg you not to let the same happen to   20
you, Madame. Your gentle soul would suffer too much from
a supposition that all likelihood belies.

Letter LV
Aline to Valcour

Paris, 24 February

What's this I'm told? They tried to hide it from me. You whom I love and wish to forever adore — idol of my heart —, you were beset with dangers yet without me beside you. You shed blood for and because of me — yet where was I? I cannot watch over you or lend help; I want to fly to be with you but am not allowed; I will take no rest or have no respite until I see you. Even if my life and honor and everything I hold most dear be compromised, I must see you with my own eyes and be sure you're safe. *Barbaric father: if I believed you did this, my love for Valcour would stifle Nature's voice.*

Where now and next in my sorry state! When I weep, tears flow but don't soothe; so oppressed my heart, my senses are all destroyed. What was the reason behind this dreadful incident? I will learn what it was or die. Just how much I love you, Valcour! Your pain inflames my ardor and the fatal blade penetrates my heart and the blood that surges from it mingles with tears that drop down upon the words I write! How do you fare? Inform me every hour... every hour I'll send someone to your home. Except when you must take your rest — that I would come provide myself at the expense of my own and indeed of life itself. And why wouldn't I? What do I care? Or fear? The only thing that frightens me is your suffering. Without you nothing matters. All talk of respect, sentiment, decency, and duty are just so many cold vain considerations, without compare to my love for you. Those who do take care of you are so very fortunate. I'd give anything to share their lot! What I am saying? Ah! Were my happiness not denied, I alone would care for you and I'd stop anybody who kept me from it.

Will you even be able to read my words and make out my
jumbled scrawl? My head is bursting with savage despair. Do
the expressions of my heart lost in love and all that I feel even
reach you? Sometimes my soul abandons me to unite with
your own. At those moments I stop breathing and am nothing
but a sad machine. The wellsprings of it can be found deep in
your heart. My mother tries to console me and wants to dry
my tears. If my disquietude were susceptible to her ministrations, what hand could be more comforting? Alas! I can barely
hear and hardly see her — she, the kindest person in my whole
life. Dearest soul and sweet hope of my sorrow-filled days!
Why didn't the cruel blows to my lover not strike and lacer-
ate me instead! I'd suffer less than you from inflicted agonies.
Eternal One: *Avenge him, avenge outraged love no matter who
pays.* Your sensitivity conceals from your soul the real perpetrators of the crime while, so absorbed by your tragedy, mine
is not permitted the same illusions. I see the tyrant — see him
putting knives in the hands of the miserable scoundrels who
assaulted you. *Aim those cruel blades at me, you depraved
man. Pierce the breast of she who adores him. Rip it open, I
say, if you want to banish its burning love! Violent love that
fires me is the sole principle by which I live; it will end only
with my death. And why spare my blood when you shed that of
Valcour? Don't you know it's the same? Don't you know my life
flows in his veins and when you slice them open you spill my
life too? Finish me off if you can but don't try to separate us —
for the souls whose bonds you want to break are forever united.
God only created them so they could be together, and He gave
to each a portion of the other; and these two halves must be
reunited in spite of monsters who want to tear them apart —*
    Wait! *Someone's coming... indeed, back from seeing you.*
And I'm told you're well but don't believe it. They're treating
me badly here. Everybody connives to keep me in the dark.

If you're really well, why don't you write me yourself? Your condition might have changed since he left you. *Go back, foul beast. Go back and tell him to write a note himself to Aline. Let him say in his own hand that he feels better and that he loves her.* Everybody here turns a cold cheek to my tears and cares nothing for my suffering! Only my mother understands me and only her soul is like mine. Even so I'm cruel! She kisses me yet I push her away. I want Valcour. Why does she not take me to him? *If you refuse me, it's because he's no longer alive and you're hiding it from me. You fear I'll follow him down. Don't doubt it! Don't even try! Nothing could stop me. Live without Valcour? In a world he no longer graced? Whatever would I do on earth once he was gone? Send me Déterville, I'll deal only with him. Let him go and take with him the fiery breath of my love. Let him see you and then come back to reassure me — or take me down and strike me dead.*

Letter LVI
Madame de Blamont to Valcour

Paris, 28 February

Stay calm. Aline is better. Her first reaction was terrible — a letter she did not want to show me, written and sent without my consent. It must have convinced you she was in a frightful state after learning of the assault. For a whole day she had convulsions that alarmed us; but now she's as well as can be expected. She wanted constant assurances from you by mail and now has them and finally believes them. You learned what she desired and know me well enough that, if it were possible, there would be no obstacles from my side. But the dangers! I hope you've no doubt that we're being watched. Just imagine what could happen next, after all you've been through. But illusions not permitted! Words, indiscretions, secret information — all cast a ghastly light on a tragic situation, so dire that we can neither scream nor even complain. Will I besmirch the honor of Aline's father? Shall I drag my husband's name through the mud?

He's not been so bold as to make me accommodate his pleasures after inflicting such pain. And just as well because I think it would be impossible for me to dissimulate any longer.

I fear new pitfalls, my friend. I fear a plot upon your freedom. Yet let's not frighten ourselves. I have reliable people who follow my husband's every move and keep me informed. Wait for further clarifications and meanwhile take care of yourself. The scoundrel! He hatched two plots in tandem — attempting to be rid of his daughter's beloved and unburdening himself of a poor young woman he feared might interfere with his perfidious plans.

How can we hope to avoid so many traps? We're surrounded and can never be sure we're safe. Providence may be right as rain, but *vice will crush virtue* — such is the warning I take from the latest news we have of poor Sophie. Allay my suspicions if you can, dispel my fears. Make me see they're unreal. Reassurance is all I need. But such furtive cunning! My friend, you can't imagine my disquiet. If what I suspect is true — if he's capable of absolute horror, then for safety's sake Aline and I should get away from him immediately.

Read on and decide for yourself.

The President and Dolbourg left here on the 21st at six in the morning to go to Chateau de Blamont. After they arrived, about seven in the evening, Sophie was moved to another bedroom, which made it impossible for my dependable fellow from the village to talk to her by her window. This man, with whom I have a personal attachment, did all he could to observe closely and enlisted help of friends.

I enclose the result of his efforts. From his letter you might better judge and even penetrate the thick veil with which these scoundrels enshroud their behavior.

Letter LVII

Addressed to: Madame de Blamont*

Nearby the Chateau de Blamont, 26 February

[...] Following your orders, Madame, I pass without further preamble to the daily record you requested I keep.

On the evening of the 21st, Monsieur le President and his friend arrived at the chateau between seven and eight o'clock. At that hour I would usually see a light in Sophie's bedroom — but not tonight. The upstairs apartments which Monsieur prefers were brightly illuminated; I strained to hear but at that distance, despite the quiet surroundings, I could make out nothing. I returned to Sophie's window three times but it remained dark; she must have been moved to another bedroom.

The morning of the 22nd I learned that our travelers had only a single lackey with them, the same who last time had arrived with Monsieur le President. I also discovered that nobody besides the concierge who prepares their meals was allowed inside the chateau, not even the gardener, from whom I had these details. He needed to meet with Monsieur on urgent matters but could not obtain an audience. Today I renewed my efforts to signal your protégé six different times beneath her window but received no answer. Meanwhile, much was happening in the upstairs bedrooms, where there was a fireplace kept burning and consequently much light in the evening. At nine o'clock the windows were opened in order to close the exterior shutters, then shut again and the blinds were drawn. Darkness was complete. My presence seemed useless, so I left.

---

* This letter was sent together with the previous one. It does not begin as it does here; we leave out the information Madame de Blamont summarized at the conclusion of her last letter.

The same night I asked four friends to watch each of the four roads leading to Chateau Blamont, and made them promise not to return until I told them to. Their orders were to pay most scrupulous attention to every passing carriage and provide an exact report on the occupants.

On the morning of the 23rd the concierge, opening the shutters of Sophie's bedroom, seemed to be alone; he left the windows open until the gentlemen departed, then closed them tight, just as when the house was vacant. That evening I did not catch sight of a fire or any light in Monsieur's apartments. But what surprised me most was to see, on several occasions, light coming from the murder holes, located by the underground caverns.* I approached them as near as I could, close to the moat; but I heard nothing throughout the rest of the evening. I thought everybody must have left. Nevertheless, I asked two men to stay at the chateau just I as I had done the day before; they reported everything remained quiet.

The 24th was also calm; no one occupied any of the rooms with a fireplace; absolutely nobody entered or left. I stopped by under pretext of paying my respects to Monsieur le President, but the concierge told me I was mistaken, that he was nowhere to be found.

At two in the morning on the 25th a coachman arrived leading three horses. Quickly and quietly let inside the chateau, he harnessed the animals to the same carriage that had brought the gentlemen, and it left before daybreak. From behind a tree I saw both men climb into the carriage; assuredly no woman was with them. I had them followed and the coach drove very slowly to the end of the avenue and from there

---

* Embrasures for cannon, frequently found in fortified castles. Some served simply for musketry; while those found in ancient fortresses, before the invention of artillery, were used by archers and for observing enemy forces.

set off at a gallop. At that point I ordered for my four friends   o
to return and while waiting kept watch outside the chateau.
Nobody appeared at any of the windows. They could not have
hidden Sophie from the gardener; he knew she was there
and told me so. I asked him why we no longer saw the young
woman, what had happened to her. He first replied with an   5
air of mystery; then he said she'd left on the evening of the
24th by carriage with a lady who came from Paris to fetch her.
I did not dare tell him that I hadn't left the grounds of the chateau for four days and was absolutely certain what he told me
was false. But I assure you, Madame, that no carriage came   10
by here from the 21st to the 25th. Except for the coachman just
mentioned, absolutely no one entered the chateau during that
time and nobody came out.

Seeing as the gardener wanted to say no more and even
tried to change the subject, I left him and went off to question   15
my friends. Along three of the four roads, only carts trundled
by save for a carriage bearing two old priests. On the other
road, which leads to Lorraine, there passed on the evening
of the 24th a light two-horse coach driven at a slow pace by a
coachman in peasant dress; inside was an old woman, dressed   20
like a villager, and a young woman in a white bodice who was
about the same age and appearance as Sophie. My friend, just
so he could give me further details about the two women, pretended to be drunk and purposely fell beneath the wheels of
the coach. When the women screamed, the coachman pulled   25
up the horses and they got out. My friend rose to his feet and
played the clown so they would talk, and the old lady started
laughing and replied to his nonsense. The young woman's clear
pronunciation bespoke good education: "I am pleased, dear
Monsieur, you did not hurt yourself." But she never smiled or   30
partook in the vulgar gaiety of the older woman who, after a
moment, said suddenly: "Come on, let's go. Nothing can cheer

you up. Your sorrow's going to be the death of me." With a sigh, the young woman returned to the coach.

The more there seemed to be some resemblance to Sophie, the more I questioned my friend. A thousand things proved it was her but another thousand absolutely refuted it. If I had to wager a fortune, I'd do so as to convince you it wasn't her; or, if it was, she must have been spirited from the chateau by flying through the air. If I were deeply persuaded otherwise, I would have mounted my horse and set off in fast pursuit; but I was so sure of what I'd not seen that it didn't occur to me to take such a step.

There you have it, Madame, all I've done in conformity with your orders; I await further instructions to take action, either from within or without.

Post-scriptum by Madame de Blamont

So, Valcour, tell me what you think. Judge as best you can. Sophie was at Chateau de Blamont; no one saw her leave but nevertheless she no longer seems to be there. Where is she? What have they done to her? Is she even still alive? I stop here, for my unfortunate position in all this forbids conjecture. For all that I'd prefer not to suppose evil deeds, the more plausible they seem and force my mind to concur; no sooner does my heart alleviate my suspicions than reason revives them. The fellow ought to have followed the young woman and verified whether it was her. Why couldn't we take care of these things ourselves, in such delicate matters?

Upon the President's return, despite the constraints I am under and words that prove only too well the part he'd played in the attack upon you, I had questions. His journey to Chateau de Blamont, which he in no way concealed from me, enabled me to pose them. He told me Sophie had left there

and was to be placed in a convent in Alsace, where she will   o
be all the more comfortable because Dolbourg would warmly
commend her to the prioress, to whom he is related. Here
my doubts resurfaced: the woman encountered on the road
to Lorraine could have been on going to Alsace; on the other
hand, it seems that she wasn't Sophie. I have no reason to   5
question the work of the man who has been helping me. But if
it was Sophie, why has she not written me? Amidst worry and
anxiety, I dared more questions:

"In whose hands did you entrust care of the young lady?"

"A reliable man," replied the President. "We wanted a woman,   10
which would have been more appropriate. But we could find
none equal to the fellow we had."

"O! Monsieur, forgive my questions, it's childish, I know.
But I had a frightful dream concerning the poor girl and your
responses help dissipate my awful imaginings. What kind of   15
carriage took her away?"

"A light two-horse Phæton."

"How was she dressed?"

"In a blue Levite gown. But, really, your questions!"

"Forgive me, I shall stop. In my dream the poor girl was   20
with a woman and dressed in white."

My friend — please, tell me what you think because, for
myself, I don't dare. It sounded like the same carriage, same
horses. Only the companion and the way she was dressed
seem different. With my questions I'd hoped to dispel my dis-   25
tress but they only made it worse. If you write Aline, say nothing about all this. We are concealing it from her. She's already
devastated by what's happened to you and could not endure
this new shock; there's no point in telling her about it. She
already has too much cause to fear her father; we mustn't give   30
her more reasons to hate him. She is told Sophie was sent to a
convent in Alsace; that's all she needs to know.

o

The President gave the impression he was touched and affected by his daughter's condition. He pretends to not know its cause but this week Dolbourg did not make an appearance. *Adieu* — and by my anxiety you can imagine the impatience with which I await your next letter.*

---

* As it reveals only various dilemmas and resolves none of them because the veil is impenetrable, we have decided to omit this letter from Valcour, together with the first lines of the next, which only concern the uncertainty of Sophie's fate. We resume in Letter LVIII just after Madame de Blamont puts aside that discussion which, though episodic to be sure, is essential. Whoever would fear for Aline must shudder for Sophie. Were this a novel, we would not hesitate in saying there is much art in suspending Damocles' sword over the heroine's head, conveying alarm as to her fate by crushing everyone around her. *Editor's note.*

Letter LVIII
Madame de Blamont to Valcour

Paris, 6 March

....
....
....
.... In Brittany everything goes exceedingly well.
In three months Mademoiselle de Kerneuil will come into
possession of all the assets of her supposed mother; and to
add to her happiness and that of her spouse, the King of Spain
has announced that they can expect 2,000,000 more. The Inquisitor objected directly to the King, contending that the gold
ingots found in Sainville's trunks were not worth that sum;
however false that statement, we are only too happy with the
result. Sainville has written me several letters with *much more
feeling* than those of his dear wife; he did the same vis-à-vis
Count de Beaulé, who continues to serve him most zealously.
    As for the young woman — mannered as ever, witty and
cold hearted — she has engaged in some little villainy quite
revealing of her soul. Certain to soon begin receiving an annuity of 2,000 to 3,000 livres, and having learned of the return of a portion of the gold ingots, she decided to bring suit
against a poor relative with an annuity of 600 livres from the
late Madame de Kerneuil's estate. The poor man, with only
that to live on, will die from hunger if he loses — as by law
he must, for only the legitimate heir's good will could make
a difference. But my dear daughter has formally announced
that she has no mercy for anyone, not for him or anyone else;
consequently, the poor fellow, certainly more deserving than
she, has been forced to renounce a marriage his legacy would
have permitted, and he will be obliged to return to the plow

or look for work to survive. This characteristic of the woman is despicable and most assuredly makes her the daughter of Monsieur de Blamont, but I am sorry to say she's mine also. How is it possible to act so harshly after having been so unhappy? I'd always believed misfortune nudges open the soul, that remembering the pains we ourselves endured, our heart grows more sensitive to the suffering of others. I was wrong. Unhappiness hardens people, dulling them to their own pain; one grows accustomed to be unmoved by that of others, to remain impassive in the face of attack and therefore indifferent to blows that strike others. All this makes me even angrier for having consented to our reprehensible arrangement; I cannot begin to tell you how much it displeases me. But what would have happened to Léonore without it? There were too many good reasons to *not* recognize her as mine and who else could she have belonged to except Mademoiselle de Kerneuil? And that being the case, she must inherit the estate.

When I told the President about her despicable tendency, he was delighted and walking on air. He praised her for an hour.

"There is no circumstance," he told us, "when we must leave others in possession of our assets. It's not a question of whether we need them or not; they belong to us, and that's enough; it would be wrong to give them away. Six months ago I did something much worse at Chateau de Blamont concerning some land I needed in order to enlarge a terrace — a touch of luxury, to be sure, and in the end perfectly useless. For 60 years this bit of land had been the property of a penniless family that lived near the chateau. I searched my title deeds, suspecting usurpation, and found that it was mine free and clear. Immediately I evicted the man, his wife, and a whole gaggle of children, despite their screams and complaints, to which I paid no attention. They were gone and I had my terrace."

"Such is the way the poor fall victim to despair."

"As much of it as you like — but I have my terrace. To all these things reason must be applied. I invoke it for everything, even pleasure and desire; it's the best way to make decisions. Depriving myself of a beautified terrace was a painful sensation; depriving the poor peasant of land was unfortunate for him but necessary. Tell me, if you will be so kind, why I must accept sensations of sorrow on account of this poor Pierre? Why, I ask, do you want me to act charitably toward one who means nothing to me? To anybody with an ounce of sense, I'd be a fool."

"That's unjust. You must compare needs. Pierre's were those of life itself, they must be met. Yours were but a whim you easily could do without."

"You're mistaken, Madame. Whims constitute a habitual need for those of us who are wealthy, just as pressing as what poor fools need to stay afloat. For me, deciding in my favor scarcely requires our needs be equal. Pierre's pain is nothing to me; in no way does it touch my soul. That he eats or not causes me not the slightest anxiety, while that's not the case if I'm deprived of my terrace. Why should I prevent someone from suffering something that I myself don't feel, at the price of something I do? It would be an unforgivable fault in reasoning. When you yield to the sentiment of pity rather than the counsel of reason, and listen to your heart rather than your head, you cast yourself into in an abyss of error, for no organs are more false than those of sensitivity; they lead us to the silliest decisions and most ridiculous actions."

"O! Monsieur, if that's what it means to listen to your heart, let me be a fool my whole life long. Your cruel sophisms will never bring me half the pleasure of a good deed. I'd prefer to be a sensitive imbecile than to possess the genius of Descartes if it must come at my heart's expense."

"It all depends upon the organs themselves," replied the President. "Differences in morality owe entirely to the physics of the thing. But I beg you never to conclude, as I know sometimes happens with you, that one's a monster for not weeping like you over some tragedy or making sacrifices to help some poor lout. Accept that one can exist without being like you and, as a gentleman, I'll agree that amiability belongs only to someone like yourself."

Now comes a false caress, his watch snaps to hand, and he rings the bell. The coach is waiting — off to the opera. This is the man, my friend, the dangerous being with whom we must contend. But I tell you again, don't worry for I shall find out more. There is something in the air, assuredly. He clearly intended to take your life and is quite angry for having failed. Still more certain, he hopes to counteract the blunders committed by the scoundrels he hired to attack you — despite all of which, I assure you, he will do nothing without your being wholly informed.

Letter LIX
Madame de Blamont to Valcour

Paris, 15 March

Fortunately, my dear Valcour, your complete recovery permits
me to tell you about everything that's happened since my last
letter. As concerns you, I've just received the soundest advice
possible. The 500 louis you were offered did not find a home
among souls as delicate as yours. Rather, the money went to
purchase an *order* clearly sought to curtail your freedom.
You are now a wanted man and must leave Paris. You've not
a moment to lose. Take a trip — to Italy, for example. You've
long wanted to go there; it will be edifying, enjoyable, and
safe. You shouldn't suppose we will stay in Paris after you've
gone; by consenting to endless demands I have obtained a few
things myself and can well imagine that what made him agree
to some of them was the hope of soon being rid of you. No
matter, I came away nicely. Here are the articles we agreed to:

1st — I will make no inquiries concerning Sophie. He
has told me where she is and I mustn't worry. Here he was
eager for me, by signed agreement, to renounce the idea that
she might be my daughter. I did not do it.

2nd — I will not allow you to visit us at any time in the
country, where I have asked to go immediately. What treachery! While requiring this clause, the viper has in his pocket
everything he needs to have you arrested!

3rd — I will not get rid of Augustine — despite libertinage
and espionage — everything dreadful you can imagine. At
first I did not believe it but now have unquestionable proof.
Such turpitude!

4th — Next September, without further delay, I will consent
to Aline's marriage to Dolbourg.

In return for accepting these four clauses, I obtained, *first,* as you can see, a delay I consider very important; *second,* authorization to leave immediately for Vertfeuille, where we will have more peace than here; and *third,* I will not have to see either him or his friend until the time I must consent to the marriage — a concession, let me confess, that I find the sweetest. The entire agreement was signed by each of us and witnessed by Monsieur de Beaulé.

Once this was done, the Count told the President that it was impossible to conceal the fact that he was suspected, albeit quietly, of two things; and he begged him, for the sake of his friends, to justify his actions. The first: a plan to assassinate Valcour; the second, to obtain a *lettre de cachet* that would imprison him. You can scarcely imagine with what impudence the man, so accustomed to crime, defended himself.

"I am a man of justice, 20 years older than Monsieur de Valcour," he said. "Despite which, you can be perfectly certain that if I wished to be rid of him I'd employ no such base means like the ones you dare accuse me of. I would propose pistols and, as you force me to explain further, that will indeed be the path I choose if he does not desist in his pretensions, which I do not like, or if he ventures to obstruct in the slightest the arrangements we have agreed upon here today."

"You say nothing of *lettre de cachet,*" said the Count. "I learned of it through official channels."

"You were misled, Monsieur," replied the President. "Perhaps you were told about the order obtained against Sophie, but I certainly did not request another."

"If that is the case," said the Count, "be so kind as to write to the minister, before me as we speak, to tell him we have accused you of plotting to deny Valcour his freedom and you beg him to assure me it's not true."

"On points such as these," replied the President, furious, "my word must suffice." And so he left matters. The Count, who had no desire to break with the President but only wished to be persuaded by him and yet — owing to the latter's demeanor, behavior, and the way he answered — had become quite certain of the facts and told him curtly:

"I must believe you, Monsieur, but I am displeased you do not want to satisfy something as simple as my request, if you really had not acted against our friend. But whatever the truth of your assurances, I declare to you that he shall always have my support."

Here was an end on it. The Count, quite convinced the President has in his pocket a *lettre de cachet*, is the first to advise your departure. He requested I write precisely to tell you to go away, adding that you can count on his help during this period to preserve your safety and well-being.

Now this is our plan, as approved by our mutual friend. I will use the first four months to perfect and secure our project, deploying all available weapons. At the end of July I shall return without warning to Paris and during the last month of tranquility provided by the signed agreement, will contest everything. The salvo will be fired. I will hesitate no longer. My whole family will support me. We will expose the President's conduct. We shall reveal his odious intrigues with Dolbourg and the reasons he wants Aline to marry him. We will point to the unhappy young woman's extreme disgust for the vile creature and make public what justifies that disgust: in a word: *Sophie*. We will quite simply insist that she is mine. This contention will be instigated by my family for I've already agreed otherwise — a tricky step, I know, but sure to succeed. Once the affair has been joined, just mention of her name will so shock the President that he'll do everything he can to forestall the claim. We'll likely never need to go that far for, as you must know, some people are certain he could never produce the creature if required to do so.

Such a horror, let me add in all honesty, whatever we think of all this, I must truly doubt. It is difficult to even imagine things so revolting and it pleases me that the Count de Beaulé, in all sincerity and candor, can no more conceive of it than I. I've long noticed that people apt to suspect crimes are the same who commit them; it is easy to imagine what we can accept but not what we find repugnant. We would not have 10 death sentences in a century if the judiciary was entirely composed of honest men. Instead of claiming, like those wretched scoundrels, that a man once guilty of a crime is bound to remain a criminal his whole life long — an abominable absurdity — I should say that a man, on the contrary, reprimanded or punished for any kind of crime, will surely not do the same thing again as long as he lives. Such is the opinion of good men while the other view is that of those who, knowing they themselves are vicious and capable of recidivism, imagine that others must be like them. Such people ought not to judge men; they will always be severe. And severity is powerfully dangerous; it is surely infinitely better to save a guilty man by indulgence than condemn an innocent one too harshly. The greatest danger of indulgence, to set free one who is guilty, is relatively unimportant, while to destroy the life of one who is innocent, that is a terrible thing.*

Now, my friend, I've a favor to ask. May you love me enough that I need not fear refusal.

---

* Gentle and wise maxims, you have for too long been estranged from our nation: so kindly return to inscribe yourselves eternally upon its spirit, and would that the nation no longer be an embarrassment in the eyes of the universe for having cruelly disregarded them.

As you read this letter, a man I trust, waiting in your an- o
techamber, is charged with providing you with 1,000 louis. I
can only imagine that on the eve of a hasty departure you may
not possess the necessary funds for the voyage I advise. To
whom belongs the responsibility of seeing to your needs if not
your best friend? Valcour — I know you and your refusals. But 5
I must insist. Listen to me. The man you'll see will demand
a quittance for the sum you receive. If you count the money
as an advance upon my daughter's dowry, so be it. But only a
cruel friend would dare refuse.

Letter LX

Valcour to Madame de Blamont

Paris, 16 March

All gratitude, Madame! Is there any need to augment your liens upon my soul? You almost make me cherish my sufferings since through them I obtain such sweet proofs of your excessive kindness. Clever subterfuge, pleasant expectation. In offering help, great sensitivity. Yes, Madame, I will be going away — and leaving immediately, too — because my safety is important to you. Until the moment I depart, I will lodge at a friend's house and remain incognito.

Must I admit, Madame, to something more? Your kindness emboldens me to demand further proof of it. To be so far from you for so long, to go away without seeing you or be allowed to cast myself at the feet of those whom I worship — would your rigor be so severe to condemn me thus? From my heart a most desperate cry: I ask a single favor. In the first days after you arrive at Vertfeuille — when you'll be alone — grant me one hour — even a single minute. How can I tear myself away from my country without a blissful brief visit with the only one that binds me to it? You won't deny me, will you? You won't condemn me to a privation more painful than death itself? Tell me what precautions I must take; show me the road to follow. I'll do everything required and obey you in every respect. There's nothing to which I would not submit to obtain the favor I implore. I await the verdict. Announce it — and be certain that with a single word, you will make me either the happiest of men or the most wretched of lovers.

Letter LXI
Valcour to Aline

Paris, 16 March

If I've been able to instill concern for me in your sensitive soul,
would you deny the new proof of it I implore? You can readily guess what I want; the same desire must stir in your own
heart. The favor denied me last year I painfully remember. But
deign to consider it anew, Aline, for the circumstances today
are much different. I'm wary of this period of apparent calm.
Though I dared not say so, it seemed to me that the renewal
of postponement was granted too lightly. Can we believe in
promised tranquility while taking all sorts of precautions
and permitting all kinds of indignities? If the President did
not want to hurry things along, why does he range such force
to suppress every obstacle? Would that all my premonitions
go for naught but, as I take my leave, I tremble. I can't hide
it from you: the more alarming my fears, the more pressing
my desire to see you. What if we're being deceived! What if
the cruel man's horrible schemes will soon deprive me of the
one I worship! That dreadful thought enters my heart like a
red-hot iron and tears it apart, infusing it with shuddering
death. First let me see you, Aline. Allow me to profess my love
once again, content with your kindness and sympathy, happy
that you admit me into your heart. Then I could at least better
contend with your absence. It is with blood shed for you that
I trace these words, my eyes filled with tears and in my soul,
unbridled desire. If you refuse, Aline, I will go far away, as I
must, but never see you again. Believe me because, however
chimeric the thought, it obsesses me and I cannot suppress
it. In a word: I must see you. My need is so great that I'm not
sure I could even obey if you refuse. Indeed, I would rather

disobey and see you than to die in compliance. My cruel life is dear to me only for the interest you take in it. O Aline! Witness your lover on his knees before you, tearfully imploring a simple favor — to see you for a single minute. See him tremble at the blade wielded by the author of your existence, hoping for a single favor to compensate for his pain. Where would you have me go without seeing you first? Weakened by despair, misled by love, what will become of me if I am, alas, deprived of the solace I seek? Either you never loved me, or you will obtain your mother's permission. I ask and want to kiss you both or die.

Letter LXII
Madame de Blamont to Valcour

Paris, 20 March

Two leagues from the chateau at which your two friends will be staying, between Vertfeuille and Orléans, is a hamlet bordering the forest known as Haut Chêne. On an isolated hill at its outskirts may be found the cottage of an old woman who lives with her daughter, whose name is Colette. She is Aline's friend, whom we mentioned last year; it was on our way back from seeing her that we came upon poor Sophie. Arrive there on April 15th between three and four in the afternoon. Come disguised as a hunter; Colette will know. There you will find two persons for whom you are the dearest in the whole world — two friends who accede to your demands de- spite every danger.

    We leave the first of next month. Until then we should keep wholly silent. Leave Paris as soon as possible, the danger increases with each passing day. Be on your journey when you come to the place mentioned above and from there plan to leave France without a moment to lose. *Adieu.*

Letter LXIII
Aline to Valcour

Paris, 20 March

So tell me: must I not love and eternally cherish this charming mother? Let me tell you what she's done for me: I shall see you. It's all because of her and to her we owe this great favor. The soul of your gentle Aline, filled at once with love and gratitude, will not know which of those sentiments she'll experience that happy day — but how short will be our joy and what dreadful torments might follow! Believe me when I tell you that our cruel separation alarms me just as much as you. I know we've had to become accustomed to living apart, but at least breathed the same air and lived in the same country. Now think of the detestable obstacles that promise to come between us!

How to endure our separation? The more I think of it, the less I'm able to face it. Long absence can give rise to so many things! Until now, though separated, when you were at least not too far away, I felt stronger and suffered with resignation. But who will now inspire me with courage? Who will act as kindred spirit and soul of my life, who will assuage my pain? Valcour! Don't tell me of your premonitions — for my own are too cruel and tear me apart. Forget them. Leave the country because you must, but go assured of my love, for I will follow, my heart tracing your steps. My gaze, ever fixed upon the Alps, shall cross the mountaintop and soar to the heavens. When you arrive at the summit, look back upon the land you've left behind and say to yourself: *There live and breathe two creatures who love and care for me, who rule my days and count every step I take, who desire with as much ardor as me that sweet happy moment when we'll be together again.*

O! My friend, if it's written in the stars that we should
never enjoy such happiness, if all our plans are only illusions,
would we then be wrong to fix our thoughts, as I've often told
you, upon celestial felicity, bound inescapably, to virtue?

To be pitied, my friend, are those who by their suffering
do not have a gratifying faith in religion, or the one who, seeing himself worn down by men, cannot find the words deep
in his heart to say: *There is a fair and benevolent God to offer
recompense for all I've been made to suffer. To his breast He
shall clasp my afflicted soul and for the price of my pain, I shall
have his consoling embrace.*

Yes, I dare affirm: knowledge of a Supreme Being is one
of the sweetest gifts we receive from Nature; there is no moment in life when that idea is less than precious and dear to
us; not a moment when we cannot find within it a torrent of
delights. What manner of being would ever imagine expung-
ing it from mankind? Cruel and barbaric! He would thereby
deprive himself of life's sweetest hope. Does he not realize
that in so doing he thus sharpens the blade of the tyrant and
arms the hand of iniquity? Or that, by lowering the price of all
virtues he opens the door to every vice and hollows out the
abyss into which his systems will cast him? To what class of
men does he belong, the miserable wretch who destroys the
idea of a just God rewarding goodness and punishing evil? Is
he wealthy? Does he oppress his fellows? Let him tremble and
shudder as soon as the man whom he wants to restrain bursts
forth unbridled, tired of being shackled, rebelling against the
yoke. Once there is no God, what risk does the poor slave run?
What's the danger in his plunging a knife into the heart of the
prideful despot who wants to subdue him? Is he poor or infe-
rior, this impious apostle of atheism's somber illusions? When
a man no longer hopes to be rewarded for the good he's done,
who exactly will alleviate his misery, soothe his torments, or

offer the hand of compassion? But why doesn't the servitude he complains about and scourge he resents only intensify when the tyrant who's the cause of it all has no avenger to fear? What is there to say but that such a sad frightful system is good for nothing? It is dangerous for all classes of men — bleak for the oppressed, fatal to the oppressor. The real philosopher must view the time that he takes hold of minds as an era of desolation, when the air, infected by pestilential poison, comes to silently annihilate generations on earth.

Will you forgive your Aline this bit of reasoning and reflection? I feared you'd find me gloomy. Indeed, a lugubrious tincture erupts despite myself and darkens all that I think and imagine; I'd hoped to brighten for a moment in talking to you but, through the words formed by my hand, sorrow flows despite myself; tears efface the lines as I write them. Who makes them flow and why? My mother loves me and my lover adores me; I'm about to see him yet I weep nonetheless. A thick veil seems to extend to the future and my sad gaze cannot penetrate it; and if my fingers move to lift it for even a glimpse, the full features of death appear before me. O my friend! What if you lost her — Aline, so dear to you! Though still young, what if Heaven wanted to call her back? Would you have courage enough to bear the loss? Would you find the strength in your soul to not be devastated? When we meet I will demand you swear to endure tragedy with resignation. Who, I ask, Valcour, can ensure life for even a moment? Frail creatures, we're on earth for the blink of an eye; the day we're born is near the day we die, and in that rapid succession of moments which cannot be fixed and which nothing can stop, we are rushed into the abyss of eternity like the floods of an impetuous torrent across the immense ocean plains. If our few moments of life on earth are so short and readily destroyed, it could happen at any time. Why should love be placed in fragile creatures like ourselves?

Yes, my dearest, I would wish that, convinced by this rea-   o
soning, you'll become the lover of the soul that shall survive
me, not the charms that wither and die in a moment's time.
I've often chided you for too much attention to fragile beauty
and I do so again.

O Valcour! Love in me just what cannot melt away; cher-   5
ish only the soul to which your own will be reunited one day.
Believe me and renounce the rest before you're forced to — by
men or by death itself. Consider the great difference between
the two objects that I offer your love: if you went fifteen years
without seeing me, I'd defy you to draw my portrait. Whilst   10
the movements of my soul and my thoughts will never desert
you. Prefer what you can keep forever to what can vanish in
a moment. Consider that if you love me this way, you'll miss
me far less if you lose me. Of what importance is a thing that
must come to nothing compared to the delicious certainty   15
that what is unchangeable will never escape us? What of me
will you love, I ask you, when matter goes to dust and there's
nothing in the coffin save the rattle of bones? Even supposing that those disfigured charms could appear to your senses,
they would only induce despair; but the expressions of the   20
soul I want you to prefer — they will flow through your own,
enlivening and fulfilling it.

It would be better, and I would love you more, it seems
to me, if you would consent to love me thus. I would so purify
the sentiments of my soul that it would bring you happiness,   25
such that the cult it created would be absolutely like the devotions offered up to God. No more separation, nothing could
trouble us, or divide us, or kill us; and our unassailable love
would live as long as God Himself.

Here I leave you. I tried putting aside my pen but, taking   30
it up again, find it still filled with melancholia's venom, alarming your soul instead of fortifying it. I cannot succeed in consoling you and that only afflicts me still more.

Letter LXIV
President de Blamont to Dolbourg

Paris, 29 March

I must see you. Can you believe it? Augustine trembles when the time comes to act. As if we're demanding of her something extraordinary. I thought she was clever, but no — she's an imbecile. When important matters are at stake, we should assign them to good minds. She wants me to come to Vertfeuille. In my presence she could act with greater courage. The idiot! You can see how we must restore this feeble mind to the right path. You must arrange for me to dine with her at your little house in the *faubourg*, tomorrow night at the latest, since we leave the next day. We will triumph, I hope, over foolish scruples. At times I've seen the small mind of a woman tempered by fire to carry out these sorts of things. Incredible what we can obtain from moments of intoxication when a woman's soul, driven closer to the state of malice for which Nature intended her, more readily accepts all the horrors we propose. I quite agree that neither you nor I should plan to pick that particular lock. Our age and our principles of sensuous delight — in a word, our way of being in the world — have a poor fit with the outrageous demands of an 18-year-old whose head we're intent on turning. For those kinds of jousts I've an incomparable valet who will fearlessly take on the physical side of things so that, when we receive her hot from his hand, we'll be able to work on her mind with confidence.

Nothing worse than this kind of vacillation, but it's what we must expect whenever we employ the female sex. Shy by nature, in spirit faint-of-heart, I've long said that women are only good in bed — at best, apart from which we must expect nothing. False or weak, perfidious or blasé: if we entrust them

with a plan, they make a hash of it through listless behavior
or else betray it by meanness. Machiavelli surely had them in
mind in saying that one must either never choose them as accomplices or else make them quickly disappear once the deed
is done.* For this task I am sorry we didn't engage that old
rascal of an alms-giver priest who was in my pay for three
years — enterprising, deceitful, cunning, and a hypocrite. He
would have pursued the operation with duplicity and vigor.
I've never seen anyone more reliable and sure-footed. To that
fine fellow alone I owe adventures enough that I — *the judge*
— could send 30 scoundrels to the gallows. As you know, my
friend, for us there's a great difference between the thing we
are forced to uphold and what we enjoy doing ourselves. Beneath the fairness in which we cloak ourselves boil passions
that melt like wax beneath the burning sun; but we nonetheless must condemn what we do and punish what we cherish;
by scrupulously displaying inflexibility in morals, we succeed
in artfully covering our own depravation. It's only a question
of laying claim to morality; when not by recourse to our virtues, at least with all possible rigor.

I've also very unhappy about this failure in dealing with
Valcour. Skillful villains though they were, too, capable of a
thousand such similar acts of kindness — from all of which I
might have absolved them for the price of just that one. Imbeciles! But at all events, we're rid of him. He must be scared out
of his wits and won't dare show his face before it's over.

Tonight I won't see you for it is consecrated to conjugal
farewells and you can easily understand why I want them to
be tender. She and I will part *for quite some time* — a pleasant
idea, to be sure, delighted I've conceived of it.

---

* The President here advances, for women alone, the abominable opinion regarding
accomplices found in Machiavelli's *The Prince*.

Indeed, from time to time it's nice to test just how far your soul will take you; you can hardly imagine how wildly happy I am with my own. In all this the only emotion I feel is a kind of unalloyed pleasure. A strange thing, analysis of the human heart! I'm perfectly sure than we can make of it anything we want; it readily receives impressions from the head and soon adapts to those movements alone, with nothing to oppose circulation of the voluptuous venom.

Hurry, though. Any delay could be fatal. I distrust my wife the President, and despite our signed agreements, will bet that she works secretly hand-in-hand with her adorable protector, the charming Count. The other day he imagined he made me uneasy! Nothing amuses me more than these debonair fellows who believe they're putting themselves over on professional rascals like us. To hear them talk, they crush us with the power of virtue; but if virtue is illusory, and if we always see it thus, there's little danger of that.

Adieu, tender sweet husband! I can see you already in the wedding embrace, lavishing kisses that draw forth, perhaps in those first days, a flood of tears which, however, are soon to be dried by the heat of your passion, as their frenzy dispels all pungency of resistance.

But no jealousy, I beg you. We can't afford something ludicrous that could stop us from mingling pleasures as we do mistresses. Remember that one of the clauses in the contract is that *1 lend but 1 do not give.* You owe me that at least, for the care I've long taken in satisfying your wishes. You cannot imagine, my friend, the desire I have to possess Aline; I find such stinging detail in the dear young thing. It must be delicious to *take her* in tears! Sophie was all very fine, but Aline! We'll never go as far with the latter as with the former; there's some sort of consideration we owe to virtue — and to blood. But let's not swear on anything because, for minds like ours, the paths we take are, as you know, *unbounded.*

Letter LXV
Valcour to Déterville

Dijon, 20 April

Arrived here and plan to leave tomorrow. If health permitted,
I might've gone directly to Savoy. But I need a few days' rest.

My dear Déterville! How ill-starred the separation! The
horror that accompanied it, my wounds not yet healed, the
awful agitation of my soul, and terrible foreboding owing
to the intricacies of these cruel farewells — everything, my
friend, has put me in a state where I can't go on. Let me take a
moment to depose before your heart some of the sorrow that
torments my own.

Listen as I recount the lugubrious circumstances of my
long-sought meeting, and tell me if you don't see, as I do, that
heaven's judgment is written in blood.

After having embraced you and said goodbye on the
evening of the 8th, to better cover my departure from Paris,
I left for the rendezvous just as Madame de Blamont firmly
instructed, disguised as a hunter. I traveled alone on foot to
Orléans while my valet, with my luggage, went to wait for me
in Montargis. Unfamiliar with the road to the hamlet that was
my destination, and so planning to give myself plenty of time,
on the 15th I left the city at about seven o'clock in the morning.
Imagine my surprise when, after walking through the forest
until near midday, I asked a passing woodsman if I was far
from Vertfeuille, and he'd never heard of the place.

Great heavens! If I didn't arrive on time, they'd be waiting for me and terribly concerned — and here I was, worried
to death myself. What would become of me? In the middle of
a forest in a place I didn't know, with not a house within three
leagues where I might hope to ask directions? One moment

I wanted to return to the city, the next I hoped to meet some-body better acquainted with the countryside. Adopting that alternative, I begged a passing peasant to guide me to the nearest house.

"I've got to be careful," he replied. "You're a poacher, aren't you? Custodians at the house where you want me to take you will show no mercy and I don't want to be the cause of your death. The best thing you can do is go back the way you came."

Although my disguise presented no great danger at Vert-feuille, I saw that wasn't the case thereabouts, especially if I couldn't identify myself. So I took leave of my man and walked four leagues further, making my way as best I could without meeting a soul. Suddenly the sky darkened. Perceiving no shelter nearby while still walking aimlessly on, I went deep into the forest. Shortly thereafter, night fast descended and little by little the cloud cover deepened and brought a sense of darkest dread.

Although still early in the season, lightning flashed across the sky and announced a frightful thunderstorm. The wind howled. With prodigious power it split trees as everywhere the sky burst forth with celestial fire. Twenty times lightning crashed close by and 20 times I thought myself lucky enough to meet my maker. Suddenly came the lugubrious sound of a multitude of tolling church bells that added more horror to the scene. Blackest thoughts shattered my mind in response to Nature's fury, with terrible quiet punctuated by howling winds, lightning bolts, and the clanging of the bells that sent majestic sounds soaring to heaven and made me fear I wasn't the only one that day threatened by God's wrath.

Ill-fated soul! I cried. The object of these sinister lamen-tations, striking my ears with mournful tropes, must be my Aline. She must be dead. Ghosts by the thousands seemed to take flight around me and I saw among them the cherished

shade of the one I adore, but she escaped my embrace in a
torrent of flames and vanished from sight. I fell roiling to the
ground, wishing the flooded earth would open to receive me.
My reason gone, I remained the rest of the night lost in pain
and despair.

The winds subsided at last, stars shone, and the sky cleared
— and so my soul, just made the plaything of insurgent elements, dared open itself to hope once more, just as branches
of surrounding oaks, bent by the impetuous north wind, recovered their majesty.

Taking to the road again, I resolved only to return to the
city. I arrived there on the 16th at six o'clock in the morning.
After a short rest, I left at eight with a guide hired to take me
to Haut-Chêne in less than five hours. Arriving there without
incident, and not wanting the man as a witness, I dismissed
him as soon as the hamlet was in sight.

"O, Monsieur!" exclaimed Colette's mother when I
reached the house. "The ladies waited for you with such impatience yesterday! They were so worried and only left in
tears when night fell. I'm sure they didn't reach home before
the storm." She turned to her daughter: "Go, Colette, and tell
them just as they insisted we do. Take off your sabots to walk
faster. Meanwhile, my brave man, rest easy." The good woman
offered me everything she could. "We're very poor, alas, Monsieur, and have not a lot to offer you — but all from the heart.
Without the charity of Madame and Mademoiselle, my child
and I would long be gone from this world. They're such good
souls, Monsieur! So many wait for the poor to come to them
but these ladies seek them out. They live to help. You can
see how we love them so. We could shed our blood for them,
drop by drop, and still think we'd done nothing."

It warmed my heart to hear such things and my eyes filled
with sweet tears. Is anything more wonderful than praise for
the ones we love?

Colette returned at last, out of breath; she'd run the whole four leagues, there and back in less than two hours.

"They're on their way," said the poor perspiring child. "They're following me, Monsieur. I made them so happy." Throwing her arms around her elderly mother, she added: "I helped them so much that Madame said she'll give me the ten sheep I need to marry Colas. I'll marry him, Mother! I will! Won't I?"

Unable to resist the young woman's innocent joy, I said: "Yes, you shall marry him. And here are 10 louis, all I've with me right now. Take them for your wedding bouquet; it's only fair that I share in the gratitude for a favor that's even more precious to me than to my friends."

Hardly were the words out of my mouth than the ladies arrived.

Madame de Blamont was the first to cast herself into my arms; just after, my Aline, in tears. After pressing both close to my heart and covering both with the delightful caresses that the soul lavishes but words cannot depict, we settled down to talk. Our respectable mother gave the best and wisest advice. She shared with me the wise counsels and prospects as she envisioned them and her plans to achieve them; she told me of everything she'd already done and of the glimmers of hope, and what must be done to succeed. In a word, to believe what she said, I may view my happiness as certain come autumn. She instructed me to come back then. We arranged our correspondence, using a map, with respect to the various cities where I'll be staying. Both made me promise to be punctual in my replies. To Madame de Blamont I brought up my concern that the interest she took in me could cause her further misfortune. What was there not to fear from a furious husband, constantly fulminating against my sentiments for his daughter? Most vividly I explained how aware and sensitive I was of the pain she experienced on my behalf. Turning to me, beautiful eyes brimming with tears, she said:

"And what does it matter, my friend, if I'm a little more or a bit less unhappy? At all events I will be miserable without you; helping you offers at least some consolation." _o

With those words she pressed tight my hand and my lips imprinted upon her own kisses of friendship and liveliest gratitude. ₅

"My dearest," said, Aline, drawing me near, "promise and swear to me you'll write without fail."

"Great heavens! Can you doubt it?"

"Well, then, take this," said the beloved young woman, presenting me with a superb letter case. "I want you to use it exclusively for my letters. I forbid any other purpose." 10

Seizing the precious object, I devoured it with kisses and opened it to reveal a portrait of Aline, exhilarating to sight and soul. Beneath the cherished portrait, the goddess I worship had written — in blood — two sentences to be em- 15 blazoned on my soul, the sanctuary in which her image shall reign forever, and which I reveal to you: *Think of me always. And let that thought be the source of your every action.* There they are, Déterville, the cherished lines — and would the hand of Eternal God reduce me to dust the moment they are not 20 the law of my life.

"The blood with which I wrote those words came from here," said Aline, pressing my hand to her breast. "They are expressions from the heart that adores you, engraved with the blood that moves it. May all this be dear to you, my friend, 25 and never forget that a poor girl will swear by her own mother that she will never live for anyone but you."

So saying, she knelt, and her respectable mother, as moved as those around her, took her daughter's hand and placed it in mine, and said: 30

"Yes, Valcour. She belongs to you. As heaven is my witness, I shall give my consent to you and you alone."

No sooner had I cast myself into the arms of these dear friends than my silence, more eloquent than words, convinced them that my impassioned soul was entrusted to theirs for the rest of my life.

Meanwhile, night portended and it was time to go. Madame de Blamont thought herself strong enough and stood up without looking at me. Her daughter understood and wanted to do the same but her knees trembled and she dropped into her chair in tears. Madame de Blamont with noble firmness:

"I must leave behind my friend, just as you must, my daughter. Hopes of seeing him again sustain me and give me the courage to separate."

But Aline heard none of it. She lay in my arms, her tears and mine flowed together, and from her arose only bitter cries of pain and sobs of desperation. Madame de Blamont sat down again and, taking her daughter's hand, kissed it with such passion that the vivid caress produced in Aline's soul the diversion that the sensitive and spiritual woman intended. She turned to her mother and buried her head in her bosom, shedding another torrent of tears. Madame de Blamont immediately stood up and all but carried Aline across the threshold while signaling me to go into another room. With an impetuous soul's sacred intensity, yet cruel foreboding that still fills my own with fear and anxiety, the dear girl turned toward the place she'd just left, thinking I was still there; and not seeing me, pulled away from her mother's arms, walked straight to where I was and fell motionless at my feet. Now my own heart burst and its effervescence could not be allayed. I swept her up in my arms and pressed her to me. Our bodies entwined like our souls as a single mass that no power could disjoin, until at last I regained my reason only by my desire to return to life the woman whose sorrow was tearing me apart — she who by her pain suspended all the faculties of my being.

"Flee!" said Madame de Blamont as she lay her poor
daughter across the bed. "Go now, for it's better she not find
you here when she awakens. Go, my heavenly friend." She held
out her hands. "Remember what happened here, recall how
much you are loved, and if you believe my daughter's dear to
me, you may be sure, lest death take me, that she will belong
to no one else but you."

Kneeling to kiss the dear hand, flooding it with tears of
gratitude and tenderness, I dared once more gaze upon my
heart's idol; and I expressed, albeit without her hearing me,
my final words of adoration before rushing off into the forest,
intent upon reaching Orléans the same night. From them I
shall hope to learn the suite of this sad and painful separation. I implore you to obtain more from them and the greatest
detail possible. But let me finish by telling you what happened
with me.

I made scarcely two leagues before nightfall made me
fearful of getting lost again as happened the day before. My
state of mind kept me from finding my way. I resolved to stay
the night at the foot of a tree, waiting for sunrise to console
the earth and, if possible, calm my beating heart. I lay down
beneath an ancient oak, downcast and plunged into thought,
giving myself over to melancholia that at the same time
seemed to dull my senses so that in my violent sorrows I saw
the prospect of a moment's rest which my soul would not have
obtained if it was less overwhelmed. I slept. But no sooner did
I shut my eyes than a dreadful ghost appeared to my fettered
senses. I can see it still. As I write I know I must have been
dreaming but can't be sure — the impression was too vivid —
no, my friend, I declare it was not a dream.

The ghost — I saw it — garbed in black with a face I can
only describe as Aline's father. His hand clutched the dear
girl's head — forgive my confusion — and he held it up by the

hair. He shook it before me and blood surged out, mingling with the blood of my own reopened wounds. He talked to me during this ghastly spectacle — talked, I say, and his harsh words struck me hard. I could not have been asleep. The cruel man said: *Here is the woman you want to marry. Tremble before her now, for you will never see her again.* I clutched at the phantom, wanting to tear from his grasp the precious head and bring it bloody and bleeding to my lips. But I only grasped at shadows as it instantly disappeared. Nothing but terror and despair remained. In mortal anxiety I rose and began to walk aimlessly. Giant dark shadows cast by moonlight through the trees all around seemed to make all the more real my lugubrious vision. At that cruel moment I would've given my life for a single word from my Aline and a mere instant to have drawn her gaze upon me. While a thousand thoughts raced through my mind, I was ravaged by a thousand torments. At times I wanted to turn back and retrace my steps, and other times I wanted to end my life the better not to survive the woman whom my imagination had just presented as dead before my eyes.

At last the sun came up and more by chance than the incertitude of my unsteady steps, I entered the city — only to depart a few hours later to join my servant in Auxerre, thereby to reach Dijon from where I write you these lines. From here I'll quit France altogether and faithfully execute the orders of my two devoted friends, so as to merit their trust and respect. *Adieu.* This has been a long letter indeed, burdened with heartrending details; but we soothe our pain by discharging it into the heart of a friend. Hurry to see the two objects of my affection; apprise me of their fate and inform them of my own; confer with them and tell me their thoughts in fine detail. And consider that to truly care for a friend, one must pit love against despair.

Letter LXVI
Aline to Valcour

Vertfeuille, 22 April

Why must my first letter to you since your departure be penned with a trembling hand? Never do my heart's expressions reach you without weeping; they always arrive with a flood of tears. Let me tell you what happened from that dreadful moment you tore yourself away from your unhappy friends. My own terrible state forced my mother to spend the night by my side in Colette's home; we sent her off with a message to the chateau so as not to spread worry, then returned by dinnertime the next day. Augustine, my father's young charge, whom I've told you about, seemed surprised by our brief absence, and my mother and I couldn't help noticing that her questions suggested infinitely more curiosity than concern. We no longer doubt but that she's watching our movements at the President's behest. We will keep her nonetheless, for my mother wants to fully respect the agreements. But we now distrust her. I don't know but since we've been back at Vertfeuille I see something deviant in her fine eyes — superb yet frightening. In the past they displayed candor, decency, and honesty in a way that enhanced her attractiveness. Today, only haughtiness and arrogance. How vice makes for ugliness! Poor thing — the same face, once lovely and good, but now we can only look upon it with disgust. You see what seduction and debauchery have wrought, how crime is so entirely Nature's enemy that its odious features ruin her charm when they don't destroy it entirely.

Everything was quiet until the 18th. That day around three o'clock, my mother felt unwell. The next day she had a fever accompanied by headache, lethargy, and intestinal trouble.

She improved on the 20th and her doctor told her it was nothing, there was no danger whatsoever. After prescribing the usual medicines to treat the feeling of heaviness, he went away. All was stable through the 21st. But today the pain has returned, in spite of the strictest diet. Her fever is higher than on the first day, the headache more severe, and intestinal pain more acute. Now we're waiting for the physician to come; but owing to the mail schedule I must post my letter to you before knowing the results of his visit.

From my father this afternoon, we received a very tender note. He says he just learned of her condition and is extremely worried. If he did not fear disturbing the arrangement, he would fly to her bedside. He asks her, considering the circumstances, if she would allow him to obey his heart. Replying on behalf of Mother, I told him he may do as he likes but she thinks her indisposition not so serious as to warrant him to come.

O! Valcour! How terrible all this for your Aline — can you imagine the torment? Can you guess the state of her soul? Although, fortunately, nothing suggests the worst possible outcome — I tremble at the thought — but if it did happen — if I lost my best and most precious friend — what dread disaster! What if the hand of God burst my life's most tender bond! You will scold me, and I deserve it — you'll say that my imagination, always dark, takes pleasure in tragedy and embraces it for its own sake.

Well, think what you like, but in writing these lines I'm not myself. Fear that makes me shudder compels me to set down the words it dictates or put up my pen.

Can you believe, my friend, that I might survive the woman who gave me life? You know how much I love her — can you even imagine? Such a frightful loss would rob me at once of my hope to devote my life to her and to spend it with you.

Do you imagine that? No! Of course not! I swear to you that   o
I wouldn't survive her for a single moment. I'd soon cut short
a life that would bring me nothing but pain.

 I am far from thinking that it is wrong to put an end to
one's life when it can bring happiness neither to ourselves nor
to others. Life is a not a burden to be borne against our will.   5
Our soul in the image that God created, early set free of its
bonds, will return no less pure to Our Father's bosom. If our
soul is only to languish, locked away for a time in our body, if
its real destination is to be near God from whom it emanates,
why should it not be reunited with Him? Can the soul's wish   10
to rejoin its author ever be a crime? It is the human being who
believes all shall perish when he dies, whose feeble imagination cannot rise to the sublime doctrine of the immortality of
the soul, who must fear death, and will tremble to end his own
life. But for one who sees only a coarse envelope that contains   15
the shining portion which belongs to God, it is as if he were
confined to a prison but not obliged to remain and can break
free from those chains when the pain becomes too great. He
who sees this life only as a passage can turn, when he finds his
path strewn with thorns, toward the final resting place. What   20
threat is there to his immortal soul? Can it be hurt by the
blows that set it free? They disorganize its material substance,
the form of which is the same everywhere in Nature. Of what
importance are the elements of which we're composed, disposed as they are in such and such manner? It's not in our   25
power to destroy anything when we bring death upon ourselves; we only vary and modify a right given us by Nature;
it contradicts none of her laws because it detracts nothing
from her foundations, those indestructible elements she herself transforms every day in thousands of different ways.   30
 Just suppose for a moment I found myself in a situation in
which I cannot go on living without being the cause of a host

of murders, and unable to avoid committing them myself. Would not that state of continued disorder and hopelessness irritate the Divinity far more than the little wrong I'd do by taking my own life? And in all possible cases, isn't one murder — if that's what you want to call it — preferable to 200? If I don't commit that latter crime by killing myself instead, if I'm firmly convinced I'm permitted to break free of my shackles when they so afflict me — is not that action, when it saves me from committing untold murders, on the contrary, praiseworthy? Doesn't it warrant the Eternal One's approbation? Is our existence so precious that one creature more or less in this universe should be regarded as something so very important?

Should the general of an army, in the name of the Prince of Peace, sacrifice 20,000 men in a single day and return from the carnage to be covered with honor and glory, while only disgrace and opprobrium await the unfortunate who eagerly eliminates himself to rejoice in celestial light, who aspires to take leave of falsity, selfishness, libertinage, and crime, destroying a single fragile life on earth to sooner join God in Heaven? To whom belongs my life if not to me, myself? Who may dispose of it if not I? If this life is a gift from God, He can only demand I look upon it with respect, so long as nothing keeps me from seeing it that way; but when that fine thing becomes an onerous burden that weighs upon and no longer serves me, I may return it without fear to the One from whom I received it. I might indeed be ungrateful if, wishing to enjoy the gift of life, which was meant to be a way of glorifying the One who endowed me with it, I defiled it with crime. If to the contrary, for fear of committing murder, I returned the gift that I would only profane by keeping it, my self-undoing would not be wrong.

Forgive these thoughts, my dearest! Some power stronger than myself inspires them. If the voice that dictates them

were to compel me — if I was going to leave you on earth — if
you were to lose the one whom you loved so — would you
forever cherish her memory? Would you ever watch over your
dear Aline? Would she live always in your thoughts? Would
she be forever the soul of your life, the elementary matter of
your existence? Dearest Valcour, if the God to whom I pray
deigns to listen, I would ask Him a favor: that the breath
which once animated the body of the woman you loved might
inhabit your own. And if I obtained such a favor, you could
observe that there were days when you would love me all the
more and remark upon those when my presence was palpable.
These would be the days, my beloved, when the soul of your
Aline would have awakened within you, and you would be
stirred by her alone.

My mother is calling — I'd taken advantage of a moment's
quiet to write you. But now she's awakened, sicker than ever.
She's shivering and vomiting. I'm ghastly unhappy. Nothing
any longer obscures the future for me. The awful veil becloud-
ing my life has been torn away and all the horrors I once only
glimpsed from afar are now advancing as the scythe of death
upon me. The Angel of Death opens the coffin. One step more
and your poor Aline will lie within.

Letter LXVII
Déterville to Valcour

Vertfeuille, 6 May

They exist no more, those happy times when I would take up
my pen to convey interesting facts and pass my days easing
your pain, amusing you with some of the same stories that enchanted those that you love so tenderly. Take the serpentine
tracings beneath this funereal pen to be as cruel vipers that
will tear your heart asunder; and opening this letter — tremble. I shall not say to you: Take courage. I have no consolation
to offer and would hold you in scarce esteem or not know you
at all if that was the tack and tone I took. No: *read this and
die.* I shall not compel you to an existence too cruel after the
losses of which you're about to learn. Time to yield, Valcour.
Life henceforth offers you none but thorns. Unite your soul
with those of your friends. Once more: read on, I say, and go
to your grave.

Hardly had I heard of Madame de Blamont's condition
than I rushed to Vertfeuille. A man on horseback came to beg
me come, for there was not a moment to lose; this courier
also brought a letter for the Count de Beaulé, requesting he
join me; but the day before he'd departed for the coast on urgent inspections. I forwarded him the letter by post with a
note from me and arrived alone on the 24th. As you can well
imagine, everyone was in a state of extreme desolation, for
what afflicted our great good friend had become very grave.
Symptoms both singular and frightening had reappeared on
the 22nd; and the doctor confided to me that if she did not
improve by the next day he would give her just three days
more to live. I carefully refrained from conveying such news
to Aline, whose heart was already full of foreboding; and as

her mother awaited me — with impatience, they told me — I   o
went to her directly. She took my hand the moment she saw
me and pressed it tight.

"O! My good friend. I'm indeed afraid we must part."

And when she saw I was trying to reassure her, she added:
"At all events I wanted to see you and convey to you my last   5
wishes."

"What useless precaution! Why such gloomy imaginings
when there's so much hope?"

"I won't die from wishes, my friend — they do no harm
but provide tranquility."   10

With those words she proffered a written document and
bade me read it. Since it contains many clauses which, despite
your attachment to this dignified lady, are inconsequential to
you, I will only tell you about the most important.

Married by an agreement that included separation of as-   15
sets, and so in possession of all she owned prior to marriage,
she leaves everything to her daughter, Aline, under a careful
clause that specifies a marital union with you; and she asks
her husband, as one final kindness, not to force her daughter's
hand in a matter upon which depended her whole happiness   20
or misery in life. In the case in which Aline is forced into a different marriage against her will, she would not be deprived of
her inheritance but it is stipulated that she is the sole legatee,
and it forms in no way part of a shared community of assets. In
addition, she leaves funds to establish a hospital of six beds at   25
Vertfeuille, solely for the use of the local inhabitants, with the
monies for this establishment to be held by her conveyancer.

Further, she wants the simplest sort of burial in her local
parish but desires that all poor people living on her land would
be fed for nine days, morning and evening, served by her peo-   30
ple in the main room of the chateau. She asks that I send you,
on the day after her death, a small box containing her portrait

in an ornate frame decorated with gems worth 15,000 francs. She wants her superb hair to be shorn and given to her daughter. She leaves a jewel worth 12,000 francs to Léonore, and to Sainville another beautiful box which also contains her portrait. The document concludes with wise advice to Aline and moral counsels full of piety; she further wishes that her loving daughter never choose another sepulcher than the vault into which her mother is to be laid. She names me as testamentary executor of her legacy and her wishes; and she begs and enjoins me, in the name of our long friendship, to faithfully execute them, all based on her written document.

As soon as she saw I'd finished reading, she asked me with great urgency if I would swear to carry out her wishes. I so promised, taking her hands in mine. She smiled and told me that I had proved to her I was her friend and, now with this assurance, she was far more at peace. She slept for about three hours, the night of the 24th into the early morning of the 25th. Awakening toward two o'clock in the morning, she called for Aline, who had sweetly refused to leave her bedside, and drew her upon her breast, telling her that she felt still worse. Her daughter dissolved into tears while Madame de Blamont controlled herself so as not to afflict the young woman who'd so cruelly suffered and shared so much of her pain. She begged her to take a short rest, assuring her that I would take her place; but Aline denied anyone the pleasure she took in caring for her mother. She said she would yield to no one, that men did not understand such things; and no orders, pressure, or pleading would make her leave.

How very fine she was, my friend, in carrying out those sacred tasks! Pale, sunken eyes, hair disheveled, dressed in a plain cotton housecoat, a chambermaid's apron fastened around her waist — all made it seem as if filial piety wanted to compete with the Graces for the right to embellish her beauty.

But the pain increased and Madame de Blamont could o
no longer conceal it. The doctor, who was in constant atten-
dance, approached me after examining her.

"Exactly as I feared," he told me. "She is lost."

"Good God!" I replied, frightened. "Lost? At her age? In
such fine health, with all her resources and goodness." 5

"She is lost."

"Why? From what disease? What can be the cause of this
unexpected malady?"

"A cause that defeats every secret of the art of medicine.
She's been poisoned." 10

"Poisoned!"

"So she is. What do you want me to do?"

"Write her husband. But withhold the cause of death from
both her and her daughter, and also from the entire household.
I think that's wisest." 15

The physician wrote down, signed and sealed his opinion;
and the letter went out by secret courier.

Intestinal pains followed an irregular course during the
day. At one of the most violent crises, Aline brought us all to
tears when she cast herself at the doctor's feet. "O! Monsieur," 20
she cried in a frightful burst of pain. "Save my mother! All
I possess is yours. I'll donate everything I have to you."

But when she saw the doctor recoil, not answering but
touching a handkerchief to his eyes, she swiftly returned to
her mother, invoking Eternal God with such compunction 25
and fervor that she was overcome with the violence of it and
fainted in my arms. We put her to bed and when she regained
consciousness, I did my best to make her understand that
she must try to remain calm, that her wild intemperance was
damaging not only her health but that of her mother. At first 30
I thought my words seemed to soothe her and so I decided to
try to gently prepare her for the terrible news to come; but she
interrupted me fiercely and screamed:

"Great God in heaven! Is she dead?"

Despite my efforts to restrain her, she escaped me and flew directly to her mother's bedside and fell on her knees, hands joined in prayer. Madame de Blamont, feeling a little better, rose up and gently scolded Aline for being so frantic, and kissing her brow, added;

"Do you no longer want us to talk calmly together?"

"O! My dear sweet mother!" Aline answered in tears: "Don't you know how much I love you? Don't you realize how your fate is irrevocably linked to mine?"

"If you love me, prove it by calming yourself."

"I am calm, Mama, I am."

Hoping to distract both herself and Aline from her pain, Madame de Blamont asked her diamonds be brought and for two hours she toyed with them, polishing them and trying them on Aline; but she was in the end still more given over to the unwilled darkness of her thoughts than by any effort to alleviate them.

"Déterville," she said to me, "do you see how beautiful my Aline would have been on her wedding day? Here is how I would have adorned her."

For both women, that heartrending notion provoked a riptide of tears.

Throughout the house, once so serene and delightful, we lived and breathed only pain; we perceived nothing but sadness and anxiety. People came, learned the news, and departed. The mood was one of utter desolation.

Amidst the crowd circulating in the house we saw a young woman enter, arms outspread and face streaked with tears. It was young Colette in whose home you made your last farewell. We tried to keep her out but she resisted and insisted.

"Let me come!" she cried. "I want to see my good mother and protectress of the poor."

She flung herself at the foot of the bed and begged a bless- o
ing of her dear mistress, kissed the ground, and went out in
tears.

"Well, there you see!" the adorable woman said once the
child had left. "Is there not some satisfaction in doing good?
And don't you agree that every touch of wealth pales before 5
homage from the poor?"

As Madame de Blamont felt taken up in her own thoughts
on the evening of the 25th, we retired before midnight; but
despite my pleas Aline refused to leave her mother. She requested I supervise the estate and allow her to take care of the 10
household. Two women from Vertfeuille took turns helping
her and fought for the honor; not one, even among the best-
off in the village or surrounding countryside, did not solicit
the privilege of watching over the angelic woman.

O my friend! Such are the effects of beneficent charity, 15
the delicious fruits of piety and wisdom! It seems that the
Eternal One, desirous of rewarding men, wants them to taste
on earth the pleasures that shall crown their virtues in heaven.
At daybreak the 26th — and a frightful day it was, my friend, a
day that God's will let innocence succumb to crime in order to 20
put men to the test or take them down. We learned that Augustine had fled. She'd said not a word to anybody and we had
no idea what became of her. This was the moment that the
veil was lifted and further doubt, even for me, was impossible.
I counseled the greatest secrecy and forbade myself further 25
inquiry.

I had Aline's honor to consider. Would I engage in something that would not spare her mother's life but also lead
her contemptible father to the scaffold? I went upstairs to
find that Madame de Blamont had passed a terrible night as 30
spasms, convulsions, all the symptoms of a cruel and incipient death, began to take hold, as a result of which the doctor

told me it was my duty to forewarn her. I approached the sick woman's bedside at a moment when Aline went to fetch some papers at her mother's request; and I entrusted the physician to delay her return so that I'd have time to act. When she saw me approach, Madame de Blamont smiled with the sublime tranquility of a soul both honest and at peace — a virtuous conscience at sweet repose!

"I'm indeed doing poorly, aren't I, my friend?" she said. "Will I never be able to see my daughter happy and content? Alas! I wanted to live for that happiness alone. I'll never enjoy it. Heaven will not allow it."

At that moment I thought nothing would be more mean-ingful than my silence. I lowered my eyes and stayed quiet.

"You don't answer, Déterville?"

I took one of her hands and pressed it to my lips.

She repeated: "You don't answer?"

Here Nature triumphed over courage: she suffered a vio-lent crisis, then opened her arms to me:

"I am ready, my friend. I'm ready. But dear Aline — I must abandon her. Leave her unprotected from the dangers all around! I wouldn't have believed that Heaven would permit it. But no matter, it's not for me to question God's orders, only to follow and comply."

She asked for her priest and charged me with keeping Aline wholly occupied for two hours and not to allow her in the bedroom. That proved to be no easy task. Immediately I sent for the priest and, assuring her that her mother was feel-ing better, I begged Aline to walk with me in the garden for I had something absolutely essential to tell her — but I knew it wouldn't be easy and, indeed, she replied firmly that she would come only after seeing her mother because it had al-ready been an hour since she'd left her; and after such a long while she trusted only herself to know how she was. She went

upstairs to bring her mother the papers she'd requested. Soon   0
after she came down I saw that Madame de Blamont had
clearly said nothing but probably advised her to talk with me.
Using vague language at first, I walked her out to a grove of
trees far beyond the flower garden, and begged her to listen.

"Well!" she exclaimed, not sitting down and in a state of   5
prodigious agitation: "What are you going to tell me? Quite
clearly there's some mystery. Must I lose her?"

"Perhaps not," I said. "But if such a tragedy were to happen —"

"She would not be the only victim. I'd soon share her fate."

"Great heavens! Is that what I ought to expect from so   10
much virtue and piety? Think of yourself and the man who
worships you."

"Valcour? He is lost to me. How can you even think I'll
ever be his? Don't talk to me about him again, I beg you. Nor
do sentiments concerning what I might owe God Himself   15
carry any weight with me. My mother is all. I think only of her
and care for her alone. Not a single idea can do battle in my
heart with the idea of her."

Clearly wanting to flee from me as if counting the minutes that separated her from her object of worship, she added: 20
"Is that all you have to tell me?"

Reaching out to restrain her, I realized that with such a
soul as hers it would be best to hit hard now rather than let
gentle evasions destroy it bit by bit.

"Aline!" I cried. "My dear Aline! The mother you and I   25
both adore — that tender object of our mutual anxiety — we
must absolutely let her go."

The words struck the most sensitive part of her soul and
she stared at me, petrified. Immediately her gaze clouded and
she appeared to be in a stupor; her breath came hard and fast.   30
Her mind, completely deranged. I regretted having acted so
impulsively and saw that she was in no way prepared; despite

what she said, she was still deluding herself. I approached but she pushed me away in a fury. Rambling on, she demanded I bring her mother to have lunch, to be served right where we were standing in the grove — alas! — just as used to happen in the past.

"But I know she won't come," she continued, pointing to the earth: "Because she wants to go *there* — *there* — *there*. But she won't go without me. So, Déterville, go fetch her. As you can see, we're all waiting for her."

Now my own tears flowed and I pressed her to my breast: "O my sweet child!" I cried. "Come to your senses! Pay attention to the sincerest friend you have — and listen to me."

But instead, still deranged and brusquely freeing herself from my grasp, she told me that since I wouldn't get her mother, she would run and do it herself.

"No," I said and held her back. "She is just now fulfilling her sacred duties and you must not disturb her."

Those words, cruel though they were and striking her soul a second time, did not annihilate hope — those very words, I say, brought her back to her senses and revived her reason. But the nerve-shattering blow brought on violent convulsions. She fell to the ground roiling and atremble, shivering from limb to limb. At that fatal moment she might have died if she'd not been overcome and relieved by tears — I was glad to see her cry. And now she flung herself into my open arms.

"O my friend!" she cried, "Must she then be taken from me? Must I lose the consolation of my days, my heart's dearest friend and arbiter of my fate? She whom I adored and whose tender and loving kindness made me happy, the woman I might have cherished 50 years more? And you want me to survive! What will become of me on earth when I can see her no more? I beg you not to ask for such a sacrifice. Don't make me. It's something I cannot promise."

Seeing that though still more afflicted, she was a little
more reasonable, I put forth all grounds for consolation that
wisdom could dictate. But all in vain. The more I sought to instill resignation, the more she evaded my pleas. What should
have eased and alleviated only served to revolt her; and I
reached her devastated soul only by aggravating her despair.
Meantime she grew impatient with her burning desire to rush
back to her mother. I had to take her and thus leave my task
unfinished. Madame de Blamont's offices were done. We entered. Aline sped to embrace the object of her heart's affection
and asked why they'd been apart for so long.

"Duties to perform."

"Unnecessary," replied Aline impatiently. "You have not
reached the place where you must."

Madame de Blamont, tenderly kissing her daughter, shed
bitter tears:

"Aline, from one another *we must part.*"

Wrapped in one another's arms, for a long moment they
remained motionless; but when Aline tore herself away, she
collapsed onto the bed and suffered another frightening attack of spasms that made us fear for her life. But, owing to
the last rites, the sweet young woman, not wanting to waste
the final moments, managed to calm down; and the doctor allowed Madame de Blamont, as she apparently wanted, a little
rice porridge. Aline, more tranquil, for she was now always
prone to illusion when not ravaged by despair, shared that last
bit of food pressed close to her mother's breast. It was a scene,
my friend, as compelling as any I ever witnessed. My own co-
pious tears stop me from trying to describe it.

Frightful weakness took hold of our dear patient at three
o'clock; she could be brought back only by powerful aromat-
ics. When she opened her eyes, she asked to be left alone with
her daughter and myself for half an hour; the doctor, when he

realized she could talk, fortified her with a few drops more and went out. She asked us to come around her bedside but Aline wanted to kneel and in that posture, clutching her mother's hands, pressing her head against the bed, she listened with utmost respect.

"My friends," said the divine woman, "here I am ready to part from you forever. At 36 years old, I might have expected life to continue; but with the misfortunes that have plagued me, it was no longer useful for the well-being of my soul. The moment I'm about to reach is a cruel one; we are not sufficiently accustomed to it on earth, and whatever our behavior here, the end, when it comes, frightens us. Wholly convinced of the existence of a just and fair God, I daresay that I shall fly into His arms unafraid. I ask forgiveness for whatever might have offended Him; true, I would have liked to bring with me a purer heart but at least the one I offer will be free of crime. I would be deceiving you if I said that I had committed no sins: what of impatience, of chafing under the yoke that it pleased Him to impose! I was sacrificed young and you know what I endured. I complained but should have instead seen that what happened was God's will. Each of my resentments represented a form of revolt I should have considered a crime. Perhaps, too, I am guilty of excessive pride, but if so, dear Aline is the cause. I was long filled with contentment for bringing her into the world and giving her life. But with all my affection came pridefulness. My extreme love distracted me from the veneration I owed to God alone: her happiness was my sole occupation; I sought it as consolation for my pain. I've not succeeded; I had yet another cross to bear. A cup of torments I was to drink to its dregs! I leave her young and helpless, prey to misfortunes that make me tremble, and I'll not be there to keep her from them. She will no longer have my hand to dry the tears shorn from her heart. O my daughter! All hope lost!

My final advice: obey your father. Surrender blindly to the   o
man he wants you to marry."

Here she saw Aline recoil in horror.

"Well, then!" she continued. "If you fear the crimes from
such a union, you are left with the choice of a nunnery. Cast
yourself into the arms of the pure Spouse on high, for the   5
heavenly pleasures He promises are worth far more than illusory joys in a world that offers nothing but crosses to bear.
If that is to be the case, Déterville, see to it that my husband
recognizes Léonore as my daughter and all my property will
go to her. Supported by a husband she loves, Léonore would   10
have nothing to fear from a father who is vicious and cruel.
Such an arrangement may be legitimized in case my Aline
should devote herself to God, and all my reasons for remorse
hitherto would disappear; her sister would receive the estate
that is her due; and so, amply compensated by my property   15
and her father's wealth, she would renounce the inheritance
she now claims. I leave this task to you, Déterville, dependent
upon Aline's decision; I fully authorize you to make the testamentary changes."

Then, painfully, she sat up: 20

"The moment is upon us, my friends," she continued.
"Very soon I will appear at the feet of the Eternal One to whom
I will pray on behalf of my Aline. Stand, daughter. Is it not a
fine thing that I have the pleasure of dying in your embrace?
That joy could easily have been denied me. Let me bless you   25
and kiss you. And Déterville, I leave Aline in your care. *Adieu.*"

She threw her arms around her daughter and pressed her
tightly to her breast. Then, seized by light convulsions, the
purest soul ever to emanate from the hands of the Supreme
Being returned to her Creator.   30

I won't describe the state I was in, Valcour; you can readily imagine it. I barely had strength enough to raise my eyes
but many things required I take courage. My first concern, as

you might suppose, was Aline. I rushed to her side, where she bowed before her mother. Alas! It was hard to tell which of them was still alive; the dear young woman had no pulse or warmth and seemed not to be breathing; and when, with much effort, I tore her away from the enfolding arms, she tumbled across the bed and lost consciousness. Servants rushed in and tasks were shared out, but the unfortunate mother had no need. She had already embarked upon that voyage which the Eternal One is duty-bound to virtue — and already it made her more beautiful.

Aline was taken to her bedchamber and delivered into the care of the doctors and Julie, her dear maidservant. She regained consciousness after an hour and, finding me at her bedside, she asked for her mother. Dazed and confused, she said it was I who'd taken her away and prevented them from seeing one another; and she appealed to the tribunal of the Lord against all the injustices I'd committed. I tried to enfold her in my arms but she tore herself away — then reversed herself with much passion and asked my forgiveness for her reproaches, a thousand times over. She told me she could not control her thoughts, that she was quite aware of the tragic loss just come upon her, but that if I loved her I'd allow her, once more, the sweet pleasure of kissing her mother. With those words, and despite Julie's best efforts, she escaped us and rushed directly to the corpse, which was just being readied to lie in state. She was blocked from doing so by Julie, who shielded the body with her own and returned Aline to her own bed.

She wept. Her tears flowed in great abundance and she cried out with expressions of pain and loss that would wrench the most insensitive mortal alive. But as a coach was arriving in the courtyard, I was forced to leave her in Julie's care to attend other tasks.

The coach belonged to the President. He had with him a single valet. He entered the front room, where he sensed the

dark timbre and heard the mournful sounds and sobs, and he   o
could see that his hideous crime had been carried out — that
the angel was no longer in the temple because the Eternal One
had called her back. I approached him. He embraced me most
phlegmatically and thanked me for my assistance while skill-   5
fully making me understand that my presence at the chateau
was no longer needed. I did not even pretend to hear him; he
could say whatever he liked but my portfolio clearly authorized my presence. He asked me to take him to his wife and I
brought him into the bedchamber where attendants were preparing the body; it was naked beneath a sheet hastily thrown   10
over it before he entered. He signaled them all to leave. When
he and I were alone the monster approached the bed and,
lifting the sheet, like Nero defiling Agrippina:

"*In truth, still beautiful!*"

He might have said more if he hadn't seen me shudder with   15
horror. Moving still closer, he closely examined her features.

"But I see nothing to suggest poison," he said. "What is
your so-called doctor up to? He's either mad or dangerous, a
fellow I ought to punish. Such talk wrongs the honest people
she died among. You yourself shouldn't tolerate it."   20

"Me? Not only did I allow it; I insisted you be informed
in writing."

"In all that I don't recognize your customary prudence."

"I've never been more careful in my life." And containing myself: "To whom should I have complained? Who should   25
I tell about an unquestionable fact if not the one who must
avenge it?"

"Unquestionable? Nothing of the sort, and it would have
been a hundred times better to say nothing. That's what I would
have called prudence."   30

"A young woman has gone missing."

"Who?"

"Augustine."

"A harlot! I know what that's about. Seduced by one of my servants, not at all fond of her mistress. She would have left no matter what, illness or no. The two of them are long gone. Believe me, I fired the valet! Is this your proof?"

"More can be found."

"Come now, let's be done with all this. Such horrors ought not to be suspected in one's home; to believe them is to compromise everybody who lives there. Where's Aline?"

Relieved to change the subject, according to the firm resolutions by which I had decided not to go further, I described the state of the dear young woman and told him I thought it prudent to leave her alone for a few days.

"A few days?" He laughed dismissively. "I plan to take her away with me tomorrow. Dolbourg awaits her at Chateau de Blamont and we'll conclude the affair directly."

"What are you saying, Monsieur! Her mother's not cold in her grave!"

"A trifle, that. A woman freshly dead needn't keep us from enabling another to bring forth new life. On the contrary, it's a sort of reparation we owe to Nature and every moment's delay is an affront to her laws. A mother is sacred, if you like — when she's alive. Once she's dead she's nothing. Listen to me: just yesterday evening as I left Paris there transpired something in a little different vein — but really quite similar — just to show you that with serious matters we won't be stopped by sentimental claptrap meant only for the masses. For a certain Monsieur de Mézane, we had a legal proceeding at the Parlement of Aix — one of the best, wisest and most honest in the whole realm —* that ruled in favor of his wife's family

---

* In its registers the Parlement records 20 executions similar to that of Calas. During the reign of François I, 80 villages in Provence were burned down and 80,000 citizens killed; at various times the Parlement threw open the gates of the city to its enemies; again in 1787 it devastated the province. Quite obviously, such an assembly deserves the praises of a monster that makes readers tremble. *Editor's Note*

and consigned him to a long prison term — Monsieur de Mé-   0
zane, I say, who'd lived in hiding for several years, was led by
his own *imbecilic delicacy* to betake himself to Paris, despite
every danger, to see his dying mother. No sooner had he entered the apartment of the deceased than he was arrested on
order of his wife's family. When he protested, they laughed in   5
his face and cast him in the dungeons of the Bastille, where he
was *very pleasantly* left to weep at one and the same time for
his lost freedom, his mother's death, and the barbaric stupidity of his in-laws. To my way of thinking, when the government
provides us with such a fine example, we do well to follow it."   10

"The case you cite is shocking," I replied. "The fellow
you're talking about must have been guilty of high treason."

"Nothing of the sort. It was writings against us magistrates and the king; some predictions, a few youthful adven-
tures readily forgivable for a 27-year-old. The kinds of thing   15
we do ourselves every day but don't want others doing."

"In that case, Monsieur, allow me to say to you that punishing a minor offense as a major crime is a revolting atrocity.* Virtue gains nothing, and it is one more appalling wrong
added to the state's great number of wrongs."   20

The shameful man changed the subject and continued:

"But what legitimizes the pain we feel at the loss of those
we cherish? What good is a sentiment that does nothing for
the dear departed but only bothers and troubles the well-
being of those still alive?"   25

"These things cannot be rationalized, Monsieur, only felt
— and woe to those who don't experience them!"

"No, Monsieur. Everything must be submitted to analysis.
What cannot be analyzed is false. Now tell me if, according to

---

* Monsters capable of such horrors: you will recognize your victim and grow pale!
But remain calm. No sooner was he set free than forgiveness was the first pleasure
he tasted.

my materialist system, with my absolute certitude that death ends all our pain and leaves us with nothing to fear — if, I say, with respect to all that, my wife, who was anything but happy on earth, doesn't now find herself at peace preferable to the perpetual state of torment in which she wallowed while alive. And that being the case, why would I miss her? Wouldn't my regret seem to say: *I'm so sorry you're no longer in an unhappy situation and it fills me with despair to see that you're no longer suffering?* Such regrets — I ask you — would you consider them so very delicate? Putting aside my own system for a moment, if I adopt yours, and believe the woman is in a better place, doesn't bereavement at no longer seeing her suffer on earth become absolutely insulting, making myself the only object of sorrow? You must admit such selfishness is revolting. What are you saying but that I should be angry for being deprived of her, afflicted only for the loss I endure without a thought for the advantage she obtains in no longer having me around. If I act that way, I'm thinking only of myself, not about her, and it looks as though I would tacitly consent if she lost what she gained and gave me back what I've lost. From which I conclude that to regret the death of those dear to us is a great injustice; for hell being impossible, the dead either are nothing, which makes them not worse off, or they're better off, which is a more pleasant alternative. In either case, we're clearly wrong to want them back, where they'd only find themselves diminished. With all this, we shouldn't be at all surprised that entire nations ritually rejoice at the death of those close to them while deploring the birth of a child. I know of no better customs than these.* We must feel sorry those born to pain;

* The Scandinavians and Germans used to weep at the birth of a child; no sooner was it brought into the world than the parents gathered around its cradle, each to rehearse, pathetically as might be imagined, all the miseries of human life, sympathizing with the newborn for the sufferings to be endured during its time on earth. These same ☞

we must imitate them and cry the way they do when they first set eyes upon the world. As for death, it's an undoubted good thing and we must not be afflicted with sorrow."

"But why not suppose that such pain is for ourselves alone?" I replied. "The delightful instinct of a tender soul. Is it not barbaric to resist it?"

"The true philosopher grows used to privations and ought not be affected by them. Besides which, I don't agree that extreme sensitivity is a good thing. It would be easy for me to prove the opposite; but what is certain is that if this emotion is a sort of happiness, at least it's not for everybody, because, I assure you, I've never felt it. There's nothing easier to fill, Monsieur, than the void left by the death of a wife, mistress, parent, or friend! We're not so upset by the loss as by the idea we'll never find in another human being the qualities that belonged to our dear departed; but that idea, not only quite personal to ourselves, is also chimeric. Habit is what binds us together far more than harmony or suitability; and careful thought shows that the pain we feel at a loss is nothing but the physical sensation of a disrupted habit. Doubtless the man most afflicted is the one unfamiliar with the art of cavorting amidst all the various pleasures, touching upon all but dwelling upon none, creating a predilection so strong he can't renounce it without suffering. If we took advantage of everything but became attached to nothing, losses would never afflict us. A new friend can take the place of an old one; a new mistress can replace the one we just lost; and we're taken on a whirlwind of pleasure that gives us no time to think. Prompt replacement means no pain from sorrow."

peoples rejoiced at the death of parents and friends; all who attended the interment would discuss the glorious exchange by which the deceased was taken from a life prone to so much unhappiness to enter a state of perfect felicity; they subsequently played, sang, and rejoiced for three days. Traces of this custom remain in nearly all the cities in northern Germany.

"But the void that's left is devastating. Just the thought of it makes my blood run cold; it debases our soul and stifles its kindest faculties. Monsieur, whatever pleasures you might put on offer, would a single one of them be worth the sensation I experience in weeping for the friend I've just lost?"

"If you cherish your pain until it becomes a voluptuous pleasure, you'll have to agree that voluptuary consolation is far better than the kind that inflicts pain."

"One comes from a cast iron soul, the other from a kind and sensitive heart."

"And how do you know, Monsieur, that the better organized soul owes to your perspective rather than by mine, if we each of us have our pleasures?"

"Mine are those of virtue, yours lead to all sorts of crimes."

"And so now we must inquire as to which of them — leaving aside social conventions — gives more pleasure: vice or virtue?"

"How can you even discuss such a thing?"

"I ask you the same question. For, if you characterize pleasure as that ticklish sensation the soul receives from whatever source, its commotion is far more violent and abundant when induced by vice rather than virtue — in which case the perfectly happy man might be the one who, upending societal ideals, would make virtues of vices and vices of all your virtues."

"Monsieur!" I said, furious and unable to listen any more of his cruel sophisms, "you'd be right to hang any miserable soul who thinks like you."

"Very well," replied the scoundrel, "but the chance to lord it over others gives one the right to think differently from them. That's the first effect of superiority; the second is to do so often, guaranteeing that one's actions fall in line with the piquant singularity of his philosophical systems. That was the way one fine man could betray the state, make his fortune, and

quit the government, claiming he'd been ruined.* Still another o
could destroy domestic commerce in France when his absurd
projects cost millions.† Not to mention a hundred more who
helped suck the life out of the people they starved by selling
the food they'd just stolen from same for 10 times what it was
worth. Do you think those men are less happy because, unlike 5
you, they fail to cherish the idealized phantom of virtue?"

"Happy? It's not possible. True happiness resides in virtue.
Remorse experienced by those rogues you describe, absent
the sword of Themis, avenge us of their crimes."

"Remorse — you make me laugh. Do you really think the 10
long habit of doing evil provokes any such thing? One of the
fellows I was just telling you about expressed some of it after
his second fall from grace, only to become a fool in the eyes
of his peers, who instantly plucked him clean and cruelly
mocked him if they didn't molest him some other way. But 15
look here, Monsieur, I see we shan't agree tonight. Kindly ask
dinner to be served; to arrive sooner I'd not taken the time to
eat before leaving and am absolutely famished. We can phi-
losophize over dessert if you like."

I ordered dinner and the villain sat down to eat with a 20
tranquility that showed me how he had acquired such a raging habit of crime as to be completely at ease just after committing one. As you can imagine I ate nothing but only kept
him company, leaving the table from time to time to attend to
various necessary tasks; but I did not go to see Aline, whom 25
my presence irritated rather than calmed; and I decided to
wait until the next day to tell her about the succession of cruel
misfortunes awaiting her. The doctor, who'd still not left, was
taking a little rest. The President wanted to see him and had
the effrontery to ask him the cause of his wife's death. 30

---

*   Such was the lie of the abominable Sartine.
†   The operations of the rascal Le Noir.

"*Poison*," the latter boldly answered.

"But, doctor, do you really think — ?"

"The surest way to convince you, Monsieur, and we shall do so whenever you like, is to open the body."

"No. With all due respect, such things have always revolted me; they're not infallible, and I find it cruel. Let's have no talk of dissection, but simply bury her."

Somewhat surprised by that retort, the doctor asked him if he planned to take legal action.

"Against whom?" asked the President.

"Such things must not go unpunished, Monsieur. Men of your profession, who punish upon the slightest pretext, know better than us the necessity of severe action against these sorts of horrors."

"All very well," said the President, "but I'm far from sharing your suspicion, which would inevitably fall upon all those good people close to my wife over the past three months. Lacking any evidence whatsoever, we can scarcely mount an example with only rumor. I'm quite convinced that the wisest course is to keep quiet and you'll come around to my view, Monsieur, that to consider such a crime, without foundation or motive, is absolutely inadmissible."

He immediately changed topics and carefully avoided any further discussion of Augustine. Finishing supper, he went to bed.

But then came the height of horror! Why must I reveal yet this final turpitude? Why must a missive devoted to sorrow and sadness be sullied by accounts of shame and infamy?

The President never goes anywhere without one of his zealous servants to attend to his master's pleasures — and one who, in order to procure them, will sacrifice honor, duty, religion, and all the virtues that characterize an honest man. No sooner does his master arrive someplace than that designated

agent casts his eyes all around and rapidly selects with singular skill any object who could satisfy his employer's filthy desires. For these two monsters, place and circumstance, or the
pervasive sorrow that enveloped all in the deepest respect —
none of that proved sacred. One gave the order and the other
acted on his behalf. To be found among the young peasant
girls, whose pity and gratitude brought them to the respectable lady's bedside, was one who, whether out of weakness or
less moved than the others, lent an ear to certain proposals.
She was an orphan, 14 years old and on her own. The zealous
manservant introduced her to his master; the latter approved
the choice and no sooner did night fall than she was brought
to the bedchamber, where the viper consummated his crime
near the still-warm body of the poor woman whose life he had
so odiously cut short. He kept the girl the whole night; I only
learned of this after his departure the next day. Had I known
or been warned, I never would have tolerated it.

Once he was gone I made it my duty to fulfill the mournful tasks assigned me, the most difficult of which was finding a
way to tell poor Aline of the new tragedies that awaited her. The
instructions were clear, the President having repeated them to
me before he left; and when I showed him his wife's last wishes,
he considered them so much gibberish, pitiable considering
the circumstances, but otherwise simply laughable.

"Regarding the assets, furniture, and property, I lay claim
to nothing, Monsieur," he told me. "It all belonged to my wife
to dispose of however she wished. But as for my daughter, she
belongs to me. Tell her as much, if you will be so kind, and
warn her that she shall be leaving tomorrow without fail."

So I had to find a way to tell her.

Not to disturb her that night, for I supposed her to be far
from tranquil, I only went to her apartment at daybreak. She
had not undressed or been to bed; bouts of cruel harsh pain

had been her lot and, doubtless even worse, for her despair was muted. Tears would not come but fell as drops of blood upon her heart. She kept asking to go kiss her mother and the resistance she met infuriated her; but she calmed a little when she saw me. She asked me why I'd left her alone for so long. I apologized, noting the tasks I was required to perform; and after having done all I could to salve her soul's afflictions, I tried to take the situation in hand. A movement of friendship escaped her and I made the best of it, taking her and holding her in my arms while she wept.

"O my friend!" Now I told her: "Summon courage to your side. I must alert you to new misfortunes."

She fixed my gaze with a such a terrified stare that I trembled — and her thoughts went to you.

"O Heaven!" she cried. "Is Valcour now with my mother? Has the same calamity reunited them?"

It is fortunate when, in such a case as this, the person to whom we want to gently reveal news of terrible things imagines the very worst. I took one of her hands in mine and offered a friendly smile:

"No," I said, "Valcour is getting on just fine. I'm certain he's concerned with you alone; but what I have to tell you may prove still more cruel than you feared. Your father has come. He plans to take you away today and wants you to immediately become Dolbourg's wife."

Never in my life have I seen a reaction as violent as this woman's, at once so courageous and unfortunate.

"O my friend!" she said, rising. "Now nothing on earth can keep me from joining my mother."

"Be seated, Aline," I replied, "I hoped to find you strong but you evince only despair. Nothing can break your father's resolve yet there are ways you can escape the union he's planned."

"And what are these ways?"

"Calm down and listen to me."

She sat and gave me every attention.

"I won't advise you as to your choice of cloister," I told her. "Proposing it to him would be useless because you'd surely be denied; but here's what friendship dictates. First, weaken your father through submission. Show only obedience and respect during the journey to the chateau. Once there, try to meet with Dolbourg alone, and make him bear witness to your insurmountable aversion to this marriage. Depict for him the certain unhappiness that would result for you both. In the end, evoke his sympathetic interest by using everything you have: nature's graces and your sweet and persuasive eloquence are qualities difficult to resist. Less violent than your father, it would scarce astonish me if he gave in. Should that happen, as I think possible, engage him with the same ardor to compel him to break it off, and perhaps he will.

"But let us imagine the worst and suppose you'll find no way to avoid destiny. By agreement your faithful Julie will be with you: escape with her. She'll have 100 louis that I'll give her for expenses. Hurry to the home of Madame de Senneval, who will know about it in advance; she'll be waiting for you on her estate near Paris. Once there, call for Eugénie and me. We'll take matters in hand and spirit you out of France. We'll convey you to the waiting arms of the husband as your mother intended and you'll in peace be able to enjoy the fortune she left you."

Even the slightest hint of happiness can raise spirits in a heart filled with despair! The dear girl fell into sweet reverie and I asked what she was thinking.

"O Déterville! The way you go about things always confuses me but let me to ask you, my friend: if you really want to rescue me from the threatening evil, as your touching kindness so clearly attests, why start the way you do? Why not spare me this terrifying journey with my father?"

"How could I?" I replied softly. "Now your father has come and you're in his power. Were you simply to disappear, I'd be suspected and without escaping you'd lose the only friend who can help you — and you'd still have to go with him. If you flee from Chateau de Blamont, no suspicion can fall on me. Your flight would be your own decision and such help as we then offer cannot be charged as bridal abduction but simply protection accorded and service rendered. Your father would have intended real harm and you had no wish to become his victim. Until now what he's done hasn't been enough to warrant flight; here it's been only bad manners. But at Chateau de Blamont there could be horrors. Escaping from here, in a word, would be a drastic move. Something far simpler could succeed; prudence admits excessive measures only when others offer no hope."

She fell again to reflect; then, after a little while:

"Déterville, I feel stronger than I would have ever believed possible; your goodness penetrates me and I shall make use of it." She rose to her feet and continued: "Yes, my friend, I will if I possibly can." She added vehemently: "But possible or not, I'll never be Dolbourg's wife."

She took my hands:

"Now tell me, my friend, if you think there's a creature on earth as unhappy as me."

"Most certainly," I replied. "Your fate is far from hopeless. Yesterday, perhaps you were to be pitied; today, less so than I'd ever have thought."

"My friend," she said, turning to look out the window, "the sun is rising and we must soon separate." Throwing herself in my arms: "O! My dear Déterville! The wrath to come will be terrible! But before it crushes me, don't deny me one kind favor."

"What, Aline? You well know you've a lock upon my heart."   o

"I want to kiss my mother once more. Either you've never loved me or you'll grant me that single consolation."

"You frighten me," I said. "Your head's too fervid, your heart inflamed. The spectacle is so painful. You couldn't stand it."

Containing herself with indescribable courage: 5

"No," she answered. "'Tis a sacred duty I must fulfill. Don't be afraid. Religion and piety will do combat with pain; my too battered soul will gather from the multiple shocks the force to recover from each of them. Let us go there. Guide my trembling steps and have no fear."   10

Leaving me no time to reply, she took my arm and we advanced upon the bier.

Madame de Blamont reposed on a bed covered with royal blue damask, which I had carefully prepared, the better to procure for tenants of the manor the satisfaction of seeing   15 her as they had begged to do with a flood of tears. She was laid out in a white taffeta dress; her hair in its natural color was neatly combed beneath a large bonnet; her head rested on a pillow adorned with lace. Her appearance was that of a woman asleep; eight candles burned around the bed, with the   20 curtains raised and tied back with large white ribbons. In low voices two priests discreetly recited prayers.

Through the door as we entered the entire scene came before our eyes, and your poor Aline no sooner perceived it than she recoiled and fell into my arms. But extreme resignation,   25 the certainty she had little time and fear of wasting it, gave her strength and we advanced as the priests briefly retired. Without restraint, Aline fell at her mother's feet and respectfully kissed them. She stood up and went around the side of the bed, took her mother's hands and solemnly pressed her lips   30 to each of them in turn with the most intense grief. She gazed upon her face, observed for a time the pure calm that reigned there, and admired the beauty that abided. At this point her soul tore itself apart. She wrapped her arms around her beloved mother's neck, shed tears upon it, covered it with kisses, and addressed her with sweet words. She put to her the most touching questions, so much so that, afraid excessive sensitivity would cause her to collapse, I approached and begged that she not let herself go on this way. But as she resisted, aware only of her pain, the priests came too and made the same entreaties. Now afraid she had showed a lack of respect, the sweet and tender young woman, forever preoccupied by her duties and always sacrificing her own soul's most fervent passions, stepped away and lowered her gaze; she kneeled before the bed to pray with the good churchmen. I took that moment to tell her in a low voice about the legacy of her mother's hair; I told her I was going to cut it now in order that she would have it. The news filled her soul with consolation.

"She makes me a gift of her hair," she said, "my good sweet mother. She was thinking of me. Let me have it, give it to me now. It shall never leave me as long as I live."

I approached the bed to carry out the operation but Aline turned away, not wanting to see me perform it; she was well pleased to have the hair but disturbed by the cutting of it, which made one more proof of her mother's death, perhaps because she entertained the pleasurable illusion that she was just asleep and dreaming. In some way it seemed to despoil the body she so adored and all such ideas must have disrupted the somber pleasure she had of this gift, and when I brought it to her she trembled to receive it. Soon, however, she covered it with kisses. Then she turned away to open her bodice and place the hair beneath her left breast, and at her mother's feet she declared it would remain there forever.

"My dear friend," I said, half an hour after this cruel visit began, "we must leave lest this moment so afflict you that it would be better if we had not come."

She shivered and it was as though I'd torn into the most   o
sensitive part of her soul; but, as ever, firm and courageous,
after once more kissing her mother's forehead and hands, she
lowered her gaze, respectfully, and left weeping, her head
buried in my arms. Once we were outside, I kissed her.

"I'm far happier with you that I would have thought," I   5
told her, "and it fills me with hope for what's to come. O! My
dear friend, you need strength — and prudence and good
sense, too — and you can be sure we'll succeed."

We returned to her bedroom; she asked where her moth-
er would be interred with a rush of emotion that alarmed me.   10
I told her about the arrangements; and, when she learned that
Madame de Blamont had expressly asked that her daughter
one day be buried with her in the same vault:

"How that too consoles me! It will be done, won't it,
Déterville? It will be — nobody can oppose it?"   15

"Certainly not."

Then, after thinking:

"Will you take care of it, my friend?"

"Adorable girl," I replied, "Nature shan't change her laws
to make it my task. Consider that I'm 12 years older than you."   20

"What difference! We can die at any age. Just tell me that
if you outlive me, you promise to bury me with my mother."

"I swear to it, but on condition that we're now going to
take care of something else."

"After you've promised, anything you say."   25

"Well, then, of course! Now I insist you take some
nourishment."

"Yes, some rice porridge. Like I had yesterday with the one
I've just lost. Isn't that right, my friend? Just like yesterday?"

And with some slight confusion: 30

"But she won't be here. It won't be with her. I'll never see
her again!"

Not answering her: "So would you like me to fetch you a little something to eat?"

"No — in truth, no."

Nevertheless, I insisted, obliging her to eat a raw egg beaten with a few drops of elixir. We used the little time left us to review our plans; we agreed that, whatever happened at Chateau de Blamont, Julie would report to me in detail from the moment they arrive; and Aline for her part promised she would write me as often as she could and observe with the greatest care everything as we'd discussed. The time grew short and she made herself ready. When presented with her black dress, she avidly kissed it.

"Ah! My friend," she said, looking to me. "This is the color I'll wear for the rest of my life."

No sooner was she dressed than the President sent word. He was waiting for me downstairs and requested I bring his daughter.

"So now!" I said to her: "How goes your heart?"

"Better that I would've thought," she replied, taking my arm. "But promise not to leave me for even a minute until I'm inside the coach."

I gave my word and we went down. When she heard the President's voice as he chatted with some of the people from Vertfeuille, she began to tremble.

"Courage," I told her. "Show respect and keep silent."

She entered, nodded at her father but said not a word. Monsieur de Blamont approached her and coldly urged her to console herself; he told her that mourning suited her wonderfully well, that he had never seen her looking so pretty. She stood still, downcast, and did not reply.

"As testamentary executor, you will indeed have some difficulty," the President said to me. "She did well to choose you, and assuredly the thing could not be in better hands. Has my daughter eaten?"

"Yes, Monsieur," I replied, sure of my response on behalf of Aline. "Have you ordered something for yourself?"

"Yes. I told them to bring me two partridges. I'm mad about the birds of Vertfeuille; they're so much tastier that those at Chateau de Blamont. Aline, will you have one?"

"No, Father."

"A long day ahead, 25 leagues with six relays but no stops. We'll have only biscuits in the coach."

The meal was served; the President ate his partridges, drank two bottles of Burgundy, and chatted with various people in the room while Aline and I remained in the doorway, talking.

I managed to keep up her spirits and she offered a thousand expressions of warmth but, just because her soul lay so open to friendship that it seemed ready to shatter, I pretended not to notice. She begged me to write you and no sooner did your name cross her lips than her eyes filled with tears. I put an end to these new effusions, fearing an awful crisis; and as the moment of departure arrived I saw that the only way to avoid such turmoil was to wound her with coldness. It tore me apart to act this way but there was no other. I approached the President; she understood and contained herself. We were informed the horses were ready. I saw her flinch but did not go to her again. The President left and Julie followed. Aline was the last to go out.

Once they saw her, the people formed two lines through which she had to pass. As she did so, the celestial angel received spontaneous homages from all. Some raised their arms to the sky, wishing her every kind of prosperity. Others wept and turned away, not wanting to see her leave-taking; others cast themselves at her feet, expressing gratitude for all of her good and kind deeds, and imploring her blessing. She passed through the crowd, eyes on the ground, evincing nothing but pain and humility. The President entered the coach and Julie followed. Then Aline looked to me and addressed a cruel fare-well that forced me to swallow my tears. I made it so she could not see me but did not lose sight of her, as she straightaway entered the coach and it took off like a bolt — leaving me confounded, crushed. I believed a star had disappeared from the heavens and the earth itself was condemned to darkness forevermore.

I went back inside, followed by her people, whose tears did not let up. Intending to bury Madame de Blamont only after 36 hours had elapsed, in accord with her daughter's insistent wishes, after carefully surrounding the bed with a balustrade covered in black fabric, I opened the apartment where her body was to be exposed. There was no one who did not come to prostrate themselves before the woman who had been so dear to all; everyone blessed and worshiped her.

O, people of this century! You who live like the monster who sacrificed her: will such homages as these be yours when destiny cuts short your days? Will you, like this divine woman, brought by her virtue into the bosom of the Supreme Being, have the sweet consolation of living on in the hearts of men, and see-ing them offer you holy tributes of their love and gratitude?

The services lasted throughout the 27th. The next morning, at ten o'clock, a funeral cortege arrived to take the body to its final resting place; everyone fought for the honor of bearing the precious burden; and only with reluctance did her people cede to six prominent men from the village. They carried her to the parish, arriving to the sorrowful tolling of church bells, whose harmony was made ever more funereal by the sobs and moans of all gathered around her. Despair grew tumultuous as they saw her disappear and sink into the entrails of the earth; and the cries and lamentations were such as to resound in the vaults of heaven; you would have said she somehow belonged to everyone there; all seemed to be her children and all wept like she was their mother.

I returned to the chateau only to endure what was cer-   o
tainly the cruelest day of my life. Having taken care of the
most important tasks, nothing to my ears resounded but
my own sorrow. O my friend! How awful! The obligation to
constrain myself, to hold back tears and weep only within my
heart, caused it to burst asunder and make of me a broke-   5
down engine. Alone I wandered through those apartments
where decency, sweet joy, and honesty once reigned, and now
found only horrible emptiness and signs of mourning.

She has passed away, I told myself: the woman who made
others happy. Heaven decided to allow her, on earth, but a mo-   10
ment. She appeared there only to do good and I dedicated to
her Fléchier's superb inspired words for the celebrated Duchess of Aiguillon:* *She was great to serve God, wealthy to help
the poor, living only to prepare to die.*

All this, my dear Valcour, has recounted only the first   15
part of the misfortunes of which you must learn. I spare you
the details that kept me busy over the next several days in
order to pass immediately to the somber and sorrowful story
that remains. It will break your heart no less cruelly than my
own when you read it.   20

The evening of May 3ʳᵈ I returned from the church — I'd
gone there every day to shed tears for two hours upon the
tomb of my unfortunate friend — to be told that a man on
horseback was urgently asking for me. I hurried to him, my
heart palpitating with fear, and found a stranger who imme-   25
diately handed me a packet of letters. Puzzled, I tore open the
package and glanced at them, reading without understanding,
finally recognizing Aline's handwriting, preceded by Julie's
carefully kept diary. I send it all to you. Read it, Valcour, if you
are able, to the very end.   30

---

* The niece of Cardinal de Richelieu.

Letter LXVIII

Julie to Déterville

Chateau de Blamont, 1 May

In carrying out your orders, Monsieur, and those of my mistress, would that you read these sorrowful lines, no sooner set down than streaked by my tears. You require details, however painful. I obey.

Monsieur le President fell asleep as soon as the coach started out from Vertfeuille and only awakened at the first relay. He put several questions to his daughter, who answered in monosyllables, so he harshly asked if she was decided upon being in a bad mood.

"I am only in pain, Monsieur," she replied, "and take it that my sorrow gives me the right."

To which Monsieur replied that grieving was the height of folly, that one must know how to lift one's soul to a sort of stoicism that enables us to look upon everything that happens in life with indifference; that, for himself, far from letting anything afflict him, he took joy in everything; and that if we carefully examine what would seem at first to be an obligation — to be cruelly distressed, for example — we would quickly find a pleasant aspect to it. It's a question of seizing upon that and forgetting the other; by such a system we can succeed in turning aside all life's darts. Sensitivity is only a weakness to be readily cured by the forcible repulsion of anything that too closely besets us, to immediately assuage with some voluptuous or comforting idea those barbs that sorrow would inflict. It requires only a little practice and, after just a few years, we achieve a hardening to the point that nothing can affect us any longer. He assured Mademoiselle that she would always be unhappy unless she adopted this wise and sensible philosophy.

When Aline replied to none of this, Monsieur turned to
me and in a loud voice began asking, concerning Mademoiselle, the most indecent sorts of questions. When he saw me
lower my eyes and not respond, he rudely informed me that
he would make my life miserable if I decided to act the prude,
and that the tenor of things in his home was far freer than the
place I was leaving so I'd better comply or would soon be gone.
Then, posing more improper questions concerning his daughter, he said that as he was about to marry her off, he must
know these things; he does not want to deceive his son-in-law
and it was essential to be sure the merchandise was without
defects. Since I refused to say, he would himself inspect the
package to see to its worth. Then, turning to Mademoiselle,
he advised her, as it was quite warm, to remove the scarfs and
cloaks in which she'd wrapped herself. But Aline, who'd chosen the small folding seat, leaning on the coach door with her
head hidden in her hands, did not listen or reply.

Upon which, Monsieur le President posed the same
questions of me, just as he'd asked me about Mademoiselle,
and he accompanied them with movements so improper amid
gestures so indecent that I threatened to call for help and
fling myself from the coach. He told me that he knew how to
put some sense into me, that I was quite wrong to think he'd
brought me along to please his daughter; and that, if it weren't
for my youth and pretty face, he'd have left me behind. He
would wait for the right moment, as I was so difficult, but he
warned me that it would always come down to the *same thing*,
and at Chateau de Blamont, there were sure and certain ways
to overcome a girl's resistance.

A little while later he dozed off again and talked very
little the rest of the day. A coach wheel broke about a quarter
league from Sens and we went on as best we could, managing
to make the post station inn, where we had no choice but to

spend the night. Monsieur spoke directly with the mistress of the place, who showed us upstairs to a bedroom with two beds, where he asked for Mademoiselle's overnight luggage to be brought, informing me that he and his daughter would stay in this room and I need only ask for one for myself. But Aline gripped me by the arm and insisted on a room for herself with me, as she could not do without a chambermaid.

"Well, then!" said the President, "we'll have a third bed installed. But you, my daughter, are to sleep nowhere but here."

"Please forgive me, father," replied Aline. Brusquely opening the door, taking me with her, she rushed into the gallery.

After calling for the mistress of the inn and requesting a room, that woman, warned by a glance from the President, replied that she had no extra bed and, as for another room, the inn was full.

"But you had a place for this young woman," said Aline, indicating me.

"Yes, Mademoiselle, but unsuitable for you."

"Doesn't matter, not a bit. I'll sleep with her. Everything is fine provided it's decent, while nothing is less so, Madame, than to force a daughter sleep in the same room with her father."

"But it happens all the time."

"Not for me."

The hostess dared not reply but showed us to a small and uncomfortable room at the other end of the gallery, and we went without the President, watching from his doorway, able to say a single word.

Mademoiselle ordered chicken for me and broth for herself. She begged the hostess to keep the key to our room and only open the door tomorrow morning when her father wished to leave.

No sooner the lock turned than, describing what happened during the day, I put before Aline her father's behavior

and told her that, with all the dangers we courted with such a   o
man, the wisest course would be to try to quietly slip off and
flee right away. I argued that once we arrived at the Chateau,
the escape we could try to make now might not be possible.
But Mademoiselle, who had no memory of the Chateau de
Blamont, where she'd gone just once with her mother as a child,   5
said it seemed impossible we'd not find the same opportunities
as here. Also, she hoped to win over Dolbourg, convincing him
to renounce his intentions; and she in no way wanted to deviate from the advice she'd received from Monsieur Déterville.

"Mademoiselle," I replied, "it seemed to me that Monsieur   10
Déterville said that to legally warrant our escape, you need
only show bad conduct on the part of your father. Didn't his
plans and what he said today all forecast horrors to come?"

"Julie," said my esteemed mistress, "do you know what it
means to accuse one's own father? You can't feel the cost of it   15
to a soul like mine, disclosing wrongs of that kind on the part
of the man who gave me life. I'd rather die than do such a thing.
Moreover, in all this there's still nothing real, nothing that I
can prove or he cannot contest. O my dear friend! Things may
go better than you think; I've every hope for Dolbourg." She   20
added: "And no matter what happens" — she seized my hand
with a look that made me tremble —, "never fear, Julie, that I'd
betray the one I love; I'll never take another besides he whom
my mother chose for me. If a victim these monsters must have,
here she is," she said, putting forth her hand. "Here is their   25
pound of flesh."

Then, without undressing, she threw herself down on the
bed and spent the night in tears.

In the morning they came to say it was time to leave and
we promptly went to stand outside the door to Monsieur's   30
room, without entering. He appeared; we went downstairs
and entered the coach, taking the same seats as the day before.

Monsieur did not say a word; we imitated his silence and near midday arrived at the Chateau de Blamont, whose tenebrous and isolated surroundings startled Mademoiselle who, as I noted, remembered nothing of where it was located. Entering the courtyard, there we found Monsieur Dolbourg. He offered to help Mademoiselle out of the coach and she accepted his polite gesture with a sweet curtsey. The carriage went off and we entered the main room downstairs.

Everything about the chateau is sad and dismal, darkening the imagination and inspiring terror; the horrible place is more like a fortress than a country house; everywhere one looks are vaults, gates, and thick doors. Once inside, Monsieur told me to have his daughter's luggage taken to an apartment reserved for her, but Mademoiselle stopped me, insistently demanding that I be allowed to stay with her always.

"Nonsense!" barked Monsieur de Blamont. "She's not going to eat and sleep with you. It seems to me a young woman ought to be safe in the hands of her father and future husband."

"Nothing to fear, Mademoiselle," said Monsieur Dolbourg, "Do believe me and let Julie go."

Aline didn't dare resist; I left to do as I was asked and soon returned to the drawing room. Mademoiselle was seated between the two men and I could see that, except for a few improper words that such men cannot forego, there was no question in this first meeting of anything much happening. As soon as Aline saw me she asked permission to leave, which was granted; Monsieur offered his arm to escort her to her bedroom. When she entered, seeing only one bed, she urgently demanded another for me.

"Impossible" replied the President. "Julie is close by and there's a little bell you can use to call her if need be."

That said, he retired and we settled into the room. While inspecting it, we discovered words written on the window sill:

It was here that I, Sophie, unhappy… The sentence was not   o
finished.

"Great heavens!" cried Aline, frightened. "Here was where
he brought the poor girl. I didn't know. I'd been told she was
in a convent. What did he do with her? Why bring her to the
chateau? Why did she only write these few words? O Julie!   5
It makes me tremble."

That is where we left things when Mademoiselle was
informed that dinner was served; she had no choice but to
appear and dared not make excuses. She recovered from her
confusion as best she could and went downstairs. She saw   10
then that the company included, in addition to the two men,
a middle-aged woman, a rather pretty girl of 15 or 16 years,
and a young abbot. Conversation in front of the servants was
mundane but when they were dismissed, at dessert, it took
on a much different tone.   15

"Aline," said the President, "this young woman, Madame's
daughter, is my mistress. I commend her to you and hope you
and she will get along nicely. The old rascal Dolbourg used
to be my rival but today, roped into sacraments, he's given
his word that only the hymen's torch will set love ablaze. This   20
beautiful child and her mother will witness your wedding and
Monsieur the abbot will officiate — a circumstance that Dolbourg at first thought to oppose, for the abbot himself is a
gallant fellow and your elderly husband, jealous as an Italian."

Mademoiselle, eyes constantly downcast, said nary a   25
word. We left the table and, claiming she was tired, she excused
herself, respectfully bowed to her father, and retired. Later she
pretended fatigue to avoid supper, and after we'd both again
carefully inspected every corner of the bedroom to be sure nobody could enter by surprise, she locked herself in with me to   30
once again spend the night. But owing to Sophie's enigmatic
words, she was all the more agitated. Thus passed the 28th.

Next morning at nine o'clock the President came knock-ing; we opened the door. He demanded I leave and after tell-ing his daughter to listen carefully, asked if she had decided to obey him and marry his friend Dolbourg — tomorrow. Made-moiselle told him that she was greatly surprised to hear such a proposition before her mother was even interred. Monsieur, considering himself his victim's master, harshly responded that such considerations were laughable, that he expected obedience and had come to ask she give her word; and if she would not he'd throw her in a dungeon where she could stay the rest of her life.

Mademoiselle did not become alarmed but showed great courage. She replied that she counted on her father's kindness far too much to fear she would be treated that way; but with such a cruel sacrifice required of her, she must be allowed to meet with Dolbourg alone. The favor was granted; the Presi-dent left. Monsieur Dolbourg arrived in short order. Aline evinced disgust for the marriage and did everything possible to put him off; love and despair lent her words great force, and she was so powerfully affecting that it would seem impossible to resist. But Dolbourg would not be moved; finally, she cast herself in tears at her tyrant's feet, begging him to renounce his intentions. All useless. He coldly told her to stand up. What was decided shall be done. He wanted from her only her *person* and not her heart; once his wife, he would find a way to overcome her revulsion or give up caring if it grew worse. As for her hatred, nothing in the world frightened him less; he would keep her in such solitude and submission that he need not dread her antipathy. He said this reminded him of his previous spouse; he was obliged to take her by assault and saw that he might have to do the same thing here. For, despite that woman's dignified character and her invincible disgust, he had succeeded after a couple of months in bringing her

to heel. He well remembered how to proceed and, as violent   o
as the means he used were, he could use them again.

Mademoiselle, disconcerted after having demeaned herself by begging before such a monster, proudly said to him:

"Well, then, Monsieur, everything has been said. My father may come and I'll give my word: tomorrow I shall be-   5
come your wife."

Monsieur de Blamont returned and she renewed her
promise in front of him and Dolbourg with a firm and tranquil
expression. The sole favor she asked was not to be obliged to
come down immediately but to be left alone for 24 hours in   10
order to prepare herself for an event of such great momen-
tousness. The President hesitated, saying that it was not for
the slave to dictate to her masters.

"As you can see," she replied quickly, "I'm only asking a
favor."   15

"Yes, go ahead," said Dolbourg, dragging off the President.
"Let her sulk for 24 hours if she likes. Besides, doesn't a virgin
have things to take care before the end to it?" He went on
with mockery both insolent and ridiculous. "Yes, my child," he
added, trying to cup her chin in his hand. *"Yes, go about your*   20
business. I'll be delighted to inspect the premises when Papa
gives me the keys."

Monsieur de Blamont, bracing the vulgar tone, added:
"A room must be swept and aired out before admitting its new
guest. And that's task a task for myself and me alone."   25

"Most assuredly," said Dolbourg. "I'm not in the least jealous, as you know. *You'll never gobble the oyster that I won't*
find the shell. Too bad, but that's the lot of Inspector Spouse."

Spurred on by such callous and obnoxious words, the
President impudently advanced upon his daughter and brutally   30
grabbed her by the arm:

"Little savage," he said, "you'll find no defense here, no
mother's breast to weep on."

At those cruel words Mademoiselle fell sobbing into a chair and would have surely suffocated in her own tears if Dolbourg, more frightened than his friend, had not called me to come back. Hidden nearby, having heard it all, I rushed back to find Mademoiselle unconscious; I quickly unlaced her. Those scoundrels — I tremble writing of these indignities — dared, *dared* cast their impure gaze upon milk-white breasts heaving with pain, flooded by tears of despair. Oh! Monsieur, don't ask more — their loathsome deeds — none worse. Through it all they kept me there. When Mademoiselle came to her senses, she immediately understood.

"Ah! My dear Julie," she exclaimed, "What did those monsters do?"

"Alas!" I answered in tears, "they exacted the toll for which they gave you 24 hours."

"Well," she resumed with surprising firmness, "I don't need any more time."

Approaching the window, she gauged how high with her eyes: more than 80 feet and, at the bottom, a moat some 20 feet wide.

"Well, Julie," she said after a short reflection, "as you can see, our plans become impossible."

"Even more than you think," I replied, distressed. "We're watched everywhere, making the horror even worse. Look," I said, pointing to the far side of the moat. "Those two men never leave sight of your window; and here within, two others follow my every step. Our situation is frightful."

"I feel it so," replied Aline. "Then, too, I've but a single choice."

Not understanding her, I ventured to say that, in her tragic situation she could only submit. Without hearing me out she angrily pushed me away.

"I thought you were my friend," she said. "But now I see. So you've sold yourself to my tyrants, have you? Did they

inveigle you to tell me that? So I'm alone on this earth? Aban- ₀
doned? Surrounded by enemies?"

"Great heavens!" I exclaimed, throwing myself at her feet.
"How can my dear mistress even think such a thing? Betray
you? Me? Abandon you! Count on me to the *death*."

At that word she trembled. Brusquely she stood up and ₅
said:

"I'll know soon enough if you're lying. You'll see if I shan't
be free of my persecutors!"

"What! You still hope to get away?"

"Yes." She smiled in a way I still remember — but was not ₁₀
sufficiently struck by at the time. "Yes, Julie. Return, I shall, to
my mother's house. What they said — that her bosom won't
shelter me still — isn't true. It will, Julie. It shall."

And after striding twice around the room she asked me
for a glass of water.

"This shall be my last meal," she told me, taking it, "at ₁₅
Chateau de Blamont."

"Mademoiselle," I said, believing she had regained a little
composure and guessing she would now tell me of her plans to
escape, "that's not a meal to give you strength for a long trip."

"Indeed, my good friend" she replied with an open and ₂₀
free expression, "I intend to go far. And from this place, never
far enough!"

She asked for her writing case, and I brought it to her.
She told me to leave her alone until she rang. I obeyed and ₂₅
she wrote until seven o'clock. She then bade me enter and sit
down:

"These letters — see who they're addressed to."

I read one of them: *To my best friend.*

"That is Monsieur Déterville, I'd guess." ₃₀

"Assuredly."

I read the other: *To the man I shall worship beyond the
grave.*

"O! For this one," I said, "Whomever you like. Let me guess."
She smiled.

As to the third: *To the divine spirit of my mother.*

"Would you deliver this one?" she asked.

"Mademoiselle!"

"Well, then — I'll take care of it myself. She stood up, powerfully agitated. "And deliver it by hand."

Why didn't I understand what she was saying? Why couldn't I?

A little while later she told me that since leaving Vertfeuille, we'd not taken even a moment to pray for her mother.

"True," I said.

"Let's put that to rights, Julie."

She kneeled and enjoined me to do the same, and to recite from my *Office of the Dead*, reading slowly to allow her to follow and carefully listen. She fulfilled her duty with such fervor and solemn intensity that it brought tears to my eyes. She then asked that we recite together the 24th Psalm: *Dominus illuminatio mea*, the sense of which is: *however many enemies torment us, we must not be afraid when we have God to protect us and hope of eternal life.* But when she reached the third verse: *When my father and mother forsake me, only the Lord will take care of me,* her eyes filled with tears. She gave herself over to the most profound dejection; soon after she stood up.

"I am more at peace now," she told me. "You can't imagine a sensitive soul's satisfaction in praying for the one who's so dear to my heart. My poor mother — sweet mother — how she loved me, what care she took me of as a child! And when I grew older, how she made my happiness her only concern. How she held me tight just before she died! Now I've nothing. Everything in the world is lost to me. Julie! I've nothing left."

And again she began to weep.

As it neared eleven o'clock she asked me if I wanted to stay up with her. That was what I wanted, and I agreed.

"Good," she said. "But, we won't pass the whole night to- ⁰
gether. A little before they come for me, I will take comfort
and have a few hours' rest. I want to be beautiful for the ceremony. *I want to be as beautiful as Nature will permit.*" After
a moment's reflection she added, "They're eating dinner and
given over to gaiety and pleasure. They won't hear. Bring me ⁵
my guitar."

She took and tuned it, then played an air from the ro-
mance *Nina, the Girl Driven Mad for Love*, and she sang
these verses:
  ¹⁰

> *Adored mother, in a moment*
> *Death took you from my tender arms!*
> *My lover — you who live on!*
> *Come back to console your mistress.*
> *Ah! Let him come back (2×) Alas! Alas!* ¹⁵
> *But my beloved does not come.*
>
> *As the rose in sweet spring*
> *Opens to the wind of Zephyrus*
> *So my soul to this sweet song* ²⁰
> *Would open to love's fervor.*
> *In vain I listen: Alas! Alas!*
> *My beloved does not speak.*
>
> *You who come to shed tears* ²⁵
> *On the coffin in which I rest,*
> *Wailing over my pain,*
> *Tell my lover, the cause of it all*
> *That he remained forever — Alas! Alas! —*
> *Beloved unto death.* ³⁰

And as soon as she was finished: "Enough!" Furiously, she broke the guitar against the wall. *"Get away from me, useless instrument! For the last time I've sung of the one I love and you've nothing more to do."*

Seeing her so troubled and agitated, I didn't dare say a word. At times she got up and strode about; other times she sat, battered by pain, moaning and screaming.

At 11, she counted the strokes of the clock.

"I've only that number of hours left," she said, "They're to arrive at 10."

Gathering her letters together, she placed them in the envelope addressed to you.

"Did Déterville not advise you to send him a detailed diary of everything that happens here?"

"Yes, Mademoiselle."

"Well! So you must. And when you send it to him, don't forget to include this envelope."

Making me swear to do exactly as she said, she put the packet in my hands.Once that was done, she was calmer. As we talked tranquilly for two or three hours, she seemed worried about what had happened to Sophie; she couldn't imagine how she came to be at the chateau or why her name was to be found on the windowsill. Since she knew nothing of Augustine's flight nor of the frightful suspicions it had raised among us, I followed your orders and continued to conceal everything from her. We talked about things of little moment, but into her words she was always injecting sinister things that much frightened me. Several times she asked me how long a body remained whole after a person takes his last breath; whether I thought a person would take a long time to expire after cutting open his veins; and if I thought that, should she die at Chateau de Blamont, her father would refuse her wish to be entombed next to her mother. She asked if I believed

Valcour would be truly angry to learn of her death — and a o
thousand things of the same ilk to which I ought to have paid
far more attention, but failed.

When the clock struck three, she shuddered.

"How time flies," she said. "When we come close upon a
great event the moments seem to go faster. By this same time 5
tonight, much will have happened."

Turning to me, she gazed at me for some time without
speaking; then she counted the years we had been together
and remarked tenderly that I'd been with her ever since she
attained the age of reason. 10

"You were almost as young as I," she told me, "I remember."
She kissed me. "Honest creature, I've never done anything for
you. I would have, had I married Valcour. I shall recommend
you to Déterville."

Of all she said, these words were the most telling, clearly 15
revealing her intentions. By Heaven's ghastly assent! I was not
sufficiently vigilant. I was convinced she wanted to escape and
only if that plan failed would she want to put an end to her
misery; and so it seemed only a question of not letting her
out of my sight. She recounted all she'd done since we'd been 20
together — her hopes, fears, worries, desires, sorrows, and
moments of peace. She left nothing out.

"Oh!" she said as she finished. "How life is short! It seems
like it's nothing but a dream."

The clock struck four. 25

"Go outside quietly," she told me. "See whether it might
be possible to flee. Look down the road that leads to the gates
of the chateau. If the way is free, come back and we'll make
our escape."

"But wouldn't be it better, Mademoiselle, if you came 30
with me?"

"No. If we're followed they'll say I was trying to get away,
and come after me and inflict some new outrage."

I went out. No sooner I had stepped into the corridor, which was always kept lit, than two servants appeared and brusquely asked where I was going, what I wanted, and why I was still up at that hour. I said I needed fresh air but they replied that it was too late and I must immediately go back to the room or they would awaken Monsieur.

I returned and gave Mademoiselle the sorry account of my efforts.

"Well," she told me, "my dear friend, we must resign ourselves. May God's will be done. Go and take a few hours' rest. I'll be happy myself to sleep a little."

Then with the greatest tranquility — and this is what misled me:

"They'll be here at ten o'clock, so come back at nine. I'll need at least an hour to dress."

I resisted her request, told her I had no need to rest, and would prefer to stay and care for her.

"No, no," she said, showing me the door, "that would keep me from sleeping. We're talking now and we'd keep talking. Go, my good friend. Go, but don't forget to come back an hour before they arrive. You know I don't want them to find me in bed."

Just as I was about to do as she insisted, she realized I'd forgotten to take the letters on the table; nervously, she retrieved the envelope and concealed it in my bosom. I started to go out and she stopped me, threw her arms around my neck, and clasped me close, in tears. Immediately aware that this new burst of pain violently affected me, she contained herself and continued to lead me gently to the door, telling me to not forget anything she said.

I went out — but troubled in a way I couldn't control. In my bedroom, you can imagine, I couldn't sleep. Several times I went to quietly listen by her door, resolved to enter at the least sound from within. I heard nothing and when nine o'clock struck I rushed to her apartment with inexpressible anxiety.

O Monsieur! What a spectacle! Impossible for me to de- o
pict. My dear mistress, that angel from heaven — for whom
I'll weep the rest of my life. She lay on the floor, soaked in
blood.

Her mother's braided hair lay carefully arranged on the
ground beside a miniature portrait of that so very fine woman. 5
Kneeling before those beloved objects, she must have stabbed
herself and, losing strength from loss of blood, fell back. That
was how I found her. The weapon she'd used was the detached
blade from a pair of scissors she had for her toilette; she'd separated the one blade from the other and pierced herself in three 10
places beneath her left breast. Blood flowed like a river from
the wounds and covered the floor. The desire to rescue her, if
it wasn't too late, overcame my fright; I rushed beside her but
she was cold and death had already cast its shadow across her
beauteous glow; her eyes were already shut against the light; 15
already the earth had lost its most beautiful ornament.

I took her in my arms, flooding her with tears, and laid
her on the bed. On the table beside it I found the following
note, which I transcribed immediately for safekeeping before
showing to anybody. Here it is, word for word: 20

*I humbly beg my father's forgiveness for the act I
am committing in his home, and for the ill-humor I
shall cause him by resisting his orders. The motives
that provoked this resistance must have been too vio-* 25
*lent, for I choose death to destiny. I implore, as final
favor, burial next to my mother, as she wished, with
her portrait and the hair upon which I pressed my
lips while hewing myself from life.*

Aline de Blamont 30

As soon as I finished copying the note, I called the President. Can you believe, Monsieur — can your sensitive soul even imagine the overwhelming inhumanity? The dark scene of woe and sorrow inspired in him only wrath and rage — and it was terrible. He blamed me. He heaped insults upon me and threw me to the floor, trampling me underfoot, and said I was the one who had killed his daughter. Overcome with pain, suffering through it all without strength to respond, I pointed to the note on the table; he quickly read it and, forced to acknowledge it, took no further notice of me. He strode around the room, evincing not a trace of pain but only fury. After a few minutes he left and returned with Dolbourg.

Who trembled. As he read the note, he cast his eyes upon Aline — and now tears fell from his eyes. Firmly, with some measure of pride, he addressed the President:

"Monsieur," he said, "this foments for me too much to bear. This dreadful thing ends by opening my eyes to the disorder of my life. 'Twas only by my vices that I inspired such horror in this poor girl. I am sick and tired of being nothing but a despised object of terror and contempt. The dying beams of unblemished virtue strike my heart. They enlighten it — and tear it apart.

"O heavenly creature!" he continued, taking my mistress's hand and shedding tears upon it, "forgive me the crime I've caused! Would that the Eternal One, whose glory you already share, also forgive me! I shall go and expiate my crime in sorrow and I shall weep until the end of my days. *Adieu*, Monsieur. I shall no longer share in your debauchery; I shall forever enshroud myself in harsh retreat. Do not follow me and you'll never see me again as long as you live."

So saying, he went out and within an hour had left the chateau for good. But the soul of Monsieur de Blamont was not so easily shaken. Become even more furious by the loss of

his friend than that of his daughter, he came after me again,   o
bellowing that if I'd kept watch over Aline it would never
have happened. I begged him to remember that he'd forbade
me to sleep in Mademoiselle's bedroom; and that, despite
his orders I'd spent part of the night there with her and that
the tragedy only took place toward morning, after Aline had   5
insisted I leave.

Still furious, he stalked out only to return shortly with
the elderly woman and the abbot — the latter, tucking and
plucking his jabot, saying it was terrible but all so important
to follow the thread of the story, and that it would assuredly   10
lead to unravelling the scheme through which the murderer
could be discovered and arrested.

But while he and the President talked in low voices, the
woman was visibly moved by the sight of Mademoiselle, and
she read the note.   15

"Monsieur," she said, "if you want my advice, the wisest and only honest thing to do is return Aline in a coffin to
Vertfeuille, where she can be interred beside her mother, as
she wished. And let this poor woman here, who's surely not
guilty of anything, quietly accompany the body. Begging your   20
pardon, Monsieur, but if you decide on some other course, I'll
follow Dolbourg and neither my daughter nor I shall remain
with you a moment longer."

"All of you can go to the devil!" replied the President, furious. "There's been a crime committed and I want to know   25
what's at the bottom of it. Only this creature can tell me and
she refuses to say. I don't know what else to do but put her in
the hands of justice."

"Most certainly," said the Abbot, "No other way's both
right and wise."   30

"I don't think so," asserted the woman — with much force
yet great composure. "This young woman has committed

no crime and confessed to nothing. Once out of your hands, she'll talk and spread word of a horrible event that you've the greatest interest to conceal."

At that the President, without answering, went away growling and snarling. The others followed and I was left alone, racked by pain and worry.

And that, Monsieur, is all I have to tell you, awful as it is. It remains for me forward to you the letters from Aline in good order and I will append a final note to this one as soon as I'm certain of sending it off safely.

Post-scriptum from Julie:

The elderly woman's advice seems to have prevailed and we're ready to leave. Aline will be taken to Vertfeuille by closed coach under my care and with a single servant to guide the way; it's to all to happen under pretense of a transport of furniture sent by Monsieur to the estate of Madame, and it will be addressed to you. Monsieur de Blamont, who's aware that I'm writing you and has made it possible for me to send this letter, requests you wait for us at Vertfeuille and not leave before taking care of Aline as you did Madame de Blamont. Thus once more you shall see your unfortunate friend — but in what a terrible state! Could you have ever thought it?

I had another letter ready to mail that was less detailed, and it would have been the one sent if Monsieur le President had asked to see what I was writing; but he did not, so I am able to send you my complete diary.

Adieu, Monsieur. Though choked with pain, I conclude with assurances of my respect.

Julie

Post-scriptum from Déterville to Valcour

I am awaiting it — her coffin — and to rain bitter tears of despair upon it, paying final respects. This baneful detail I send you together with her posthumous letters. May these cruel words forever indulge and service your pain. If you have   5 strength enough to survive the one who loved you, you'll at least lament her and consecrate every moment to her the remainder of your whole life long. I permit you no distractions other than those piety might offer. But if ever, by no matter what counsel, you should venture once more into the world   10 after such a loss, I will be the first to say: Valcour is not worthy of Aline, nor of Déterville either.

Letter LXIX
Aline to Déterville*

Chateau de Blamont, 29 April

Astonished though you may be by my course of action, Monsieur, rest assured there remained no other. Believe me: had I been able to take advantage of your kind offers, I certainly would have done so. As Julie will tell you, no possible means of escape remained that would have conformed either to your counsel or to my duties.

I most insistently entreat you that I be placed beside my mother; you will recall that she wished it. If the cruelty of those in whose house I now reside go so far as to refuse such a favor, I beg you to lay claim to me, Monsieur. Consider that I have suffered too greatly in life not to be rewarded with such a favor upon my death.

From the envelope with its letters, which you will have received before my sorrowful remains, I ask that you place the one I wrote to her in my mother's tomb, and to forward the other one to Valcour. Tell him, Monsieur, that I die to save myself for him. Tender and sensitive, he will understand. There remained no course but the one I take, lest I become a creature of infamy. How could I hesitate?

With fond memories of Eugénie and her mother, I ask that you remember me to them from time to time, Monsieur; and if one or the other condemns me, I beg you to defend me and remit all rights to do so in name of friendship, yet without compromising the person from whom Nature demands my respect, however great his faults.

---

* This and the following two missives, Aline's posthumous letters, were included in the packet that Déterville forwarded to Valcour with Julie's diary.

So kind you've been to my mother and myself, Monsieur, that to beset you with such trouble is a great indiscretion! Yet I beg you not to deny me these final wishes. I ask them of you in the name of the pure feeling you so often swore to me.

Do you remember the charming winter evenings we spent in Paris — with my mother, you and your kind family, and Valcour — when you told me that I would survive us all and that it would be left to me to write the epitaph for our little society? I deplored that prognostic, you recall, and how happily it now stands refuted! Yes — happily, I say, for the one left to mourn those dearest to him is to be pitied, the one who died, less so; and knowing how sensitive you are, I am infinitely more distressed for you than for me. But do not regret my passing, Monsieur, for the happiness I dare aspire to now is far and away greater than that which awaited me on earth. Kindly use such thoughts to soothe Valcour; I fear for him when he first learns of it, with you not be there to care for him!

Oh! Monsieur, I'm left few things indeed but at least no one can take them away. I would like my little drawings and other works to be sent to Valcour, for I know he likes them and the gift will please him; and you, Monsieur, I ask you to accept my books. You will want to divide the rest of my things, and money, between the poor inhabitants of Vertfeuille and my dear Julie; I commend her to you and ask that you find a place for her as part of my mother's pious bequests; she deserves as much both by her conduct and the care she took of me until the very last moment.

Adieu, Monsieur. Remember Aline from time to time; you never had a better friend, nor one more sincere than she.

Letter LXX

Aline to the Divine Spirit of Her Mother

Chateau de Blamont, 29 April

O you who gave me life! Whose mortal remains I embrace in putting down these final words, whose cherished shade I see before me, whose voice I hear, inspiring in me the courage to join you — for, a few hours from now, we will be together again, peacefully reunited in the maternal breast, where men's crimes and cruelty can no more lay hold of your luckless unhappy daughter. She will find within that sacred breast the restful calm which she could not attain in the world. Open your arms, Mother, that I may come to you; receive your daughter in the final sanctuary in which you lie; let us die together for, in that world, we could not live.

Savages! They wanted to sacrifice me upon your tomb. Your remains were not cold before crime was in their hearts. What do I mean? Just this: they may indeed have cut short your life to carry off their odious schemes! I resisted, Mother, yet I'm no longer worthy of you. Our flesh will lie together and decay. You preceded me into the abyss of eternity but not by long; now I hurtle after you, full of confidence in the kindness of the Divine Being. You are with Him already and I may hope He will not punish me for the wrong I do, for I come braced by all your virtues, which will bring me clemency I could not expect without them. O Mother! You will lead me before God's throne and tell Him:

"Behold a victim of men but her heart was ever your temple; you wanted her to die like Moses and 'twas your will that brought her to the mountain* and bade her gaze upon

---

* Allusion to Colette's house, situated on a mountain, where Aline saw her lover for the last time.

806

the land she could never inhabit. Happy to see her life's flame   o
extinguished scarce sooner was it lighted, do not reproach her,
O Lord, for having dared end it; do not punish her for having
disjoined mortal bonds to ask you for eternal life, where the
satisfaction of constant service unto you will be troubled no
more by her tears.   5

    "O my Lord! Must this pure soul, your handiwork, be soiled
for having spent only a short time in the frail body to which you
confined it? She knew only tears and despair from which she
fled to return to you. Perhaps weakness, perhaps lack of cour-
age. Instead of rebelling against shackles or revolting against   10
restraint, if she had called upon you in her tribulations, she
would perhaps have obtained your help. Do not punish her for
her weakness; she has more love than hope, and greater desire
to be reunited with you than strength to implore you. These are
the crimes of a tender soul; be so good as to not castigate her for   15
them. When you created her in your image, the gift of love was
the first virtue you imprinted upon her; do not punish her for
it. Do not condemn her to pain and sorrow because she feared
those sensations; let her rest in joy because she desired to know
it in you and wished to rapidly pass across the chasm of human   20
misery to find herself once again in the immensity of your glory.

    "My dear God! Don't do it for me but forgive the tears of
a beloved mother who never stopped knowing and serving you.
See us as two flowers withered by the serpent's venom, and
which the pure breath of your celestial soul can return to life   25
in the bosom of immortality."

Letter LXXI

Aline to Valcour

Chateau de Blamont, 29 April

> *Never again shall I see the inhabitants of the earth.*
> *Like a shepherd's tent, my dwelling has been pulled*
> *down and thrown away.*
>
> — Canticle of Hezekiah

Gone sweet illusion, as smoke rises and vanishes. You've lost the woman you loved. *Her days slip by like shadows, she withers like the grass.** Deceptive joy! Foolish hope! You touched her heart only to make crueler your own privation! O Valcour! She exists no longer and the fragile voice that speaks to you rises from within the sepulcher and resembles the meteor's flight as it escapes the eye's trailing gaze. Was I wrong to make you pledge to attach but little value to that vase of clay, which endures but a moment? Let your eyes penetrate the haze of death, which envelops me now, and to behold those once beloved features, now disfigured by the horror of decomposition, with nothing but the seal of indestructible feeling that my soul imprinted upon them. Yet if all is annihilated, and even if nothing is left of me except dust, yet the soul that loved you survives — immortal if not by the purity of its essence, then by the toil of your passion. And the being you brought to life in Aline, created and vitalized by your love, must subsist forever. You will see her loving soul appear to you during sleepless nights and in your dreams; it shall hover and watch over, at one with your own soul, and govern its movement like the hand of God guides the stars in the immense champaign of celestial space.

* 101st Psalm.

O my dearest! What change a few days wrought! Three   o
weeks ago we were planning love's mutual pleasures and the
tender mother I worshiped but have now lost was glad to see
us together and led us to believe, with her, that we would be
united! Fragile playthings of edicts on high — a few moments,
and what an enormous distance now lies between us! Like a   5
ship's pilot rejoices when sighting a distant harbor but foun-
dering upon the shoals when suddenly there breaks forth an
impetuous and unstoppable storm — so did we imagine at-
taining happiness that most certainly will never be ours. So
it goes with the plans of men, the sorry outcome of perilous   10
decisions! Their impotent desires, like feeble beams of sunlight during the winter signs of the Zodiac dissipate without
bringing heat to the cold thick air — they are annihilated by
the will of the Eternal One.

But suppose all had gone well for us and we passed our   15
lives in a garden of delights, where roses bloomed beneath our
feet beside fruits of palm and where the ever-fragrant cedar
lent shadow upon the riverbank and milk ran in the streams.
Are we immortal, my dearest, and must we not take leave, like
Eve, of this sweet sojourn? Don't you imagine such a sepa-   20
ration would be even crueler than the one we endure today,
fallen amidst thorns? Our bonds multiplied, our love would
have grown, making each of us dearer to the other with every
passing moment. Would it all not have made the obligation to
break those bonds still more frightful? Let us thank the Eter-   25
nal One for having presented us with the chalice before it was
filled and more bitter still; you would've wept at one and the
same time for a cherished sweet spouse, a kind and obliging
friend, and the mother of tender fruits your love would have
planted within my womb. Today your tears flow for a lover   30
you hardly knew. Who can say if my so ardent desire to please
would not have given rise to still more virtues and bound you
to me tighter still and made your loss more painful?

Ah, my dearest! Let me stop to dwell a moment on one idea that my misfortune only effaces the very moment my heart conceives it. If the sacred pledges of which I speak would have indeed brought us closer, how enchanted I would've been to guide the young fruits of your tenderness and my own! With what pleasure I would have placed within their innocent souls the divine flame I felt for you! How pleased I would have been to see them address you with expressions of my love! Are those the awful pleasures, so sweet and pure, of which God wishes to deprive me? But let us not try to perlustrate his designs. We were not born for each other. Let us worship and submit.

O Valcour! I ought now to justify to you the criminal means that I use to leave this world. If I've chosen this terrible path, if I've been forced to shatter your idol in the temple in which you worshiped it, you can be sure nothing would have saved me from infamy. Learn before condemning and don't lay blame without listening to everything that may be said. To what condition must I have been reduced to renounce the greatest good in my life only to cause the greatest grief in your own! Yes, I preferred death to the certainty we would never belong to one other. I would rather end my life than live with the double disgrace that would soil it, frightful though it may be because it will separate us — *forever!* Think of it, my dearest, but 'tis only too true. *Forever* we will be apart; it is now impossible we'll ever be reunited; years will pass, present and future generations will succeed and fall into the abyss of time. Crimes and virtues will mingle, cross-breed, and multiply on earth; everything will vary and change and be reborn, everything beneath the vault of heaven will be destroyed — yet none of it will return Aline to Valcour. No, my dearest. Every drop in the ocean multiplied a hundred million times would still not give the feeblest idea of the numberless centuries to comprise the immensity of time that will keep us apart; and during that terrible interval, no action or act of authority,

even were it to come from God, could renew the earthly bonds ₀
in which we took such foolish delight.

But set beside that idea the sweet gentle thought of the
Infinite Being in whose bosom our souls shall be reunited! So
there is one way we can see one another again, conceived and
made possible by the existence of this worshipful Being — and, ₅
for us, does that not make Him still more cherished! At His
feet I shall await you. Don't hasten the moment: shed tears
upon the wrong I've done but don't imitate it. Let me prepare
the Holy One to receive you; let me implore Him on your behalf and request your place among the angels who sing his ₁₀
praises. Don't deprive me of the pleasant hope and thought
that my prayers may contribute to your eternal felicity. Having failed on earth, I must try to find it in heaven whilst you
continue to exercise the virtues that won my heart, each one
taken up by your Aline to present to the Lord's holy tribunal. ₁₅

"All-powerful God," I shall say, "by dint of his good deeds
he expunges the crime committed by the woman who loved
him; don't expel him from your bosom but may it be by His
good works that I obtain your forgiveness and his happiness.
We love and cherish and glorify you. Together we will braid ₂₀
crowns of myrtle and lay them at your feet. We will chant
to make the azure vaults of your temple so resound that *the
name of the Lord will be declared in Zion, and his praise in
Jerusalem.**

No pity for me, my dearest — I'm not to be pitied! Think ₂₅
of what little you've lost compared to how much you'll find —
what awaits you in the bosom of the Eternal One. But to be
worthy of this celestial end, don't remove yourself from the
world in which you were born; in no way do I foredoom you
to abandon it. I ask only that you continue to live honestly; ₃₀

---

*   102nd Psalm.

the more our earthly sojourn offers occasions to fall, the more beautiful it is to evince virtue which, in this perverse world, can be found in profound solitude — and that is the wise man's heart. He enters into it, meditates upon it, and finds the strength and means to resist corruption. Let my image embellish that solitude in your place of exile; let it reign there forever. I've still pride enough to believe it will serve as a rampart against vice and that nothing shameful will ever enter the sanctuary created for that cherished image. When the true Christian wants to excite himself to acts of love toward the God he worships; when he wants to oppose that kind of all-consuming love to the burning temptations of seduction, he casts his eyes upon the image of God, who sacrificed Himself for him. He remembers the pain that God endured and tells himself: *He died for me.* If that thought does not suffice to keep your soul to the righteous path, if though beautiful it cannot fill your soul, turn then to Aline's portrait and, while contemplating it, tell yourself: *And the one who loved me also died for me, she sacrificed herself to avoid crime; and for that let us perish if need be a thousand times rather than betray her.* And with the power of that faith, we will meet again. We will live on in eternity; united by the hand of the Supreme Being, and those darts envenomed by men's evil shall be turned back upon them, just as powerless as once upon a time were those sent by the Prince of Darkness against the God who made him.

Parting ways as we must, Valcour, this separation is very different from our recent farewell on Colette's mountain; for then we still had hope and quit one another intending to be reunited — but now it is *forever.* Aline, the woman of whom you were so proud, will never again appear before you. Wasting away in the darkness of the tomb, no longer spoken of, it will be as if she never existed; she will live on only in your heart. When you receive this letter and shed tears upon it,

your imagination, so struck by the one who wrote it, will bring
her image before your senses though she will no longer be
alive; she'll have descended into the abyss. The illusion that
comes before you will be as nothing but shimmering colors
that abide upon alpine peaks long after the setting sun.

Love me, Valcour — love and cherish always the one who
preferred death to dishonor, and remain faithful to her until
the last moment of your life. The world will offer you more
beautiful creatures but never one more tender. Not even one
of the intoxicating caresses that you might find in the arms
of another would be worth a hairsbreadth of Aline's glistening flame, and opening yourself to them would tear you apart
with remorse. Think often of our old love and try to find in the
memory of past pleasures the strength you need to endure the
abiding heartache.

Adieu, Valcour! I must say that final word at last. Tears
flow as I write and my blood grows cold. My gaze turns to you,
seeks but does not find. I'm like a fawn torn from its mother.
Why is yours not the hand to strike? How is it that I won't
breathe my last in your arms? Why cannot my soul's last sigh
reunite with yours in the kindling fire of my final gasp? Why
must I die coldly and alone amidst my enemies? Why does my
body, perhaps to be profaned by their shameful gaze, not have
your own as my shield? Why aren't my last words imprinted
on your lips with the most exalted expression of tenderness
and affection? That I cannot do — no. But it is for you that I
die and that idea alone affords me the strength to do what my
love for you would only forestall. *Adieu*.

Letter LXXII
Valcour to Déterville

This day the 17th May, 1779

I've read them — the fatal sheaf, the somber words. And still I live! So vivid is love's sentiment that even in losing the woman who was its object, it is impossible for me to cut short my own life, which she will continue to animate and inflame until I draw my final breath. I will do far more than die — I shall live, Déterville, I will feed upon life's serpents — and drink the venom they spit. The sacrifice is more frightful than if I myself committed suicide. Isn't the man unable to endure the plagues that press upon him and so escapes by ending his own life infinitely weaker than the one who consents to live through pain and torment? The one fears pain and gives up; the latter braves it and resigns himself. It's not that I disapprove of the terrible choice Aline made, for though she took from me all that I hold dear, I should not blame her. But my situation is quite different and permits me to choose another way. I prefer sustaining my pain rather than doing something that perforce would put an end to it: a profound retreat that will bury me forever. I shall cast myself into the arms of God — and worship none but my Aline.

Abandoned from childhood to live and breathe only suffering and misfortune, exposed every moment of my life to the sinister flames of the Furies' torches, I came to know that reversal could come at any moment of my life — but this is one I never would have imagined. My heart could never admit such a thing. Where shall I seek asylum? Where can I go? Where to flee that her image would not be before me? I shall see her everywhere. She'll pursue no matter my redoubt, offer herself under the aegis of the Lord, in whose breast I might have found happiness.

O my friend! Lift open the tomb in which she lies, for   o
only there am I permitted to live. Let me go there to drench
it with the caustic tears of despair, every day of my life. Who
knows but that her ardent and sensitive soul, uniquely embo-
somed by love's fires, will not revive, by dint of my own violent
passion? Open her coffin, I tell you, let me bring her back to   5
life — or die. Here my reason leaves me; I must put down my
pen: too bitter, I'd soon become either stupid or cruel. *Adieu*
— love me. Forget me. Above all, never seek me out. If, despite
all my efforts, your friendship brought you to the place of my
retreat, I'd consider it proof of contempt rather than a mark   10
of kindness owed one who abjures, now and forever, anything
that might remind him of a world into which the ferocious
hand of fate had plunged him into nothing but a vale of tears.

The correspondence ends here, making the rest of the story quite difficult to recount. But inasmuch as we greatly desire to please the reader, interested, we might suppose, in the characters with whom he's been living for some time, and because certain details furnished by Monsieur Déterville make it possible, we offer several clarifications which, we hope, will earn his gratitude.

On the evening of May 2nd, Aline's body was dispatched in complete secrecy from the Chateau de Blamont; it was accompanied by Julie, upon whom the President imposed strictest silence. On arrival at Vertfeuille on the 6th of May, Aline was placed, in accordance with her wishes, in the tomb beside her mother.

Déterville brought Julie into his home, where she remains to this day, servant to his wife, with annual wages of 100 pistoles and assurances that she may remain there for the rest of her life. But he did not content himself with minor considerations and soon turned to weightier ones. Finding the President's crimes too abominable to go unpunished, he was consumed by a desire to avenge his dearest friends. As soon as he concluded his obligations at Vertfeuille, he traveled by coach to meet with Count de Beaulé, who was unfortunately detained by official duties. This excellent and most trustworthy officer swore that to help exact revenge upon the monster who had just deprived them of the two women so dear to them. Soon they returned to Paris, where initially they undertook the most exacting inquiries concerning Augustine, the accomplice of Monsieur de Blamont's darkest, most shameful deeds. She was found at another of the scoundrel's estates, in Champagne, where she was quietly awaiting her reward.

The Count and Monsieur de Déterville were wholly deter-   0
mined to avoid any sort of scandal because Léonore, in accordance with Madame de Blamont's wishes, it was now
planned, was soon to come into the inheritance that belonged
to her by birth after renouncing the other to which she had no
right. So they contented themselves with having Augustine   5
secretly interrogated before officials chosen by the ministry.
She confessed to everything and was immediately condemned
to spend the rest of her life in a cloistered convent, assigned
the lowest tasks, and may she long regret her terrible youthful
transgressions.   10

With all material evidence against Monsieur de Blamont
in hand, including Augustine's confession and other accounts
by witnesses she named, also obtained secretly, the minister immediately dispatched an order to have him arrested.
But that cunning criminal, always vigilant, carefully tended   15
to the actions of his wife's friends and schemed accordingly.
Although he could not stop them, he was clever enough to
evade them. He fled the country. The Count de Beaulé judged
further pursuit inappropriate, now they were rid of the detestable individual — they committed themselves to putting   20
Sainville and Léonore in possession of the assets of the House
of Blamont by legitimizing Claire's birth, proving with the ac-
cumulated documents that she was the real daughter of Monsieur and Madame de Blamont, not the Countess of Kerneuil.
That inheritance Léonore officially renounced, which did not   25
displease the more distant heirs.

The young couple thus now found themselves in possession of Vertfeuille, which estate they continue to enjoy greatly.
With two millions' worth of gold bars returned by the King of
Spain to Sainville to considerably enhance the family fortune,   30
we see that they have become enormously wealthy — but humanity shan't be offended by the use the young woman has

made of her wealth. The terrible destiny to which Léonore's father, mother, and sister were subject more impressed her hard-hearted and prideful nature than all the misfortunes she'd encountered in her travels. The first effort born of her return to benevolence was to seek out her father. Once she'd located him in Stockholm, she made it known to him that he must take up permanent residence in a place where he could enjoy an annuity she would provide for his care and betterment, such that she might enjoy delicate pleasures of the heart. That she did with greatest punctuality. The President, not reformed but surely more prudent, retiring to London, lived quietly for several years on an income of 50,000 livres annually. But Heaven, which never lets a criminal go unpunished, permitted thieves to murder the scoundrel during a visit he made to the north of England.

Sainville, ever honest and considerate, wished to share his dear wife's filial piety in a different way. He called for construction of a splendid mausoleum in the church of Vertfeuille, dedicated to Aline and her mother and inscribed: *Constancy, Piety, Conjugal Fidelity, and Love.* The two women, with crowns of myrtle and roses, were portrayed in one another's arms.

Dolbourg, having thoroughly renounced the path of iniquity, has gone on to live a most regular life of modest means in a small country house far from Paris, having left everything he owned to relatives and the poor.

Monsieur Déterville, his beloved Eugénie, Madame de Senneval, and the Count de Beaulé — happy to have avenged, without bloodshed, the women so dear to them — continue as before to spend part of their summers at Vertfeuille. There they quietly enjoy the company of its new proprietors and never go without offering tribute, in tears and prayers, to the spirits of those two virtuous women whom they cherished and respected.

As to Monsieur de Valcour, after terrible episodes of frightful despair, including six weeks during which he hovered between life and death, he gave himself up to God's embrace. He spent the rest of his life in the abbey at Notre-Dame de Sept-Fons, in which he was the embodiment of resignation, pure candor, and austerity most severe. His retreat was discovered only upon his death. None of Monsieur Déterville's efforts to locate him had succeeded and his whereabouts might have remained forever unknown had not Valcour written a letter, just before the end, in which he charged his friend with carrying out his final wishes; the missive informed Déterville where he was but there was no time left to come to his aid before he died. Upon his heart, until the very last, the tender and delicate lover wore the portrait of the woman he loved.

Clémentine is still living in Biscaye, happy with her husband and in correspondence with Léonore, whom she visits every other year. We do not know the fate of the other characters in this work. As concerns Sophie, we are distressed to have nothing to report; for the rest, we don't imagine the reader will regret not knowing more — with the possible exception of Zamé. We may surmise he will die amongst the people who idolize him and take with him to the grave the sorrow but also the esteem, love, and gratitude of everybody around him — adulatory compensation for virtue owed a legislator and honest man.

finis

Endnotes

Our translation, in accord with the 1990 Pléiade publication, takes the third state of the 1795 edition of the novel as the canonical text, into which Sade had introduced a small number of significant changes after the novel's first printing. Modern French editions, beginning with Jean-Jacques Pauvert's 1966 edition for *Cercle du Livre Précieux*, include useful contextual information, and we are indebted to the work of Michel Delon, editor of the Pléiade edition, and to Jean-Marie Goulemont for his notes to the 1994 Livre de Poche edition. Our own endnotes and brief explanations, which bear witness to Sade's encyclopedic mind, are designed explicitly for an Anglophone audience.

115   381.27: *"He bore the titles…"*: The system of justice at the end of the ancien régime was thoroughly disorganized, as Sade implies.

116   382.25: Brigand Louis Mandrin (1725–1755) was a highwayman who challenged the hated tax farmers and is often cited as the Robin Hood of France.

117   383.32: Île Sainte-Marguerite: an island off the shore of Cannes, site of the Fort Royal prison. The famed "Man in the Iron Mask" was imprisoned there.

118   385.14: Alguazil, a borrowing from Spanish, refers pejoratively to a constable or minor minister.

119   388.3: Combat in Germany refers to the Seven Years War (1756–63); the mention of Corsica alludes to the French conquest of that island country, 1768–69.

120   388.20: Versailles: the King's Court; the city of Rennes was the administrative center of Brittany.

121   392.13: Aspasia (c. 470–400 BC) was a lover of Pericles and played an influential but somewhat obscure role in political life in ancient Greece. She was rumored to have spent part of her life as a prostitute.

122   407.27: *"Traitorous state"*: a reference to Venice, the failed republic, as Sainville noted (see note 20, above).

123   418.24: Sade's description of the caravan and other aspects of
voyage here owes to a volume by physician Charles-
Jacques Poncet (1655–1706), who published an influential account of his voyage to Ethiopia which, in fact, was
so unique and popular that it was translated into English
as *A Voyage to Ethiopia* (1709).

124   419.26: The Grand Seigneur refers to the Sultan of the Ottoman
Empire. At the time Sade wrote, this was Abdul Hamid I
(1725–1789). Hélaoué is described in contemporary texts
as a village on the way to Ethiopia from Cairo, the last
under the Sultan's rule.

125   421.0: At the time Sade was writing, Dongola, on the Nile River,
belonged to territory that was contested by local sultans
and strongmen. Context makes clear that Sade relied on
Poncet, and perhaps other sources.

126   429.16: The Kingdom of Sennar would last into the mid-19th century, when it would become part of the Ottoman Empire.

127   429.29: City of Sennar, today part of Sudan, historically an important hub for the dissemination of Islamic religion
and culture.

128   430.7: This passage paraphrases and draws heavily upon the
discussion in Poncet; Sade adds critical commentary.

129   433.15: Impalement was traditionally performed as Sade indicates, with insertion of the pike through the anus and
extrusion through the chest cavity.

130   436.6: Giasim (Giésim) is mentioned in several accounts of
voyages in the 18th and 19th centuries. Again, Poncet
describes Serka in terms that suggest his volume is the
source for Sade. Both places are mentioned in travel-
ogues contemporary to Sade's time.

131   441.25: *"Quomodo potest hic nobis"*: The Latin translates as:
How can this man give us His flesh to eat? (John 6:52).

St. Augustine refers to the so-called Capharnaite error, with reference to Capernaum, a fishing village where Jesus Christ is said to have planned a ministry. Some inhabitants of the place apparently believed that Jesus intended to give them his flesh by actually cutting off and distributing parts of his own body.

132   442.3: *"communion of two species"*: In Catholic doctrine, referring to the sacrament of wine and bread, a practice that was much debated and even the basis of warfare in the Late Middle Ages.

133   442.25: The mythical Mountains of the Moon originated with the great astronomer Ptolemy (100–168) in the 2nd century and appeared on maps well into the 19th century until, in 1858. the source of the Nile River was finally located and mapped. As the footnote indicates, Sade was aware of the uncertain and perhaps apocryphal character of the Mountains.

134   443.2: The "extraordinary animal": Sade may have borrowed his description from *Dictionnaire raisonné universel d'histoire naturelle,* vol 5. In modern terms, perhaps the reference is to the Hamadryas baboon.

135   443.12: Voltaire mentions both Monomotapa (see also note 31 and 57) and the Kingdom of Monoëmugi in his *Philosophical Dictionary,* first published in 1764. (Incidentally, Voltaire's descriptions and ideas concerning Africans in this context invoke a form of racism that is largely if not entirely absent in Sade's portrayals.) Today Mombasa is the second largest city in Kenya; this early conquest of the Portuguese passed to Ottoman rule in the mid-18th century.

136   443.17: Zambezi River: the French text refers to the River Zebé, a name mentioned in travel texts as early as the 17th century. For the reader's sake, we use the modern name of what turned out to be a major tributary of the Nile and the fourth longest river in Africa.

137 444.12: Fort Sena: Established by the Portuguese in the 16ᵗʰ century.

138 445.0: Duke of Medinaceli: The title is genuine, though why Sade chose it remains unclear.

139 449.3: *"colony in Benguela"*: The Portuguese established the Kingdom of Benguela on what today is the coast of Angola in the early 17ᵗʰ century. Fort Tete refers to a Portuguese installation on the Zambezi River, Forte de São Tiago Maior do Tete. Tete was a Swahili town or small city.

140 450.6: Saint Mary Bay was mapped to the coast of Angola. The kingdom of Monomotapa (see also notes 31 and 57) appeared on the early maps of Africa, and in encyclopedia entries into the 19ᵗʰ century, a large poorly defined area situated southeast of Angola.

141 463.25: Emperor Hadrian (76–138) enjoyed a homosexual relationship with the Greek youth Antinous, whom he deified after the youth's mysterious death.

142 474.15: Chamber of Commerce of Africa. The chamber movement traces its roots to the early 17ᵗʰ century.

143 484.27: *"suburb of Belem"*: Located at the mouth of the Tagus River, Belem is notably the site of an impressive fortified tower built in the 16ᵗʰ century. Sade clearly chose this location as a personal, internal reference to his four libertines at the impregnable Chateau de Silling in *120 Days of Sodom*.

144 489.28: *"Four men, aged 50 to 55 ..."*: Here are the libertines from *120 Days*, in cameo roles channeled into *Aline and Valcour*. As Sade wrote, the scroll for his unpublishable novel was secreted in his prison cell in the Bastille.

145 490.30: *"bachelor of Salamanca"*: Dating to the Renaissance, the University of Salamanca was an influential center of Catholic learning that morphed into a powerful and foundational center of pre-Enlightenment thought, including secular law, economic theory, and justice.

146   501.15: *"We were first subjected to a practice"*: Sade refers to relations between the Dutch and Japanese at the turn of the 17th century with the advent of the Edo shogunate. Catholic missionaries had come to Japan and made thousands of converts until 1614, when the "great unifier" Toyotomi Hideyoshi issued an edict that banned Christianity and crucified a number of Franciscan monks. The 1636 Act of Seclusion ultimately made a qualified exception for the non-Catholic Dutch.

147   502.29: *"When Bulgarians flooded the East"*: Sade provides a plausible historical gloss on the history of Romani culture and the dispersion of gypsies in Europe. Founded in Persia in the third century, Manicheanism was heresy in Europe and provoked conflict beginning in the Middle Ages. The Pillars of Hercules refers to promontories at the Strait of Gibraltar, the boundary point separating the Iberian Peninsula and Europe from Africa.

148   504.7: Palus Méotides is an ancient name for the Sea of Azov, atop the Black Sea, bordered today by the Ukraine and Russia.

149   504.29: Regarding Assyrian law, Sade is probably referring to the Code of the Assura (c. 1075 BC).

150   505.28: St. Thomas Aquinas offered several reasons for prohibiting incest and the idea that it fosters immoderate lust was indeed one of them.

151   506.5: *di Manes*: In Ancient Rome, the gods of the underworld, including souls of the deceased; hence, ancestor worship as a precursor of all religious doctrines of immortality.

152   506.12: quotation from *The Æneid*: "She wakes nocturnal Spirits / you'll see earth yawn under your feet" (A.S. Kline translation [2002]). From Horace: "Blood into a ditch they spewed that so they might compel / the ghosts to give them answers out of hell" (Christopher Smart translation [1767]).

153   506.19: St. Cyril of Jerusalem (313–386), a father of the church, argued for the real existence of the Holy Ghost.

154   508.18: Candle of Cardan: in supernatural lore, a candle made from human flesh or fat.

155   508.30: *"ex semine hominis..."*: the passage translates as "from the seed of a man who has been hanged or otherwise punished by death."

156   510.19: *"Sappho never showed as much with Damophyle..."*: Here we correct all previous editions, which give *Démophile*. Sade undoubtedly meant Damophyle, a lyric poetess, companion to Sappho.

157   513.19: *Holy Brotherhood*: a constabulary inaugurated in the 15th century by monarchs Ferdinand and Isabella to insure law and order in Spain. Elsewhere Sade uses the Spanish *Santa Hermandad*, see p. 376, 524.

158   515.20: *"a bar of gold and two hundred shekels"*: Joshua 7–8. *"Saul consulted Samuel's ghost"*: 1 Samuel 28.

159   516.18: *"Just a word..."*: The Palladium of Athens (Pallas Athena) was a cult image said to protect the city state. The Colossi of Memnon still stand in Luxor, Egypt. — The "stone storks" of Apollonius refers to the *Ciconiæ Nixæ*, a statue or relief in ancient Rome. The poet Virgil forged a "brass fly" on astrological principles and displayed it in Naples, said to be thereafter have been free of flies, thanks to the Roman God Myagros; he also recounts that he saved Naples from a plague of bloodsucking leeches by casting a "golden leech" into a well. Lucius Ælius Sejanus (20 BC – 30) was friend and confidant to the Emperor Tiberius, and prefect of the Prætorian Guard, so powerful and popular as to inspire statues; and he himself had supposedly owned a statue of the *goddess of Fortuna*, giving rise to the notion of swearing by the "Fortune of Sejanus."

160   516.28: *"Talismans Justifiés"*: The book, published in 1653, is by a bishop of the church, Jean-Albert Belin (1615–1677).

161 521.22: Knights of the Order of Alcántara, founded in the 12ᵗʰ century, wielded considerable power and were long involved in Spanish politics.

162 522.0: *"Pearl of the Two Spains"*: Sade's use of the term "Two Spains" predates much contemporary historiography and etymology, which tend to date it to the 19ᵗʰ century and to political divisions culminating in the Spanish Civil War. For the broader view, see e.g. C. Douglass, *Bulls, Bullfighting, and Spanish Identities* (1999) 62.

163 522.26: *"We've just seized Mahon"*: The major town on the strategically important island of Minorca. France and England contested possession before, during, and after the Seven Years war until, in 1782, after a siege and battle, a French-Spanish coalition took it over from the British.

164 523.4: The British Constitution: Brigandos is referring to 1689 Bill of Rights.

165 523.30: Strabo (c. 64 BC–24 AD), the Greek geographer and historian, indeed describes gold found in ancient Spain. The Phoenicians colonized parts of the Iberian Peninsula in the 10ᵗʰ century BC.

166 523.18: *Pacte de Famille*: In 1779, the French and Spanish crowns renewed their 1761 alliance against Britain in the context of the American Revolution.

167 524.4: *"the universal monarchy"*: Spain was the base for Holy Roman Emperor Charles V (1500–1558), who in the 16ᵗʰ century developed the visionary concept of a supreme sovereign.

168 524.8: *"Santa Hermandad"*: see note 157.

169 525.11: The Tarquins were two of the seven kings of early Rome.

170 526.7: Tartary was the term long used in Europe to refer to the whole of northern and central Asia stretching from the Caspian Sea and Ural Mountains, all the way to the Pacific Ocean.

171 526.12: *Agnus deis* refers to sacramental disks, imprinted with the figure of a lamb, treated as a Catholic relic.

172   526.24: Danzig: Sade was writing in the context both of medieval history and of the first partition of Poland. Danzig
(Gdansk) had special status as city-state dating to at
least the 15th century; it was seized from the Russians
by the Kingdom of Prussia in 1772. But Sade's reference
has a peculiar quality of prescience: Napoleon Bonapar-
te would establish the "free city of Danzig" in 1807; it
became officially known by that name again after WWI
in the wake of the Versailles Treaty. Nazi Germany tar-
geted the city as soon as it invaded Poland in 1939.

173   526.32: Abbé de Saint-Pierre (1658–1743), an Enlightenment
author whose influence extended to Rousseau and Kant
alike, was essentially the first to suggest a European
union and international order. His project for perpetual
peace was published in 1713.

174   528.10: The University of Compostela is located in Galicia,
which in the 18th century was still a kingdom in north-
west Spain.

175   528.18: *"first-class noble"*: Nobles or grandees in Spain were indeed divided into first, second, and third class.

176   529.2: *"Rabelais' quarter hour"*: the hour of reckoning, the bill
to be paid. The popular expression derives from an anecdote about Rabelais when after an excellent meal he was
presented with a bill he couldn't pay.

177   535.31: Bartole: see also also note 9; Cujas, note 15. Both serve
Sade as eponymous beacons of law with a vengeance.

178   537.24: Sartine, Sade's nemesis and arch enemy, indeed employed spies to provide King Louis XV with tales about
sexual behavior. See also notes 39 and 90.

179   538.4: *"Philippe IV long imprisoned…"*: Adventurous nobleman Charles IV (1605–1675), the Duke of Lorraine, tilted
against France, then Spain. During the reign of King
Philippe IV of Spain and in the wake of the 30 Years' war,

he was imprisoned in Toledo, from 1654 until 1659. Sade might well identify with Charles who, as Voltaire said when he died, had spent his life losing his estates.

180   538.8: *"Close by are the ruins ..."*: King Roderick and The Enchanted Tower refers to a legend reformulated by Sade both for a tale in his *Crimes of Love* and as the setting for the story which he here interpolates into the main text. A recent investigation of the tale of the Roderick legend by Elizabeth Drayson would indicate that Sade employed a medieval tale that was also used by Robert Southey, among others. See *The King and the Whore: King Roderick and La Cava* (2007).

181   540.31: Statesman and Cardinal Ximenes de Cisneros (1436–1517) was a key figure in the historic rise of Spain. As archbishop of Toldeo, he protected Mozarabs (Iberian Christians who had lived under Moorish rule) and founded the chapel, as Sade indicates, as a means of but perpetuating knowledge of its rituals.

182   545.30: Procopius of Cæsarea (c. 490–560) wrote about the reign of the Emperor Justinian (483–565) and his wife Theodora (500–548), sometimes described as co-regents. His *Wars of Justinian,* which appeared during the Emperor's lifetime, was a panegyric; the *Secret History,* which was not published for more than a thousand years, was by contrast highly unflattering, just as Sade describes. See also note 199.

183   550.28: Léonore's narrative resumes on page 564.

184   572.20: Construction of the Royal Palace of Aranjuez, with its huge and famous gardens, commenced in the 16th century but only completed 200 years later.

185   576.28: *"His son said"*: Matthew 10:34. We use the translation from the *New American Standard Bible.*

186 582.5: *"Silence was observed"*: Sade was using a secondary source, Bernard and Picart's multi-volume *Religious Ceremonies and Customs of All the Peoples of the World* (1723–1743), an early and famous comparative survey of religions. As Sade notes, details cited owe to Jacques Marsolier (1647–1724): see *De l'origine des inquisitions: Histoire de l'inquisition* (1693). We eliminate from the translation a brief reference to the Spanish author Miguel de Monserrate (Pléiade p. 906 and notes to the passage, pp. 1324–25).

187 590.31: Don Carlos (1545–1568), was the heir-apparent of King Philip II of Spain. His imprisonment by his father and subsequent death while confined sparked a legend.

188 602.1: *"I sighted to my left El Escorial"*: the massive castle complex which Philip II had constructed in the 16th century. San Il defonso is located north of Madrid. Léonore is making her way across Spain, southwest to northeast.

189 602.8: *"old and new Castile"*: The vaguely defined but traditional central region around which Spain was formed. New Castile, the southern portion, was incorporated into what became known as Old Castile in the 11th century.

190 618.18: Diderot hailed the famed actress Mademoiselle Gaussin (1711–1764) as "beauty personified"; Mademoiselle Doligny (1746–1823) was said to have debuted "with unusual success," according to F. Hawkins, *French Theater in the Eighteenth Century* (1968); Madame de Préville, wife to a famed actor, was herself an actress of dignity and renown.

191 620.26: *"We tremble and weep…"*: A reference to a cruel scene in *Atrée et Thyeste*, a tragedy by Prosper Jolyot de Crébillon (1674–1762) in which, famously, Atreus offers to his brother Thyestes a cup filled with the blood of the latter's own son. The further quotation is from *Alzire*, the tragedy by Voltaire that invokes the Spanish conquest of Peru. For the English translation we use the 1904 edition of Voltaire's collected works.

192 621.29: Luc de Clapiers, the Marquis de Vauvenargues (1715–1747), a philosophical author and aphorist.

193 622.6: *parlements*: Parlements prior to the French Revolution were regional and provincial appellate courts. Sade's animus is clear: he was convicted by the one at Aix, sentenced to death, decapitated and burned in effigy. The sentence was subsequently overturned.

194 626.26: *"Melpomene's somber tones"*: Melpomene was the Greek Muse of Tragedy while Thalia, another daughter of Zeus, presided over comedy.

195 630.7: Sade borrows heavily throughout this discourse from *L'esprit des usages et des coutumes des différents peuples* by Jean-Nicolas Démeunier (1751–1814). Herodotus discusses the Scythians, an ancient nomadic people, in his account of the Persian wars. *Pegu* refers to the ancient city in Burma, capital of the Mon kingdom. But all this can be found in slightly different form and emphasis in Démeunier's text.

196 630.20: *"cult of Astarte"*: Astarte was the Phœnician goddess of fertility and war; Byblos was an ancient port city.

197 630.24: "priests of Tanais": Located on the Don River in present-day Russia, Tanais was an ancient trading settlement for the ancient Greeks, and also the name of a goddess worshipped by the Armenians, who indeed used to consecrate virgin daughters to the priests, according to the historian and geographer Strabo (c. 64 BC – 24 AD).

198 634.0: The various plays represent popular 18th century theater: *The Oracle*, by G.F. Poullain de St. Fox; *Britannicus*, by Racine, a tragedy; *Zénéide*: a light comedy by Louis de Cahusa; *Mélanide*, a tearful comedy by Pierre-Claude Nivelle de La Chaussée; Chamfort's *La Jeune Indienne*, and *Le Père de famille*, the 1758 play by Denis Diderot.

199 639.10: Theodora (c. 500–548), the powerful empress of the Byzantine Empire and wife to Emperor Justinian I, was

accused by historian Procopius in his famous *Secret History*. Messalina (c. 17–48) was the third wife of Emperor Claudius, said to be ruthless and sexually promiscuous (see also p. 545).

200   638.28: *"An excess of sensitivity…"*: Encyclopedist Jean-François Marmontel (1723–1799).

201   639.29: Marquise de Brinvilliers (1630–1676), accused of conspiring to murder her father and two brothers, was tortured and executed after a sensational trial. Her alleged crimes led to the "Affair of the Poisons" in which La Voisin (Catherine Monvoisin), a fortune teller, was accused and executed for witchcraft in 1680.

202   639.30: *Le Père de famille*, see p. 634; *Lucile*, a comic opera by André Grétry with a French text by Jean-François Marmontel, first performed in 1769.

203   661.19: "Asiatic method of strangulation": Strangulation with a handkerchief, such as employed by the Thugs of India.

204   663.30: Blamont's use of the term *singularities*, which resonates with Léonore's usage of the term, which we translate for her as *most singular impressions* (p.644.11), alludes to highly refined properties of perception and imagination and, at one and the same time, to "bizarre" sexual acts; it may also be translated as "eccentricities."

205   665.32: Another reference to Sade's nemesis, Antoine de Sartine, who reported to the king concerning the sexual extravagances the police collected concerning various nobles.

206   670.25: *"the wife of the Marquis de Karmeil"*: Here we correct all earlier editions, including the Pléiade, which give "Kerneuil" in place of Karmeil.

207   687.30: Paolo Veronese (1528–1588), Italian Renaissance painter.

208   693.4: *"Sister of the Shears"*: The Parcæ of Roman myth were the three goddess sisters of fate, and Daughters of the

Night. Nona spun the thread of life, Decima measured it, and Morta, to whom Sophie alludes, cut it.

209   714.11: *"murder holes"*: an architectural feature of the medieval castle. Sade's explanatory note underscores his tendency to embed meaning in physical detail. Cf. Folichon, p. 34.

210   723.10: *"order"*: Our italics. The reference, according to Pléiade, is understood to be a *lettre de cachet*.

211   737.32: Machiavelli does not discuss accomplices per se in *The Prince*, so Sade's reference here is unclear.

212   765.13: After having murdered his mother Agrippina, with whom he had an incestuous relationship, Nero was said to have inspected her body and praised her beauty.

213   766.26: *Monsieur de Mézane*: Sade is talking about himself. He was judged guilty by the Parlement of Aix, and eventually arrested in Paris when he went to visit his mother on her deathbed.

214   766.30: For Jean Calas, see also note 108. In 1545, during the reign of François I, many villages were indeed burned (and inhabitants murdered) in an example of religious persecution of the Protestant Vaudois population. The Parlement of Aix followed the king's lead and participated in the killings.

215   767.31: *"Monsters capable of such horrors"*: Sade is addressing his wife's parents, who were responsible for his long imprisonment, and alluding to himself. After he was freed, political leverage as a revolutionary would have enabled him to exact revenge on his former in-laws, but he did not.

216   768.25: Sade may have in mind, among other accounts, a passage from Book 5 of *The Persian Wars*, in which Herodotus notes a custom among the Trausi people to collectively weep at the birth of a child, and to rejoice at death.

217   770.31: *"singularity of philosophical systems"*: Sade makes allusion in this paragraph to the Flour Wars of 1775, which

indeed implicated the police officials he detested (see footnotes to this page), Sartine and Le Noir. A laissez-faire effort to de-control the price of flour, the main staple of the average French diet, was overseen by the police and afflicted by speculators, causing dramatic popular discontent.

218   771.32: *"Such was the lie"*: A final salvo: After his stint as Chief of the Paris Police, Antoine de Sartine remained prominent in government, serving as Secretary of the Navy. His tenure was controversial and he later claimed that his work for the French government had ruined him financially.

219   771.33: Jean Charles Pierre Lenoir (1732–1807) succeeded Sartine as Chief of Police in Paris.

220   783.12: Duchess of Aiguillon (1604–1675) was famed for her charity and good works. At her funeral service, Esprit Fléchier (1632–1710) gave the oration; he was widely known as an eloquent pulpit orator; compilations of his funeral speeches were published during his lifetime and well into the 19th century.

221   785.30: *"quarter league from Sens"*: The old cathedral city of Sens is located about 120 km outside Paris.

222   789.20: *"hymen's torch"*: marriage. Hymen, the god of the marriage ceremony, is sometimes depicted with a torch in hand.

223   794.14: *Office of the Dead*: a prayer cycle in Catholic Church liturgy, said on behalf of the deceased.

224   794.17: 24th Psalm. Sade is actually referring to the 26th Psalm in the Latin Vulgate Bible.

225   795.8: *Nina, the Girl Driven Mad by Love* refers to the popular 1786 comic opera by Nicolas Dalayrac (1752–1809) with an original libretto by Marsollier des Vivetières. In 1791 Giovanni Paisiello's opera, derived from that source, created a scandal owing to copyright legislation, enacted during the French Revolution.

226   797.10: *Age of reason*: Sade again refers to Catholic doctrine, which declares that a child at age seven years has reached the "age of reason." See also note 48.

227   808.3: *"Never again"*: From *Isaiah*, ch. 38, we use the recent Catholic translation, *The Christian Community Bible*.

228   808.33: The footnote cites the 101st Psalm, which refers to the Vulgate bible; for other translations, it is the 102nd. Our translation is from the French.

229   811.23: *"name of the Lord"*: We use the translation from *The Catholic Christian Community Bible*.

230   819.4: Notre-Dame de Sept-Fons: A Trappist monastery dating to the 12th century. Although still operating when Sade composed *Aline & Valcour*, the Revolution confiscated the monastery in 1791, prior to its publication. The Trappist monks lived in silence.

Acknowledgements

Our deep thanks to friends and colleagues who provided help and moral sustenance over the long course of this translation. Donald Nicholson-Smith offered advice throughout and we benefitted greatly from his long experience and constant enthusiasm. Our appreciation extends most sincerely to Allan Graubard, Caroline McGee, Alyson Waters, and Christopher Winks, for reading and evaluating substantial portions of the manuscript. In France, Philippe and Françoise Barque patiently responded to queries. Brief extracts of the novel appeared in *Brooklyn Rail*, for which we owe warm thanks to Donald Breckenridge. We are grateful as well to Steven Moore, who used our translation-in-progress to discuss *Aline and Valcour* in his *The Novel: An Alternative History*. Our work benefitted greatly from a translation grant awarded by the National Endowment of the Arts.

Bringing a work of such length and complexity to final parturition required vision & fortitude, which Rainer J. Hanshe supplied in abundance. For no less requisite invention and skill in design & typography, we are grateful to Alessandro Segalini, whose creative efforts and appealing solutions would surely have delighted the novel's first modern editor, the legendary Jean-Jacques Pauvert. Thanks too for guidance to our agents Amy and Peter Bernstein.

Finally, our gratitude does not end here but only begins with a disparate and wide-ranging group of readers who, long ahead of publication, contacted us with encouraging hopes and queries about its eventual availability, now answered at last.

Illustrations

"May our distinguished rascals see how innocence and virtue triumph over villainy!"

fig. 9 ⊗ p. 491

Can it be? Have I cut short the life of the one to whom I was to sacrifice my own?

fig. 10 ⚜ p. 561

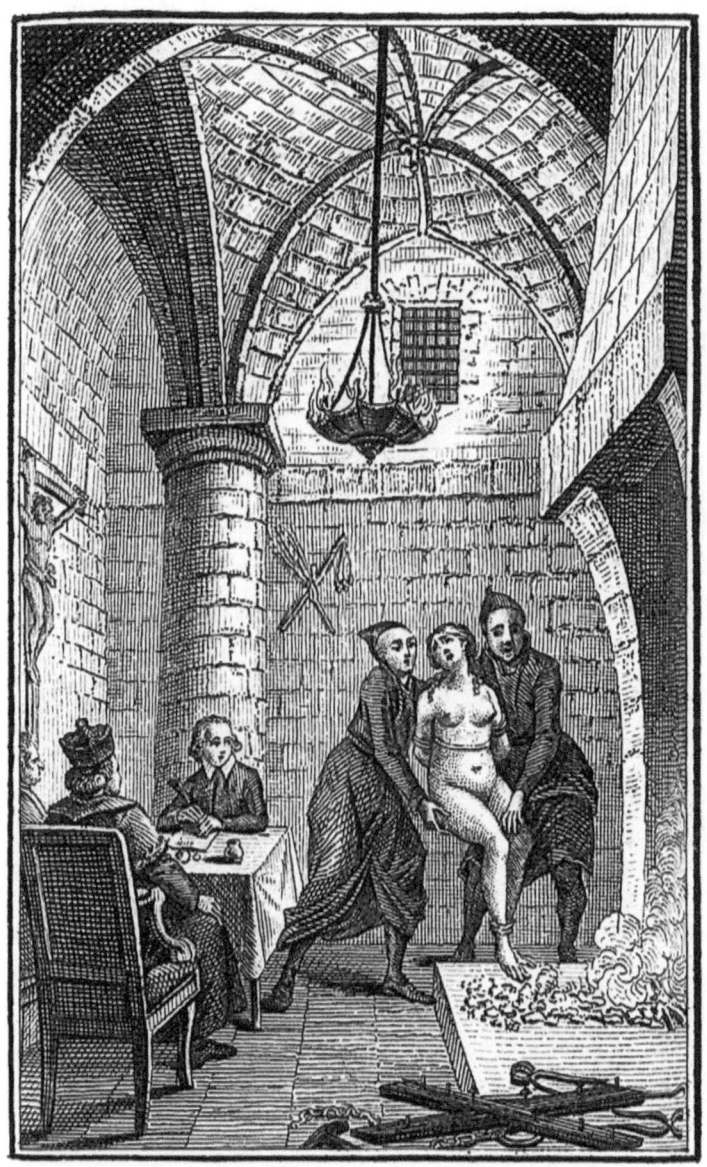

"How can Heaven abandon virtue to dreadful torments?"

fig. 11 ⊛ p. 586

"VILE CREATURE. HAVE YOU FORGOTTEN WHOSE HOME YOU ENTERED?"

fig. 12 ⚜ p. 680

Four men, armed with swords, crossed the street and
came at me so swiftly that I received the first blow
before I had time to defend myself.

fig. 13 ⊘ p. 706

COLOPHON

ALINE AND VALCOUR
was handset in InDesign CC.

The text is set in *Adobe Warnock Pro*.
The illustration captions are set in *IM Fell Pica*

Book design & typesetting: Alessandro Segalini

Cover design: CMP

Cover image: Federico Gori, "Sade" (2019),
36 × 23 cm, ink & enamel on paper,
federicogori.org

ALINE AND VALCOUR
is published by Contra Mundum Press.

Contra Mundum Press   New York · London · Melbourne

CONTRA MUNDUM PRESS

Dedicated to the value & the indispensable importance of the individual voice, to works that test the boundaries of thought & experience.

The primary aim of Contra Mundum is to publish translations of writers who in their use of form and style are *à rebours*, or who deviate significantly from more programmatic & spurious forms of experimentation. Such writing attests to the volatile nature of modernism. Our preference is for works that have not yet been translated into English, are out of print, or are poorly translated, for writers whose thinking & æsthetics are in opposition to timely or mainstream currents of thought, value systems, or moralities. We also reprint obscure and out-of-print works we consider significant but which have been forgotten, neglected, or overshadowed.

There are many works of fundamental significance to *Weltliteratur* (& *Weltkultur*) that still remain in relative oblivion, works that alter and disrupt standard circuits of thought — these warrant being encountered by the world at large. It is our aim to render them more visible.

For the complete list of forthcoming publications, please visit our website. To be added to our mailing list, send your name and email address to: info@contramundum.net

Contra Mundum Press
P.O. Box 1326
New York, NY 10276
USA

OTHER CONTRA MUNDUM PRESS TITLES

SOME FORTHCOMING TITLES

THE FUTURE OF KULCHUR
A PATRONAGE PROJECT

LEND CONTRA MUNDUM PRESS (CMP) YOUR SUPPORT

With bookstores and presses around the world struggling to survive, and many actually closing, we are forming this patronage project as a means for establishing a continuous & stable foundation to safeguard our longevity. Through this patronage project we would be able to remain free of having to rely upon government support &/or other official funding bodies, not to speak of their timelines & impositions. It would also free CMP from suffering the vagaries of the publishing industry, as well as the risk of submitting to commercial pressures in order to persist, thereby potentially compromising the integrity of our catalog.

CAN YOU SACRIFICE $10 A WEEK FOR KULCHUR?

For the equivalent of merely 2–3 coffees a week, you can help sustain CMP and contribute to the future of kulchur. To participate in our patronage program we are asking individuals to donate $500 per year, which amounts to $42/month, or $10/week. Larger donations are of course welcome and beneficial. All donations are tax-deductible through our fiscal sponsor Fractured Atlas. If preferred, donations can be made in two installments. We are seeking a minimum of 300 patrons per year and would like for them to commit to giving the above amount for a period of three years.

WHAT WE OFFER

Part tax-deductible donation, part exchange, for your contribution you will receive every CMP book published during the patronage period as well as 20 books from our back catalog. When possible, signed or limited editions of books will be offered as well.

WHAT WILL CMP DO WITH YOUR CONTRIBUTIONS?

Your contribution will help with basic general operating expenses, yearly production expenses (book printing, warehouse & catalog fees, etc.), advertising & outreach, and editorial, proofreading, translation, typography, design and copyright fees. Funds may also be used for participating in book fairs and staging events. Additionally, we hope to rebuild the *Hyperion* section of the website in order to modernize it.

From Pericles to Mæcenas & the Renaissance patrons, it is the magnanimity of such individuals that have helped the arts to flourish. Be a part of helping your kulchur flourish; be a part of history.

HOW

To lend your support & become a patron, please visit the subscription page of our website: contramundum.net/subscription

For any questions, write us at: info@contramundum.net

www.ingramcontent.com/pod-product-compliance
Lightning Source LLC
Chambersburg PA
CBHW031025030726
47497CB00004B/1011